PERFECT PURSUIT

PERFECT PURSUIT

A SMALL TOWN, AGE GAP, FRIENDS TO LOVERS, SECRET RELATIONSHIP ROMANCE

MIDAS SERIES
BOOK 7

TRACEY JERALD

Tracey Jerald

101 Marketside Avenue, Suite 404-205

Ponte Vedra, FL, 3208

https://www.traceyjerald.com

Editor: Melissa Borucki
Proof Edits: Holly Malgieri, Comma Sutra Editorial
Cover Design by Tugboat Design
Photo Credit: Wander Aguiar Model: Joe M.
PR & Marketing: Linda Russell - Foreword PR (https://www.forewordpr.com)

TRIGGER WARNINGS

Thank you for reading Perfect Pursuit. I hope you embrace the relationship between Fallon and Ethan even as they find love while answering a question many of us struggle with every single day—what would you do for love?

As some readers may experience some sensitivity regarding some of the subject matter contained within these pages, some trigger warnings are being provided:

- Cancer (*not of a main character*)
- Chemical assault
- Car accident (*not of a main character*)
- Death (*not of a main character*)
- Grief
- Hospitalization (*not of a main character*)
- Miscarriage (*not of a main character*)
- Sexually Explicit Employment
- Terminal Illness (*not of a main character*)
- Underage drinking

Thank you,

Tracey

DEDICATION

If you will do anything for the ones you love, this story is for you.

PLAYLIST

Lou Gramm, "Midnight Blue"
Alanis Morissette, "Hands Clean"
Sarah McLachlan, "Hold On"
Taylor Swift, "Cruel Summer"
Joe Jordan, "Big Enough Mountain"
Indigo Girls, "Galileo"
Taylor Swift, "Guilty as Sin?"
Emika, "Wicked Game"
Bastille, "World Gone Mad"
Miley Cyrus, "Jaded"
Heather Nova, "I Have the Touch"
Meredith Brooks, "Bitch"
Sarah McLachlan, "Full of Grace"

ALSO BY TRACEY JERALD

MIDAS SERIES
Perfect Assumption
Perfect Composition
Perfect Order
Perfect Satisfaction
Perfectly Free
Perfect Pitch
Perfect Pursuit
Also, Perfect Proposal

AMARYLLIS SERIES
Free to Dream
Free to Run
Free to Rejoice
Free to Breathe
Free to Believe
Free to Live
Free to Dance
Free to Wish
Free to Protect
Free to Reunite

AMARYLLIS HERITAGE

PERFECT PURSUIT   5

Free to Fall

GLACIER ADVENTURE SERIES
Return by Fire—Available in audio!
Return by Air—Coming soon to audio!
Return by Land
Return by Sea

DEVOTION SERIES
Ripple Effect
Flood Tide

STANDALONES
Close Match
The Ultimate Challenge

Go to https://www.traceyjerald.com/ for all buy links!

THE MIDAS TOUCH

In Greek mythology, Midas, wandering one day in his garden, came across the wise satyr Silenus, who was rather the worse for wear. Midas treated him kindly and returned him to his great companion, the god Dionysus

In return for this, Dionysus granted Midas a wish. The king, not realizing the repercussions of his decision, chose to be given the magical ability to turn any object he touched into solid gold. Simple things, everyday things, Midas took for granted were instantly transformed by his touch into solid gold.

The full consequences of this gift soon became evident. At the barest touch, flowers, fruit, and water turned to gold. Food took on a metallic taste the moment it brushed his lips. Midas became sick of this world he surrounded himself with and sought to relieve himself of it.

Those finding themselves burdened with an abundance of perfection gifted to them by the gods often seek relief to reverse their fortune.

Except when that gift is love. Then, treasure is considered to be of unfathomable value and it's absolutely something you never want to rid yourself of.

CHAPTER ONE

KENSINGTON, TEXAS

Ethan

American singer-songwriter Garth Brooks received the Library of Congress Gershwin Prize tonight at the DAR Constitution Hall in Washington, D.C.

—Nashville Nights

Five Years Ago

I GORGE ON THE SIGHT OF HER LOOSENED HAIR. GOLDEN LOCKS CATCH in the precious breeze, lifting fine tendrils away from a face I'm confident artists once fought wars to carve from marble.

Because it's almost certain the young woman standing a few feet in front of me is a witch. *Otherwise,* I think bitterly, *How could she have merely sauntered through my father's front door and cursed me?*

In a past life, Fallon Brookes must have been Venus or Aphrodite. Almost certainly, men pursued her as much as I'm heaping blasphemous thoughts upon her now. But is it really her fault she was gifted with such exquisite beauty?

I try to suppress the growl rising from deep in my chest at the yes that wants to erupt. No eighteen-year-old should be blessed with such a fatal combination of features guaranteed to turn a man rock hard. No, Fallon's no witch. Perhaps she's related to Medusa. Like the mythical Gorgon power I'm presuming has been passed down her family lineage, Fallon turns a man to stone from the moment he lays eyes on her.

Namely, me.

Even knowing her effect, and despite resenting it, I study her unabashed sexuality safely from behind my darkly tinted lenses. I suppose I should be grateful. Close to two thousand years later, at least it's only my dick that hardens when I look at her instead of my whole body.

My niece shared a great deal about her before I actually met her when I acted as chauffeur for the two of them a few months ago. "Fallon is smart, dedicated, loyal, and determined."

I remember flicking an avuncular smile in Austyn's direction before my Jeep door flew open and a goddess slid into the back seat. With a lightning quick wit, she drawled, "So, you're the infamous 'Uncle E' I've heard so much about."

Dumbstruck by her beauty, I nodded.

Feigned innocent eyes met mine in the rearview. "Are you the kind of uncle who wants us to make polite conversation with you until we get where we're going or are you more comfortable being ignored? I can do either."

Austyn howled even as my gaze challenged hers. Softly, I questioned, "Think you can ignore me so easily, Ms. Brookes?"

She shrugged, as if the warning in my voice meant nothing to her. "You're a man. It won't be terribly hard."

My tongue almost fell out of my mouth at her insolence. It was then she smiled smugly before winking at me.

In an attempt to forget the deity who made herself comfortable with my family, I forced myself to go on several first dates with women who in no way reminded me of Fallon. Revulsion surges through me as I recall the way I felt after those evenings out—as if I had the wrong woman on my arm. Now, seeing her, I know why.

My body was admitting what my brain wouldn't. A "Do you really think so?" or a "Wow. Is that just you or all men who are so arrogant?" from Fallon can stir more emotion than lengthy exchanges with other women who might be closer to my own age but did nothing to raise any part of me—body or mind.

If it wasn't for her damn age. If Fallon wasn't my niece's best friend. Fuck, who am I lying to? I might be willing to risk my family's shock and abhorrence if I didn't think Fallon planned on putting Kensington into her rear view the very second she had the chance. After all, from everything my niece has been saying, they plan on living it up at UT in the fall.

They deserve to, I chastise myself. They deserve the rush of the first college party, the first time they forget to bring their keys to dinner and beg someone to let them back in the dorm. My eyes skim over Fallon as I recall a memory from my own college days—the fun of a fire drill when you're in the middle of a shower.

Now all I can picture is Fallon wrapped in a towel, struggling to keep it tied around her ample breasts despite gravity . . . Maybe the burn in my gaze makes her skin warm. Singularly stunning eyes cut in my direction. Plump lips curve upward, revealing a dimple before she nods in the direction of where her and Austyn's graduation cake rests. "Are you certain we have to wait?"

Fuck no. I don't want to wait. I want you now. I study the table the cake rests on. If it were up to me, I'd have the excuse of a dress covering Fallon's body rucked up past her hips before bending her over near her cake. One of my hands would pluck at her nipples while the other fought with hardware and fastenings until my pants dropped over my shoes. My hands would smooth over her ass cheeks before I forced her back to arch slightly. I'd slide myself deep. Hard. Fallon's hands would reach out, inadvertently slapping at the cake. When she lifts her hand away—gaze dazed, fingers smeared with frosting—I'd grab her hand and suck her fingers clean, causing a deep moan to emerge from her throat.

And that's before I began thrusting.

Shit. If my cock isn't twitching visibly beneath my dress slacks as my body gives way to my fantasies, I'll take my rightful place in hell.

Fallon lifts a knee to reach the strap on one of her sandaled heels while we wait for everyone to emerge from the house. All it does is send another shaft of lust surging through me as the hem of her skirt edges even higher. Taunting me. Filling my mind with more explicit thoughts I shouldn't— can't!—act on.

Wanting to fuck my niece's best friend crosses every code of fucking morality—most of which I was certain my soul had forgotten long before this vixen was born. I know I can't have her, but that didn't stop my thoughts on the nights I came home from those pointless dates and stroked my cock, imagining the warmth of her mouth covering it. Right before I find the first flat surface, hoist her up, spread her thighs apart, and penetrate her.

Fallon gasps, pulling me from my fantasy. Her body sways violently when her sandal catches in the string of a cluster of balloons. Just as she's about to fall headfirst into the three-tiered cake, my hands reach out and grab her around the waist. Hauling her against my chest, I'm close enough to interpret every emotion in her indigo eyes.

Sharp pain wars with biting pleasure. I growl, "Are you okay, witch?"

Her hands reach up and clasp my shoulders for purchase. I have to bite the inside of my cheek to avoid howling when the points of her nails penetrate through my suit jacket. Equal amounts of pleasure and pain have me cursing.

Flushing, her face contorts. She rasps, "Dandy."

Without thinking, I scoop her up. Her hands slide around the back of my neck into my hair. She grasps for purchase even as I stride toward a chaise lounge. "You're dangerous in those shoes." You're dangerous in anything.

"Ethan! Put me down!" she orders.

"After I check out your ankle," I reprimand her.

Unceremoniously, I deposit her, but just as I'm about to stand, her fingers tighten around my collar before they release. A current of electricity arcs between us. I try to control my breathing just in case I'm the only one who recognizes it for what it is.

Quickly, I kneel and capture her ankle in my hands. My imagination isn't nothing, judging by the sharp inhale she takes. If I wasn't already on my knees, I'd be dropping to them within seconds of her reaction to my fingers grazing her perfect skin. Gritting my teeth, I apply pressure in different spots to test for weakness—almost hoping I find some reason to order her out of these ridiculous heels worn to entice the stupid jackasses that are coming to celebrate their graduation tonight.

She allows me to poke and prod for a few moments before finally soothing me. "I'm fine. I just got my foot caught."

"And almost went flying into a cake," I say sternly.

"You came to the rescue."

Not knowing where the words come from, I blurt out, "I always will."

She reaches into her purse and whips out her cell phone. Immediately, thumbs move. I roll my eyes. "What? Are you telling Austyn about this?"

Giving me her patented smirk, Fallon drawls, "Hell no. I'm just marking the date and time in my calendar so I can use it against you in the future."

"Oh, give me that," I growl before swiping her phone out of her hands. Knowing I'm not just going to hell, I'm making a reservation for my space, I program in my phone number before sending a text to myself.

Fallon quirks her brow. "And you did what, exactly?"

"When you and Austyn get into trouble at UT, text me. Do not contact my sister or your mother. They'll have a heart attack at your shenanigans." My experience with the high jinks the two young women could get into sends chills down my spine when I picture the number of times I'm going to be hit up for bail money.

Instead of laughing, Fallon's face sobers. I'm about to rescind my offer when she whispers, "Why am I not surprised? Before you, no one's ever tried to rescue me before."

Straightening to my full height, I stare down at the crown of her head. I'm rocked by the admission this strong-willed reincarnated goddess lets slip. But now's apparently not the time to explore it. The back door to my father's house bursts open, and a plethora of kids spill out. In most cases, proud parents file out right behind them.

Fallon locks away her momentary fragility before bounding out of the chaise and enthusiastically greeting her friends and fellow graduates.

As for me, I berate myself for showing even a modicum of weakness toward a girl who has no intention of looking back once she leaves Kensington.

CHAPTER TWO

Fallon

Could a Tweet by a pop star change the outcome of the 2020 presidential campaign? Taylor Swift shared a 38-word Tweet upbraiding President Trump for his provoking comments about the Minneapolis riots.

– StellaNova

I'M AFRAID TO STAND UP, TERRIFIED I'LL BE SPORTING A WET SPOT ON my silk dress when my pussy began leaking after feeling Ethan's hands on my bare skin after he checked out my ankle.

Christ, now how am I supposed to take one of these stupid high school boys seriously when they try to make a move on me later? It's going to be impossible now that his strong hands have smoothed over my skin letting me feel both the tenderness in the gesture as well as the callouses along his fingertips—something unexpected. I would have predicted his hands would have been smooth as he's a man who works with computers day in and day out.

I'm so glad I'm wrong.

As I stare down at his bowed head, I'm not entirely certain I'm breathing as another surge of lust blasts through me. Up until this moment, I'd always categorized the way I fantasized about my best friend's uncle much the same way I lust after Beckett Miller—the world's hottest rock god—or his country counterpart, Brendan Blake.

Something any female would turn to her partner and say, "They're on my celebrity hall pass." That's how gorgeous Ethan Kensington is. Celebrity or not, the man absolutely makes my top five.

What I felt before was something I had no problem falling asleep to when his emerald-green eyes flashed behind my closed ones, and his face flashed into my mind as I orgasmed in my room late at night. My attraction was something completely controllable.

That is until he touched my skin with his hands.

Now, the only thing I can pray is that Ethan can't smell my arousal from his touch—the way my breath hitched when he smoothed his hands up and down my calf after he caught me in his arms when I tripped in my heels before almost face planting in the graduation cake I'm supposed to share with my best friend—his niece!—and about a third of our high school.

At the moment, I need to put some distance between the two of us before I do something like jump up, wrap my legs around his waist, and dig my heels into his lower back. Trying to calm his agitation, I soothe him. "I'm fine. I just got my foot caught."

"And almost went flying into a cake." At the stern tone of his voice, my nipples pebble behind the lace of my demi bra.

"You came to the rescue."

His next words almost make me fall off the lounger I'm sitting on. "I always will."

Trying to regain some semblance of calm, I drag my clutch from where I tossed it at the lounge bend. Snapping it open, I whip out my cell and immediately begin texting. An aggravated expression crosses his face before his eyes roll heavenward. "What? Are you telling Austyn about this?"

My lips twist. "Hell no. I'm just marking the date and time in my calendar so I can use it against you in the future."

He wants to laugh. Like so many nights since we met officially a few months ago, I really want to be that person who breaks through that wall and is the one who makes him do just that. Instead, he swipes my phone from my hand.

Curious, but not concerned, I ask, "And you did what, exactly?"

"When you and Austyn get into trouble at UT, text me. Do not contact my sister or your mother. They'll have a heart attack at your shenanigans."

A warmth that has nothing to do with sexuality spreads through me. I reach for my phone and for a moment, our fingertips touch. Neither of us moves away.

Our eyes lock—blue to green.

His words were a kind of gift—a protection I've never experienced. I grew up without a father, not because he didn't want to be there, but due to a freak trucking accident wasn't able to be. My mother mourned him in ways I never quite understood until I got older. He was the love of her life and she wasn't about to dishonor his memory with stand-ins when she knew what true love was.

Still, it left me never knowing what it was to have a strong man to catch me when I fell, to lay my worries on. Or to just wrap my arms around. Ethan can't appreciate the beauty of what he just offered me, but I can't let it go unacknowledged. "Why am I not surprised? Before you, no one's ever tried to rescue me before."

His brow furrows. I know he wants to ask more, but the back door of the Kensington estate seems to explode as kids from my senior class come racing out. With much practice, I lock away my frailty and bound over to my best friend to celebrate the next stage of our lives.

The unknown.

CHAPTER THREE

KENSINGTON, TEXAS

Ethan

Snowy-T's team allegedly sent emails from 270 fake accounts to stop "Campaign Snowstorm." For those not in the know, Snowy-T has been accused of adding stimulants to guests' drinks without permission, as broken by celebrity news reporter Joanna Heart. The intent of these emails was to discredit the reporter.

Sorry, Snowy. You're still stuck in the blizzard.

—Sexy&Social, All the Scandal You Can Handle

Five Years Ago—September

I PULL BACK FROM LEANING IN TO GIVE MY DATE A PERFUNCTORY KISS on the cheek when I hear a distinctive ping on my cell phone—the one assigned to the witch who has been invading my thoughts since she left Kensington a few weeks ago for her college adventure. Stepping back, I excuse myself. "I apologize. I have to look at this."

The kindergarten teacher who has been dropping in to the shop with varying equipment from her classroom and chatting me up narrows brown eyes at me. Her previously dewy expression to in the past turns mutinous before she snaps, "Who is it?"

I don't acknowledge her acerbic comment before I read the outcry of help from Fallon. An amused chuckle escapes from the back of my throat after my heart calms down.

FALLON:

Help.. Save?

ETHAN:

What the fuck happened?

FALLON:

Heel. Pless help?

ETHAN:

Christ, witch. You're not making sense. Do you have a dog?

FALLON:

Hang onder.

ETHAN:

Hangover?

FALLON:

K.

ETHAN:

You scared the piss out of me.

FALLON:

Shhh. Yipping too loud.

ETHAN:

You mean typing?

FALLON:

Sure.

ETHAN:

How is it you can hear my typing?

Over and over Fallon sends me an emoji of a bell, telling me without exerting effort every message I send pings her phone. Part of me takes a perverse satisfaction knowing she and Austyn are feeling the agony from their morning after. A chuckle erupts from the back of my throat after my heart calms down.

FALLON:

Oh. God. Hurts.

ETHAN:

You know the answer?

ETHAN:

Don't drink that much.

FALLON:

DIDN'T!

FALLON:

Two.

I smirk. Two drinks that likely knocked her and my niece on their asses. That is, if she's telling the truth.

ETHAN:

You two must be the biggest lightweights in history.

FALLON:

No funny.

FALLON:

Worse than hairy balls.

I really want to ask her how she knows about a man's hairy balls but now isn't the time to send the little witch retching and likely starting a chain reaction with my niece two seconds after her

I back up another step and nod at my date. "I had a nice time, but I have to go."

Brown eyes I thought for a brief instance when they came into my shop the first time might be able to distract me from the woman presently texting me widen before they narrow into slits. She says nastily, "Did you double-book yourself? Get a better offer?"

I clear my throat and try not to come off as a total dick though I really don't give a shit now about finding my way into her bed. "Actually, my niece needs me."

She sneers, "Your niece is three hours away in Austin, Ethan. What could she possibly need?"

I'm about to explain when she pounds the final nail in her coffin, "Besides, rumors around town about your niece include she has a *mother* who can take adequate care of her."

Stepping close, I hiss, "I really hope you remember when it's time for your *probationary* contract to be reviewed. As you might recall, every member of the Kensington family sits on the local school board. Talking smack about my sister—a doctor—isn't a way to guarantee you're going to be renewed."

Her mouth opens and closes like a fish before she whirls around and unlocks her apartment door. Flinging the door open, she slams it behind her with an enormous bang. Right after, I hear a scream of frustration.

I don't give two shits. Glancing down at my phone, I realize it's been six minutes since I texted Fallon. My recommendation:

Ethan: Keep a bucket close by. I'll be there as soon as I can.

Three hours later, I laugh at the disaster before me. "You two look like you're auditioning for a Cyndi Lauper video."

My niece, Austyn, opens her mouth before slapping her hand over it and gripping the mop bucket closer to her. My face morphs into a frown. "Two drinks? What kind of act are you two pulling?"

"Juss two. Sw-Sw..." Austyn's voice fades off as her eyes fixate on her desk.

"Austyn?" Now fear is sending alarm bells clanging in my head.

Fallon, dressed in a blue sundress has her head resting on the lower bunk. Her whispered words are slurred. "Nesser."

"You mean never?"

Her face is chalk white, but she nods.

Concerned, I reach for one of their desk chairs and spin it around, straddling it. In doing so, it dragged across the floor, causing both to moan. I feel relief when Fallon lifts her head marginally to fry me with a glare so scorching I'd be incinerated if she actually had the witch powers I attribute to her. I confirm, "You're never drinking again?"

She shakes her head before her eyes roll back, and she passes out.

I leap from the chair and lean over her, terrified. "Fallon."

"Ssome...," Austyn starts before gagging.

Calculating how many hours it's been since midnight, I come to the conclusion that nothing about this is right. Not one thing. These aren't two women who had too much to drink. A sour feeling churns in my gut. This isn't a simple hangover. This is something worse—so much worse.

Thank God Fallon texted me.

"P-p-punch, Unca E," Austyn's words, as disjointed as they are, barely let me understand her.

I'm grateful as fuck when Fallon moans.

Fury replaces my initial disappointment in the two young women before me. Instead, the analytics training the Navy paid too much money to hone in me kicks in. "Is anyone else sick?"

"Y-yeah." I absorb Austyn's words before she leans over and hugs the bucket. Nothing comes up, but the sound causes a chain reaction in Fallon, who just dry heaves in place. I take careful note of their demeanor. They're both sweating, stains easily visible along the sides of their dresses and where the dresses catch in varying locations. Their eyes are glassy. They're both disoriented.

I swap out their buckets for individual bowls. A sneaking suspicion is rising inside me, but I don't want to make a big deal of it.

Yet.

Neither realize what I'm doing when I bag some of their conjoined vomit in a ziplock after slipping my hands into sterile gloves. Then I text a number I never thought I'd ever be using again.

ETHAN:

I think my niece was dosed w/GHB. I need some testing done.

AGENCY:

Fuck. Do you have the samples?

ETHAN:

Yes

AGENCY:

Closest drop off?

ETHAN:

Airport. Austin.

AGENCY:

Vomit, urine, or blood?

ETHAN:

Vomit

AGENCY:

I'll have the agent test on site.

AGENCY:

How certain are you?

ETHAN:

Over 95%. May be other victims.

AGENCY:

Someone will meet you there in thirty.

ETHAN:

Roger. Owe you one.

I crouch down to the two women who likely feel like their insides are coming out their mouths. "I have to run out."

Fallon pries her eyes open and I'm confronted with emotions in no way is my heart ready for. Her eyes are swirling with a mix of agony and fear, plus something I refuse to let myself see—a feverish, naked longing. God, I want to consume the last of what I see in her eyes more than I want my next breath, but I don't want it because some son of a bitch drugged her.

I reach for her free hand—the one that isn't clutching the clean bowl and explain, "I wanted to check your condition before I bought any food—

especially if I had to take you two to the ER. Now, it's time to go get your hangover provisions."

She relaxes. Her lips curve and her eyes drift to half-mast. "Taking care."

I relish the feeling of her flawless skin beneath my fingers as they stroke down her cheek. "I promised you I would."

"Close my eyes and die now." At that, her long lashes drift fully downward and hide the unique shade of blue from my view.

My heart flips in my chest at the flippant words knowing if I'm right, there was a damn good chance of that or something else having happened to her and Austyn last night. Leaning over, I press a kiss on her forehead before I do the same to Austyn. "I'll be back within the hour."

I get to my feet and am opening their dorm room door when Austyn mumbles, "T-t-take m-m-my k-k-keys."

I'm about to leave when I hear Fallon manage, obviously still drugged. "He came."

It isn't until I'm in the hallway, a hallway I note is filled with the noxious smell of puke, I confirm aloud, "Just like I always will. No matter what you need, witch."

With that, I go to meet members of my former team for answers.

CHAPTER FOUR

KENSINGTON, TEXAS

Fallon

Every time I hear Erzulie's name, I think of Stevie Nicks.

Every time I hear her sing, I know I'm right to do so.

—@PRyanPOfficial

Five Years Ago—October

TREPIDATION.

It's an emotion I'm not used to feeling.

My emotions since the night a group of us at a party were deliberately drugged have caused my sense of self to evaporate. I'm no longer striding across campus without a care in the world. Instead, I'm checking in dark corners, even in the middle of broad daylight. Even with hours of counseling, I can't find my balance any longer, despite my desperate need to locate my sense of self.

It's gone.

I've changed.

All because of one night.

At home in Kensington for parent's weekend, I find myself keeping makeshift weapons in my pocket as I stroll down the streets. Fear can be tangible when you can feel your heart pound out of your chest when you walk alone in a dark corridor to get to a classroom, and you don't know if your nightmare is going to jump out and grab you. Still, it's exhausting.

Something has to give.

Part of my brain wants to hide away from the reality of the outcome of the university's investigation into the college party Austyn and I attended. We didn't get sick on the punch—we were drugged. If it wasn't for how little we drank, who knows what would have happened to us.

A subdued whisper tells me, *More than just your feelings would have changed.* I know that to be true, based on the stories that have come out. The only thing is, no one is blaming anyone except the guys who spiked the punch.

Our reasoning and control were stripped from us.

I clutch my coat around me tighter before racing the rest of the way home. Bursting through the front door, I quickly drop into a chair.

Within minutes, my mother sits down on the ottoman as I huddle, knees to chest. I'm home because the last place I wanted to be was at school. I had to have a safe place to expel the emotions swirling inside me since that party. Anger surges through me, making my muscles tense. "I refuse to weaken at a time I'm supposed to grow into a woman of strength."

My mother grips my fingers. "Then what do you want to do, sweetheart? Do you want to leave school? Take a year to regroup?"

"Yes. No." Silence follows my confusing response. I feel the pressure of my mother's hands, the comforting scent of her perfume wash over me. In the bubble of peace she's created for me, an idea comes to me. I consider it, twisting it around in my mind before I give it voice. "What if I were to transfer?"

"Fallon, these kinds of problems may occur at any school," she logically points out.

I concede her point before pointing out, "But, Mama, you know I struggled to decide where I should go. I went with having a built-in friendship and proximity to home over my future ambition."

Her eyes widen fractionally. "You're thinking of transferring to Seven Virtues."

"Think about it. It's less than an eighth of the student body. It has the major I want—"

"Something you would need to go to another university for graduate school if you remained at UT."

"If I find an off-campus apartment, I can declare residency after a year, so I'll only need loans for out of state tuition for a year." I quake at the idea of taking out a loan for that amount, but I won't let that deter me. This feels right—the first thing that does since that fateful night spent puking.

My mother tugs my fingers. "What about Austyn?"

I open my mouth and snap it shut. That's the major crimp in my plan—explaining to my best friend I need to leave UT. Then I voice my last concern. "Truthfully, I'm more worried about leaving you here alone."

My mother pushes to her feet. "Give this a lot of consideration, Fallon. Then, once you've had a discussion with Austyn, we'll talk some more."

Staring into nothing, I realize the next move is mine if I want to stop worrying about my immediate future.

"You're not the only one thinking about leaving." Austyn takes my announcement with surprising ease. I should have expected no less from my best friend, but I'm stunned by her counter. After all, she's made a huge name for herself as a DJ on campus. Her plans have always centered around music. She's a damn prodigy, able to pick up any instrument and play it at an expert level.

Not to mention what she can do behind a sound booth, I think with pride.

Right now, we've slowed our horses to a walk through the sunflower fields behind her family's farm, discussing our next steps. "I'm not?"

She shakes her head, causing her braid to swish back and forth. "I'm putting together a plan."

Curious, I rein in so I can concentrate on what she's saying. "For Paige to send you to a different school?"

She snorts. "I want Mama to cash in my college fund so I can move to New York and try DJ'ing full time."

My jaw drops as my mind explodes in shock. I'm unable to formulate a reply until Austyn asks with more than a hint of amusement, "Should I use your reaction to gauge Mama's? You think it's a bad idea?"

I walk my horse as close to hers as I possibly can and lean to the side so I can grab her arm. Tugging her close, I rasp, "It's the best damn idea you've ever had. You're going to set the world on fire, Austyn."

"Come with me. New York has some of the best museums in the world. We can still live together. Both of our dreams can come true."

I contemplate my words carefully because a part of me wants nothing more than to go with her to maintain the connection we've had since I moved in across the street. "Seven Virtues is one of the best schools in the country for what I want to do, Austyn. If they accept me for a mid-year transfer, that's the path I need to take. I thought I could go about it a different way, but I think we both found out that was a mistake."

"Understatement of the century," she mutters.

"Austyn, I have to tell you something."

"What's that?"

"If I knew then what I know now, I might not have gone with you to Austin."

"What?" She screeches so loudly, our horses begin to shift beneath us.

After we get them settled, I explain how I found out that if I go an extra year to school, their accelerated master's program feeds directly into the Biltmore Estate. "My dream, Austyn."

"I know." Her head lifts and I can't miss the tears on her cheeks. "So, this is it? This is where we end?"

I jerk her forward into my arms. "No, you goof. You and me? We'll never end."

She turns her horse around so we can feel the warm Texas sun beat down upon us as we ride back toward the stables for what may be one of the last times in the foreseeable future.

For both of us.

CHAPTER FIVE

SEVEN VIRTUES, NORTH CAROLINA

Fallon

Saratoga Springs, N.Y. Cybersecurity attacks can happen anywhere. Even e-readers can be hacked just by opening a single e-book infected with malicious content, according to research published at Defcon.

#defcon29

—Castor Newsroom

Four Years Ago—January

WRAPPING MY SCARF TIGHTER AROUND MY NECK, I TAKE A MOMENT

to inhale the cool air in my lungs before making my way across campus so I'm not late for my art history lecture.

If I were still living in Texas, I'd be in shorts and a T-shirt, I think with some amusement, despite the fact that it's January and noticeably cooler. It's one of the many changes I've quickly adapted to since moving to North Carolina. That and the rolling mountainous landscape in the small college town near the infamous Biltmore Estate is as far from the never-ending plains of Texas.

Texas. Kensington. *Ethan.* A tiny ping in the region of my heart stabs when I think about how long it's been since I've received a text from him—even just a cheesy GIF or funny meme. Despite the obvious, I can't stop my heart from being disappointed by the fact that now that I'm out of his family's vicinity, I also guess he feels he no longer needs to keep his promise to me even to check in.

I mutter to myself, "I could be dead for all he knows. Then again, it's not like I expect a man to look out for me anyway."

Squaring my shoulders, I toss my hair and flash a smile at a handsome guy I recognize from my dorm who holds the door for me as I race up a flight of stairs to the second floor of Constantine Hall.

After what happened last fall at the party, it was hard to remain where I knew I didn't want to be. I contacted the admissions office at Seven Virtues University and quietly arranged for a mid-year transfer the week I returned from my visit home during parent's weekend. Though her timeline wasn't as set in stone as mine was, Austyn was working as diligently as I was for her move to New York.

Both of us were done with the life we were living in Austin and each of us had plans that led to our dreams coming true. I championed her decision to seek out the bright lights and big city—a place I promised her I'd visit once I got settled—even as she offered up recommendations for me to help me with mine.

Finally, it was just the two of us together, right before holiday break, toasting each other with chai tea. "The one thing I'm going to miss about moving is you."

"You don't have to worry about that."

"I don't?"

"Nope. Want to know why?"

I lean back and watch as she picks up her guitar and plucks the strings. An Indigo Girls song that Austyn swears is our secret soulmate song fills the air. Just after the intro, her incredible voice belts "Power of Two."

I am helpless to do anything but sing it back to her.

When it's done, Austyn sets her guitar aside before her wet eyes meet mine. "It's like the last stanza of that song, Fallon. We're closer to being free than ever before, and if we have each other, we can do anything. We don't have to be together to do that."

Careful of her guitar, I dive across the space and wrap my best friend in a hug that seems to last forever back then but wasn't near long enough, considering I haven't seen her face in weeks.

Now, having moved, being first stunned then elated when my mother followed me to Seven Virtues since her job as an IT auditor permitted her to work anywhere, signing up for new classes, and having a front-row seat to Austyn's New York adventure with the world in the palm of her powerful hands, life is good. I haven't lost any of the important relationships I feared I would by moving to North Carolina.

Austyn and I talk almost daily—swapping stories about everything between what we're doing every day to the men sliding in and out of our lives. Whereas Austyn is meeting smoking hot older men—the kind of guys right up my alley—I have a ready-made smorgasbord of hot young bodies, all of whom appear to be interested, but it isn't in any way reciprocated.

I might break down soon though because, truly, there are only so many batteries I can order from Amazon before the shipping giant starts to target sex toys as my primary advertising.

Truth be told, I'm not playing hard to get. I'm just looking for a man and nobody I've met here has made me want to spread my legs to let him pump his cock in and out of me. I don't want some boy who has no clue what to do with their scrawny bodies. They can shoot me puppy eyes and flash their dimples—it will be a long wait before I let one charm me into bed. For right now, it's easier to ignore them all. Like me, Austyn is selective. She seems to have set her sights on a singularly arrogant, disappearing mess—her roommate's brother.

To say we're both sexually frustrated is an understatement. I wondered aloud to her on the phone the other night, "I have enough problems getting laid at this school."

A welcome bubble of laughter escaped her lips. "Well, what did you expect?"

"I had such hopes some hot professor would bend me over his desk. Maybe I'd tempt one of the priests into thinking they'd made a mistake when they'd joined the seminary," I flat out told her. Her laughter almost took out my hearing. In my head, I tacked on, *I want someone who makes my clit tingle the way Ethan did at our graduation party.*

That's when Austyn chooses to remind me, "You go to a university whose name has the word 'virtue' in it."

"Trust me, that isn't as much of a problem as one might think," I informed her dryly. Then I proceeded to tell her about the number of condom wrappers in the bathroom every Sunday morning and her laughter again pealed out.

"So...your problem?"

A pair of green eyes flash from the depths of my memory as he knelt in front of me at my high school graduation. "Huh?"

"Hello, Fallon. Why aren't you getting any?"

"What is my problem, you ask?"

"Oh, please tell me." I heard her comforter rustle as she got comfortable.

"I can suck a dick and finger a man's ass without breaking a sweat. But ask a man to manage to suck my nipple at the same time he's fingering me—it's a no go. They can't manage two body parts at once. And we let these men operate heavy machinery?"

Austyn screamed with laughter, her beautiful voice panting out my name, "Fal-Fal...oh my god."

"I mean, let's face it. Most of them can barely have their heads between our legs and remember to slide their fingers in and they're incompetent."

After I proceeded to tease her out of her bad mood due to her own man not calling her, I buried the hurt feelings I felt when I reminded myself Ethan had forgotten all about me and his promise to be there for me when I drawled, "I'll continue to hold out hope your uncle is secretly pining away for me because the pickings around Seven Virtues are slim."

Austyn snorted before changing the topic. What she didn't realize is my ideal man is someone I can lean on, someone who isn't afraid to take on me and my attitude. Ethan Kensington was the current bar, but that didn't mean there wasn't a man out there who couldn't top him.

Or that I shouldn't be looking for him, according to my mother.

Talk about a shock—I about passed out when I was helping my mother unpack my dorm room at the beginning of the semester and during a conversation where she was placing photos around my mid-year dorm room, she casually mentioned how much Ethan reminded her of my father.

Lifting one of me, Austyn, and Ethan, she mused, "There's just something about him—whether it's that silent strength or his great butt—that is certainly attention grabbing."

Choking on my own breath, I managed, "Mom, are you involved with Ethan?" Because if that was the case, I'd sure as fuck be abandoning my new dream and joining my best friend in New York. School or no school, I wouldn't be able to be around the man I've been crushing on for well over a year if he and my mother were getting horizontal together. Fuck, is that why he stopped texting me? Has he been texting her instead? I turn around and study her face to find her studying me intently.

Objectively, my mother's a beautiful woman. About ten years older than Ethan, there's nothing to stop a relationship between the two of them.

Nothing at all.

Her wise eyes met mine. "No, I was merely making an observation, darling."

All the air seemed to rush back into the room at once.

"But Fallon…" she began.

I held up a hand. "I already know what you're going to say."

She placed the frame down and came closer. Taking my hand, she led me to my bed before sitting on it and pulling me down next to her. Cupping my cheek, she said, "You remind me so much of myself at your age."

I opened my mouth to thank her, but I was flabbergasted when she continued, "My interest in older men was because I didn't have a good opinion about myself, Fallon. My home life wasn't the best. I was determined to escape it. It made me feel older than I actually was. Maybe that's what attracted your father."

"Or maybe it's because you're you—remarkable, smart, and gorgeous," I corrected her.

Her eyes were unfocused as she recalled memories I'll never have. "Your father was my everything. He had this way about him that made me feel like I was more than enough. He was willing to give up—"

I reached up and covered her hand with my own. "What did Dad give up?"

Her eyes blinked back into focus. "That's a story for a different time."

"Mama?"

She squeezed my fingers. "That's the kind of man I want for you, Fal. One who cherishes every part of you. Nothing else about him matters."

"Truly?" I hesitated before rushing out, "Even if the man were older than I was?"

"The only thing the man who captures your heart has to do is to make certain that after he makes my daughter fall in love with him that she never doubts it." Mama leaned forward and pressed a kiss to my forehead.

Now, as I scoot past some of my fellow classmates, I ignore the vibration in my jacket pocket. The important people in my life know where I am and what I'm doing. If it's Mama and it's an emergency, she will call.

With that, I whip out my laptop and begin to take notes on St. Jerome's oil on wood by Da Vinci at the Vatican.

Two hours later, I'm saving my notes when I recall the frantic buzzing at the beginning of my lecture. Hoping it's just another news alert about my best friend, I'm shocked at the message on my Lock Screen:

ETHAN:

Are you ignoring me, witch?

CHAPTER SIX

KENSINGTON, TEXAS

Ethan

Rumor has it that indie goddess Erzulie—a.k.a. Kylie Miles—doesn't have to work another day in her life based on the amount she inherited from her sister, Leanne. That amount was made public with the final filing of the stock transfer on behalf of the Castor Trust. However, Erzulie continues to dedicate herself to her music.

The real question is which Erzulie will be showing up at the Grammys? Will it be the seasoned performer or the woman rightfully still in the throes of grief?

—StellaNova

I FALL FACE FIRST ON MY BED AND GROAN, GRATEFUL TO BE BACK home and in the comfort of my own apartment. When I agreed to return the favor for the Agency running the tests on behalf of Austyn and Fallon—setting up a shitstorm of an investigation at their old college—who fucking knew the favor I'd be asked to assist with would take so fucking long? Especially when I had limited access to every person I knew—including my family—as I lived under an assumed name while I was spending the better part of a month in the picturesque town of Silverthorn, New Hampshire, trying to fly beneath the radar of the paparazzi as they descended like vultures after the death of CEO and world-renowned white hat, Leanne Miles.

Having met Leanne professionally and collaborated with her company, Castor, on a few contracts for the Department of Defense since I left the navy, I'm one of the many members of the tech community collectively reeling at the implications of her murder.

Even before that, my father's massive coronary directly as a result of my sister confronting him as a result of a lifetime of lies he subjected her to, a holiday where my sister rekindled her relationship with her daughter's father, and my niece grew closer to her father every second she spent with him, I was grateful to put Texas behind me for a few weeks.

The second I received the call from my former boss just after the first of the year, I knew why I was sent to hunt any and all information I could in Leanne's hometown as there are any number of national agencies and international enemies eager to determine not only the cause of her death but also unearth what secrets would be available to the highest bidder. And they all wanted to cast the blame on each other as quickly as possible.

But things never stayed clean when the Agency was involved. I practically snarled over the phone at the big man behind the desk when he admitted, "I need you to do more than just your normal sweep."

"What do you mean?"

"One of my agents went missing the day of Leanne Miles' funeral."

"What the fuck were they even doing there?" I scrubbed my hand over my face as I sat in the small, nondescript motel room in Silverthorn. "You're determined to give me a damn coronary, just like my father, aren't you?"

"Hopefully you're in better shape than that bastard."

"Fuck you. Now, why was your agent here?"

"Watching what went down in Silverthorn at Leanne Miles' funeral."

"And?" Knowing there was more to follow.

"Someone tried to run them off the road." In response, a deep snarl of disgust erupted from my chest, something the man on the other end of the line approved of.

"How many did they get?"

"Cleanup crew found three. I need to know if there were more."

"Do you think there are?"

"Does it matter what I think? I need to know."

"You always do."

"Dig down. Use whatever resources you have access to, and I don't care if they're legal to do it," the man snapped before disconnecting the secure call.

My thoughts flashed briefly to my family and...her.

Fallon.

For the first time ever, she wasn't at my family's annual Christmas Eve party. I didn't get to see her shaking her amazing body to whatever song Austyn was singing. I didn't get an opportunity to try to maneuver her beneath the mistletoe. Instead, I propped myself up against a wall, nursing a single whiskey while keeping a sharp eye on the door, willing her to come through it.

She never did, and neither did her mother, which caused its own spurt of surprise. Helen Brookes has been my sister's neighbor for as long as I can recall. A quick peek out the front window showed they were home as a tree was prominent in the front window, though there appeared to be new sheers across the windows.

Still, neither woman showed.

Damn, I'm thinking about her more and more despite the fact she likely found some college guy at UT closer to her age and is living it up—like she should be, I remind myself. Just because I'd sell my left nut to have her in my bed doesn't mean she'd want me to be there.

Shrugging the disturbing thought of some guy touching her perfect skin when the truth is I'd give anything if I could find someone to wipe the fantasies of her from my mind, I figured this might be a good break. Satisfied at my silence, I was told, "Then keep your ass there and do what you do best."

"What's that?" I asked, curious.

"Clean up other people's shitstorms." His words remind me of how we met. Back when I was just an ensign—a hacker to be sure, but nothing in comparison to the men and women from the contracting team who stormed aboard the bridge of the *USS Lassen*—an Arleigh Burke missile destroyer I was serving on. The Alliance crew immediately drew notice from every man and woman serving on deck, in particular from the SEAL team, as they took over our consoles. Back then, the man was the hardened SEAL team leader—a lieutenant who had survived more combat action than I could fathom at the time. And when it was over, the two of us and a shit load of others working to keep hostages alive—not to mention the world at large— came off that particular cruise changed after we witnessed the desecration of human life for the madness of greed. My life mission drastically changed and I never questioned it.

Not once.

Not until I saw Fallon standing in my father's backyard.

Now I wonder what the fuck is wrong because this is the longest we've gone without contact since we met. I don't miss the opportunity to give the man on the other end of the line a raft of shit because I know I'm one of the few who can. "I gave you puke to test. You sent me as part of a clandestine, off-books, HUMANIT fact-finding fuckup." The truth is, the human intelligence gathering mission yielded little, but it did give us a few leads, all of which I already passed along. What I'm pointing out is what he asked for wasn't balanced in the slightest.

His, "You're good at it," made me bark out a laugh. The problem was, what should have been a seven-day job took weeks longer than expected. The agent I was supposed to be locating was never once found on camera. She was smoke. All I found once I hacked every security camera I could from street cameras to personal doorbells, was blond hair caught in a glimpse out a car window as she drove away from the fatal shooting sight. It demonstrated the agent in question is a fucking bad ass who managed to survive by the skin of her teeth. Not to mention, we share a mutual mentor if her driving skills are anything to go by.

Which also means she's lethal.

Pulling my phone from my back pocket, I ring my sister to let her know I'm back in town from the computer system consultation she believes I've been working at, only to find out she's in the process of packing up and heading back to New York soon to be with my niece and her man. I groan before rolling over to my back. Despite my exhaustion, I offer, "Need any help?"

"You sound exhausted, Ethan," she scolds.

"Yeah. This contract was a bitch," I admit, without elaborating. My family has no clue about the work I did for the Agency. They *think* I own a lucrative consulting business with a storefront open for local computer repairs in our hometown of Kensington, Texas. I snort. As if that would be enough to occupy my time.

They have no idea what happens in the back room.

They have no clue about the jobs behind the secure doors.

No one does but the man who sends me orders from safely behind his desk in northern Virginia.

If they did, I wonder if they'd hate me as much as I do myself, I think despairingly. When I think of all the pain I could have saved my sister if I verified the source of the information that guided all of our lives...

I broach the topic of my father's deceit with my sister carefully. "Have you talked to him?"

I hear her murmur to someone she'll be right back before she replies, "If you're referring to our father, then no. Not since before you left. I'm arranging for his home health care for when I'm gone."

"I still can't believe you're leaving."

She's silent for a long while. "It feels right to be with him, Ethan. How many years have Beckett and I lost?"

"Because of lies and deceit perpetrated by our father?" I was on a tour of duty when my father lied to my sister about not being able to find the father of her child. In the years in between, we all accepted his word only to find out he lied about so much.

Too much to forgive.

Paige breaks into my thoughts. "Yes."

"Too many." The answer comes easily.

She sighs. "I just wish you could find your happy."

Immediately, Fallon's face flashes into my mind. I'm about to reply back when she says to someone helping her pack—most likely our brother, "Put that one in the pile for Fallon so I can mail it to her."

My brows snap together when I realize I haven't received a single message from the little witch. Casually, I ask, "How is she doing?"

"I assume fine. Why?"

"Just curious," I try to fob off the question.

Paige unknowingly becoming a fountain of information. "Helen didn't say anything before she moved and Austyn hasn't said anything about her being unhappy since Fallon transferred schools."

What? Moved? New school? Instead of verbally vomiting those questions and being subject to an interrogation, I manage, "That's good to hear."

"It really is. Listen, I have to go. Jess and I have plans in a couple of hours. Why don't you join us?" Her excitement is practically palpable and I want to bask in her happiness—after I find out what the fuck happened to Fallon.

"Sounds good. Text me where to meet you."

"Talk soon." My sister disconnects the call.

Immediately after ending the call, I open my text string with Fallon. My heart drops when I realize I haven't texted her in close to two months. The last thing she sent me was a text:

Fallon: I have some pretty big news to share. You around?

My stomach churns when I realize I didn't respond. Not only that, but I know I deliberately ignored her incoming message because I was on a date with another woman in another futile attempt to forget what Fallon made me feel. It went nowhere—none of them ever do. It's a self-flagellation, a torture I submit to because I can't have what I want—a woman I friend zoned because of her age.

Even then, I've been a shitty one at best. I have no idea what's going on in Fallon's life and it's my own fucking fault. My fingers text before my brain can catch up.

ETHAN:

Are you there?

ETHAN:

Where are you?

ETHAN:

I heard you left school? What the fuck happened?

ETHAN:

Fallon?

ETHAN:

Is everything okay with your Mom? With you?

ETHAN:

I know I owe you a huge apology for ghosting you.

ETHAN:

Are you ignoring me, witch?

An hour later and there's still no response. Frustrated, I yank my laptop from my bag and start hunting her without a single qualm about invading her privacy. Most people would be scared if they knew how easy it is to be traced online using simple technology—let alone the shit I know how to do. With a few simple keystrokes, I get my answers, but I'm dumbfounded by what's on my screen.

"Fallon's in Seven Virtues, North Carolina? Where the fuck is that?" A simple Google search tells me the university town is located right outside Asheville, not far from the Biltmore Estate.

She left.

She's gone.

My phone is lying next to me on the bed when it vibrates. Snatching it up immediately, I read her response.

FALLON:

I had something to say a few months ago.

ETHAN:

Like your whole family moving?

FALLON:

Obviously it wasn't that important to you. No big.

ETHAN:

Fallon...

FALLON:

Don't worry about losing my digits.

FALLON:

I can take care of myself, Uncle E.

ETHAN:

I'm not your damn uncle.

FALLON:

Already figured out you're not anyone to me,
are you?

Shit. What did I do to break even the tentative bond between us?

CHAPTER SEVEN

SEVEN VIRTUES, NORTH CAROLINA

Fallon

Ever since the Grammys, Beckett Miller and DJ Kensington are in each other's back pockets. Is this a potential collaboration or something more? I wouldn't mind more of either of them, if you take my meaning.

—Moore You Want

Four Years Ago—February

I'M HUDDLED IN OUR ON-CAMPUS COFFEE SHOP WITH MY FLOOR-mates Ruby and Layla when they mention the most notorious Seven Virtue's watering hole, Galileo's, needs waitresses. Ruby gushes, "I heard there's an actual pendulum you have to navigate through to get in and out of the bar."

Layla, much more pragmatic, drawls, "I need money for books next semester. Who cares what it looks like so long as it's safe and pays well?"

I agree with Layla. "Besides, can you imagine the liability? One drunk tries to navigate it and it would be like a bad shot on a mini-golf course hole." I slap my hand against the side of my head and topple sideways. "*Whack!*"

That sets the three of us off in giggling fits. It's Layla who probes hesitantly about the boundaries between me and Austyn, "Couldn't you ask Kensington for money?"

"I could."

"So why don't you?"

Now that Austyn's become a household name, everyone has questions for me about her. I shrug. "She's my best friend."

"Then why work?" Ruby persists.

"If it was some kind of life or death thing, I wouldn't need to ask. She'd just be there trying to shove it in my face. But our bond isn't because of who she is but who she's always been to me," I chastise them, trying to do it gently. These two are asking questions of me instead of asking them behind my back like most of the campus is doing.

That gives them food for thought allowing me a moment to ponder whether I can maintain my perfect GPA and work a job to offset some unexpected living expenses I don't want to burden my mother with. It's Ruby who points at my face and announces, "You're thinking about it."

I don't deny the charge. "I am."

Layla shoves to her feet. "Then let's go find out if the rumor is true."

"What rumor?"

"That the owner is a gorgeous, misogynistic prick."

"Oh, goodie. Just the kind of man I always wanted to spend my free time with," I clap my hands together eagerly as if someone told me Santa was a silver fox from a Vegas strip show.

Ruby perks up. "Maybe he's so gorgeous, it won't matter."

I shrug into my lined barn coat and tug on my hat and gloves as Ethan's face flashes into my mind. A spear of pain tries to pierce through the armor I've built around my heart. "It always matters."

Layla laughs. "Then what are we waiting for?"

An hour later, Levi James—the owner of Galileo's—has already interviewed Layla into a quivering mess. He now has Ruby in the back room presumably doing the same. As gorgeous as the man is—for once, the rumor mill wasn't wrong—his rabid grizzly bear attitude detracts from his sexual appeal.

While Ruby's being verbally filleted by someone who likely learned their interrogation tactics from a three-letter agency, I admire the style the bar has. Layla and I were right—Ruby was way off base about walking through the pendulum to gain access to Galileo's. Still, I was floored to see there actually is one in the courtyard as we were escorted beyond doors painted with the Renaissance developers coat of arms.

Slipping off my outerwear, I stand to get closer to the *Moon from Sidereus Nuncius* meticulously painted behind the stage when something within me calls for me to hum the famous Indigo Girls anthem about the inventor.

That's when I hear a strident, "You! What are you singing?"

Whirling around, I find myself face-to-face with Levi. If I wasn't looking at his face, I'd swear his teeth would have either Ruby's blood or drool coming from a fang as he debated his next tasty snack. Without thinking, I get right in his face. "What? Too good for a little girl-on-girl musical action in this place?"

Levi rolls his eyes before he walks over to the bar and rings a bell three times. Immediately, as if the staff and patrons are trained monkeys, they all belt out Galileo's refrain. He shoots me a reproachful glare even as everyone turns back to their drinks. I shrug before offering a suggestion, "You should do it at a certain time, like a toast."

Levi's brows snap together. "This is how we've always done it."

"And every other bar uses a bell for the bartenders to thank their patrons for large tips."

The bartender, a gorgeous redhead, slow claps. Levi turns his feral snarl in her direction, "Shut it, Caroline."

She rolls her eyes and goes back to taking stock, his attitude not disturbing her in the least.

He steps closer to get in my personal space. "So, how do you un-train people who have been coming here for years?"

Think, Fallon. Think. Then something from my behavioral science class pops into my mind. "You have to consciously discard your actions."

"Excuse me, college girl?"

I roll my eyes. "It's easy."

His voice gets deadly when he whispers, "Is that so?"

"Yes. Stop ringing the damn bell. You're turning people into Pavlovian dogs." Behind him, Layla and Ruby snicker.

He whirls on them and they both try to stifle their laughter, but not the bartender. She chortles, "Surprised your big...brain didn't come up with that one, Levi. Must have had it thrust into other things at the time when they taught that in psych."

"Shut. The. Hell. Up." He bellows.

"Yeah, the chances of that are slim." She comes from around the counter and holds out her hand. "Caroline Mars."

"Fallon Brookes."

Without waiting a beat, she says, "Ignore Levi. Y'all are hired."

"Goddamn it, Caroline," he snaps.

"We need waitresses, and we need ones who think with their brains and not feel the need to fall to their knees to suck your cock first," she fires back. She points at me. "She thinks and presumably so do her friends. Stop dicking around—or worse yet, hiring our staff with your dick. Bring people on who will keep bodies in the seats before our profits cause us to close the doors."

If this was a cartoon, steam would be escaping from Levi's ears. Still, he tempers his ill will down enough to grit out, "It would be appreciated if you could start training this week."

I shrug. "Sure. Do you need our school schedules?"

Levi throws up his hands. "Work that shit out with Caroline." Then he storms off and slams out the back door.

I'm about to repeat the question to Caroline when one of the few daytime die hards hands me a twenty. I cock my head to the side. "What's this for?"

"A thank you. If I don't have to sing that song every time some drunk asshole rings that bell, lassie, I'll consider it a miracle. A few times a night, sure. Every bar has its shtick. Last weekend, those drunk dipshits rang it fifty-seven times." His voice is aggrieved.

"You deserve a medal."

He lifts his beer. "I'll take a refill."

"I'll get right on it." I pat his shoulder as I make my way toward the high-polished mahogany bar. As soon as I reach it, Caroline finishes pulling a fresh draft. Immediately I drop the twenty into her tip jar. She winks before declaring, "I'm going to like you, Fallon."

"Same."

"You don't seem to mind shoving Levi into place."

A flash of Ethan's face comes and goes in my mind before I reply, "I've generally found most men are worth screwing well."

Her lips curve into a smile that transforms her face from stunning to exquisite. "Oh, this is going to be fun."

I wave Layla and Ruby over. "It's going to be a hell of a lot more than that."

CHAPTER EIGHT

SEVEN VIRTUES, NORTH CAROLINA

Fallon

Sometimes stepping away from a situation can give you an entirely new perspective.

—The Fireside Psychologist

Four Years Ago—May

LAST NIGHT, MY BEST FRIEND BLEW INTO TOWN AND NOW FINALLY, MY apartment above Galileo's feels like home. Austyn admired the space I decorated in my quirky, signature style. "This place is exactly like you described."

I sit down on the guest room bed and curl my leg beneath me. "I love it here, Austyn. I never expected to."

Her penetrating blue eyes—eyes she inherited from her infamous father—spear into mine. "You're the one who left UT."

"Did it feel right to you after everything that happened?"

"Nothing would have felt right except being in New York." A flash of sadness ripples across her face.

I quickly change the subject so she doesn't need to discuss the reason she's on this short tour just yet. "I don't know why, but being in Seven Virtues feels right."

Her face brightens and she teases, "So much you don't feel like moving to New York with me this summer?"

I fan myself. "Now, I'm not opposed to meeting your hot as fuck father, but still, this place is home." I pat the bed next to me and she sits down. When she does, her dress catches beneath her and I spy the bump just below her waistline. My voice trembles, barely managing to confirm the name of the father—the rat bastard she caught cheating on her at the nightclub she was performing at, no less. The magnitude of the secret she's hiding from the world explains the deep shadows beneath her eyes and the sallow color of her skin. "Does Paige know? Your father?"

"Mama, yes. Not my father. I'm not sure how he'd react."

I scoff. "Like he has room to talk. You're walking, talking proof of him being a hypocrite if that was the case."

She shoves me, but I spy the twitches of a smile trying to lift the corners of her mouth. We talk about who does or, more importantly, who doesn't know. Especially the baby's father. I snarl out, "The bastard doesn't deserve to know."

Wearily, she pushes a hand over her multi-colored hair. "Eventually, you know I'll have to tell him."

I smooth my hand over her hair, offering her what comfort I can. Then my body shakes with suppressed laughter. "I do have one question though."

"Ask away."

"Are all you Kensington women so damn fertile?"

Austyn chokes back a laugh before she replies, "We must be."

She lays her head in my lap and we talk about some of the more crazy aspects of her pregnancy. Finally, she blinks up at me, tears making her eyes look like big pools. "What the hell is wrong with me?"

Ferociously, I say, "Not a damn thing. You fell in love with a douchebag. Someone you're better off not having in your life." Kind of the way I've forced myself to close myself off from communicating with Ethan unless it directly pertains to Austyn.

There's no need to feed my soul with hope. But as much as I feel that way about my own love life, I pour every ounce of hope into my best friend because she and my future niece or nephew deserve all the love the world has to offer.

After blowing my mind with news the world hopefully won't be aware of for a long time to come, I finally ask Austyn, "What's it like on the road?"

"Riddled with glitz and glamour. Party every night."

"Uh-huh. Try selling it to someone who hasn't known you as long as I have."

"God, you're such a bitch. I've missed you so much."

"I missed you too." Never have truer words been spoken.

CHAPTER NINE

Fallon

There are so many songs about lost love. Do people really FUBAR that much?

—@PRyanPOfficial

You're one to ask?

—@CuTEandRich3

AS SHE SIPS A CUP OF DECAFFEINATED CHAI FROM A WINE GLASS, Austyn asks, "How did you find this place?"

"I work downstairs."

"Galileo's? The infamous Galileo's is right downstairs?"

I wink. "Makes for a rough commute on those nights when I don't finish until close to three."

"Was it always a rental?"

I nod. "Caroline, a knockout redhead and our lead bartender, was the previous tenant. She moved out after taunting Levi—"

"That's the owner?" Austyn interrupts.

"Yep." I wait for Austyn to sort out all the players she'll meet tomorrow.

"And this Levi doesn't do it for you on your 'bang a hot older guy' radar?" Austyn eyes me over the rim of her glass.

I snort. "He's one of the most gorgeous men I've ever met."

"Yet, you told me there wasn't a man in Seven Virtues you'd bang?"

"Still true."

"What's wrong with him?"

"If I had a choice of doing a boy who couldn't find my clit or doing Levi, I'd do the boy every time and twice on Sunday."

At that, Austyn does a spit take into her glass. "Oh, crap. That says a lot about him. What makes him such a douche?"

I place my glass on the table. "He interrogates women like they're going to rob him blind or he's slotting them into his calendar for their assigned fucking. He has no business sense and demeans everyone who works for him. He—"

She lifts her hand. "I get the point. Has he ever tried to hit on you?"

"He might have tried if I didn't put him in place the day I interviewed." I explain to her the tradition of the Indigo Girl's song.

Austyn's interest latches onto what I noticed immediately. "There seems to be something between him and this Caroline."

"Like bad Nickelodeon slime. It's front and present, and you can't get away from it," I agree.

She grins and every time it happens, something inside me relaxes infinitesimally. This is what we both need—each other. "Have you ever asked her about it?"

"I hinted once."

"When?"

"When I asked her why she was moving out."

"To which she said?"

"'I don't need my 'landlord' to be close enough to screen my dates.'"

Austyn's face turns thoughtful. "Does he interrogate yours?"

"If it wasn't for the fact he deducts my rent from my tips, I'm not certain he'd care if I lived here."

She purrs, "Oh, this I can't wait to see. I sense musical inspiration coming on."

"So, you're for certain coming with me to work tomorrow night?"

"I wouldn't miss it for the world."

I tell her more stories since I started spending every available spare minute working at Galileo's. She's enthralled about the idea of the toast. "I'd swear, the big bad boy of Seven Virtues pouted every day no one sang his infamous bar song."

Austyn clucks, "Poor baby. What did you do to soften the blow to his male ego?"

I explain. "After a month, Caroline shoved me up on stage at forty-one minutes past the hour with a Coke in hand. One minute later—in honor of the year Galileo died: 1642—I was singing Galileo's theme song *a cappella*."

The crowd joined in—lifting their glasses as well. The commotion dragged Levi from his office. His eyes bugged out. Caroline merely walked by and slapped him upside the head before she taunted, "Now, maybe listening to a woman will cause something to penetrate other than your dick."

Austyn's leaning forward like we're watching a Turkish drama through our chai. "He must have been ready to have clubbed her and dragged her off by her hair."

"The sexual tension is ridiculous between those two."

"I can't wait to see this myself."

"In the time I've worked here, I still haven't figured out how he can ignore what's right in front of his face."

"Maybe he's deliberately choosing to ignore it," Austyn remarks. Her voice cracks when she says wisely, "Caroline has the right idea, though."

"What do you mean?"

"If you're waiting for a man to make you feel like enough, you'll wait forever. They may be the hunters, but only in their own sweet time. Otherwise they can't be bothered putting in the effort to maintain a relationship."

Later, as I lie in bed, Austyn's words run through my head. As much as I hate it, she's right. Still, I can't help but reach for my phone.

FALLON:

I've got eyes on our girl tonight.

I wait for a few minutes before giving up on him. It comes to me that Caroline and Austyn have the right idea. I've worked hard to have a beautiful life and I've done it without a man at my side. I'm done trying to hold on to the threads of what may be and am ready to grab onto the fabric of what is—possibilities.

I lay my chin on Austyn's shoulder as we wait alongside the stage the next evening. "Last chance to maintain your anonymity."

She leans her head back and gives me a play on the words she said earlier to convince me, "You and me together, Fal. Let's show Galileo's what we're made of tonight."

Levi weaves through the crowd and Austyn murmurs, "Yeah, I'm definitely getting hot but you totally nailed the slime vibes. Except when he looks at Caroline."

"When she's not looking."

"Pfft. Of course."

I throw my head back and laugh just as he reaches us. His lips part at the way we're snuggled together in the wings of the stage. Levi James at a loss for words is something I'll cherish for some time when he stammers, "Ms. Kensington..."

Austyn holds up her hand. "It's just Kensington. Or DJ Kensington, if you must."

I bury my head into the crook of Austyn's shoulder, trying to hide my ear-to-ear grin. I think I have it locked down, but when I raise my eyes, I meet Levi's and know I've completely failed. Shrugging, I beam at him. "What can I say, Levi? My girl is a badass."

He might require a trip to the dentist by the time he walks out to introduce us. He looks like a barracuda whose teeth have been wired shut, trying to not piss off the hottest star to hit the planet since, well, her father hit the music scene almost twenty years ago. "Right. Thanks, Fallon. As I was saying, I'll introduce you both. Play for as long as you like."

Austyn drawls, "Oh, I only plan on stopping when I have to leave. You, Fal?"

"I can keep up." I run my hands over her hair before I purr, "I always could."

Levi's eying me like I'm some two headed creature who just escaped from an alien spaceship before he spins on a heel. Austyn waits until he's out of earshot before she wonders, "Do you think he wonders if we're together?"

"Nope." I smack the "P."

Her brow furrows. "You don't think so?"

Levi begins our introduction as "two long-time friends who have decided to avail us with the gift of their music tonight. We'd like to welcome one of our own, Fallon Brookes and..."

Just before he announces Austyn's name, I mutter directly in her ear, "He's trying to figure out a way to get in between us in bed."

Austyn almost falls flat on her face due to laughing while walking out on stage in her Louboutin heels to the screams of the crowd as Levi barely gets her name out. We're both holding our guitars aloft as we stride toward the microphones set up in front of bar stools center stage.

I catch her eye and we immediately launch into one of our favorite song—Alanis Morissette's "Hands Clean," alternating verses back and forth and coming together for the chorus.

Hours. We sing together for hours. But knowing what I do about Austyn being pregnant, I don't know how she's enduring the spotlight beaming down on us. Sweat beads along my hairline as we keep the crowd on their feet, singing along with us. When Austyn takes a long drink of water, I tell the crowd, "I think y'all are the first crowd we've sung live for since high school."

Austyn grins before reminiscing while I take a slug of my own drink. "It was a father-daughter dance neither of us wanted to go to."

Someone shouts from the crowd, "Why not?"

I twist my head ready to give up the information about my own life to protect her, but Austyn replies, "At that time in my life, I wanted to make music more than I wanted to dance to it."

Good one, I think. Knowing everything about her life is subject to media exploitation, and who her father is, I think her answer is the truth but won't hurt the people who love her. I, however, give a straight up answer. I have no one to hurt. "My father died when I was very young. Events like that weren't easy for me. Austyn—her family—made them easier."

With that, I strum the opening notes of "Fugitive" and my thoughts turn to Ethan and the message I received from him before we climbed down the stairs.

> ETHAN:
>
> I wish I was there with you both, witch.
>
> ETHAN:
>
> You're going to knock 'em dead.

Since I broke my silence with him weeks ago when I texted him on Austyn's behalf due to an issue her parents were having, I've been keeping it light.

> FALLON:
>
> Thanks.
>
> FALLON:
>
> Austyn mentioned it's been a while since she's seen you. I know she misses her Uncle E.
>
> ETHAN:
>
> And you? Do you miss seeing me?
>
> FALLON:
>
> It's always great to see friends.
>
> ETHAN:
>
> Right. Friends.

The crowd who has made it behind the medieval-type doors painted with Galileo Galilei's crest are rightfully going insane between getting an inside scoop on the music world's newest wunderkind and an unprecedented live performance.

I step up to the microphone and harmonize to her melody, my fingers strumming over the guitar as fast as hers are. Unlike my best friend, I'm no music prodigy, though I do come by my talent as naturally as she does. My ability to play the guitar is something special—a gift from my deceased father. The one I'm jamming on right now was one of the few my mother kept so I could have something of his yet still have the money to feed his child.

I manage to pick my mother out of the patrons in the crowd and spy the tears in her eyes. It might well have been a night like this when they met. A night when my father was singing on stage and my mother stared up at him with the same awe on her face that is now shining up at his only child who was conceived years later—not in the heat of rock 'n roll passion, but long after my father traded in his music career for that of a trucker. Long before he was involved in a massive pileup on I-95 that ended up destroying my mother's world and upending her future.

I wink at her and watch her smile—a smile she passed along to me—spread across her face as she watches me and my best friend tear up the stage in a manner that must bring back memories of heartbreak as well as incredible joy.

If only heartbreak decided it had taken enough bites out of us and stayed where it belonged—in the past.

CHAPTER TEN

SEVEN VIRTUES, NORTH CAROLINA

Ethan

**The time to think about how to handle an emergency is
not when you're in the middle of one.**

—StellaNova

Time isn't on your side when death is a very real possibility.

Racing at a breakneck speed toward Seven Virtues Hospital, my brother's
and my feet cross the barrier at the emergency room doors at the same time.
My body locks at the scene before me. My niece's bodyguard steps forward
and jerks his head. "Come on. We have a private family room while we wait
for the doctors to give us more information about Austyn's condition."

Numb, I let him guide us down a hall that feels like its never-ending—much
like this nightmare. Even at the height of the emotions I'd felt at the age of
eighteen, knowing over a hundred people were murdered on a luxury

passenger cruise ship, I'd felt heartbreak and anger. But until this moment, until one of ours has been attacked, I never realized that agony and despair were woven into the core of those emotions. That wave after wave of emotion intent on destruction began with a single phone call.

It halted footsteps.

It eliminated oxygen.

It stopped my heart.

Not to mention, during the two-and-a-half hours it took for our chartered flight to make it from Austin to Asheville, I was riddled with shame. When I answered Fallon's hysterical call earlier, I was chastising myself over and over. My gut churned at how far I sank at even considering picking up a woman at the local dive bar with the intent of forgetting Fallon due to her friend-zone messages earlier in the night. My heart froze inside my chest even as the woman's insipid hand rested on my shoulder. *Whose fault is it I felt like that?*

Mine. I ended up standing, stepping away from the lady in question after mumbling some kind of excuse, dropping cash on the table for her drink, and bolting before I did something I knew I'd regret. As I stalked off, I was already making plans to see Fallon so we could work things out between us.

Unfortunately, Fate stepped in to assist in the worst way possible.

Anguish layered over fear threatens to paralyze me as Jesse and I storm into the family room in the hospital. The second I see the crown of her blond hair, the wave crashes and I'm almost brought to my knees. I mouth her name, though no sound comes out.

Jesse scans the room looking for our sister and Austyn's father. He barks at Fallon, "Where did they go?"

Wearily, Fallon lifts her head. The second her eyes meet mine, they flare before blanking when they focus on my brother. "The doctor just came in. They took Austyn's parents to discuss...the recent changes."

I'm about to ask what changed when I notice how Jesse's color pales. "What direction did they go in?"

"They asked me to tell you there would be a message at the nurses station."

"Right," he mutters before stepping outside the room, closing the door behind him. Closing us in.

Together.

Alone.

We are no more than a room apart, but there's a distance between us that never existed before I went on my assignment to Silverthorn. I open my mouth to break the ice, but Fallon beats me to it. "There's coffee down the hall."

I move a step toward her. "Any good?"

She shrugs. "It's hot and caffeinated."

"Right." I open my mouth to demand answers to a million questions when Fallon draws up her knees and lowers her head to them. A harsh sob is ripped from her chest. Her hands fly to her knees, pulling them up to her face to muffle the sound.

I want to go to her, to comfort her, but with the stilted way she's been communicating with me as of late, I'm uncertain if she'd welcome me with open arms. That is until I notice there's blood beneath her fingernails.

My niece's blood.

I'm across the room in seconds, pulling her to her feet and into my arms. I croon, "Shh. Let it out."

Fallon's body sags into mine as if she's unable to hold up the weight of the burden any longer. The door opens behind us and Jesse pokes his head in. His stern countenance softens when he spies Fallon in my arms. He mouths the word, "Surgery," to me before disappearing down the hall.

Fuck.

After their show tonight at the bar Fallon's apparently been working at—Christ, how much of her life have I missed?—some crazy ass drunk came barreling down Columbia Street and hit Austyn head-on as she was working the crowd before she was set to leave with her security detail. Fallon, not more than fifteen feet away, was the first to get to her. Fallon stripped out of her own top—uncaring she was naked except for a strapless bra—to use the clothes to apply pressure on the wounds my niece sustained.

While the idea of drunk idiots getting a look at Fallon's luscious body sets my teeth grinding, the idea of this woman doing any and everything she could to save Austyn until the EMTs could get there to transport her to the hospital causes me to shudder.

Fallon burrows deeper against me—seeking out my warmth.

I rub my hand up and down her back, now covered in hospital scrubs. "Hey, witch. She'll be okay."

Fallon lifts her face up and the utter devastation on it sends a shaft of fear through me. I grasp her chin. "What? What don't I know, Fallon?"

She stubbornly refuses to speak.

"Tell me," I demand.

Before she can utter a word, the door is flung open behind us and my sister's voice is broken when it rings out authoritatively, "Fallon, I'll handle explanations."

Fallon tries to shift away, but my hand captures hers. With a look, I pin her to my side, pleading with her not to leave me. Not now. Not when I'm so terrified at what Paige is about to say. Indecision is written all over her face until I verbalize my request in a tortured whisper, "I need you."

Pain and a swirl of other emotions flit across her face. But remains still, holding her stance. Just having her this close gives me a strength I didn't know I needed as my sister delivers more devastating news. "Austyn's safe, but the baby she was carrying is gone."

There's a keening wail of pain from Fallon. Still, it's the verbal echo of what's in everyone's hearts at that moment.

CHAPTER ELEVEN

Ethan

Sometimes, shock drives you to destinations you never believe you'd visit.

—The Fireside Psychologist

FATE HAS A WAY OF TRYING TO RUIN THE BEST OF MEN. OF TEMPTING them beyond the bounds of propriety.

I know this because in the next few days, I find myself again alone with Fallon in the family waiting room. Part of me wants to lash out at her for not sharing Austyn's condition and the other part of me knows I have no right. I have no right to know what Austyn didn't want shared and I have no right to argue that Fallon should have told me.

None.

The problem is, there's what my head thinks and what my heart feels. One understands and the other thinks she's guilty as sin for not talking to me.

She's bleary eyed, looking as if nothing will soothe the pain coursing through her soul. It's like looking into a mirror because I know exactly what will help her because it's what will help me.

Just then, she glances in my direction and for the first time since I walked in, I capture and hold her gaze. It's the first time I've really seen her since that day in her dorm room over a year ago. I catalog all the little differences —how her hair has been cut differently, how her hips curve slightly different. There's no makeup on her naturally dark lashes, framing gorgeous indigo eyes. I wonder if her lip, swollen from repeatedly being chewed on, will look the same if I kiss it. Or would it take a night of my lips on it?

Fucking hell. I turn hard as a rock, even as guilt claws at my insides for the inappropriateness of my reaction to her at a time like this.

The waiting room suddenly feels like the air is being sucked out, leaving nothing but the allure pulsing between us. I clear my throat to break the heavy silence. "Fallon, we should talk."

Her eyes don't waver from mine. "About?"

"Us."

Her bark of laughter, which should hold a peal of amusement, is devoid of that rich emotion. "Us? What us could you be referring to, *Uncle* E?"

I surge to my feet. Taking the few steps to place myself directly in front of her boot clad feet, I snarl, "I'm not your damn uncle. Let's get that straight once and for all. You're..."

"What?"

"Special, Fallon."

Instead of being intimidated by me, Fallon tips her head back before her lips twist in a sneer. "Actions speak louder than words."

My eyes narrow now that I've revealed a mere portion of what I'm feeling. She mocks, "Ethan, if I'm special, then you can keep your brand of it for the rest of Seven Virtues when—when, not if—you hit on them."

"What in the fuck are you talking about, Fallon?" My temper flares.

Her eyes are cold. "If you think this is treating me—or any woman—like they're special, you need to up your game. We're not in a committed... anything. Thank God. Otherwise, I'd have no problem shoving your balls down your throat so you choked on them when I forced you to swallow them."

"I have no idea what the fuck you're talking about."

"Do you remember what you told me and Austyn about social media?"

"What the hell does that have to do with this?" With us? The words are on the tip of my tongue, but I leave them unsaid.

"For someone good at dishing out the advice, you might want to follow it."

My mouth falls open. "Excuse me?"

Fallon quirks a brow before she slides her phone from her sweatshirt pocket. After a few quick swipes, she flips the phone around. And there for her to see at Rodeo Ralphs—Kensington's local dive bar—is picture after picture of me with various women. Then with a flick of her finger, I see others from different nights. Some of them I recall were just sitting nearby me and some who were very much in my space.

None so incriminating as the woman from the other night leaning forward, her body language declaring her intent.

Fuck.

Unfortunately, Fallon's not quite done with making me feel like a jackass. She offers me advice, "I'd check your six. The latest one—the one whose hand is precariously close to your butt? She's the recently divorced mother of one who used to torment your niece on a daily basis for not having a father."

Hearing that makes me defend myself. "I was there for a damn beer."

"Ah, but they intend to trap you so they can become Mrs. Ethan Kensington. Hope you're supplying your own condoms." Her wink would normally disarm me if it wasn't followed by a blank mask.

I lean over her and get in her face, willing to do anything to bring back the fire. I'll do anything to keep Fallon with me in this moment. "While we're on the subject, the first night you texted me—"

"The night we were drugged?"

"Yes."

Her brow furrows. "What about it?"

"You alluded to your hangover being worse than a man's hairy balls."

Fallon's stunned. "I did?"

My hand slides up and into her loose bun. I yank her head back. "Yeah, you did."

She glares up into my face. "What do you care? You're the man who never noticed I was out of your life for almost six months."

With that accusation, my control snaps. I bring my face so close to hers, inhaling her every exhale. I let her feel every ripple and shudder as our labored breaths entwined with one another. Long moments pass where we don't say anything. I vow I'm going to taste her, imprint myself on her when someone bangs up against the door.

I jump back, letting her go.

Fallon clocks my reaction, a sad smile crossing her lips.

The moment between us is lost. *Will we ever get it back?*

Fallon uncurls herself and lays her hand on my forearm. "Talk to me, Ethan. What is it you want?"

I stutter, the words catching as I creak open the vault that contains my emotions for her. "I've been feeling things..."

"Things?"

"Things about you. Things I shouldn't."

"Last I checked, I'm a full-fledged adult," she counters.

"I mean, you're my niece's best friend."

"And?"

"And the feelings I have about you are decidedly not related to my being an 'uncle.'" I wait for her to get the point.

"I fail to see the problem."

"I think about you. More than I should."

Her eyes give way from confusion to anger. "So, in your little fantasies about me, does caring about me come into play or just wanting to fuck me?"

"Damn it, Fallon, you know I care about you," I roar.

"Ahh," Fallon mocks. "Ethan Kensington can't handle the guilt of wanting a younger woman. Got it now. Now I know why I'm a convenience for you."

My voice is strained. "You are far from a convenience. Every time I'm near you, I...I feel this pull."

"What a damn hardship that must be for you when you're screwing your way through every eligible woman back home," she drawls.

My jaw tightens. "There haven't been as many as you think, and they're not you."

Fallon approaches me with a glint in her eyes. I know the next words out of her mouth are going to piss me the hell off. "Then you're going to be fine knowing I let men make me come with their fingers."

My fists clench.

"Mouth."

I force my arms to relax at my sides. I know she's deliberately trying to antagonize me and I'm falling right into her trap.

Then she slides her hands to my chest before she hisses, "Before they fuck me with their cocks. That is after I've sucked them off...Ethan!"

I whirl her around so her back is to my front. One of my arms is wrapped around her collarbone, the other forces her hips back against mine. With my back to the door, no one can see the position we're in. My lips graze the patch of skin taunting me at the back of her neck.

She lets out a small moan before her whole body stiffens in realization at what I just did. She struggles to break my grip. "Ethan?"

"What, witch?" I want to spin her around and kiss her. Brand her as mine.

Her voice is riddled with unmasked agony when she forces out, "This isn't the time or the place for this."

Slowly, I let her out of my arms, ensuring she can stand. She's right but there's a part of me that physically doesn't want to let her go. Unable to fully release her, I continue to grip her hand, leading her over to the farthest set of hospital chairs from the door. I drop into the seat and drag her in front of me. My head crashes into her stomach. As I suck in deep breaths, absorbing her scent as I do, Fallon lifts her hand to run her fingers through my hair. Finally, I admit, "You're right."

A sob escapes. "You'll get used to saying that. Austyn has."

A shudder runs through my body thinking the driver could have taken Fallon out just as easily as my niece. Her fingers in my hair soothe my craving to deliver pain, my need to be punished. She just eases the ache inside of me. I lift my head and drown in blue, finally admitting something to us both that I hope she remembers long after we leave this room. "No one is like you, Fallon."

Her hand trembles as she pushes away a stray lock of hair from my forehead. "What do you want from me, Ethan?"

My hand stills hers. "I want you to be happy, witch."

She rears back as if I've just shoved her out of my life. And maybe for a while, I need to. "What are you trying to say, Ethan?"

"I don't want you to regret what you're supposed to experience. I want to hear about it. I want to be your best friend, your confidant. Down the line, if..."

"If what?"

"If we find we're still here...if that leads to more..." I let my words hang heavy in the air between us.

"I don't understand. Why not now?"

Frustration twists my features as I think of all the obstacles we'd have to overcome to be together while she's still twenty. "Because now's not right."

"That's not just your decision!" she shouts.

Silence settles between us. Each passing moment where I don't say anything to reassure her that she's the one I want. Each moment of silence drives more of a wedge between us instead of demonstrating the desire I feel for her with a relentless force. Finally, I whisper, "I just...I need you to know... to understand..."

"What, Ethan?" When I don't explain further, she sneers, "Right. Thanks for clarifying." Fallon turns away, but I whip her back around and bury my face against her stomach.

"Everything in me wants to claim you as mine." The words come out muffled against her sweatshirt, but by the way she's no longer fighting to get away from me, she heard them.

The admission hangs between them, heavy and raw, exposing vulnerabilities neither of us is prepared to confront. Outside, the world buzzed with life, oblivious to the silent battle raging within the confines of the hospital waiting room.

Finally, I pull back so she can hear me clearly. "But I lived my life already, Fallon. I don't want to rob you of yours. You *need* to be certain. Do you understand?"

She meets my gaze, a silent acknowledgment passing between them, a fragile connection forged in the midst of chaos, uncertainty, and shared family agony. "I understand," she whispers.

"Don't cut me off. God, don't cut me out of your life again, witch."

Her fingers drag down my cheek. "I won't."

In that moment, as the world outside continued to spin, I found a pocket of solace in a fragile bond, a flare of hope amidst the darkness that surrounded the four walls of this room.

CHAPTER TWELVE

NEW YORK CITY, NEW YORK

Ethan

Comfort food is called that not because of the ingredients but because of the people who bring it to you.

—Fab and Delish

Four Years Ago—August

EVEN THOUGH I WAS BROUGHT HERE TO COURIER SOME FOOD FROM our hometown to my niece since returning from her stint at the hospital, I have this overwhelming need to escape the emotions suffocating my brother-in-law's penthouse. Fuck. Seeing Austyn so broken is cutting me deep.

Even knowing I'm the one who stopped what could have happened in Seven Virtues, it makes me wish Fallon were by my side—not only to deal with her best friend but to help heal the ache in my heart. I know she could, simply by being in the same room as me.

Instead, I looked up an old friend, knowing he relocated his family years ago after his company merged with the largest investigative firm in the nation. As I stand in the pristine office, I mutter, "You've come a long way, buddy."

"And if you think this is my office, you're off your rocker, Kensington. I'm the mad scientist they keep locked away for good reason."

Crossing the room in a few strides, I clasp the dark-haired man's hand before lifting it to my chest and bumping his chest against mine. "It's great to see you, man."

"Same, Ethan. It's been too long," my hero and mentor Sam Aiken replies.

"Wish it was under better circumstances."

"Me too." Sam gestures me back so he can shut the door behind him.

"Sweet view," I remark as I gaze out the window at the view of Rockefeller Center.

Sam twitches at all the sunlight. "You know, I think it was supposed to be my office. By now, one of Caleb's or Keene's kids has appropriated this space. Maybe Cal's?" He scratches his head as he rattles off his partners.

I snicker. "For real? You got booted out of your own executive suite and you're not even certain by whom?"

"Let's be real. I'm never in here." He tries to keep his lips from twitching when he admits, "My real office has a four-foot air gap with copper mesh wires shielding it."

I lean back in the visitor chair and thread my hands behind my head. "Ahh, sounds just like my place back home."

"You have the same kind of setup in Texas?"

"Had to build it if I wanted to partner on some of the work with Castor as prime," I admit, not without some rancor. "Between you and me, Leanne Miles can be a real pain in the ass about the specs she demands. I technically am a small business."

Sam, bless him, chokes on his laughter as I blast one of the DoD's darlings of software development, who I know through family connections has indirect ties to the company he's part owner of Hudson Investigations. "I see you haven't changed much, Ethan."

I cajole him. "Come on, Sam. Tell your wife you want to come to work with me. It will be just like old times."

He shoots me a filthy look at the reminder. "The last time you and I worked on an op together, it was life and death, and we were *with* my wife being screamed at in Italian in the middle of the Atlantic Ocean. I much prefer when she yells at *other* people in foreign languages."

Rocking the chair back on two legs, I grin at him. "Yeah, me too. Much better for my stress level."

"You ain't kidding." Sam leans against the front of the office desk, crossing his ankles. "So, what brought you to visit me? Why aren't we having this reunion somewhere fun?"

I let the chair legs fall back down before I push myself to my full height, and I stroll over to the window. "I could say I'm looking to get back in the game."

"Getting bored working as a contractor?"

"Let's just say I thought I'd be seeing some of the action you did," I admit.

He snorts. "That's because of what our company did. We were...hold on." He reaches across the desk and taps a few buttons on an iPad and in seconds, locks on doors engage and the view I'd been admiring disappears as shutters lower.

I spin on my heel to face him. "Impressive."

"All the executive suites have it."

"Do I want to know how much it cost to install?"

"Talk to Cal. His wife did the upgrades here and in our office in D.C." I make a mental note to stop by my other friend's office before I leave. Sam continues, "What I was saying is before our part of the company was acquired, what we did was dangerous."

My jaw tightens. "I'm feeling that way right now."

"No, what you're out for is vengeance," he counters.

"Is it that obvious?"

"If what happened to your family happened to mine, I'd be seeking the same, Ethan." He stands and clasps my shoulder. "You need to be there for your niece. Let us go after who did this to her. Don't blur the lines."

"Because you all follow your own advice so well," I fling back at him. The first time I met the man before me, we helped rescue his cousin from a hostage situation.

"I never claimed to, but at that time, I was the only one with the skills to get the job done." It isn't Sam's arrogance talking—it's fact.

Spinning away from him, I plant my feet apart and cross my arms before admitting, "I hate that you're right."

"But you'll do it," he declares confidently.

"How do you know?"

"Because if you were going to interfere, you'd have already done so and I'd have received a call from our former boss, pissed as shit."

The groan I release may be heard in the Bronx. "You just had to mention *him*." A man who played fast and loose with people's lives so often they should give him a gold-plated wrench as his next anniversary gift at the Agency.

Sam chuckles. "Of course I did." Then his expression morphs into one of concern. "How's your niece?"

I think back to the explosion in her father's penthouse yesterday when I showed up between her lover, her mother and father, and her family from back home, and how all it needed was my favorite witch to descend to turn it into sheer chaos. "She's desperately trying to heal, to not give the bastard who ran her over any more of herself." Sighing, I scrub my hand through my hair. "She's in pain, but her man's helping."

"And you? How are you holding up?"

I think back to the text I received from Fallon earlier checking in on our girl.

FALLON:

It's okay if her tears are falling.

ETHAN:

That's good, right?

FALLON:

That means she's not hiding them.

ETHAN:

Thanks, witch. X

FALLON:

You're welcome. X

"I think we're all devastated, but we'll all be okay." At least, I hope we will be. This latest setback just detoured off the road to get there.

CHAPTER THIRTEEN

SEVEN VIRTUES, NORTH CAROLINA

Fallon

Truly? Is there any competition when it comes to best dressed couple for the Met Gala?

Let's stop the fighting and admit Danielle Madison and her husband, Brendan Blake, win every year by default. It truly is much more mature that way.

End of.

—Moore You Want

"Now tell me you're calling me just to share how much you've missed me," are the first words out of my mouth when our call connects.

"No, I just needed a friend," is Ethan's deadpan reply.

"Oh." His response deflates my excitement like a balloon that's sustained a direct hit by a machete.

When I don't say anymore, Ethan's voice softens, "Fallon, you know I wish I was able to be with you every day. I want nothing more than to wrap you up in my arms, hold your body next to mine, touch your skin. I want to determine if what happened at the hospital means more."

"Is it just sex?"

"No. I want to experience life through you, with you. It's no longer enough to wait for your words through texts. We've been doing this back and forth for years and now and..."

His voice trails off, so I pick up where he left off. "And now?"

"Now, I crave to be where you are. Hold you at the end of a long day. Hear about what you found at the museum that fascinated you the most today. By the way, what unusual fact did you unearth about the Biltmore House today?" His voice softens as he quizzes me about the place I want to land my dream job.

I blurt out, "There are sixty-five fireplaces."

Dead silence.

"And forty-three bathrooms."

Suddenly a chuckle begins on the other end of the line. "Well, I suppose after making love to a lady of quality in front of a roaring fire, at least Mr. Vanderbilt had quick access to dispose of his sheaths."

I burst into laughter at his quick charm and bawdiness. "Cute, Kensington."

"See, now you're getting with the program. I am cute. I remember my mama telling me so," he announces haughtily. Just as quickly, his laughter evaporates.

Suddenly, I just want to hear him talk about the nebulous Melissa Kensington. Gently, I pry, "What was she like?"

"Who?"

"Your mother."

"You mean Austyn's never mentioned her?"

That's when I drop him into a vortex of emotions. "Ethan, how could she when even what Paige knows about her is hearsay?" Paige—Ethan's younger sister and Austyn's mother—has no memories of her mother. How could she when her whole life she'd been told her mother died because she was born? All she knew was that her mother was beautiful and worshiped, and losing her had reduced their father to a mess of quivering toxicity.

But Austyn's father surprised his family when he went into intensive therapy to sort his functional immorality out. Now, there's a cautious acceptance by most of the Kensington's. Judging by his undisguised anguish, Ethan's not over his duplicity.

The springs beneath his mattress squeak as his weight settles. Then, he tells me something I never expected to hear. "Mama loved flowers. She used to pick them and put them in a pitcher on our kitchen counter."

Having been out to the Kensington farm to ride with Austyn many times, I dredge up the empty bed. In my mind I can see where bright Texas flowers would have been beautiful on the corner of the bustling kitchen—a welcome to neighbors and friends who came to the farm. "I don't recall them ever being there."

There's a long pause before, "That's because I forgot, witch."

"What do you mean?"

There's a long pause before he manages, "I forgot that. I forgot my mother took me out the morning she died to pick flowers in the field. What kind of son does that make me?"

My heart breaks for the toddler Ethan was. "One who was too traumatized to function."

"Don't make excuses for me, Fallon."

"If something similar happened to a child—whether one of your own or someone else—wouldn't you?" I counter quietly.

His silence is the only response I need. So I probe a bit deeper. "Have you remembered anything else about her?"

"Paige looks just like her. It hurts sometimes to look at my sister." His confession, whispered, tells me it's a deep, dark secret.

"Or you could look at your sister and see all the good your mother left with her," I counter gently.

He sucks in a breath so sharply I can hear it from a thousand miles away. I'm functioning on instinct when it comes to Ethan, not much else. But tonight, he doesn't need flirty banter, he needs a friend and I'm determined to be that person for him.

I'll always be someone strong for him, no matter how much my heart may be crushed in the process.

Finally, he whispers, "Thank you."

"I didn't do anything."

"Yes, you did," he counters. "That special voodoo that belongs to only you is helping clear the cobwebs away from my old brain."

A soft laugh escapes. "You said it, not me."

He lets out a rough chuckle. Then, for the rest of the night, he regales me with stories about his mother as he remembers them. I hear the longing in his voice for something he can't go back and change, but I know one thing from my own experience with coming to an understanding about my father's death. With knowing Ethan just wants to be friends.

Pursuing dreams that can't come true has a high price to pay. It's better to focus on what's attainable.

With that, I listen to my friend as he celebrates the more painful parts of him celebrating his sister's birthday—and the day his mother died.

CHAPTER FOURTEEN

SEVEN VIRTUES, NORTH CAROLINA

Fallon

Try new things. Listen to your body. Be the healthiest you that you can be.

—Fab and Delish

Three Years Ago

OVER TIME AND DISTANCE, ETHAN AND I BECAME AS CLOSE—IF NOT closer—than me and Austyn. There wasn't anything I didn't share with him. And in retrospect, he gave me the same honesty.

This isn't going to work with us in the places we're presently at in our lives.

We rarely give specifics but I know him and try my damnedest to deny the crazy jealousy where he's concerned.

He tells me about his dates. I've...shared some about the guys I see. I just don't share when, on the rare occasion, I let one in my bed. I assume Ethan's doing the same. We each lean on the other about why the people in each other's lives is completely wrong for the other and why.

Long distance, I've forced him to consume tubs of ice cream when I need him to commiserate about my dates and he's demanded I join in on whiskey nights when he needed to bitch about "—ditching some bitch." Like tonight. "Christ, Fal, she went cuckoo for Cocoa Puffs."

The burn the whiskey made as it came through my nose when he drops that line made my eyes tear up. "What did this one do?"

He goes on to explain how she unplugged all the cords in his office and used them to tie herself in some ritualistic bondage in front of the desk. "In front of the plate glass window on Main Street?" I screech.

"None other. And of course people took pictures of that shit and kept trying to post it to social media. Want to guess how I've been spending my day?"

"Deleting any dick pics she had possession of?" I smart, trying to tamper down the seed of jealousy that always arises.

"Do I look that stupid, Fal?" he snarls.

"Listen, if she was disturbed enough to be naked..."

"I haven't had *any* woman in a manner long enough for her to get a dick pic, Fallon." His voice drips ice.

"Well, excuse me for asking. Why else would someone tie themselves naked to the front of your store?" I hiss.

"Perhaps because they're insane." His voice could chill the burn from Szechuan chicken.

I mumble, "Insane over your cock."

There's a splash, a guzzle, then a slam before he shouts, "Goddamn it, witch! We've been so good about not going there with each other."

Not by my choice. But thank God I keep those words to myself. Instead, I give him his meltdown before I try to bring him back on topic. "I think you're being nice when you're saying cuckoo, E."

"Maybe I'm the one who's losing it."

"What? Why's that?"

He mumbles something under his breath that involves being hexed. All I can do is smile and sip my drink while Ethan gets himself smashed and continues to fight the evils of social media against the drama of a woman who feels she's been scorned.

CHAPTER FIFTEEN

NEW YORK CITY, NEW YORK

Fallon

I might date @PRyanPOfficial if I could get into the #beckettmiller VIP section tonight at #redemption

—@CuTEandRich3

If it gave me half a chance to join you, I might let you, @CuTEandRich3 Did you hear about who is in there.

—@PRyanPOffical

Yes, Ryan. Thus, why I'm desperate.

—@CuTEandRich3

Two Years Ago

Hanging out in a VIP lounge at a nightclub with my best friend, her husband Mitch, her parents, and their friends, I tease, "I'll say one thing about your life."

"What's that?"

"It certainly doesn't lack for eye candy."

Austyn bursts into gales of laughter. "You can thank my dad for that."

I cut my eyes over to Austyn's father and let loose a heartfelt sigh over his own gorgeousness. "Yes. It's going to bother me terribly to have to go converse with your father."

Austyn's about to open her mouth to slap me down when her eyes widen dramatically. Then she shouts, "Uncle Jess!" before taking off at a run.

I twirl around on four-inch heels just in time to catch sight of Jesse Kensington. He lifts his niece and swings her around before shouting above the din, "Happy birthday, kiddo!"

A quick glance to my left shows Austyn's mother is just as shocked. She leaves her husband's side to dash over to her brother and greet him warmly. Meanwhile, I'm scanning the entrance frantically to see if someone else is behind him. I mean, he would have told me, wouldn't he?

I give it a few minutes before I send a text.

FALLON:
Mama Paige. Uncle Jess. What? No Uncle E?

ETHAN:
Not tonight.

FALLON:
No?

ETHAN:
I won't be there. I already have plans.

FALLON:
Sorry to bother you.

ETHAN:
You're never a bother, Fal.

FALLON:
Except when you're out on a date?

ETHAN:

Fal . . . no.

FALLON:

Pretty bad timing on my part, Ethan. Sorry for the intrusion.

I slip my phone back into my clutch and lift my cosmopolitan to my lips, contemplating my text to Ethan. *It's not jealousy*, I assure myself. It's about being here for Austyn's birthday.

Still, as much as I would love to have seen Ethan and my enduring hots for him, I decided to take Ethan at his word and not pine away for him during my college years. My lips curve as I recall the scorching hot sex I had with my TA last semester after I agreed to model nude for one of his art studies classes. I wonder if the art department is aware the abstract they so revere is not tantamount to Saint Augustine but more an "oh my god, more" religious experience.

Still, it wasn't Ethan. I'm aware all I'm doing is scratching an itch, not searching for a soulmate. My heart's aware I've already found him and ultimately what I want is for him to be happy.

Screw that. I want him with me.

Despite the deep-seated jealousy I refuse to acknowledge, no one with Ethan Kensington's looks should be without sex—*good sex*, I amend. I lift my glass in a silent toast he gets some. Since I first met him, I'd have to be blind not to notice how fucking gorgeous the man is. Who cares that he's twenty years older than me? Hot is hot, and the man has the face of a rugged Hollywood star combined with the body of a rodeo god. Truth is, Jesus wept when he made Ethan because he knew he wouldn't be on the earth long enough to bang him.

I giggle at my train of thought, drawing the attention of several of the people milling about to celebrate my girl's birthday, including—holy bat shit—country music star Brendan Blake. Turning away from the revelry, I saunter over to the bar where a behemoth of a man named Louie is manning the station for the night.

Winking at me as I approach, he immediately begins pulling the ingredients together for my next cosmopolitan as soon as my glass hits the leather counter. As I wait for my drink, I wonder what Ethan might think of this crowd. Music legends, lawyers, doctors, and, well, me. Another bubble of laughter escapes.

If he's not pissed at me for cock blocking him, I'll text him later in the week and tell him the details.

Louie sets my drink in front of me before his eyes dart over my head. An arm slides around my shoulders, and I twist to meet Jess's familiar green eyes. His gaze drops to the drink in front of me before he shakes his head. "Where did the nice, small-town girl I know go?"

I back away and hold out a hand. "Have we met? I've never been a 'nice' girl."

He jerks my hand and wraps me in an enormous hug. "It's good to see you, Fal."

"You too, Jess," I tell him honestly. We chat back and forth for a few minutes before he mentions his assigned role is to get pictures for Austyn. He leans over the bar and yells, "Hey, Louie. You mind?"

"You mean since there's a no photo rule except the one your family persistently breaks?" Louie growls.

Jess and I laugh. Wrapping an arm around my waist, Jess tugs me firmly against his body. I grin until the flash goes off, after which Jess promptly lets me go. "You have to send me a copy of that," I tell him.

He gives me a quick one arm hug before offering his excuses. "Will do. Now, I need to go say hey to a few people."

I wink. "We'll catch up at later."

Reaching for my glass still on the bar, I take a sip, letting the chilled vodka slide down the back of my throat. A few seconds later, a blond dashes up before introducing herself as Leanne Miles. After we each make our connection to Austyn known, I fascinate her when I let her know I'm about to start my fourth year of an accelerated master's degree program to become a museum curator. "How did you fall into that?"

I admit, "I wanted to jump Riley from *National Treasure*."

She hoots before lifting her finger to order a drink. "Going for the hot hacker. I like you."

When Louie hands her a glass of wine, I tap my glass to hers. "Same goes."

Leanne notes, "Your handbag is sending out strobe signals. Someone trying to get in touch with you?"

I frown. "That's not a good sign." Quickly, sliding my empty glass on the bar, I whip out my cell phone, hoping everything is okay with my mother. But it's not her frantically trying to reach me.

It's Ethan.

> ETHAN:
>
> What the hell?
>
> ETHAN:
>
> Why the fuck is my brother holding you?

My eyes bug out at what I'm reading. A wave of emotions washes over me, the most prominent one being confusion. How in the hell does Ethan know anything about me talking to Jess? Finally, I type back.

> FALLON:
>
> Excuse me?
>
> ETHAN:
>
> Come on, Fal.

I then receive the picture of me and Jess that Louie had taken earlier. I take a deep breath and decide to take the high road.

> FALLON:
>
> Cool. Jess was going to send that to me later.
>
> ETHAN:
>
> YOU TEXT WITH HIM TOO?
>
> FALLON:
>
> Are you kidding right now?
>
> ETHAN:
>
> Not even close, witch.

Suddenly, anger courses through me. Ethan may be everything I want, but he's made no proclamations of happily ever after to me even after the emotional encounter we had during Austyn's hospital stay. We're *friends*. We have a mutual love and affection for his family. My thumbs move furiously beneath Leanne's fascinated stare.

FALLON:

Why are you turning into a green-eyed monster?
Because it's Jess?

ETHAN:

I always have green eyes.

FALLON:

Stop. Just stop. Okay?

ETHAN:

I'm not joking.

FALLON:

You should be.

ETHAN:

This is a load of crap, Fal.

FALLON:

Excuse me?

FALLON:

You're typing this while you're on a damn date?

ETHAN:

It's not a date.

ETHAN:

I'm working.

FALLON:

It was a platonic picture.

ETHAN:

Fine.

FALLON:

That was way uncool, Ethan.

ETHAN:

I'm sorry, but, Fallon, my brother?

I don't know what makes me say it, but I do.

FALLON:

Then you should have been here to put your own
damn arm around me.

Shoving my phone back in my bag, I ignore the buzzing that starts and beam at a patient Leanne, telling myself I won't let Ethan ruin my night. "So, what do you do, Leanne?"

Her laugh is filled with amusement. "Oh, that's a long and complicated question. I'll sum it up by saying I tinker with computers."

Fucking fantastic. Something to remind me of Ethan. Still, I remain tuned in as Leanne explains she's the CEO of a company that does contract work for the US government. Still, I have to admit I'm grateful when Austyn rescues me so we can dance.

I leave my purse behind because the buzzing hasn't stopped.

Not once.

CHAPTER SIXTEEN

SEVEN VIRTUES NORTH CAROLINA

Ethan

From all of us at StellaNova, we would like to offer our sincerest congratulations to all of the graduates of the class of 2024.

Surprise us. Do great things.

—StellaNova

Present Day

AN ENORMOUS SMILE CREASES MY FACE.

ETHAN:

> I still can't believe you managed to graduate from a school called Seven Virtues.

FALLON:

Really? Are we still doing this?

ETHAN:

Virtuous is the last thing you are, Fal.

FALLON:

It takes one to know one, E.

ETHAN:

Hmm. That it does, witch. :)

ETHAN:

What time is graduation tomorrow?

FALLON:

Six.

ETHAN:

What are you doing until then?

FALLON:

Working. I picked up a shift at the bar.

ETHAN:

Are you kidding?!?!

ETHAN:

What happened to celebrating?

FALLON:

I need rent money. My new job doesn't start for a month.

ETHAN:

You should be doing something to celebrate.

FALLON:

I am. Dinner tomorrow.

ETHAN:

I meant with friends.

FALLON:

See comment above.

ETHAN:

Proud as fuck, Fallon.

ETHAN:

Straight out of college and hired to be an associate museum coordinator for Biltmore?

ETHAN:

That's a long way from the girl I rescued from her first hangover at UT.

FALLON:

Stop, E.

ETHAN:

Stop what? Reminding you of your first college 9-1-1?

FALLON:

No, the compliments.

ETHAN:

Why???

FALLON:

Well, for one, you're making me blush.

ETHAN:

I didn't think that was possible.

FALLON:

You've just never seen it.

ETHAN:

Does it cover every inch of you?

FALLON:

Wouldn't you love to find out?

Yes. The answer leaps to the forefront of my mind. I can't believe it's been five years since Fallon and I began talking outside the confines of our defined roles within my family. Yet, we still haven't crossed that final boundary with each other. I haven't seen the glory of a blush spread across her perfect skin.

I haven't touched it.

Kissed her.

That's going to end soon.

When she texted me a 9-1-1 emergency request for help due to a hangover that turned out to be so much more, I know I shocked both her and my niece when I pounded on their doom door three hours later. Eventually, once I was certain the GHB was out of their system, I fed them my surefire hangover cure of Funions, Gatorade, and Ho Hos. Both women, still trussed up in the clothes they'd worn the night before, were passing a mop bucket between them as they puked something called "Witch's Brew."

Appropriate for my witch—my Fallon.

After I got them both moderately sober and left, Fallon texted me her heartfelt thanks on my way back to Kensington.

> FALLON:
> Don't know what I would have done without you. I have an exam on Monday.

> ETHAN:
> Take it from someone who knows—avoid the mixed drinks, Fallon.

From then onward, our relationship bloomed. We became friends that have aroused, amused, and irritated the fuck out of each other. Case in point, I scroll back and chuckle over the snap and GIF of the West Wing, where the president is banging his head on the desk.

> FALLON:
> I'm so close to doing this. Why did I agree to be fixed up?

> ETHAN:
> Ditch him.

I sucked in a breath at the selfie I got at that point of Fallon decked out in an excuse for a dress.

> FALLON:
> Because I look good, E.

> ETHAN:
> You look better than good, witch.

> FALLON:
> Sweet talker.

> ETHAN:
> Want me to tell you what I'd do if you were nearby?

> FALLON:
> That sounds more interesting than hearing about stock futures.

> ETHAN:
> Then ditch the date.

FALLON:

Fine. So bossy.

ETHAN:

You have no idea.

FALLON:

You'd better make good on some of these promises.

FALLON:

I need something to fantasize about.

ETHAN:

You're just looking for trouble tonight.

Her response caused my cock to stir.

FALLON:

The trouble I want has been too chicken shit to be with me.

Almost a year old, I wasn't certain why I saved it—then. Now? I know the answer. Fallon was brave enough to step out on the edge with her emotions. She recognized where we were going.

It's why I'm camped out in a hotel room a few miles from her apartment, debating how to answer her last text.

Yes, I want to discover everything about her, but is now the right time to smash through the thin wall we've kept between us? It's been on my mind more and more as of late.

A new text comes in.

FALLON:

Anyway, I have to go.

FALLON:

Will you be up later to tell me a "bedtime story"?

She blows me a kiss and sends me an eggplant emoji.

I text her the rolling eyes emoji in return before giving her my response.

ETHAN:

You are the antonym of a good girl, Fal.

FALLON:

Do you want me to become one?

ETHAN:

I'm not holding my breath.

FALLON:

Good. You know me better than that.

She's right. I do. Our friendship means so much more. She's woven herself into my life, and I don't know what will happen if I take a shot and she bolts.

She's family, but she's not.

She's a friend, but she's more.

She's just Fallon. And I'm still me.

But this can't be put off much longer. When the time is right, I'm willing to take a chance on us if she is.

My thumbs fly.

ETHAN:

Try to be good?

FALLON:

I'm always good.

ETHAN:

No, you're exceptional. Never forget that.

Fallon doesn't reply. Knowing I'll see her tomorrow—even if she doesn't—I decide I'd better get on with the work I was contracted to provide.

Booting my computer in my hotel, my fingers dance over the keys as I reread the assignment through my secure email. Still, Fallon lingers in my thoughts even as I prepare to go into deep hunting mode. I forcibly shove her to the back of my mind and concentrate, knowing I was brought into the assignment for a reason.

A painful one that's going to resurrect secrets and demand further justice for a death of someone lost far too soon.

Even though the citizens of Kensington, Texas believe I repair computers, the United States Navy didn't stop at that kind of training. It's a good thing most people can't tell the difference between a computer repair shop and a server room that lurks just behind it.

When I recall the volume of government officials and private agencies who have come under deep cover to Texas to procure my services, I'm amused. I specialize in cybercrime investigation and too often come across data no one expects me to unearth. Such was the case with the information I found recently, which is how I ended up being contracted by my current employer.

Still, despite the implications that are flying fast and furious through the dark web, I needed to be here to see Fallon graduate. Because somewhere between her first 9-1-1 text and now, I've fallen for the little minx.

As I predicted, she never returned to Kensington. But hell, how could she? She was offered her dream job just after spring break. Nor do I blame her; I just want to figure out if it's possible for us to blend our lives together—if that's what she wants.

I contemplate the kind of family outrage I'm going to stir up when I finally come clean about her, about the depth of my feelings for Fallon. *But what if she doesn't want to be with you? What if you wasted too much time? Dragging your feet, waiting for her to live her life before you moved in?* I slam the door on that idea. I can't—won't—let myself think like that.

We're going to face enough problems as it is.

My heart clenches painfully when I recall how she reacted when I declined her invitation to attend her graduation. Still in my world of denial, I demanded, "What would you have me say, Fallon?"

"That we're friends? Friends show up when they're asked," she retorted.

"*I* know we're friends. *You* know we're friends. My family has no clue." A pin dropping could be heard at a hundred paces with the silence between us after I released that bomb.

She whispered, "Still? I told my mother about you and me a long time ago, Ethan."

That flabbergasted me. "You did?"

Her next words were like a knife driven through my heart. "*I'm* not the one ashamed of our . . . friendship."

I heard the hitch in her voice by her choice of word right before she disconnected our call. I let out a blazing "Fuck!" even as I dialed her back.

I was sent directly to voicemail.

It took me two weeks of almost constant persistence to get her to speak to me again—even through text. I finally let out some of what my heart was feeling in voicemail, admitting, "Before you, there wasn't anyone I wanted to protect, Fal. It's instinctive. I don't know what to say where you don't get hurt."

She begrudgingly came around. When I finally talked to her again, she texted me something I'll never forget.

FALLON:

Don't be ashamed of who I am.

ETHAN:

I was trying to protect you. I care too much for you not to try to, Fal.

FALLON:

If I care for someone, I'll go straight to hell for them. I want them to know they're in my thoughts on the way down.

Frowning at the computer screen at the information I've located, I should be leaping with joy. Instead, a knot of worry has slithered into my stomach. The part of me that knows Fallon is the end of my heart's journey—despite my underlying worries—is the man sitting in the hotel room, waiting to surprise her at her graduation.

The part of me hunting down the people who ordered the death of an Agency's relative so they could pull her out of her special identity on the dark web makes me wonder how Fallon's going to react when I can't tell her about these assignments. Will she understand? Will she be able to handle the pressure? Will it just be one more burden on top of the twenty-year age difference between us?

Either way, I'll know when I see her face tomorrow when she realizes Austyn's husband Mitch isn't the only man attending her graduation.

CHAPTER SEVENTEEN

SEVEN VIRTUES, NORTH CAROLINA

Ethan

"I'm sorry, I will not comment about whether or not DJ Kensington is at Seven Virtues University graduation. If she is, it's not in a professional capacity."

—**Paula Stone**

Wildcard Media Representative

WITH A RAINBOW OF CORDS PROCLAIMING HER SUPERIOR ACADEMIC excellence draped around her neck, Fallon's mother and I take photo after photo of two women hamming it up outside Seven Virtues Stadium. The crowd shifts and bulges around them as they carry on. *Especially once they realize who is posing with Fallon,* I think sardonically.

Austyn demands I get into a picture with Fallon. "After all, Uncle E. If it weren't for you taking care of us, who knows if we'd have ever survived that first hangover," she mocks, tongue in cheek.

Fallon's mother snickers. "I'm just grateful I never knew about it, Ethan. I'd have been mortified."

Fallon bursts into gales of laughter. The brightness of her smile lights the dark corners of my soul. My whole body stills when Helen Brookes murmurs, "Ethan? Can you promise me you won't hurt her?"

Slowly, I lower my cell phone and face her mother's directness, realizing Fallon has told her everything. Her mother's knowing eyes meet mine. Still, I give her the only thing I can: honesty. "I can promise to try."

Her chin jerks. "That will have to be good enough." Her attention returns to Fallon, whom she taunts, "Well, at least I know who instigated your obsessive-compulsive love of Ho Hos."

Fallon doesn't hesitate before calling back, "Thus why I kept it from you for so long, Mama."

"Austyn, switch places with your uncle. He needs to be in some of these photos," Helen commands.

Austyn's melodic voice purrs, "I couldn't agree more."

I roll my eyes. "Brat."

"But you love me," she sings—on key, as always.

I hand her my phone and approach Fallon—whose smile hasn't wavered since she spotted me sitting beside her mother and her best friend. Wrapping an arm around her shoulders, I murmur, "Good surprise?"

Her arm slides around my waist and she tilts her face upward. Her mortarboard shadows her eyes, but not the blazing emotion bursting from them. "The best, E. Better than anything."

My fingers clutch her shoulder. My gaze spears down into hers even as her breath fluctuates slightly.

The world fades away as I'm lost in pools of indigo.

Then, in front of the people who mean the most to her and in front of a million strangers, she shows she has more courage than anyone I've ever met. Fallon leans up and brushes her lips against my cheek. "Thank you for being here for me tonight."

An ache races through me as her lips touch my skin for the first time. Now, I know what that feels like, and that too, will factor into the dreams she stars in every single night of my life. In that moment, I clutch her to me, bury my face in her neck, and give her everything. "There's nothing I wouldn't do for you, Fal. I hope you know that."

I watch her struggle as she tries to interpret my words. For just a moment, I let the facade I've been wearing all these years slip. Whatever she sees on my face causes her eyes to flare. She opens her mouth, but I shake my head. "Not now."

Her head tilts. "Then when?"

I tighten my arm so she's notched against my side, facing forward. Finally, I give in. "I'll come to you later."

Together, we face the camera, each of us clutching the other, knowing the temptations that lie between us will be given into the moment we're alone.

CHAPTER EIGHTEEN

Ethan

When Amaryllis Events, local coordinators of Collyer, Connecticut's GradNight, were asked about why the all-night event works, they gave the following quote, "The GradNight celebration is always a success because of the commitment from everyone involved."

Though serious about the rules, they teased future graduates about parents begging them to add items to the list of requirements to participate in GradNight, such as reduced gaming time, increased reading, and double dating with parents.

—Fab and Delish

After we all celebrated with a late dinner at the Ritz Carlton, I pull my rental up to Fallon's. Climbing out, I find the discreet PRIVATE plaque marking her entrance. After plugging in the code Fallon texted me earlier, I bound up the stairs leading to Fallon's apartment, anticipation building.

Particularly when I glance up and spy her waiting for me in the open door, still in the sexy as fuck blue silk dress she was wearing beneath her graduation robe.

I murmur, "Hi."

Happiness blooms across her face, causing my stomach muscles to clench, my cock to harden, and my balls to draw up, and I haven't even laid a finger on her. What on earth does she want with a man like me?

She cocks her head to the side. "What are you thinking?"

I let her close the door before I admit, "I'm tired of pretending I don't want you."

"What do you mean?"

"Do you remember your graduation party?"

A frown pulls her brows down. "Since it was all of an hour . . ." Her words stop mid-sentence.

"Not that one."

"The first one?" At my nod, comprehension lights her features. A smug look replaces the temporary awe. "It wasn't just me."

My lashes lower as I take in the wicked combination of beauty and frustration vibrating off her skin. "No, it wasn't just you, Fallon."

She rolls her eyes, making me want to light up her ass for her impertinence. "Then why wait? We could have . . ." Her lips press together, squashing her words inside.

But I know her thoughts without her finishing her sentence. After all, the hunger living inside her, the lust dying to break free, I've been on the other end of it for just as long as she has. I take a step forward and proclaim, "Our time is now."

Her choppy breath threatens to cause her breasts to spill out of her halter top—not that I'd mind since her dress is going to end up on the floor in a few moments anyway. Still, I want to seduce her—our first time anyway. We're both so worked up after years of texts that I know I could simply take her hand and lead her into the bedroom, but Fallon deserves more. Frankly, so do I.

Instead, I step back and ask, "Are you certain you want this? Me? Us?"

A slow smile graces her lips as she glides toward me with confidence. When she stops directly in front of me, she presses her hands against my chest.

My arms bind around her waist to haul her to me.

Rising on the balls of her feet, she brushes her lips against mine—her eyes holding mine the whole time. I taste the sweet cru she drank earlier mixed in with all that's Fallon. My blood beats fast in my veins as she lowers herself down before asking, "Does that answer your question?"

"Not even close to enough." I haul her back against me and slant my mouth over hers.

Lips parting, I'm not certain who moaned. I am certain I don't give the first fuck. My tongue demands her response—licking, tasting, sucking.

As Fallon's head falls back, exposing the line of her throat, I wrench my mouth away and trail my lips down the long, graceful column. My breath wafting over her skin causes her body to shudder in my arms.

And this is only the beginning.

She reaches down for a hand that is clutching one of her ass cheeks and tries to lift it to the globe of her breast. I let her, knowing it's what we both want. But even as my hand cups her fullness, she snarls her frustration. "It's not enough."

"Then tell me how to get you out of this fucking dress."

Fallon steps back and lifts her arm to unzip a hidden zipper. Once that's done, she reaches around the back of her neck. As soon as the knot is freed, the entire column of blue slithers to the floor, leaving her in nothing but a barely there scrap of lace and the silver heels she wore to her graduation ceremony.

I want to lunge, but instead, I savor the work of art in front of me, circling around her. My fingers trail over her marvelous ass, the curve of her hip, and tweak her nipples until I'm back in front of her.

When I meet her burning eyes, I know my life is forever changed. If you're lucky, there's an instant where a single look in your lover's eyes communicates everything else before you is forgotten. This is that moment with Fallon right now.

No regrets. No recriminations.

Just us.

I clasp her waist, feeling the thunder of her heart against my chest. Her indigo eyes blink languidly at me. "Ethan?"

As my lips descend to the curve of her shoulder, I cup her breast and rasp my thumb across her nipple.

"Oh god."

"I'm not a god, witch. Just a man."

Her hands lift and she flicks the buttons of my shirt open as her hands move on a downward glide. "My man."

"Be very sure before you say things like that, Fal."

"I've been certain for a long time. I was being gentle, easing you in, Ethan."

Uproarious laughter bursts from me. I nuzzle her temple, appreciating her candor and tenacity.

She arches her back like a cat.

I'm humbled and exhilarated by her response at the same time.

Reaching up, I comb my fingers through Fallon's heavy, blond hair, causing it to ripple down her back. Her unblemished skin flushes slightly. I drag a finger along the edge of her collarbone. "You do flush everywhere, witch."

Her indigo eyes flash with humor over my reminder of our text from yesterday. Then, their midnight depths morph into tenderness when she leans forward and presses her lips to the center of my chest right before she clasps my hand and leads me into her bedroom.

CHAPTER NINETEEN

Fallon

I am quite frankly appalled at what was beneath some of the class of 2024 graduation robes. It wasn't just T-shirt and shorts. Many of our graduates appeared to have slept in their clothing.

—Eva Henn, Fashion Blogger

HE'S EVEN MORE GORGEOUS NAKED THAN I PICTURED.

Ethan's holding my hands imprisoned over my head as he leans down and suckles one of my sensitive nipples deep into his mouth. My body arches, pressing the fullness of my breast against his lips in a plea for mercy.

He releases my hands, and I sink my fingers into the thickness of his chocolate-colored hair. His fingers drift down over the planes of my stomach as his mouth switches to the other breast.

My legs part, one lifting to hook around his lean hip. I'm barely aware of breathing when two fingers graze over my clit. Still, a broken "Ethan" escapes when his fingers find my soaked entrance. Instead of just shoving them inside like so many guys have, Ethan slowly grazes his fingers back and forth between my clit and my entrance, adjusting me to his touch. The way he plays my body makes my pussy weep.

I clasp his face and pull him up so I can smash my mouth against his. It's against his lips, I beg, "I need more."

I feel his smirk when he pushes just the tips inside. My head falls back against my pillows. "Stop being such a damn tease."

Since my eyes have closed in my desperation, I feel his lips surround my nipple. When he draws on the tip, it's then he thrusts his fingers deep inside —rotating them so he can brush them against the front wall of me.

My thighs quiver. My leg falls off his hip as I dig my heels into the mattress, straining for more—for the ultimate.

But Ethan's not about to let me run this show. His lips release my turgid nipple with a pop before he begins a descent down my body with his lips. I lift my head and meet his deep green eyes just before he makes room for his shoulders between my thighs.

My hands raise to my breasts and pull and twist at the nipples.

His eyes catch fire as he watches me take care of myself just before his tongue darts out to flick over my clit. With the first pass, he turns me to mush. With the second, he commands ownership of my body. With the third, I willingly hand myself to him as he thrusts his fingers inside, and I see stars behind my eyes as ecstasy explodes.

One of my hands falls to the side. The other lands on Ethan's head, where he continues to flick gently at my clit with his tongue—keeping me heightened but not in a painfully aroused state. Tiny ripples continue to run over my skin even as Ethan kisses first the inside of one thigh, then the other.

His lips against my inner thigh, he murmurs, "Protection?"

I tilt his face to meet mine. "I get the shot every three months and have always used condoms. You?"

He surges up my body, his bare cock brushing against my folds. I rub myself shamelessly against him. Bracing himself with his forearms, he clasps my face between his hands. "Fallon, I haven't had sex with a woman since well before the night I blew up at you for taking that photo with my brother."

My head rears back into the pillows. "Excuse me?"

"Swear to god." His eyes bore into mine.

I immediately wrap my arms and legs around him. His lips drop down to mine, his shaft working its way in as his tongue darts in and out of my mouth. In and out, going with the movement until the thickest part of him is seated inside me.

The walls of my vagina spasm around his girth. I tear my lips away and bury them against his neck. I slur, "So good."

As if on cue, Ethan pulls out and returns with a thrust that has me arching the tips of my breasts into his chest hair. Each time he repeats the motion, I feel the world spinning—or maybe that's just my heart flipping over and over in my chest. Scoring my nails down his back and over his buttocks, I gasp, "Don't stop."

"Not. Gonna. Stop." He thrusts with each word. He shifts and hooks both my knees beneath his arms, deepening the depth of his thrusts.

I have no way of stopping the depth of his penetration. As he quickens his pace, I writhe beneath him. I've never felt anything this primordial, this brutal. It's sensory overload.

And when I'm flung into the whirlwind, I fall over the edge into oblivion.

Ethan's not far behind me. He grunts through a few more thrusts before his ejaculation floods my inner walls. When it does, the weight of him collapses against me. After a few moments of compressing all the air from my lungs, he shifts to the side.

In the shipwreck of our lovemaking, I skim my hand up his body until I can force his face to look at me. Then I decide to drag on a pair of good old-fashioned big girl panties. "It's time to stop playing games via texts, misinterpreting each other."

His eyes crinkle in the corners. "I think that's a good idea."

"Then is this an end or a beginning?" I demand.

He leans down and captures my lips. For long moments, he does nothing more than pluck at my lips. Then he blows my mind. "I've had feelings for you for much longer than I allowed myself to admit, Fallon."

I blink. "You have?"

He rolls to his side, bringing me with him. "I know your life is just beginning here . . ."

My heart thumps wildly in my chest. "Ethan—"

He lays a finger across my lips. "No. Listen. This is still too new for us to bring us forward to my family. It's for you and for me. I want to explore what's between us, Fallon—no lies, no subterfuge. Just a few months of privacy to figure things out."

"And then?" I hold my breath.

His finger traces an outline before he replaces it with his lips. "Then, I swear on my life, I'll make certain you'll be happy for the rest of yours."

A single tear rolls down my cheek. He smiles at me tenderly. "I hope that means you agree."

"I do."

He winks. "Save that for a bit. Okay?"

Did he just say that? I'd float from this bed if Ethan wasn't in it with me. I vow to myself I don't care how hard I have to work or what I have to sacrifice to have him, but I'm ready to offer it.

No matter what it is.

CHAPTER TWENTY

KENSINGTON, TEXAS

Ethan

Sometimes, the speaker says it better than I do.

"In a year where we've lost so much, to have our community surround us is the cushion after the fall. Day after day, they've kissed our healing cuts. We appreciate those who have donated everything from the venue, goods, services, and, above all, their time to support Greenwich Hospital. But there's always more to do. We're not the only organization that needs help. Send Me An Angel—chaired by the incredible Ursula Moore—is one such organization. If you're looking for other ways to help, I'm certain StellaNova will have their information included on their website tonight, as well as ours."

Our gratitude to Dr. Laura Lockwood, affectionately known by all at StellaNova as "Queen Gore." Earlier this year, Gore's life was threatened by terrifying events at Greenwich Hospital.

—StellaNova

JESSE SLIDES ME A BEER ACROSS THE TABLE BEFORE ACKNOWLEDGING the disgust on my face at the woman I finished chasing away with a few well-placed harsh sentiments. "Not interested tonight?"

"Not interested, period." It's the truth. I want nothing to do with middle-aged women looking for whatever they think they'll find. All I want or need is waiting for me to call her back when I'm done catching up with my brother.

"Interesting."

"What is?"

"You."

"What about me?"

"You're throwing off 'taken' vibes."

I tip my head back for a long pull before asking, "Is it that obvious?"

"Only to someone who knows you as well as I do." He takes a drink of his own longneck before remarking, "Of course, it might be because the chick didn't notice the mark on your neck. Got yourself some while you were in Seven Virtues?"

I'd just taken another slug of beer and—fortunately for my older brother—twist my head before the spray of it flies out of my mouth. Pulling from the roll of paper towels Ralph keeps on his beat-up tables in lieu of wasting money on something as classy as napkins, I wipe up my mess when I grit out, "Christ, Jess."

He holds up his hands in mock surrender. "Just making an observation, brother."

"How about not doing it when I have a mouth full?"

He smirks. "Seems to me you likely had your mouth full plenty recently."

"Watch what you say," I warn, an undercurrent in my tone that brooks no arguments. I won't let my brother demean Fallon in any way.

"So, she's someone special?"

You have no fucking idea. I shrug, trying to pull off nonchalant.

And apparently failing miserably when Jesse counters with, "You're so full of shit, it reeks from this side of the table."

"Jess—" I begin.

"What?" he questions, confused. "You've never not shared about a woman with me. I mean, it's not like you fucked our Fallon."

I avoid his eyes, concentrating instead on peeling the label back from my dark ale.

"Ethan, tell me you didn't."

I decide silence is the best answer but in my head, I'm shouting to myself, *It wasn't just fucking. It can't be something as dismissive as that when your heart's involved.*

Jesse's sigh is so enormous you can hear it over the rodeo competition on the big screen. "Tell me you wouldn't be stupid enough to do something like that."

"What would make Fallon and me—two consenting adults—coming together stupid?" I question. Then I hasten to add, "Not that I'm admitting to anything, mind you."

"Right." He drawls the word out long enough to extend it into next week. Then he hits me with a few hard truths that have lived in my head for years —preventing me from taking what's mine years ago. "Maybe it's the fact you're old enough to be her father? Or the fact she's our niece's best friend?"

I wince, knowing both to be true.

"Let's not forget she's about to take her first baby steps in life and we're about to teeter into retirement?"

"Speak for yourself, old man," I retort.

His smile is smug and I want to throw a punch across the table to wipe it off his face. "What?"

"You didn't deny it was Fallon."

Crap. Crap and triple crap. I meet his gaze head-on and find concern and love but not what I expected to see, which was judgment. "Not a single word, Jess."

His brow creases. "Why not?"

My mouth opens and closes before I come up with a plausible reason. "It's new."

Christ, is it new. So new I'm certain the texture of her skin beneath my fingertips is still there. This paradox of a woman is consuming my thoughts. I only flew home this morning and already resent the distance between us.

Just then, a text causes my phone to vibrate.

FALLON:
I wish you were still here.

ETHAN:
I wish it was different.

FALLON:
Regrets?

ETHAN:
No. You?

FALLON:
Only that time didn't stand still.

ETHAN:
We'll figure this out, Fallon.

FALLON:
For some reason, I believe you.

ETHAN:
Probably because I've never lied to you, witch.

When I place my phone face down on the table, Jesse gives me a knowing look. "Was that her?"

"Yes." Judging by the expression on his face, he's waiting for me to elaborate. "She was asking if I have any regrets."

"And do you?"

I meet my brother's challenging gaze before I give him the truth. "No."

Jesse's tight facial expression eases. "That's all that matters."

"Is it?"

"Yes. Keep treating Fallon that way and I won't have to kill you."

My jaw drops as I verbalize, "You're not pissed at me being with Fallon. You're worried I'm going to hurt her."

My brother's eyes bore into mine, the truth clear as day.

I stand up and pull out my money clip. Tossing a few bills onto the table to cover both our tabs and the tip, I lean forward to hiss, "You have nothing to worry about."

He offers me a sad smile.

"Spit it out, Jess."

He lets out a long sigh. "You're not here, E. You're not here to listen to the old man's ramblings about Mama at home and in his therapy."

Ice chills the heat in my blood. I slide back into my barstool, not saying a word.

Jesse takes that as a cue to go on. "He loved her so much he lied to our sister, kept her from her soulmate for decades. His pain turned him inhumane."

Recalling the way he lied to our sister as she tried to find her baby's father to notify him of her upcoming pregnancy in her late teens, I wince. The knowledge of the ways he systematically degraded her to make her co-dependent on him makes me roar in fury. The fact Paige forgave him says a lot about my sister.

As for me, "I harbor so much resentment about what he did to Paige, I'm not certain I can get past it."

Jesse leans forward. "See, that's just it."

"What?"

"How can you pursue Fallon when you can't give her your full heart?"

"I'd be giving Fallon everything I have," I snarl.

"Would you be giving her your blind trust?"

Shock holds me in place when Jesse stands. "Right or wrong, Dad had his reasons. You need to listen to them."

I dismiss him. "He's made his peace with Paige. She's the only one who needs to forgive him."

"And the longer you keep thinking like that, the more your relationships are going to suffer." Just as I'm about to argue some more, Jesse turns. "I've got to go. Are you done?"

I surge to my feet, ready to bury this topic and wishing I had a way to bury my cock in Fallon tonight. God knows I need her and only her.

ETHAN:

Can you get away for a few days?

FALLON:

Seriously?

FALLON:

When?

ETHAN:

Next weekend?

FALLON:

I'll switch shifts?

FALLON:

Where are we going?

ETHAN:

Would you care if the answer is nowhere?

ETHAN:

I just want to see you.

FALLON:

That sounds perfect.

FALLON:

I miss you lying next to me.

ETHAN:

Five days.

FALLON:

Seems like five million but it's a start.

Encouraged by her response, the ache of discussing my father's betrayal eases as I make my way out of Rodeo Ralphs to my truck. Knowing I'll speak to Fallon daily between texts and phone calls, we can make this work.

We have to.

I can't live without her any more.

CHAPTER TWENTY-ONE

SEVEN VIRTUES, NORTH CAROLINA

Fallon

My favorite color palate is always fall.

—Eva Henn, Fashion Blogger

MAGIC. IT'S NOT JUST IN THE CHANGE OF THE SEASON RIPPLING across the mountain leaves, leading them from an almost iridescent green to an array of colors that range from the palest yellow to the deepest red. It's in the way I feel when Ethan slips into my bed late on a Friday night and we remain wrapped up in each other until late Sunday when he returns to Kensington.

Cocooned in our bubble, we exchange whispers of truths. I tell him about the pileup that killed my father, how I have no contact with my paternal grandparents—which he questions. I shrug without much force. "I guess if they really wanted something to do with me, they'd have tried long before now, Ethan. Mama and I are a large enough family. We have each other; that's all that matters."

He frowned before saying words that buried himself to the core of me when he reaffirmed something his sister said to me thousands of times. "You're part of a much larger family, Fallon. You're one of us—and that includes your mother." Then he ducked his head down and pressed his lips to mine in a languid kiss that clearly demonstrated he meant in a way different than the way I was accepted before.

Months have passed since that first weekend he flew back to see me. Months of incandescent joy intermingled with loneliness every time I drop him off at the regional airport for him to fly home. It's forced me to think long and hard in the time when he's not here. Have I convinced myself my career will make me happy because I couldn't have what I really want —Ethan?

Do I want something different? Something I could have had if I hadn't left Texas?

The thoughts persist as I pick up a few shifts at Galileo's—something I haven't done since I took my job with the Biltmore. But I couldn't refuse when Levi called pleading since, "Half the staff is out with this motherfucking bug, Fallon. Even Caroline is down, and you know she never calls out."

My nose wrinkled. "Did you fumigate the place?" The last thing I wanted to happen was catching whatever was going around and I'd be too sick to appreciate Ethan's upcoming trip.

"You bet your sweet ass, I did. Every surface has been cleaned, every bottle, and I've had every glass sanitized five times. I'm debating having one of those temperature check scanners installed at the door so none of those dumb fucks from the university can come through if they have a fever."

I snorted at Levi's vehemence. "Those 'dumb fucks,' as you just called them, pay your bills."

"Yeah, but now I'm having to resort to begging to keep the lights on."

"This was begging?" My voice was incredulous.

"About as close as it's going to get." Just as I was about to lambast him, he quickly wrapped up the call. "See you at six."

I shoot off a quick text to Ethan to tell him to come straight to Galileo's when he lands and why.

ETHAN:

Sounds good, witch.

ETHAN:

See you then.

FALLON:

Fly safe.

After warning our security team I have a guest arriving and when so they let him directly in, I call out to Levi, who is already slinging drinks behind the bar. "You planning on sharing your tips with me tonight?"

He rolls his eyes at me before winking at a pretty brunette who asks for a pina colada.

Sick or not, Galileo's is filled to capacity when seven forty-one rolls around. Maneuvering my way over to the stage, I swing by the bar and grab a cold can of cola before ascending the stairs.

Thirty seconds.

I snag the guitar that waits on stage. It's not my father's, but it will do. Over the din in the bar, no one can hear me doing a quick check to ensure the strings are tuned perfectly. Then, the house lights flicker.

Twenty seconds.

I slide in the cord to hook the guitar to the amp. Cheers erupt just as a man slipping in the entrance catches my eye. My heart speeds up when I realize it's Ethan. It takes everything inside me not to leap from the stage and into his arms.

Ten.

I hear a piercing whistle and know that's Levi's way of calling the bar to attention, ripping mine away from Ethan.

Five.

Four.

Three.

Inhale.

Two.

Exhale. I flick on the microphone.

One.

My lips part and I sing the first word at exactly forty-two after the hour. "Galileo's..."

Within milliseconds of my voice emerging from the speakers, the rest of the bar picks up the popular tune. All except for Ethan, whose eyes are trained on me for the four minutes of the song.

The second it's over, raucous cheers break out and I take a quick bow. I lean into the mic and remind everyone, "We'll be back to toast this amazing bar and its patron saint in the next hour."

Another cheer goes up as I slip from the stage. I track Ethan as he makes his way around to me. A small parting of people gives me the chance to sprint in his direction, so I take it.

He plants himself, but that still doesn't stop him from staggering back a step with the force of the impact I hit him with. Wrapping my arms and legs around him, I bury my head into his neck and absorb the fact Ethan's here with me.

For me.

He spins me around and backs me up against the bar. "Fal? Witch? Is everything okay?"

I cup his cheek before my lips curve. "Now it is."

That earns me a delicious kiss that sets fire deep in my core. It's a good thing I know Ethan will quench that particular flame or I don't know what I'd do.

I don't know what I'd do without him. Not anymore.

CHAPTER TWENTY-TWO

SEVEN VIRTUES, NORTH CAROLINA

Ethan

There are some things I'm grateful for in life.

1. Being alive.

2. Being healthy.

3. One time, just once, being smarter than StellaNova.

I can't share the reason why, but because Arek Ronan owes me, I'm cashing in. This guy is going to see Beckett Miller and Brendan Blake play at the American Music Awards!

—Viego Martinez, Celebrity Blogger

I HOLD FALLON CLOSE TO MY CHEST AS SHE RESTS, HER BREATH

evening out after our last round of making love, and admit to myself that's exactly what it was—making love. I refuse to lie to myself any longer.

But I can't outrun the doubts that creep in when I'm not connected to her body, doubts my brother pointed out early in my relationship with her but I already knew.

"How can you pursue Fallon when you can't give her your full heart?"

Rolling to my back, I keep her body pressed against my length even as my other arm raises to my forehead. I stare up at the shadows shifting across the ceiling as the trees dance outside Fallon's bedroom window.

I wish the night sky and the gods that roam through them could give me insight into the future, if not answers to the questions my heart has. But as hours pass, I lay there with Fallon's breath wafting across my chest, forcing my mind to subdue my emotions spiraling out of control. Even with as much as I love Fallon, I need to pursue her slow and steady to ensure I stack the deck against our age difference and the distance between us each day.

When we finally conquer it, I'll never let her go.

CHAPTER TWENTY-THREE

SEVEN VIRTUES, NORTH CAROLINA

Fallon

Unexplained weight loss should be discussed with your doctor. While it's normally nothing to be alarmed about, it may require adjusting some medication. You always want to be your healthiest you.

—Fab and Delish

"THERE ISN'T A BIG ENOUGH WORD TO DESCRIBE WHAT HE MAKES ME feel," I admit to my mother as we eat lunch at Blue Ridge Brews & Bites. I sip at their seasonal pumpkin ale before leaning forward to swipe a bite of pepper through their sunflower hummus before letting out a moan of pleasure.

My mother, amused, asks, "Is there any chance you're pregnant?"

I still, just as I was about to pop another bite into my mouth. "What the hell would make you ask that?"

She inclines her head in my direction. "You're devouring our appetizer like it's our last meal."

My face flames. "Well, umm...you see." How do I tell my mother my boyfriend—if that's what I call him?—wouldn't let me out of bed long enough to down a few bites of food and drink a bottle of water.

Still, as the dawn burst across the morning sky and I studied his profile in the shadows of my bed, the peace that consumed me was immediate. Food was an easy sacrifice for having Ethan in my heart, in my bed.

"What are you daydreaming about over there, sweetheart?" Mama questions.

Pulled from my reverie, I grin. "One guess."

She opens her mouth but before she can ask me anything, our mains are delivered. I happily dig into my cheeseburger and relish the burst of flavor from the fire-grilled meat as it hits my tastebuds. After wolfing down a few bites, I notice my mother hasn't touched her salad. "Is there something wrong with your meal, Mama?"

A wan smile creases her lips. "Just not hungry, sweetheart."

I frown, even as my burger hits the plate. "Is there something wrong?"

"Nothing that can't wait. I want to hear everything about Ethan," she encourages me.

"Ask away," I offer.

For the next little while she does. Then she asks me a curious question. "What would you give up to have him in your life?"

"What do you mean?"

"There's a lot riding on your relationship whether it succeeds or if it fails, Fallon. Do you stay in Seven Virtues? Do you take a job somewhere else? Does your relationship with Austyn have the same dynamic? What if you end up married to Ethan?"

I smirk. "I'd be her Aunt Fallon."

She snickers. "Okay. I concede, that one is funny to consider. But what about things like children?"

Exasperated, I throw my hands into the air. "Mama, we've been together for a few months. Do all couples discuss these things within the first ninety days? Is there some sort of money back guarantee on relationships if you file for an incompatibility refund by then?"

She bursts into laughter. "You always could make me laugh, Fallon."

I reach across the table and squeeze her hand. "Until you're one hundred, I'll have the chance."

Her fingers tense around mine. "I hope so too, sweetheart. Now answer the question. What would you give up to have Ethan in your life?"

Giving the question the seriousness it merits, I think about it before I answer, "The answer's simple—likely everything."

A blinding smile crosses her face. "Good. That's what I was hoping you would say."

CHAPTER TWENTY-FOUR

Fallon

Send Me an Angel charity board member, Dr. Clarabel Lam, has taken a sabbatical from her position at SMAA to join the program at the St. Peregrine Cancer Research Institute in Seven Virtues, North Carolina. When asked why she chose to make this move, Dr. Lam indicated. "Pain isn't limited to those we treat at SMAA. If I can both help and learn at St. Peregrine, then aren't we all better off?"

Dr. Lam's rotation will last for one year, though she will retain her board seat on SMAA. We wish her nothing but the best of luck.

—StellaNova

IN THE TAPESTRY GALLERY AT BILTMORE HOUSE, I'M AN OBSERVER today as much as any of the tourists who will saunter through within the next few hours. My boss wants me to become even more comfortable with the history and maintenance of these priceless pieces left as part of the Vanderbilt estate. I hear a guided tour walk by and, for the third time, hear one of the incredibly trained tour guides explain, "No complete set of The Triumph of the Seven Virtues exists today."

"Which one is missing?" a man asks.

"The Triumph of Temperance no longer exists anywhere in full glory, although fragments which have been salvaged have been sewn into other tapestries at Biltmore House."

My heart flips every time I hear that. Those simple words remind me of how I feel when Ethan isn't by my side—a part of him is with me. A part of me is with him.

In fact, he said something similar to me on the phone last night.

"You're always on my mind, witch."

Settling in the oversized chair in my living room, I hold his gaze while I ask evenly, "Is that a good or bad thing?"

"It's a good thing. It's like…" His voice fades off.

"Like what, Ethan?" I push, thinking of my conversation with my mother. There are too many things we haven't yet said, haven't asked. When we're together, we burn— consumed by passion. While I never want that to change, I want the warmth of the embers when I know I can be in his embrace, watching the antics of our family, each of us sporting at least one or several gray hairs.

"Like pieces of us were made for each other."

I suck in a deep breath at the depth of his words.

His face twists in distress. "Too much too soon?"

"If you only knew how perfect that was and it could never be soon enough."

The crow's feet next to his eyes crinkle when his strong lips curve.

"Fallon? Fallon?"

I'm ripped from my recollection when I hear my name being called. Giving myself a hard shake, I answer the office staff intern, Julianne, with a smile. "Yes, I'm sorry. I was woolgathering."

"Rather appropriate to do in this room, I would think," she replies with a quick longing glance at the tapestries created in the 1520s.

"Is there something I can help you with?"

"I apologize. You received a call. I was asked to notify you it is urgent." I'm handed a folded slip of paper.

I wait for her to step away before I unfold it. The second the words register, I reach out for the arm of a green club chair—so great is my shock.

And my fear.

Your mother passed out at work. Get to SV Hospital immediately.

Without a word, I race for my desk to grab my purse before dodging employees and tourists to get to my car.

And my mother.

"Helen Brookes?" I fling my words at the individual manning the information desk the second my body collides with it. I can't recall how fast I drove the roads to leave the Biltmore Estate, how many speeding laws I broke, how many stop signs I blew through just to get here one minute faster.

My experiences with this hospital aren't kind memories despite the hard-working staff.

"One moment, please." Every second the computer is being checked, I'm dying a small death. Finally, "Room 402."

"She's been admitted?"

An expression of sympathy crosses her face before I'm given directions to the elevator bank—not that I need them. Not unless they've moved since Austyn was admitted as a patient. Without a second glance, I take off in that direction, barely managing to slip in as the doors close.

A quick look at the panel tells me the fourth floor has already been pushed. I hold my breath as patients and doctors perform a shuffle and dance as they get on and off at floors two and three. Finally, I burst out at floor four and make a left in the direction of room 402.

Before I get there, I'm stopped—not by a person at a desk but by the most beautiful, yet hideous marble etching. My lips form the words but no sound comes out.

St. Peregrine Cancer Research Institute.

"No. It's not possible." I duck back and ensure I didn't head in the wrong direction. Finding what I believe to be is a floor nurse, I demand her to look up my mother's room. "I was just called because she passed out at work." Holding out my cell phone as if there must be a grand mistake.

There has to be.

Instead of confirming or denying anything, the woman squares her shoulders. "Why don't I walk you to your mother's room, Ms. ...?"

"Brookes."

"I'm Dr. Claribel Lam. I'd be happy to escort you to your mother."

She leads me in the direction opposite of the cancer ward and my heartbeat slowly settles down as we make the first right. "What do you do, Ms. Brookes?"

"Make it Fallon. I work at the Biltmore Estate as a curator."

"That must be an interesting job. I recently transferred here—a temporary assignment to study...well, that's not really important. Let's get you to your mother."

"Do you like it?" I ask, making polite small talk as we turn the next right bend.

"So far. I've only been here about a week. I used to live and work in New York."

"Big change."

"I accepted the offer after...well, I just needed to get out of the north." She uses her badge to take us through the next set of closed doors, where we make another immediate right. Now, the rooms are different. Each has a sink outside and a warning posted. Every patient's door is closed. Most individuals moving in and out of them are gowned.

As we approach room 402, we slow down, and I realize I can see the marble etching from the back. My gut churns bile when I realize we've done nothing but make a gigantic circle. "The cancer ward? Is my mother going to die?"

Dr. Lam rests a hand on my shoulder as gently as a butterfly. "I need to walk you through the protocols, Fallon. Then you can go in to see your mother."

She doesn't answer my question.

For the next few moments, I manage to keep from screaming as I learn how to scrub my hands, how to dress in a gown, how to slip on a mask—quickly tied by Dr. Lam. Before I can shove through the room, Dr. Lam offers me a small bit of insight. "You will never know how strong you can be until you fight for the person you love to live just one more day."

Immediately, I decide she's right. I square my shoulders. "I'll do anything to ensure that happens." And I do mean anything.

Her lips lift at the corners. "Then, are you ready to see your mother?"

I nod.

She knocks at the door before pressing the door open. "Helen? You have a visitor."

I thought I was prepared to see my mother hooked up to an IV or two. What no one prepares you for is there are going to be times when you bitterly regret every moment not cherishing the person you love. For me, that time is now. I step forward and reach for her hand. "Hey, Mama. Something you forgot to mention when I came over for dinner last week?"

She lowers her facial oxygen mask before smiling a weak ass smile at me. "Yes. The meatloaf leftovers I had for lunch were dry."

My laugh is ruptured by the tears I'm shedding. "Of course they were."

Dr. Lam backs out of the room to give us privacy. Only, I don't know where to start or even what I'm supposed to ask. I do know what I'm supposed to say. Stepping forward, I reach for my mother's hand.

She immediately takes mine. It's as strong as it's always been. *There must be some kind of mistake.* The thought floats through my mind until I spy the IV in her hand.

I study the needle and follow the line. It's attached to a bag of fluids as well as something with a name and a warning label on it. Fear squeezes my heart when I suspect I'll learn what all the bags that are hanging up are. In this moment, I stubbornly refuse to ask. Right now, only one thing needs to be made clear. "I love you a whole lot, Mama."

She swallows repeatedly before rasping, "Never more than I love you, Fallon."

Leaning forward, I rest my head next to hers on the pillow and murmur, "That's just not true."

CHAPTER TWENTY-FIVE

KENSINGTON, TEXAS

Ethan

According to the University of Kassel (2023), one-third
of romantic partners engage in deceptive tactics.

—The Fireside Psychologist

I TRIED TO REACH FALLON EARLIER, BUT SHE HASN'T ANSWERED HER
phone or replied to any texts.

"That's unusual for her. Even if she picks up a shift at Galileo's, she
normally lets me know." Still, a grin crosses my lips. My Fallon doesn't
know the meaning of the word relax. I saunter into my kitchen to grab a
beer when my phone pings.

FALLON:

Sorry. I was caught up with Mama.

ETHAN:

No worries, witch.

FALLON:

Can I talk with you tomorrow?

FALLON:

I'm going to be here with her for a while.

ETHAN:

Everything okay?

The dots move as Fallon formulates her next thought. I wait with more than a bit of concern, knowing that Fallon is as close to her mother as my niece and sister are—both women treating their mothers like best friends.

FALLON:

She's caught up in something, so I'm keeping her company.

ETHAN:

Enjoy your night with your mother, witch.

ETHAN:

We'll catch up later.

FALLON:

How many days is it until you're here?

ETHAN:

Two weeks.

ETHAN:

Hand to god, I can't wait until we're in the same room together.

FALLON:

Me neither.

Satisfied with that, I leave Fallon to spend time with her mother since I plan on consuming every inch of her body, mind, and soul the minute my plane touches down in North Carolina.

I just hope Fallon's ready to leave every thought behind because I don't plan on letting her think about anything but us.

CHAPTER TWENTY-SIX

SEVEN VIRTUES, NORTH CAROLINA

Fallon

I recently received an email. I so rarely answer them, but felt this was important. "Where can I get fashionable clothes for a friend who is having a mastectomy?"

Try AnaOno. Founder and CEO, Dana Donofree knows exactly what a post-surgical patient needs.

—Eva Henn, Fashion Blogger

THERE'S NO WAY I'M HEARING HER CORRECTLY. "MAMA, YOU *WANT* ME to go away for the weekend with Ethan?"

Dr. Lam—Clarabel, as she ordered me to call her after our initial meeting—just left my mother's room after relieving my heart. "Your mother's on a definite upswing. With luck, since the surgery went so well, she should be ready to be discharged early to mid next week, Fallon."

But none of that explains my mother trying to get me away from the hospital. She grasps my hand and entwines our fingers. "Fallon, you've done everything possible to ensure I'm comfortable. You've been here every available moment."

"Mama, I'd give up everything for you." It's no less than the truth. Fortunately, the team I work with at the Biltmore found a way for me to catalog some data only requiring me to take minimal time off. Grateful, I've barely had to leave her side since the doctors went in and removed her uterus.

"I don't expect you to." Her voice is firm. Before I can counter her words with reassurance, she goes on. "That being said, the exact same is true. I'd do anything for you, baby."

My facial muscles relax. "You already have. You've always loved me."

"I always will, Fallon. Still, you've barely left my side."

The relief that sweeps through me, cleansing away the pervasive fear is tremendous. I'm about to suggest we celebrate when she beats me to the punch. "You heard Dr. Lam; I'm not going anywhere. Go meet up with Ethan."

Guilt wars with my own need to be held and have my heart healed. It comes out as a huff. "I need to be here for you."

"To hover over me as I watch a Peter Freeman marathon on Food Network? No," she concludes before I can speak. "You need to pursue wherever your heart leads you, Fallon. Especially now."

Especially now. I lean forward and lay my head against her stomach. "Mama?"

"What, baby?"

"Will you tell me why you're not afraid?"

"You think I'm not afraid?"

"You are?" A part of me feels relief I'm not the only one, but knowing it makes me feel guilty for placing a chink in the armor she's been using to get herself to this point. Surging to my feet, I move toward the window.

"That's because I'm focused on fighting to live."

Eyes narrowing, I dare her to lie to me when I face her before challenging, "Are you keeping something from me?"

My mother rolls her eyes. "Fallon, I have been diagnosed with a very aggressive form of Stage IV uterine cancer. While I don't want anyone to know about it yet, I think I'll be okay sitting here for a few days until my blood levels even out enough for Dr. Lam to feel comfortable sending me home."

I try to determine if there's any subterfuge in her words but find nothing but sincerity there. With a sigh, I capitulate. "Only if you swear you'll have the hospital call if anything happens."

She holds up her hand and says solemnly, "I swear, if I try a new flavor of Jello for dessert, I'll have them call you."

"Not funny."

She pinches her fingers together. "A little funny?"

My lips twitch. "Maybe just a bit, but only because I'll be jealous if you finally get the orange flavor."

We both succumb to laughter. While I'm grateful for the laughter, I hate this. I hate our banter has been reduced from discussing jobs, TV shows, and men to mocking the fear building up within these four walls.

Maybe that's a good sign. Maybe cancer should be afraid of two Brookes women set out to destroy it. I want it eradicated, eliminated, pulverized to nothing but a distant memory. I don't care what it takes—what specialists or medicines my mother requires. No matter the cost, no matter the toll, I'll do what I need to pull her from the edge of death to the safety of life beyond.

Austyn won't hesitate, I know. She'll raise an army to get my mother well, with Paige leading a brigade of doctors right behind her.

That's why my senses go on high alert when my mother cautions me. "Fallon, I need you to make me a promise."

"What?"

Tension snaps my back ramrod straight when she requests, "Don't say anything to anyone about this."

"Not even Ethan?"

"Not yet."

Incredulous, I stare at her with my mouth agape. "You've got to be kidding."

She shakes her head.

I sputter, "B-b-but why?"

Her voice is sharp as a knife when she scores my heart with it. "Because until I've accepted exactly what I'm facing, I'm not ready to field a million questions? Because it's my decision? Because it's my choice and not yours?"

Every word out of her mouth causes her voice to rise and causes me to shrink. She's right. Of course she is. The problem is I just don't know if I'm strong enough to handle her prognosis on my own. Surging to my feet, I walk over to the window overlooking Seven Virtues—a place that's both given and ripped away so many dreams.

I only pray today the saints that supposedly protect our sleepy little town hear my prayers to give me the strength I need to carry my mother through her battle.

"Fallon?" My mother's voice is filled with regret. "I'm sorry I snapped at you. It's just...it's a lot, sweetheart."

"I know, Mama." *Boy, do I get it.* "And I won't say anything to Ethan." *Not yet, anyway.*

Relief flashes across her face. "Thank you."

I make my way back to her side and take her hand. "Should I be annoyed you're watching Peter Freeman without me?"

"No."

"Why not?" I tease her—anything to distract her.

"Because you're going to forget all about me the moment you fall into Ethan's arms," she declares confidently.

Rolling my shoulders, I feel some of the tension ease with my decision. I'll be able to lean on someone soon. My someone. My Ethan.

Despite the desire to lay my head on his chest and sob out my pain, with my mother's recent decree, I'm not certain I can. I bite my lip uncertainly. Some of what I think must be visible on my face because my mother amends her statement. Gently, she gives me, "Fallon, you can let him know I'm not well."

I open my mouth to agree but I stop myself. If I open that door between me and Ethan, I know myself. I'll tell him everything. There's no in between. I'll never honor her request for silence about her prognosis. I have a choice of betraying my mother or holding back her secrets from my lover—which is no choice at all.

I have to keep this news to myself for a little while longer.

"You just worry about your crush on Peter Freeman and let me worry about Ethan and the rest of the Kensingtons."

"I still don't understand how you don't find him as gorgeous as the rest of America does, sweetheart."

Just then, a commercial pops up touting the star's newest episode. While yes, he's attractive, he just doesn't do it for me. "You can share your man, Mama. I'm a one-man kind of woman."

Her lips purse. "But."

That causes me to grin. "Okay, you have me there."

One heartbeat. Two. Then we both burst into laughter just as Clarabel comes striding in. "Don't worry, Fallon. I have no problems with sharing some quality Pete Freeman with your mother."

My eyes narrow on the pretty doctor. This isn't the first time she's shortened his name as if she knows him. Could the handsome star be part of the reason she's here? I'm distracted from my train of thought when she continues, "Her numbers just came back. No discharge for Helen until Tuesday for certain."

I throw up my hands, knowing I'm beat but grateful for the respite at the same time. I need Ethan—not just for sex, but for the feel of his arms around me when I sleep. I need the tangible reminder that there's more to pursue in this life than a race into death.

After a quick stop by my apartment, I drive four hours to Charleston with my mother's request not to share her medical turn with my second family permeating my thoughts. *Why? Why would she want me to hide this from my best friend? From my lover's family?*

The question tumbles over and over in my mind until I start seeing signs on the highway for Charleston. Then my heart quickens when I know I'll be wrapped up in Ethan's arms within the hour.

Feel his heartbeat beneath my ear.

His body pressing mine back against the mattress.

His fingers dancing along my skin.

My foot presses against the accelerator to shave minutes off an already long drive because suddenly each minute between us is too much. I wish I could levitate from my car and land in front of Charleston Place, but my body's bound by gravity even if my heart knows it can fly.

Finally, I turn off and hand my keys over to the valet. Ethan had texted me our room number earlier, which I give them. Grabbing my weekender from the backseat, I stride confidently into the hotel and make my way to the elevator to the seventh floor.

The second I'm off the elevator, my stride picks up until I'm jogging to reach the end of the hall as quickly as I can. My breathing is erratic when I reach it. Unable to put a brake on my body or my emotions, I slam up against the wall next to the door. Before I even have the chance to curtail what I'm feeling, the door flings open.

And there he is.

Waiting for me.

He inspects me from head to toe without saying a word before stepping forward and clasping his fingers around my wrist. I'm not sure what he sees when he stares at my face, but for certain, he feels the leap of my pulse the second he opens his mouth and mutters, "It's about time you got here, witch."

Then he yanks me into the suite's foyer, slamming the door behind me before his lips crash down on mine. Everything but this man is obliterated from my mind the second they do.

I should feel guilt, knowing my mother's only a few hours away and deathly ill, but if Ethan can be nothing more than my silent strength through this ordeal, I need to absorb him into me for all the days I can't have him.

Dropping my bag, I boost myself up and wrap my legs around his waist. He spins—not lifting his lips from mine—and heads for the bedroom.

CHAPTER TWENTY-SEVEN

KENSINGTON, TEXAS

Ethan

Saratoga Springs, N.Y., CEO Leanne Miles has released an official press announcement. She and her husband are expecting their first child.

—Castor News Room

GETTING ON THE PLANE TO LEAVE FALLON WAS THE LAST THING I wanted to do. I know she was reluctant to leave me at the Charleston airport if the amount of time she spent kissing me at TSA was any indication. But we both needed to return to work today—particularly after Fallon admitted to missing being in the office because her mother was unwell these past few weeks. I make a mental note to send Helen some flowers after I get off the conference call from hell.

Mondays can suck it.

"Whose idea was it to schedule this dumpster fire for first thing in the morning?" I demand.

Sam Aiken snorts with his typical good humor. "Be grateful it wasn't earlier. *Qəza's* normally up as early as Thorn." Sam casually drops Agency's director Parker Thornton's nickname as the two have been friends for over twenty years.

I shudder. "There's something wrong with the lot of you people."

The woman in question snarks from behind her privacy screen, "If you were growing a small human who uses your bladder as a timpani drum, you'd say to hell with it and work too, *Whiskey*."

Hearing my Agency code name fall from her lips feels unusual. When I remark on that, she retorts sweetly, "Oh, my bad. Was it supposed to be some sort of secret?"

"I mean, who the hell cares about a little thing like the National Security systems that have to be hacked into."

Cheerfully, *Qəza* switches to video. She's obscured in shadow, but my brows draw together as I study her. It was meant to distract me and it's working. "Tell me about it. When I hacked—" A sharp cough from Sam has her selecting different words. "I mean, when I 'accessed' the DoD database to find out more information about my husband, I never would have believed I could be both dead and my clearance still active."

My jaw's on the floor, but I manage to push out a rough, "Pardon me? What were you doing looking up your husband?"

She twists to the side and actively ignores my question.

It's Sam who gives me the answer. "*Qəza* was involved with a different op where she met her husband."

Patiently, as if she's talking to two-year-olds instead of men who deal with the ramifications of cyber hunting every day, she reminds Sam, "I'd met him before."

"Yes, but he thought you were—"

Just then, Thorn joins the call. He interrupts smoothly. "Someone else."

Her husky laugh comes out. Then she kisses her fingers and raises them to the sky in benediction and thanks. She whispers something but at the end I hear, "Right, Lee?"

Lee? Who the hell is Lee?

My identity, which is supposed to be concealed behind my code name and a million safeguards, but I suspect the intrepid *Qəza* knows good and well who I am. When I say as much, both Sam and Thorn respond with a shrug. Still, I'm irritated I can't piece together who *Qəza* is. My voice is petulant when I demand, "Why can't I be in the cool kids club and know who she is?"

It's Sam who is the most political. "Information about *Qəza* is need to know."

Thorn mutters, "Besides, nobody *shares* information with *Qəza*. She ferrets it out all on her own, whether you want her to know or not."

Qəza simpers. "Oh, Thorn. A compliment. Let me mark the time and date."

He chuckles. "I should have left you for dead."

Dead? Wait, that wasn't a joke?

"Just think of all the fun you and I have had over the years," she retorts.

"Fun?" Thorn roars before he hisses, "I almost lost my job because of you."

"Keyword being almost."

"I had to do paperwork," Thorn's voice is nothing less than disgusted.

"For what? A week?" she retorts.

Sam mutters, "Here we go."

"Am I going to need some popcorn?" I ask the older man.

"Possibly."

I'm stunned when *Qəza* and Thorn bicker back and forth like siblings. Remaining mute, I pick up keywords like singing, tabloid, and shot. Then *Qəza* brings me directly into the conversation. "I do owe you an apology, Agent Kensington."

"For what? And while we're speaking of it, I'm not an agent any longer."

Qəza singsongs, "That's not what your file says."

Thorn's cheeks flush when I glare at him. She snickers. "I, myself, tried to tell Thorn that years ago. Look where we are at right now. Together."

I growl, refusing to cede anything. "What's the apology for?"

She hits a button and the blur of her features disappears. I find myself face to face with a familiar one—a pain-in-the-ass business partner I bitched about to Sam what feels like yesterday. My mouth manages to push out her name. "Leanne?"

"Surprised?" Leanne Miles wiggles her fingers at me.

"That's a bit of an understatement." My head spinning, I ask one question, "How?"

Before I can formulate a reply, she sweeps my feet out from under me. "Sorry I left such a mess for you in Silverthorn. I couldn't keep my cover and stay." Her eyes flood with tears. "There were reasons I had to leave quickly."

The "mess" being after she was attacked during her identical twin's funeral —the famous musician Erzulie. It was a funeral the world thought was hers —famed CEO Leanne Miles, owner of the US government contractor, Castor. It shook the market for weeks until a successor was named and even then, until Leanne came out of hiding and took back her company, Castor felt the impact of the repeated attempts on her life.

Thorn butts in. "Now that we all know who each other is, can we get down to business?"

Leanne's dramatic sigh is amusing. "Still working on those people skills, I see?" She shifts in her chair and I notice her body is ripe with pregnancy.

It immediately makes me wonder what it would be like if Fallon fell pregnant with my child. My dick becomes iron hard in an instant at the idea of her body swollen with our combined seed, her nurturing our son or daughter against her luscious breasts.

While I'm dreaming of a future, I need to be focused on the present. Leanne's switched from picking on Thorn to the reason the four of us are on a secure compartmentalized call being bounced off a satellite. "Here's the problem." She explains that when she was in hiding from the death threat against her own life, she'd been hunting day in and day out. For five months, she did nothing but eat, sleep, and breathe, the threat against her while trying to protect her now husband.

The irony of her placing herself in harm's way to protect her husband when he's a trained bodyguard isn't lost on me and I don't hesitate to say as much. She offers me a wry smile. "He had several things to say on the subject when I took a bullet for setting off the failsafe inside of Dioscuri." Leanne names software her company built specifically for the Agency that's host to some of the highest classified information in the world.

A snort escapes my lips, causing hers to curve upward. "I just bet he did." I suspect her "recovery" from that stunt was closely monitored by her then boyfriend—who happens to head my brother-in-law's personal protection detail.

Small world.

The humor leaves Leanne's face as she caresses her stomach. Her thoughts are more musings. "Do you know how Kane and I got together, Ethan?"

"Other than you impersonating your sister to draw out her killer?" That part was widely reported in every media outlet across the globe.

"Hmm. That's the public version." Across my screen comes a request to join a chat in a part of the dark web that won't leave a trace of our conversation when it's over. Leanne winks at me. "Meet you there."

Then she's gone. Sam and Thorn follow. I click the link and find I'm the last to join. As soon as I do, I find the background behind Leanne has shifted. No more smoke and mirrors, she's clearly framed behind her desk at the New York City branch of her multi-billion dollar company, Castor. Musing, she shares, "I've never been satisfied Linus Messina was solely behind the attack against me."

A pin could drop before Thorn thunders, "And you didn't think to share that with me before now?"

She shrugs, fearless in the face of his temper. "All I had were suspicions, Thorn. I've been monitoring them..."

"Not through Dioscuri or I'd have known," he cuts in.

"No. Through another piece of software I've been tinkling with."

It doesn't take a genius to observe Thorn alternately wants to throttle her for not keeping him in the loop while at the same time bombard her with questions about the new software she's building. But it's her words that shake us all because of their truth. "Your predecessor never would have accepted either of us back if someone still wanted me dead."

The scandal surrounding Leanne's involvement in her sister's murder was contained due to a lack of police investigation and family grief. However, she's right. If the Agency was caught continuing to operate an op on US soil without sanction, all bets would have been off. It would have set off a series of internal investigations that would have sent whomever was after Leanne underground—more than they already were.

In other words, despite living, she's been doing it with one eye over her shoulder. There's never really been closure on who hired the hit on her in the past. I jump in as devastation falls across Thorn's face. "Does your husband know?"

She nods. "We don't keep secrets from one another."

Sam clears his throat. "Tell us everything, Lee."

Leanne lays out exactly what she was investigating in the months she was in hiding—the money transactions both on and off shore. The people involved. How she survived. As she details how she endured, I couldn't quite reconcile the businesswoman with the agent. Now, I'm irritated with myself for missing it. I don't beat around the bush. "I'm in. What do you need?"

"Why, Ethan, I'm so glad you asked." Leanne sketches out some initial thoughts about how to eliminate who might be hunting her. Sam and I debate the merits of which areas of the dark web we each will wallow in.

Much to my surprise, it involves a phone sex business based in North Carolina. "You're kidding. Those still exist?"

Sam chuckles. "Internet porn just isn't good enough for some people. They like a live voice."

Thorn names the amount this business rakes in and we each whistle. "More than just a few people like this business. *Qəza* already determined most of their clientele is from overseas."

Leanne confirms, "Someone on the inside isn't just laundering the money; they're dry cleaning it and wrapping it up with a pretty bow."

I question, "You can't get in deeper?"

"Not on my own."

"You won't have to," I assure her decisively not just because of the fact she's been a colleague but because of the fact the company in question is based in Seven Virtues.

And I'll do anything to protect my Fallon.

CHAPTER TWENTY-EIGHT

SEVEN VIRTUES, NORTH CAROLINA

Fallon

HomeGoods is having a sale this weekend. We expect to see every family member associated with the Freeman/Marshall/Hunt clans shopping.

Stalk your favorites with a modicum of class, people.

—Viego Martinez, Celebrity Blogger

"I've got to be boring you with all these talks about tapestries, Ethan," I joke as I lift my iPad closer.

He brings his drink closer to his lips. My eyes drift over his face as he lifts the highball to his lips, takes a drink, and licks his lower lip before placing the glass to the side. "Not at all. To be honest, Fal, it's not something I know much about."

"Really?"

"I could tell you how to disassemble and reassemble a desktop in about thirty minutes."

"Now you're talking sexy, Mr. Kensington," I tease him.

He rolls to his side, and I get a frontal view of his delicious body. I whisper, "Is it any wonder I can't get enough of you?"

"Hmm. That goes both ways, baby."

I turn into a similar position, my robe gaping open when I do. It causes him to groan. I bite my lower lip before I direct our thoughts away from an intimate one and ask more about his work. "So, is that what you do in your store all day? Rebuild computers?"

"Sometimes, though it's rare," he replies, vaguely. "Sometimes, I help when people have problems with their systems. Things like that."

Instead of coming off as not smart enough for a man like Ethan, I joke, "My major requirement when it came to my computer was that it didn't crash after I turned it on."

He smirks and it causes the gusset between my panties to dampen. "That's the way most people are, witch. You're not alone."

"So, based on that, I assume your job isn't that portable."

He shocks me when he says obliquely, "You'd be surprised. Most of what I do actually can be done from anywhere inside the US."

"Even computer repairs?"

"Well...that part I might need to look into having someone take over." His eyes bore into mine. "When we're ready for that next step."

My heart pounds in my chest when I realize Ethan's truly on this crazy expedition with me. When I say as much, he murmurs, "Absolutely."

"It's as if one of my favorite fantasies about you is coming true."

"Mmm. More like a dream." There's a pause before he puts together what I said. "You fantasize about me?"

Mortified, I flop backward, causing my robe to open completely. Ethan's breath hisses out between his teeth. "What are you wearing?"

I lift my head and glance down at the cream-colored bra and panty set I threw on this morning. Then I recall why I bought it and emit a soft chuckle.

"Fallon...," he warns.

"Honestly, E, I didn't realize this was the same set I had on beneath my graduation dress until just now."

Silence. There's an eerie stillness on the other end of the line. Finally, I dare to look over at him and he's fisting his cock. He manages to grit out, "You mean, beneath the dress and heels you were wearing...?"

I flick my hand to indicate my body. "Yes."

"Now I'm going to add that to my fantasy about *you*," he moans.

"You fantasize about me?"

"All the fucking time. In fact, it starts at that damn party."

"My graduation party is your fantasy?" I can't help the amusement from seeping into my voice.

"Shut up, Fal. It could be any party. All that matters is it's you and me in the back. Alone. And you're wearing that dress and those fucking heels," he grits out.

Playing along, I twirl my hair around my finger and interject, "You don't notice me. You never do. I don't know if that's because I'm younger than you or because you're just not interested."

"Oh, baby. I notice you. There's never been a moment since we met I haven't noticed you." His green eyes lock on to mine. The power behind that causes my nipples to pebble. Cautious, I reach down and brush my fingers against the turgid tip.

The nerves disappear when he moans at what I'm doing. Awareness and desire are heady drugs as I tug my bra down just low enough for the nipple to pop out. I exclaim, "Oh, shit!"

His hand, still strangling his cock over his boxer briefs still, "What?"

"The heel I'm wearing caught in the edge of stone. I'm pitching forward."

"I've got you, witch." His words come out as a rasp. "Let me get you over to the lounger."

"You deserve a reward for that, Ethan."

"You can't give me what I want."

Hurt begins to spread through me until he continues, "Your ankle is swelling and I want you to suck my dick, Fallon. How are you going to manage that?"

Hmm, a challenge? Well, since this is a fantasy. "The lounger is high enough for me to be at the right angle to take you in my mouth if you'd just cooperate with me."

"What does that mean?"

"I need you out of those pants."

Holding my eyes, Ethan shifts his hips so his cock springs free. He wraps his hands around it and I wish I was really there to nuzzle against the musky scent I know he's throwing off. "What's next?"

"You tell me?"

"I want to fuck you so badly, Fallon, but I can't let you put pressure on that ankle, baby." His words are punctuated with the stroking of his cock from balls to tip.

I slip my fingers into my own panties and make a *pfft* sound. "My ankle is sore, but you're touching me. Pain is the furthest thing from my mind. What I want you to do is to spread my legs apart and take what you want."

"And what's that?"

"My pussy. Just like you did the last time we were together."

"Hmm, I have a better idea."

"Oh? What's that?"

"If you think your ankle can handle it, I want to bend you over the table. I want to fuck you just like I wanted to that first night."

"You wanted to..." My voice falters.

His face is carved in stone. "I wanted to pull your skirt up and spread your legs apart. I wanted to thrust inside you so hard your pretty face told the tale of how your cake ended up on the floor." At that brutal honesty, a spurt of pre-cum leaks from Ethan's cock.

I shimmy my panties down so he can see what I'm doing to myself for him, what he's doing to me. "Dirty girl."

"Your dirty girl," I remind him.

"Hell yes, you are. Now play with those nipples and grind your hips back against me."

We go back and forth like this until I have three fingers buried inside my pussy and am clenching around them and Ethan's shot off a load. Sleepily, I murmur, "What would you do if you were here?"

"I'd suck off your fingers. I'd lick each and every one of them clean...fuck, Fallon." His voice is reverent as I do just that. "I don't know how much longer I can be without you, witch."

"So, don't be," I make it sound simple when I want to face-palm myself. Between my mother, my day job, and my night job, finding time to just talk with Ethan is a struggle.

Still, to see the smile cross his face when I make that remark, it's worth it.

He's worth it.

CHAPTER TWENTY-NINE

KENSINGTON, TEXAS

Ethan

On average, most Americans spend 3 hours and 15 minutes on their cell phones daily.

What's your over/under?

—**Moore You Want**

ON THE PHONE WITH FALLON THAT NIGHT, I DECLARE, "I'VE BEEN thinking."

"Well, that's dangerous."

"Funny."

"I am." Then there's a slight pause. "About?"

I sit with my phone in my hand, my mind swirling with concerns about the obstacles between us—the distance, the age gap. For years, Fallon's been my closest friend and despite the fact we've changed our relationship, thoughts of how it's going to affect other people we care about weigh heavily on me. "For starters, our age difference."

I can almost feel her confusion through the phone. Finally, "What about it?"

"I've been thinking..."

She interrupts. "You're repeating yourself."

"A sign of my age."

"Again, that's dangerous."

I ignore her. "About how it might affect things. Our dynamic, how people see us..." When she says nothing, I trail off, uncertain about how to vocalize the concerns clawing at me.

"Ethan?" Her voice is a balm to my nerves.

"Yeah?"

"Is this about what other people think or what *you* think about us?"

Offended, I bellow, "I'm not questioning us, Fallon."

"Are you certain?" That's when I hear the first hint of vulnerability in her voice since we became an us.

"Christ, witch, I've wanted you since the night of your high school graduation. Do you think waiting for you has been easy?"

Her amusement and her acceptance cleanses something in me I didn't know felt dirty until she teases, "In between your sexcapades?"

"They were before you, Fal. And once I admitted to myself how I felt about you, there hasn't been anyone since."

Her breath is audible. "When was that?"

I set aside my pride and admit, "The night of Austyn's party."

"Right when our texts changed."

"Yes."

"Why didn't you make your move then?" Fallon's frustration is evident.

"Because I needed to be certain some rising douche nozzle wasn't going to come in and sweep you off your feet."

She chuckles through her tears. "Listen, I understand your concerns. But age has never been an issue for me. I care about you, not the number of years between us. And second..."

"There's a second?"

"Yes. This is the one and only time I want to discuss it." She pauses for emphasis. "There have been boys, an occasional man. But none of them were you, Ethan."

Her words started out like nails on a chalkboard and immediately turned into a ballad. "Thank you," I tell her sincerely.

"For?"

"For your unwavering honesty. Still..."

"Still what?"

"I can't shake this feeling that there's something trying to wedge its way in between us."

Her voice is quietly powerful. "I get your concerns. But if you want to pursue this, us, realize I refuse to let something as trivial as age and distance stand in the way of something I have wanted since I was eighteen."

Her words hit me like a revelation, and I comprehend just how lucky I am to have her in my life. "You're right. I'm sorry for throwing up obstacles where we don't need them."

"Don't be. Just focus on us, on what makes us happy. The rest will fall into place."

We talk for a while longer before Fallon yawns and I force her to get some sleep. As we hang up, I feel a weight lift off my shoulders. I know that as long as we hold tight to what we have, we can withstand whatever the world throws our way.

Ethan

Saratoga Springs, N.Y., A site, claiming to have harvested over one million classified chats from the US government, was threatening to sell them. Minutes after the claim was made, the site was obliterated by Castor Industries.

With thanks from a grateful nation.

—InfoSec Gov News

"I'VE FOUND A PATTERN AGAINST THE OPERATION IN SEVEN VIRTUES," Sam announces after I get back from my much-needed vacation with Fallon.

"Talk," Leanne demands.

It's just the three of us. Thorn is undergoing the preliminary part of his semi-annual national security clearance re-up. When we connected with him earlier, he whined worse than a dethroned prom queen. "I'm followed every fucking day by agents of our own government, agents of foreign governments. They maintain a damn tick tock of my whereabouts, my wife's whereabouts. Any day now, I'm expecting a report telling me when my kid takes a crap. Is this really fucking necessary?"

Sam and I both laughed heartily before he dropped to talk to his team of investigators. With the way Leanne's lips curved as we relayed the story, she was going to enjoy tormenting her friend and handler later.

Sam tells Leanne, "The IPs at Devil's Lair—all belonging to their phone sex operators—match up to those Messina used in every single attempt he made to hack Dioscuri before he decided to—"

She doesn't let him soften the blow. "Murder my sister and try to kill me for it?"

"Yes."

"So, was he infiltrating the phone system to steal data, or was he using the connection to mask his own activity?" she muses.

"We'll never know since he's dead," I remind her.

"Think it's not worth giving a shot, Ethan?"

I snort. "You want to replicate an attempted hack from close to five years ago?"

"Since everything from Dioscuri has been backed up from the moment I stood it up, why not?" Her eyes gleam with the challenge.

Sam's lips purse as he wipes both our screens and creates a sandbox for us to play in. Then he attempts to connect to one of the IPs within the Devil's Lair.

```
[198.51.100.2/24]
```

```
[Connection Refused]
```

Leanne purrs, "Well, isn't this interesting. I thought you had more talent than this, Sam."

"Bite me, Leanne." His eyes widen before. "Son of a bitch. Now they're counterattacking and trying to access Hudson's IP."

"Oh, hell no," I snarl. "You don't get to have all the fun, Sam."

"Fun, my ass. They're trying to drop two Zero Days and some Ransomware on my system. Christ!"

"Sam, hold on a second," Leanne cautions him. Then, a moment later, it's like a game of Space Invaders when Leanne aims her brainchild, Dioscuri, at the intruders attacking Sam's company network and picks them off one by one.

"Lee." I don't recognize the voice that comes over Sam's line. "Are you fucking around in my network for a reason?"

"Hey, Keene." I subdue my smile when Leanne morphs from cool agent into happy-go-lucky friend. It's like watching a German shepherd roll over onto their back for some tummy rubs from their owner. Her cheerful demeanor is for none other than Keene Marshall—a man I know gives zero shits about my former boss. Something Thorn shared one night with me with great amusement after our first call when he explained that Leanne had her own personal entanglement with the investigation giant, outside of her husband being one of their best bodyguards. Leanne blithely assures him, "Nope. Just keeping up my end of our bargain."

"Which is?"

"To keep you protected after you did the same for me," she swears.

Keene's sardonic tone drops. "Keep up the good work, Lee. I came by to drop some paperwork off for Sam and received quite the show."

"What do you mean?" I ask curiously.

Keene's amusement is evident. "Sam rocking back and forth in a corner."

"Aww, Sam. Did we get too close to your precious server," Leanne coos.

"Yes! And this ass won't let me buy a new one," Sam accuses Keene.

"Not if you're violating our acceptable use policy. Remember, Sam—the phrase is limited personal use."

I can't keep my snicker in at this point. I call out, "Sam, what happened to all the guts you used to display so brazenly?"

He calls out, "I joined Hudson and Keene made me sign away my soul. Not long after, I met Leanne at a hackathon where she kicked my ass barely out of her diapers."

All of us, including one of the renowned owners of Hudson Investigations, double over laughing. Keene offers us some sage advice before leaving us to scratch our heads over what alarms we tripped. "Don't get caught."

We wait for him to leave before discussing in detail what happened. Finally, we agree to think about it some more before trying again.

But try again we will.

None of us are planning on giving up because of one little scare.

CHAPTER THIRTY-ONE

KENSINGTON, TEXAS

Ethan

The belief associated with having regular family dinners is grounded in research on the physical, mental and emotional benefits of regular family meals.

Sometimes, it can cause more mental anguish than it's worth.

—Viego Martinez, Celebrity Blogger

"WHAT IF—" SAM STARTS.

"It won't work." Leanne shuts him down.

"The code is right," he argues.

"I'm not saying it isn't. I'm saying we're missing something." Frustration fills Leanne's voice.

Just then my actual office phone rings. Reaching over, I grab it, "Yeah?"

"Son?" My father's voice comes out weak. "Hi."

"Dad. I'm kind of busy at the moment."

There's a gasp behind me. Ignoring it, I try to get my father off the line as quickly as I can. "Can I call you later?"

"Of course. Would you be willing to come to dinner this weekend?"

I think about my flight to see Fallon on Friday and tell him, "I'll be out of town."

Defeat fills his voice. "Oh. I see."

I hate I feel the bonds of my childhood with this man who almost ruined my sister's life—a life where she's ecstatically happy with the man she should always have been with. "Is there anything else?"

"I'd love to see you, Ethan."

The last time I saw Fallon, she told me Helen wasn't shaking her illness easily. I frown. I don't want to spend time with my father, but I don't want regrets knowing since his stroke, he hasn't been in the best of health. I give in, just a bit. "How about we meet for coffee after I get back from my business trip?"

"I'd like that, son. I'll let you get back to work."

"Thanks, Dad. I'll see you soon." Not waiting for him to say more, I disconnect the call and I turn back to my fellow white hats. I'm about to offer a suggestion when I see Leanne looking at me solemnly through the screen. "What? What is it?"

"Ethan, your father sounds as if he has something he needs to tell you."

Fury at her judgmental words boils my blood. But before I can say anything, she lifts her hand to stop me from speaking. "I know the whole story from your sister, so don't feel I'm taking sides. I'm only speaking as a person who knows what it's like not to have the answers and be left wondering."

My anger immediately deflates. "Yeah." Mentally I replay the conversation over and over in my head. I lean forward, resting my elbows on my knees and bury my face in my hands.

"Ethan?" Now it's Sam who is butting into my personal business.

"Yeah?"

"Where are you going out of town to?"

"Christ, did you two listen in on the whole conversation?" I growl.

"Well," Leanne drawls. "Funny you should mention that because we did. By the way, I think you should up your bid for the Atticus project."

"If you read it, you'll see I'm not..." Tingles run up my spine, causing the fine hairs on the nape of my neck to lift. I twist my head to the side and my eyes meet Leanne's. There's a gleam in hers that can only be achieved when a successful hack has occurred. "How did you get into the bid proposal system?"

Leanne shrugs while Sam clears his throat. "Back to the task at hand. We were missing one component."

"What's that?" But something low in my gut tells me I know what it is.

"Someone has to be on the phone with Devil's Lair on one of the affected IPs. Then we can access what the IP is connecting to—other than their own systems."

I joke, "So, who is going to be calling the phone sex hotline?"

Leanne says flatly, "Do you think you can out hack me, Ethan? Sam?"

Fuck. "No."

Leanne hums, "Then better get some hot tea and honey to warm up your vocal cords. You go on in just a few hours. Let's pop that sex hotline cherry, Ethan. What fantasy are you going to ask to play out first?"

Then, all I hear is her cackling right before disconnecting from the call.

CHAPTER THIRTY-TWO

SEVEN VIRTUES, NORTH CAROLINA

Fallon

Meatloaf said, "I would do anything for love."

-@PRyanPOffical

Ryan. Get a grip. Try a dating app.

-@CuteandRich3

DEVIL'S LAIR. THE NAME ALONE STRIKES UP IMAGES OF A DUNGEON filled with all different types of BDSM apparatus when the reality is, it's in an office park on the outskirts of Seven Virtues with some very impressive security roving the parking lot and mobile security towers strategically placed to ensure all employees make it safely to and from the building.

It's hard to believe I really took a job working here, but as Aesop once said, "No act of kindness, no matter how small, is ever wasted."

Maybe sacrificing my pride by working for a phone sex operation to afford my mother's health care is an act of kindness and not the sin so many would judge it to be.

Devil's Lair may cater to the creature comforts of their clientele, but they far and above care for their employees' well-being. From everything to hot tea and honey in our break room to medical benefits that rival those of Biltmore, I understand why some of my coworkers would rather work in the shadows of this nebulous field versus a straight nine-to-five job, especially with some of the other limitations on their lives.

Florence, the owner who has grown into a mentor, knows I have a time limit for how long I intend to work for her. She appreciates I fully plan to make good on the promise I swore to when I agreed to become one of her phone sex operators: my mother's life.

But that's it.

She chuckled when I explained that I had no plans to renew my contract. "We're not the mob or a gang, Fallon. I know who you are and why you're doing this. None of what you'll say out there will ever bleed into your actual life, nor will it change how you're seen." Her chin lifts. "If you didn't know, would you have expected it from me?"

I drag the contract and check across the surface and sign my name boldly to the bottom of the document. "No, Florence. And thank you."

"After what your mother is asking of you to keep this a secret, well, the words 'my pleasure' are completely inappropriate. But I won't see you suffer any more than you need to." She collects the papers, leaving the cashier's check in front of me. "Let me go and put these in my office and then we can talk.

"Okay." Leaning my head back against the rich, cream leather of her desk chairs, I recall the agony of the last week in technicolor behind my eyes. After my mother's oncologist visit in the hospital, I immediately began to discuss our financial options and floated the idea of borrowing the money from the Kensingtons. I wanted to tell them—specifically Ethan—about what was happening. It was less than a second before my mother shot me down firmly. "No, Fallon."

"But . . . why?" I cried.

"Because I refuse you for you to be in that kind of debt when I'm gone. Having to pay the Kensingtons back when I'm dead?"

"Stop talking like that, Mama."

She stood, clutching her IV pole for stability, before gripping my biceps. "Listen to me, Fallon. No. I refuse to let you. I don't want it."

Lips trembling, I said, "But if I can't find the money . . . you'll die."

Her head—hair that used to be the same texture and color as my own until she began chemo—fell forward to hide her face. "Then that's God's will."

"God can suck my dick, Mama."

"I'm sure you'll try to make him do just that, darling. In the meantime, let's enjoy the time we have left."

Flatly refusing to let her go that easily, when I left her to her daily bath, I hoofed it to Galileo's. I pleaded. I tried everything but dropping to my knees to get Levi to agree to let me work for him for free for whatever duration of time it took me to repay a loan. I even offered my car as collateral, but he didn't bite.

Despondent, I heard my name being called by one of Galileo's regulars, Florence. She huffed, "Were you serious?"

Without hesitation, I replied flatly, "As a heart attack."

She crooked her finger until I moved closer. Then her voice changed before she threatened, "If you ever share a word, I'll deny everything."

My brows lowered into a V before I decided I had nothing to lose by listening to her. I've never been so grateful to keep my mouth shut then learning how to use it.

When I realized she was handing me an opportunity to pay for the full amount of Mama's treatment, my jaw hit the floor. "You mean you can just fork over the full amount for the meds Mama needs?"

"Yes."

"Then why didn't you tip better at Galileo's?" I demanded truculently.

Florence threw her head back and roared before giving me some additional details. "The number to Devil's Lair isn't published anywhere except on the dark web."

"Oh. So, we're not going to get some perverts?"

"Don't you worry. You're definitely going to get those. They're just going to be *extremely* wealthy perverts."

Truer words were never spoken.

CHAPTER THIRTY-THREE

Fallon

The number of total enrolled post-secondary students declined by 4.9% from 2019 to 2021, the most significant rate of decline in enrollment since 1951.

While that statistic may shock you, who can remember what significant pandemic was occurring concurrently?

Ahh. Yes.

Here's a question. Are statistics merely a way to look at information to favor the person running the poll?

—Moore You Want

It shocked me that I had to study, take an exam, and train for weeks before Florence would let me even listen to one of her calls. She sniffed. "Devil's Lair has a reputation to protect."

Counting thirty-five of us on shift at the time, I murmured, "Apparently, a good one."

After acing Phone Sex 101, I was trained by "Becca," Florence's manager, who informed me, "None of us use our real name here, doll. You need to pick one to go by."

"Such as?"

"Anything you want."

Whipping out my phone, I Googled the Latin translation for daughter. Then, I pronounced my alter ego to be "Filia."

Becca noted it before giving me a set of milestones, including, "Prepare a character profile because you *will* be asked about what you look like." Not to mention the psych and medical evals, plus a security briefing in the event we got any whack jobs.

I admit I balked a little. But then I was reminded, "These men and women are *elite*," Becca emphasized. "It's why we charge such a ridiculous initial five-minute rate and our per-minute rate after is twice the national average." She then went on to explain pre-payments, gift cards, and other options first level operators offer our callers.

"What happens if you get someone who can't pay?" I questioned.

Becca's laugh bounced off the walls. "Well, let's just say they're welcome to find their own 'happy ending.'"

It didn't take long to settle into my routine—working at the museum or taking Mama to treatment during the day, Devil's Lair by night, and calls and texts to Ethan through it all.

So far, it seems to be working.

Men, women, aliens can spend as little or as long as they want on the phone in an attempt for me to pull from them anything, be it a prolific conversation about art history to a "cum-and-go" where the person just wants a quick jerk off before they hang up. Nothing's taboo on a Devil's Lair call. "Your job is to keep them talking," Florence reminded me pragmatically.

So, talking is exactly what I do, just not with the one person in the world I need to—my boyfriend. Each night I do so, I subtly shut out Ethan at a time when I need him the most at my side. But it's my mother's request for silence that holds me prisoner when all I want is to bare everything to the man I love and not listening to strangers I'm helping vocalize their fantasies in a desperate attempt to keep her alive.

Something I know deep down is failing.

CHAPTER THIRTY-FOUR

KENSINGTON, TEXAS

Ethan

Kevin Mitnick, who pioneered the technique of tricking employees into helping him steal software and services from big phone and tech companies in the '80s and '90s, making him the first hacker to ever appear on the FBI's Most Wanted List, died last year at the age of 59 of pancreatic cancer.

However, many question the relevance of his teachings in light of today's more damaging technical payoffs, such as Ransomware. CEO Leanne Miles, Castor Industries, a staunch Mitnick opponent, was quoted as saying, "Attend DefCon and you'll see firsthand the lessons Mitnick taught still apply today. He only wrote the first chapter of a very detailed playbook. My problem is I hate that the book even exists."

—InfoSec Gov News

I SHOVE THE KEYBOARD AWAY FROM ME IN FRUSTRATION. "WE'VE tried everything!"

Sam's snaps at me. "We haven't, or we'd have cracked the code."

"Well, what do you want to do? Call up Devil's Lair and ask them for their fucking passcode?"

There's a pregnant pause before, "That's not a half bad idea, actually."

"Sam? Did your wife talk to you in too many languages this morning?" Sam's wife, Iris, is the lead translator for the Secretary General at the United Nations.

"No. Kevin Mitnick."

"Black hat. First hacker to be on the FBI's Most Wanted List. Dead."

Sam interrupts the bare bones statistics I'm reciting about the son of a bitch who persistently hacked some of the largest tech companies of his time. "Think about *how* he did it, Ethan. Why was Mitnick so successful?"

I pause. "Social engineering. He charmed his way into gathering the information he needed."

Sam's excitement is palpable. "Exactly. So, how do you think we get inside a place called Devil's Lair?"

"We give them what they want."

"Which is?"

"Money. They want to be paid."

"By the damn minute," Sam confirms.

Immediately, my mind starts piecing together possibilities. "How many of those individuals do you think actually enjoy their jobs, Sam?"

"No telling, why?"

I immediately begin typing. A few minutes later, I share my screen so Sam can view the phishing exercise I'm crafting. After a few seconds he demands, "Now why weren't you this smart when we were working together the first time we met?"

"Give me a fucking break, Sam. I was eighteen when I joined the navy. I'm now forty-three. I've learned a hell of a lot in the years in between."

"Still, this kind of coding is shit hot. It might even impress Leanne. Maybe you can ask her for a job when it's all over."

"Fuck off, Sam," I grumble.

"Kidding, but I'm kind of not."

"Give me one second...I just have to...right there." Now that my hands have been lifted off the keyboard, I can't help but smirk. "The email's ready. We'll get a copy of each one when it goes out so we'll have the email addresses they go to."

"Good. Let me get the background to substantiate it." In a matter of minutes, between the two of us, we've stood up a site on the dark web very reminiscent of Devil's Lair. The hosting name boasts of a ridiculous number of made-up visitors.

By the time Leanne joins us after a meeting she has at Castor, we're ready to cast our net. She changes her voice and gives us the green light before declaring, "I hope this works."

I chuckle darkly. "Whoever falls into this trap deserves to."

I press send and the email bounces off the back end of Devil's Lair's website. For a second, just a second, I hold my breath—praying my coding goes through. Then, my elbow jerks back and I hiss, "Yes," before realizing emails are coming back to me. "Holy shit. Over two hundred people work there? Why would people demean themselves to work for a phone sex hotline?"

That's when Leanne verbally slaps me from thousands of miles away. "Why? Who knows. But I'll bet you one thing."

"What's that?"

"At least one person working there is doing so because of love. And I know better than anyone that love will drive a person to do desperate things."

CHAPTER THIRTY-FIVE

SEVEN VIRTUES, NORTH CAROLINA

Fallon

How did I fall in love with baking? Sweets were a rarity in my childhood. I wanted them to be a part of my daily adulthood.

—Executive Chef Trina Paxton, Narcissus Restaurant Group for Food Network Magazine

---

"I GOT A JOB OFFER LAST NIGHT," I TELL CLARABEL AS WE WALK INTO the kitchen not far from where my mother's getting chemotherapy.

"You'd leave the Biltmore?"

I shake my head. "I'd move into Biltmore if I could. It would only cost me about one point seven to renovate it."

"Million? That's not too bad."

"Billion. That's with a 'b.'"

She trips on the squeaky-clean floor. I catch her before she face plants. "Christ. Are you raking in that kind of money at your second job? Maybe I should come to work with you instead of this place."

My whole body shakes at the very idea of the brilliant, scholarly, Dr. Clarabel Lam answering phone calls for people who want to be spanked. She wrinkles her nose. "Yeah. Forget living at the Biltmore. I'm good at my apartment."

I chuckle at her reaction as I take a sip of my coffee. "You know what I like about you, Clarabel?"

"I'm easing the strain of your mother's life as part of her care team in this new clinical trial since I ran away from my life?" Clarabel shared with me not too long ago she was the head physician at a prominent charity—Send Me an Angel in New York City. What she didn't know was that I know the charity—and its benefactor—well.

Once we realized we had that connection, we both opened up. Over the months of my mother's treatment, we each shared our darkest secrets— mine about my second job instead of just asking Austyn for the money, hers about how her family shamed her after she broke up with her fiancé after she walked in on him cheating on her. As I told her, "Whatever the reason that led you here, I'm grateful you're by our side."

Still, I wouldn't mind if Ethan went and punched out her ex-fiancé if we ever go to New York to see Austyn and her husband.

Clarabel blows across the top of her coffee. "Are you going to take it?"

"To be honest, it was a generic recruiting email."

"Like ones from Indeed?"

"Exactly. I mean, how many of them are out there for phone sex..." I pause when one of the nurses comes in to snag a bottle of water. "Operators. You know?"

She frowns. "It doesn't seem like there's a huge market for that."

"I wouldn't think so either. Besides, nothing about my working at DL has to do with money."

At that, Clarabel's brows skyrocket. "It has everything to do with money. You're just not seeing a dime of it."

I lift my coffee in acknowledgment.

She stares down into her cup. "Are you planning on telling your boyfriend?"

"About Mama?"

"About all of it, Fallon." Her distraught eyes meet mine. "As much as I understand why you're doing this, what would he do if he ever found out?"

With her simple question, the airy kitchenette feels closed in. I set my coffee down before choosing my words carefully. "Ever since Austyn became famous, he's been protective." *Not to mention his niece's father coming back into her life, finding out his own father deceived all of them, and his beloved niece almost dying*, I think to myself.

Clarabel's eyebrows skyrocket. "And you don't think he'd flip about this? The woman he's claimed is getting people off on the phone for money."

My eyes flit away. "How, Clarabel? How do I tell him?"

"You just do?"

My eyes meet hers. "How do I tell him when I swore to my mother I wouldn't share with *any* of the Kensington's until she told me it was okay to?"

She opens and closes her mouth. "Why? Would she do such a thing? Place you in such an untenable position?"

I scrub my hand across my forehead to relieve the tension as I recall her snapping the order at me before the first weekend I spent away with Ethan, when I held him and wanted to blurt out everything. "She said it's her choice, not mine."

"Fallon?"

"Yeah?"

"I've never broken an oath."

"I figured as much."

"I'll pray for a miracle."

"Please do." That's my only hope—that a miracle happens so I can quit my job at Devil's Lair or Ethan miraculously understands. As it stands, there's no way this ends well regardless of the fact that I love them both.

CHAPTER THIRTY-SIX

SEVEN VIRTUES, NORTH CAROLINA

Fallon

I heard a rumor Beckett Miller is back in the studio. Hope isn't lost for the music world.

—Viego Martinez, Celebrity Blogger

THE LAST FOUR MONTHS HAVE BUILT MY HEART UP, YET THEY WEAR on my hope.

I've done everything to accept I've sold my soul to keep my mother alive, though God only knows for how much longer. I've deceived and lied to my boyfriend as we maintain our long-distance relationship. I told him that due to Mama's additional medical bills, I've picked up more shifts. He assumes at Galileo's; I've let him think no differently.

Instead, I've taken part in all kinds of kink calls from the basics to where a woman wanted me to describe what I would do if I was in front of her and ordered me to drop to my knees before sucking her clit until she came.

I've vocally described how I'd give a blow job—with or without prostate massage.

I've indulged caller's fetishes, including being a hunter and capturing my prey, tying them to a table, and cutting off their clothes with my Bowie knife.

And I had a baby who soiled his diaper and who wanted to . . . my stomach churns when I think about what he used as a lubricant.

Then I went home, called Ethan, and let out my emotional turmoil—couching all of it beneath worrying about my mama and how a little humiliation is worth the one thing I need.

My mom.

Everything's worth that.

"Devil's Lair, this is Filia," I purr into the phone.

There's a tinkling of ice against a glass before a whiskey-honed voice that sends primitive chills down my spine rasps, "How you doin' tonight, darlin'?"

I bite my lip as a full-body quiver this stranger's voice evokes in me every time he calls—and he calls me quite a bit. "I'm good, honey."

His dark chuckle causes me to clench my thighs together. "That bodes well for tonight."

"How was your day?" I let a bit of my native Texas drawl flow into my voice because Whiskey, as I've taken to calling him because of the smooth, smoky vision it evokes, likes it.

I both love and hate when he calls because while it's so natural to talk to him because something about him reminds me of Ethan, it just makes me miss him more. Since I have no face to go with Whiskey, I conjure up Ethan's image as I reach for the lawnmower-loud vibrator I purchased off the web.

Focusing on my call, I reach over and open the top desk drawer to find my "toys" and suffer mightily for it. With Ethan's face in my mind, my clit grazes my jeans and a moan escapes. My nipples pebble up.

I miss my man.

I hate that we haven't been able to see each other in the last few weeks between the catastrophe of my life and the contract he's buried under. Our phone calls are limited between my work and his, but our texts are heating up in a way I fantasized openly about to Austyn years ago.

I just never expected him to want me the way I do him—as something more.

Still, even as I twist the vibrator on and talk to Whiskey, I conjure up an image of the way Ethan looked when I stared down into his face as I sat astride him the night of my graduation. His dark chocolate brown hair only showed a few strands of silver at the temples. His green eyes bore into mine like they could penetrate my soul. God, just thinking about him has my breathing shifting into overdrive, my thighs pressing together.

Long ago, I admitted to myself the kind of man who did it for me—older, commanding, taking charge in the bedroom. I suspect Whiskey's like that, which is why it's easy to superimpose the beloved face of the man I've wanted for forever on top of his voice.

Especially when I can taste Ethan in my dreams. I sigh because I want it all —my mother healthy, the man I adore in my life, and the freedom to admit to the world how I really feel.

Then I'm yanked back into my reality amid a scene he chose, when he says something that steals the breath from my lungs. "If I drag down that scrap of lace, will I see a sprinkle of freckles on your pelvic bone as I make my way to your pussy, Filia?"

Ice floods my veins. I can't speak, can't reply. I'm now terrified in the kind of way I was trained to report immediately. Fear coats my skin as I wrap up the call with me giving monotonous responses and him coming in my ear— the first time he's ever done this.

Ripping off my headset, I flag his file so Becca knows there's a potential security issue. Giving myself a moment, I take a deep breath before I dive into the next call, which thankfully, is a bored rich kid looking for a quick hand job. Becca approaches just as I'm wrapping up. The second I disconnect, she orders, "Follow me."

She waits for me to clear the doorway before asking, "What happened?"

Pacing back and forth in front of her, I try to put my gut churning into words. "I can't quite explain it."

"Try, Fallon."

"It's impossible, right?"

"What?"

"That he knows me?"

She straightens in her chair. "Excuse me?"

I nod, frantically. "He made a remark that only a few select people should know about."

Her eyes narrow into slits. "You've never had a conversation with him outside of the Lair?"

I shake my head. "I know the rules."

She storms behind her desk and begins typing furiously. "A full investigation into this man's calls will be kicked off, Fallon." She taps her finger against her lips. "IT is looking into it. He's also spoken with other operators. They're going to screen his calls to see if he's mentioned the body marking. It is possible it's a complete coincidence his fantasy and your body resemble one another."

Despite the well of disgust that causes, I hope it's the case. Shivering, I wrap my arms around myself to offer myself some comfort. "And in the meanwhile?"

"In the meanwhile, I will personally monitor your calls. If we have to, you'll be escorted to and from work."

"You can't be serious," I scoff.

Her mouth turns grim. "And I want to make certain your place hasn't been bugged."

I feel the blood draining from my face. My voice can barely be heard when I whisper, "What?"

"We had a supremely successful operator here years ago—Scarlett." Becca's eyes close and the look of pain on her face is tangible.

"Is she okay?" I ask tentatively.

"That depends on your definition of okay. She was attacked outside the office by a stalker. When that happened, her boyfriend dumped her—claiming he couldn't deal with her working for us."

"What a douche canoe," I snarl.

Her smile is faint but her eyes hold sad memories. "She's okay. She's done well for herself, even if she's closed out most of her friends—including me."

Without thought, I reach across Becca's desk and squeeze her fingers. "If you're half the friend to her as you've been to me, it's her loss. Thank you for looking into this for me."

"Just doing my job, Fallon."

It might be my imagination, but as I'm leaving Becca's office, I think I hear, "This time we know what to do in order to protect you and everyone you hold dear."

As soon as I finish meeting with Becca, I head out to my car. After I reach my apartment, I send a text to Ethan.

FALLON:

Are you up?

ETHAN:

With you, that seems to be the permanent state lately, witch.

ETHAN:

Want me to do something about it?

FALLON:

Yes, please.

ETHAN:

Fuck. Call me.

CHAPTER THIRTY-SEVEN

KENSINGTON, TEXAS

Ethan

Oxytocin and vasopressin are two other chemicals released during orgasm which are also associated with sleep. These differ highly from tryptophan, an amino acid released after eating yourself into stasis.

—Fab and Delish

AFTER AN INCREDIBLE ROUND OF PHONE SEX, FALLON'S CURLED ON her side. I take a long look at her. She's practically asleep, poor thing.

Actually, now that I study her face, she might as well be passed out. Her face, relaxed from its typical animation, appears fragile—the skin beneath her eyes almost bruised. "Why are you so exhausted, baby?" I murmur, not quite loud enough to wake her.

I study her face for a long period of time before letting my gaze drift over to long blond hair cascading over her shoulders, almost but not quite hiding her perfect breasts. Trailing my gaze down over her flat stomach, I stare at the place between her legs where her hand is protectively notched.

Where my hand should be, I mentally correct myself.

If I was close enough to hold her.

I kick myself for not making time to get out to see her in the last few weeks. If I was holding her, she would be able to let go of the burdens she's carrying, share them.

Since she's so zonked, I lift my fingers to my lips and press them against the screen. My voice is barely audible when I whisper, "I love you, Fallon. There isn't a damn thing I wouldn't do for you." I inhale sharply before asking, "So, what are you hiding from me?"

She doesn't twitch or stir, letting me know my secret—that this young nymph has captured my heart—is still safely tucked away because now I know it's not safe to share.

CHAPTER THIRTY-EIGHT

SEVEN VIRTUES, NORTH CAROLINA

Fallon

If holiday colors start appearing in stores any earlier, we may as well ignore the fall season. If that happens, I will not be pleased.

—Eva Henn, Fashion Blogger

IT'S UNUSUAL FOR ME TO HAVE ANY TIME TO MYSELF, LET ALONE ANY spare money. But after a restful night's sleep, I woke up to an email where Becca had gifted me with a Visa gift card and ordered me to spend the day pampering myself instead of racing hither and yon trying to be all things to everyone.

Tears welled up in my eyes. I'm not quite certain what I stammered out, but she took pity on me. "Fallon, you're doing a great job being primary caretaker."

"But, Becca..."

"Each week, everyone here goes home with enormous paychecks. You come in here with an incredibly heavy load on your shoulders. You don't judge any one of us. You bake the best chocolate chip cookies for Bryndle's little girl because she had a bad day at school."

"How did you know about that?" I ask. Bryndle, one of the other phone operators, offered me some advice on making my phone calls more realistic.

"I know everything that happens here. Now, go treat yourself. Nothing good happens if you get sick on your mama."

Unable to respond, Becca ordered, "Go, Fallon."

After calling and chatting with Austyn during a manicure and pedicure, she convinces me to splurge on something decadent, "Something you wouldn't normally buy yourself, Fal."

"You know that's not what I should be doing with the money."

Her disdain was evident when she replied, "It was a gift. No one is going to be saying, 'Oh, Fal. That electric bill looks so hot on you.'"

I burst into laughter. "Okay. I'll go shopping."

I ended up in a lingerie boutique in Seven Virtues by virtue of the fact they had a silk robe in the window that perfectly matched the green of Ethan's eyes. Wishing my mother could be with me, I take a picture of the sets I'm debating buying and hit the first face that pops up.

FALLON:

Which set do you think I should buy?

I attach two photos and press Send. Figuring it will take my mother a few minutes to reply, I move into a different section of the local boutique and flip through racks of lingerie.

ETHAN:

Christ, Fallon. Are you trying to give me a heart attack?

FALLON:

Oops. Wrong text. Sorry. My bad.

ETHAN:

Your bad?

ETHAN:

Why the fuck are you taking pics of yourself in lingerie?

ETHAN:

And just who the hell did you mean to send those pics to? 🙁

FALLON:

Mama.

ETHAN:

Oh.

Fallon:

Oh? That's what you have to say?

ETHAN:

Hi to your mother.

FALLON:

Not, oh sorry? Not oh, you look hot? Not oh, yeah, I was a jealous ass?

ETHAN:

Take your pick.

ETHAN:

Christ, Fal, when the hell are we going to be in the same room again?

ETHAN:

I know it's been my work that's kept us apart

FALLON:

I've had other commitments as well, Ethan.

ETHAN:

I want to hold you in my arms, baby.

ETHAN:

I miss you

FALLON:

I miss you too.

ETHAN:

Soon, Fal.

FALLON:

Soon, E. I'll look up flights for you when I get home.

Right after I stop by and see my mother, make sure her port line is clear and that she's eaten, and try to eat something myself before my shift at Devil's Lair. Still, it's worth it when I get back his text.

ETHAN:

Thank fucking God.

CHAPTER THIRTY-NINE

KENSINGTON, TEXAS

Ethan

Sexy #redemption club owner, Marco Houde, wife, Lynne, and daughter, Danica, were spotted in Collyer, Connecticut at the annual Fall Festival. They made an immediate beeline for the Amaryllis Bakery booth.

Then again, who wouldn't?

—Sexy and Social, All the Scandal You Can Handle

"So, are you two certain we're going to get through tonight?" I cringe. I was supposed to meet my family for dinner and hearing the disappointment in my brother's voice when I called to say I couldn't make it almost caused me to change my mind. Almost. Instead, I'm glaring down at my two associates, who are looking at me with something akin to consternation.

"We've practiced all week, Ethan," Sam reminds me.

"It has to be three separate IPs engaging the line simultaneously—one phone, one unlocking the VoIP connection, one computer pulling down the data," Leanne states flatly. "And Thorn..."

"Can't." We all know the reasons why Thorn can't. If his IP is ever traced in any way back to a phone sex hotline, his career—the career that saved all of us—will be tanked. A gust of air releases from my lungs. "When do we start?"

Sam looks at his watch. "Thirty minutes. I'm going to go spend some time with my wife before we get down and dirty." He disconnected immediately after saying that leaving me and Leanne alone on the line.

She studies me quietly. "You've gone above and beyond, Ethan."

"Whatever," I brush off her praise.

"No. This needs to be said." She inhales sharply. "I appreciate how much deep cover you're doing. I know you're in a committed relationship."

I wince as guilt floods each and every one of my veins when thoughts of Fallon come to mind.

"Yeah," Leanne leans forward. "That's why I'm thanking you."

"Lives are at stake."

She hums her agreement. "Mine and my unborn child."

I meet her gaze head on. "Not to mention the unknown number of people whose lives you save with your wizardry. So, no, Leanne, I'm not doing this just for you. I'm doing this for them. That's how I'm getting through."

She pauses before asking me, "Has this affected your relationship?"

I bark out a laugh. "With Fallon?"

"Is that her...wait, what? Fallon?" Leanne is incredulous.

"You say her name as if you know her."

"If it's the same woman, I met her at a party at Redemption."

I snort. "If it was at Redemption, that's highly likely."

An unfettered smile breaks across her face. "I liked her. We talked for a while after someone was blowing up her phone."

My head tilts as I study her face. "Why were you there?"

"I was invited for Kensington's birthday."

A short laugh escapes. "Then you're right on all accounts."

"Those being?"

"That's my Fallon and yes, I was the one blowing up her phone." Leaning back in my desk chair, I admit, "I'd said some pretty shitty things to her after she asked why I wasn't there."

Leanne tsks. "Finished groveling yet?"

I sputter. "It's been years. She can't still hold that against me."

She calls out something to someone off screen. The next thing I know, I hear a quick agreement and a door slam. Leanne's smile is strained before she confides, "I wanted some privacy, so I just begged for some lasagna. Since my husband can't cook, that means he's heading to Daniela Trattoria to get it for me. We have a little bit of time."

I wait for Leanne to gather herself before she begins to tell me how she and her husband got together. It's a story of subterfuge and vengeance that spanned a year and left both of them buried beneath emotional baggage. "He knew what I was doing and why, Ethan. But when push came to shove, his past got in our way. I don't want to see this set you down the very tumultuous path I went down."

"It won't happen. Fallon trusts me," I declare confidently.

"She knows what you do? What you *really* do? What you're doing *now*?"

I hesitate for a second too long and Leanne jumps all over it. "You can't hold back any piece of your heart if you want her to trust you with hers."

Long after Leanne hangs up, her words play over and over in my head. Leanne's right. I know I love Fallon because over the last five years, she's become one of my closest friends as well as the missing piece to my soul. But since we've become lovers, our conversations have taken a turn.

Fallon and I need to talk about more than sex.

And soon.

She needs to know how I feel about her and I need to know where her heart is at.

CHAPTER FORTY

SEVEN VIRTUES, NORTH CAROLINA

Fallon

This is a public service announcement.

Pour Vous is having a sale.

Grab your reusable shopping bags and run, don't walk, to pick up their custom-made lingerie. After all, Christmas isn't that far away.

—Moore You Want

"I DID SOME SHOPPING," I SHARE WITH WHISKEY IN A CONFIDENTIAL tone, attempting to hide my anxiousness at his call. I was comfortable with having not heard from him. Yet, he was back. Even knowing Becca was monitoring the call wasn't helping.

Even thinking of Ethan had me barely holding on.

Whiskey purrs appreciatively. "Are you wearing it?"

I glance downward at the leggings I have on beneath an oversize sweatshirt and playact for all I'm worth. "Beneath a robe. Do you want me to take it off?"

"Yes. Lose the robe," I'm immediately ordered.

Standing, I slide my fleece sweatshirt off, so the swoosh of the material sounds as it drops against my desk. Then I gaze at it as the color reminds me of Ethan's eyes and the boundaries we crossed my graduation night. A strained laugh escapes.

"What's so amusing?"

"I didn't realize it when I made the purchase, but I certainly hope you like the color green."

"Love it. Why?"

"My body's covered in green lace." I can't help the satisfied twist of my lips when I hear his harsh expulsion of breath.

There's a contented hum before his dark voice asks suddenly, "Is it really?"

"Is what?"

"Is your lingerie really green?"

"It is," I confirm.

He mumbles something I can't quite make out before I hear, with significant authority, "You deserve a treat for being such a good girl, Filia."

"What do you want me to do?"

There's a heartbeat of silence before he orders, "Crawl to the foot of the bed. When you get there, I want your head and shoulders down so your hands can be free. Can you do that and still be on the phone with me?"

My heart thumping against my ribs, I rasp, "Yes," before I, orally, do exactly as he says.

Later, I'm going to have to replay this scene with Ethan, knowing he'll be the only person to see me in the items I bought.

What does it matter if I just described them to a stranger?

CHAPTER FORTY-ONE

KENSINGTON, TEXAS

Ethan

Show me photos of the worst Halloween costume your parents subjected you to. Celebrities, you first!

—Eva Henn, Fashion Blogger

"WHAT'S YOUR FAVORITE FANTASY?" FILIA ASKS.

I rattle the ice and whiskey in my glass, causing it to make a tinkling sound against glass. I have to keep this bitch on the phone for twenty minutes before Sam and Leanne are safely out of the system. "Oh, I have quite a few."

"Any you want to live out with me?" She purrs into my ear.

"Too many." This is the way I've let our conversations go. I give her just enough rope to lead us through one of these calls so Leanne and Sam can use the third access point to gain access into Devil's Lair's system to plant the code we need to.

Soon all this pretense will be over. After tonight, I pray we'll have all the access we need. Thank fucking God. I feel so dirty after having these conversations knowing the only woman I want like this is my Fallon.

Mine.

God, I love her.

Closing my eyes, my head tips back, and I tell the target, "Why don't you share one of your favorites with me?"

"If you want." She hesitates. "We're at a party."

I smirk. "A party? That's your fantasy?"

"Hush. All the men are dressed but the women are wearing scraps of satin and lace."

I immediately visualize Fallon in the sexy lace she sent me the photo of by accident. "Intriguing. Keep going."

"You don't notice me. You never do. I don't know if that's because I'm younger than you or because you're just not interested."

A tingle of awareness pricks at the base of my neck even as my cock stirs to life at the familiarity of the scenario. Despite wanting to step back from the situation that's growing increasingly uncomfortable by the second, I can't stop Filia from going on. "Suddenly, the heel I'm wearing catches in the edge of the stone and I just know I'm going to pitch forward."

"What do I do?" My words come out as a rasp. I shake my head. It has to be a coincidence.

Right?

"You're chivalrous. It's in your nature, despite how depraved you love being with me. You catch me up in your arms and deposit me on the lounger to make certain I'm not injured." She pauses. "That's when you notice what I've put on. I wore it especially for you, but I'm not certain you've seen *me* before this moment. If nothing else, my inherent clumsiness has garnered me your attention. I can't say I hate it."

"Are you okay?"

She makes a *pfft* sound. "My ankle is sore, but you're touching my leg. Caressing it. Pain is the furthest thing from my mind. What I want you to do is to spread my legs apart and take what you're so clearly hungry for."

I swallow hard at the scene playing out in my head despite the klaxon of bells going off. "And what's that?"

"What's covered by a scrap of green lace."

"I obviously don't do that?"

"No," her voice is riddled with amused disgust. "Instead you check on the food to make certain my tumble hasn't ruined the masterpiece of a cake and appetizers. I push you aside and tell you I'll do it since I'm the one who helped set it up in the first place."

Bile rises in my throat but I choke out, "And is it? Did you make a mess, Filia?"

"Not yet." Her voice is coy.

"What did you say, little girl?"

"I said, not yet. Not until you come up behind me when I'm straightening out the precisely lined napkins and you smooth your hands up the back of my thighs." There's a slight pause before, "I feel the heat of your body through your thin dress shirt, the buttons pressing into my back."

"And my hands? What are they doing?" I taste the salt of my tears on my cheeks.

"One of them is fiddling with the lace of my bra before you ask me if I bought it for you—I did, by the way. The other is plucking at my nipple as I buck my hips back against you."

My dick is spike hard despite myself. I toss back some more whiskey and wait knowing no one is better at this than she is. After all, night after night when we FaceTime, it isn't just the sight of her gorgeous body that gets me off.

It's her mind. Only superseded by her treacherous, disloyal heart.

"Soon, you're fighting with your pants enough to let out your rock-hard cock. You drag it over my thong..."

"Your set is a thong?"

Her voice is a pout. "You like me to show off my assets in front of your friends."

The depravity behind that statement is like a slow stroke to my already tortured cock. I can feel the pre cum building deep inside. "Do I guide myself inside?"

"After you suit up," she snips.

"Of course." I pause to give more credence to this wicked call. "Your pussy weeping for me. . . Filia?"

"I want you so badly."

I grunt. "Good enough. Take me."

She moans as I tell her I'm slamming into her. "Arch your back, baby."

"I am. God, you're going so deep. I feel you almost to my womb."

With an added rasp to my voice, I snarl, "These panties offend me. I'm ripping them off."

"I'm yours to do with what you will."

Damn straight. You have been since the first night we were together. "I'm taking you hard," I warn her.

"Do it. Take me." Then after her rapturous breathing comes through the line. "Oh, no!"

I pause, as if there's an actual sexual act occurring. "What?"

"I just ruined the cake. You kept shoving me forward and my hand slapped into it."

Shaken, I desperately search for the time. I have mere minutes before I can end this call. "Give me your fingers."

"What are you doing with them?" she asks, genuinely curious.

"I'm sucking them into my mouth. I'm licking each and every drop of icing from them."

"Every time you do, my pussy is clenching tighter around you," she moans.

Just like I thought it would. The insidious thought pops into my head. Unable to shake how she's ruined this for us, I grunt and let myself enjoy her.

One last time.

"I'm going to fuck you hard for this, Fa—" I start when I'm reprieved by the automated voice telling me I'm out of time. I'm so damn grateful I pay in advance because I was about to blow everything by saying her name.

With that, I disconnect the line and immediately hurl my glass against the wall, my anger a palpable force.

CHAPTER FORTY-TWO

KENSINGTON, TEXAS

Ethan

Is truth really self-evident?

—@PRyanPOfficial

Dude, we need to get you off this kick. You were funnier when you were depressed.

—Viego Martinez, Celebrity Blogger

FILIA IS FALLON. AFTER WIPING MY BROW AND ABSORBING THE BLOW, I can't do much but sit in shock. The absence of noise almost makes the buzzing in my mind as loud as a sonic boom.

My eye gravitates just beyond my spread legs, where a secure coded laptop and new glass of whiskey sit on my coffee table after I delt with the mess of the first one I destroyed. When I first poured it, there was an ice cube in it. It melted while I was trying to give the team precious time to upload the final code to persistently hack into their database. It ended with my future blowing my heart up in my chest.

Over and over, my mind rejects what just happened.

Filia and Fallon telling me about their green lace.

Filia and Fallon sauntering across the patio.

Filia tripping, me catching her as she fell.

Aloud, I whisper, "Maybe they know each other?"

Fallon, the woman I love, can't be working for the phone sex company I'm investigating for a possible connection to the individuals out to harm Leanne. But how is it possible "Filia" and Fallon both walked me through the exact same sexcapade? "The odds don't even exist."

And I've learned the hard way there are no such things as coincidences.

Reaching for my computer, I gather my bearings before I ease my way into the employee files of Devil's Lair. My throat closes over a knot so large that I'm surprised I'm not choking on it.

The proof is irrefutable. I snatch up my cell phone and send a text.

ETHAN:

I am going to have some business in Seven Virtues soon.

FALLON:

ARE YOU SERIOUS?!?! When?

Her excitement is palpable. My own, much less so because once I see Fallon face-to-face, I know what I'm going to have to do.

The very idea of which feels like I'm ripping off an appendage.

ETHAN:

Soon. Real soon.

Suddenly, I'm grateful I never shared my true relationship with Fallon with my family because if my devastation is anything to go by, their disappointment in my lack of judgment might be too much to bear.

CHAPTER FORTY-THREE

SEVEN VIRTUES, NORTH CAROLINA

Fallon

@PRyanPOffical, Let me assure you, not all men are created equal.

—@CuteandRich3

@CuteandRich3, Now see? That was funny.

—Viego Martinez, Celebrity Blogger

I ROLL OVER, PLUCK MY PHONE OFF THE END TABLE, AND SILENCE THE alarm. Quickly scanning for texts, I see Ethan checked in this morning already. Deciding I want to hear his voice before I start another day, I dial his cell.

Before the first ring is over, I hear his sexy voice in my ear. "Hey, darlin'."

I let out a huge yawn before asking, "What are you doing up so early?"

"Never went to bed," he admits. "I've been working with the company I'm contracted to and inspiration took flight around midnight."

Right around midnight, I had my last call at Devil's Lair—with Whiskey. Emotions I'm not prepared for make my stomach churn—anger at a God who could make my mother so ill. Resentment at my mother for not allowing me to share the burden of her illness. And worse, an unceasing guilt at not telling Ethan the extent of what I'm doing to try to prolong her life.

Pressing my head back against my headboard, I whisper, "I miss you."

"I'm right here, witch," he murmurs.

"I mean in my bed, my arms."

There is a pause before he asks, "Fal? Is everything okay? You know you can talk to me."

I feel the liquid of my tears against my lips before I even acknowledge I'm crying. Lifting my free hand, I dash them away. "Yeah. Just a long day yesterday."

"Is your mama not feeling any better? Do you want me to call Paige to see if she can come shake up the medical personnel in that godforsaken town you inhabit?"

My sob is masked by my laughter. Wouldn't that just be a pisser? My mother wants to hide her condition from Austyn's family to avoid pity and here's my lover offering to send his sister—a doctor. The grin he elicited allows the tears to leak into my mouth. "I can just see the doctors hiding when they hear Dr. Paige Kensington is back in town."

Ethan sips what I know is his morning go-to—strong black coffee. "Whatever you need, witch."

I whisper, "I need you right now more than I've needed you since we met."

His voice drops. "As soon as I wrap up this new piece of work. I promise I'll be there soon thereafter."

"I know, it's selfish...," I begin.

His soft laughter warms my cold body. "It's not selfish that you need me? Want me? Never that, Fallon."

"Make me a promise we'll talk later," I plead. I don't want the last voice I hear to be that of one from Devil's Lair. "I need to hear your voice so you follow me into my dreams."

"Done," he agrees immediately. "I'll call no matter how late it is."

I glance at the clock and sigh. "Then I suppose I need to get going."

"Think of me today, Fal."

"I always do." I want to say more, tell him how much I love him, but I'll save that for later. Reluctantly, I end the call and throw my legs over the side of the bed to begin my routine of Biltmore, hospital, and phone sex before I get a chance to come home and have a few minutes of being responsible for exactly one thing.

My heart.

CHAPTER FORTY-FOUR

SEVEN VIRTUES, NORTH CAROLINA

Fallon

I heard if someone ghosts me, I'm supposed to treat them like they're dead.

By using that logic, that would mean I should ignore Beckett Miller.

Nah...

—Sexy And Social, All the Scandal You Can Handle

WHERE CAN HE BE?

It's been two days since we last spoke. With one hand, I slip my phone from my pocket so I can check to make certain I haven't missed a call because the ringer is required to be off while I'm visiting my mother.

Nothing.

In fact, I open our text string and frown when I realize the last I heard from Ethan was after I stumbled into bed last night when I was done with my shift at Devil's Lair.

"Where is he?" I mutter under my breath so I don't disturb the hand I'm holding in her hospital bed, and then I send him a text.

FALLON:

Is everything okay, E?

ETHAN:

Fine. Why?

A two-word response after five years of texting non-stop where our messages ranged from the nonsensical **How do I cure this hangover?** to fierce arguments over Ethan's place in my life and mine in his.

We've rarely gone more than a night in five years without speaking to one another except when he made me feel disposable when I concluded I was nothing more to him than a dirty little secret. For that, I gave him exactly what he deserved—silence.

A silence that stretched for two weeks while he pleaded with me to explain the complicated mess bouncing around in his enormous brain.

Now, I've been treated to two days of silence; however, unlike when I ignored him, I have no understanding as to why.

I review the two words he texted me back and search for hidden meanings buried in their simplicity, giving up when I find none. They're two words he could have sent to anyone—a colleague, hell, a total stranger. These are not words he's used with me ever

Fine. Why? Those aren't words you reply to someone with after passion-filled nights and whispered dreams cemented what your heart already knew—you were born to be his. And you're only sorry you were born decades later than he was and he had to wait for your hearts to find each other.

Those words aren't what you expect after worshiping the other's body after years of subtle jealous texts leading up to the realization where you can't imagine a future where your complicated emotions are free to burst forward instead of being locked deep inside your heart.

My heart leaped for joy at the idea of being able to hold him again—sooner than expected. *We can fix what's wrong, make this work,* I vowed fiercely. There would be no before and after version of the man whose body, heart, and soul I desperately need now more than ever.

I just can't understand why I'm being frozen out.

What happened? What did I do?

Part of me wants to jump on FaceTime and blast him. I'm not certain what kind of games he's playing but I have more pressing priorities right now, including the hand barely clasping mine after the last injection of poison into their system. Assuring myself I'll deal with my man and whatever his issues are later, I shove my phone back in the pocket of my sweatshirt, wishing the nurse who promised she'd grab me a blanket would hurry back.

It might be summer, but inside this damn hospital, the temperature's dropping.

Just like my hope that sacrificing what might be left of my morality for love was worth the cost.

Later that evening, after I'd been reassured my mother would rest comfortably for the night, I sit in Florence's office at Devil's Lair. Scrubbing my hands over my face, I share her prognosis with Florence and Becca. "The treatments aren't working the way the doctors hoped."

Florence reaches out and squeezes my shoulder, empathy clear on her face. "Do you need the night off, Fallon?"

Becca chimes in. "Taking calls here on a regular basis is exhausting on a normal night."

"No, I need to keep my mind busy." I offer them both a wan smile. "But if I duck out early, you won't be angry?"

"Never that, Fallon. We appreciate the burden you're balancing between spending time with your mother, your day job, and working down your debt." Becca's voice is sympathetic.

Becca speaks no less than the truth, but despite my desire to go home and just cry, I need this job. The contract I signed when I agreed to work at the Devil's Lair means I'm not being paid a formal paycheck. Instead, I bring them any medical expenses my mother has accrued to keep her in the best cancer treatment facility with the hope of beating back this awful disease. I refuse to let her die when she told me how ill she was. I went to her doctors personally and confronted them about treatment options with her permission.

At the time, I was told her coverage wouldn't include certain medications which offered her a chance.

A chance to live.

A chance to continue to love.

It seemed so easy when Florence approached me with a solution—work for her and join her cadre of phone sex operators at Devil's Lair. Boy, was I both right and wrong.

Yes, Florence put her money where her mouth was, and she opened my eyes to a whole new world, one I'm still not certain I wanted to know existed. It was all about selling a fantasy.

A fantasy that we charged by the minute for.

Something I'm apparently damn good at according to the review Florence and Becca just gave me.

Although I'm not technically being paid, in the short time I've worked here, I've garnered the highest number of requests for repeat clientele, ranging from household names to the sick and deranged. Not to mention *him*— Whiskey. My brows draw down when I recall Becca's assurance Whiskey came up perfectly clean. "We used our normal investigators, Fallon."

"Are they reputable?" I demanded.

She nodded. "It's a large firm out of New York City."

"And you trust them?"

She hesitated before nodding, "Florence does. She has a...family member who works there."

I pressed a hand to my stomach. "Okay."

With that assurance I resumed accepting calls from Whiskey. After all, since the incident, I've since learned even more about Devil's Lair. Even though I've never had it officially confirmed, Becca's face lit with amusement when she'd listen in on my calls and I'd ask after if certain callers were in fact celebrities, politicians, or—swoon—a member of a royal family way down in the line for the throne. "And now you know why your NDA is so ironclad," Becca smirked.

Since that confirmation, I've never questioned the identity of my callers. I don't want to know. In fact, they've just become another facet of the disease ripping through my mother's body.

I twist my face toward Florence and Becca and admit, "I thought it would save her. I thought I was giving her a chance to live."

Florence smooths her hand over my back before reminding me, "You tried. It's just that someone else is fighting to end her suffering."

I fling my arm around to encompass the sins occurring around the call center in Devil's Lair. "Should I move so I'm not shocked when God sends that lightning bolt?"

Her lips twitch. "I think 'Oh god' is heard more in here than in the church on the Seven Virtues campus."

The three of us toss our heads back and laugh at her blatant blasphemy. For just a moment, I'm thankful I have this group of edgy men and women at my back when my world's falling apart. Even though they know they're a means to an end and that I have other plans for my future, I hold them in the highest esteem. I know how ridiculously difficult their job is and how much they care for one another.

When I started working here, the team at Devil's Lair offered me a glimmer of light at the end of a long, dark tunnel as I stared down the odds of my mother beating her cancer. Now, even as that tiny bit of light is flickering out, they still support me amid their own personal nightmares.

Because in a town like Seven Virtues, no sin can hide, at least not for very long.

Lifting my headset, I say. "Let me get to work so I can get out of here."

Florence and Becca step away. Becca warns, "If you need to leave, just let me know. I'll take your calls, Fallon."

Warmth surges through me. "Thanks. Hopefully, after I'm done here, I'll be able to go home for a few hours and crash before I need to head to the hospital."

Once I walk back to my station, I give myself another moment before I log into my system. Then, I accept my first call. Reading the brief—a couple looking for a third for a virtual polyamorous three-way with a woman—I accept the call with a husky, "Devil's Lair, this is Filla. Would you like to have some pleasure this evening?"

Soon, I'm guiding the couple on the phone to a happy ending as I talk the woman through what it would feel like if I sucked on her tight nipples and her throbbing clit while her husband thrusts up into her until they both orgasm in my ear.

Once they moan in completion, some twenty-five minutes later, I disconnect the call and check my cell phone. Nothing from the hospital and nothing from Ethan. I mutter, "At least someone had a happy ending."

CHAPTER FORTY-FIVE

KENSINGTON, TEXAS

Ethan

Be still my mourning heart.

DJ Kensington and Amanda Reidel, part of semi-retired Small Town Nights, are officially going to collaborate on an entire album, according to a press release from Wildcard Entertainment.

According to Paula Stone, "The as yet untitled album will drop sometime next year."

If there's a tour, I'm not above using some inside connections for tickets.

—StellaNova

I've been avoiding Fallon for days, limiting my response in texts to one or two words. Every time I see her beaming face from the photos I took at her graduation on my phone screen, every time a new text pops up, I want to do nothing more than hurl the offending device across the room into the nearest wall, shattering it into a million pieces.

It's close to how my heart's felt since I realized she's working for the cesspool, Devil's Lair.

My original intent when hunting with Sam and Leanne was to help protect Leanne and her unborn baby. "Sam, there are whispers of Devil's Lair's calls leading the child traffickers. I'm hunting back to this phone sex operation."

"I'm not surprised."

"That's not why I'm calling."

"Then what is?"

"Hudson Investigations' name is everywhere." I scan the screens in front of me. "If it wasn't for the firewalls Leanne put in place after we ran our initial test, you'd be under a brute force attack by some people who want very sensitive information about your company."

Then I hit pay dirt—or mud splattered in my face, depending on how you look at it—the night when "Filia" described a scene I'd only told Fallon about. How I wanted to bend her over and fuck her the night of her high school graduation.

How, after she described every last detail of Fallon's new lingerie down to a *T*, the insidious thought exploded into something much worse.

Betrayal.

Without hesitation, I used Sam's window into Devil's Lair and entered their HR files long enough to confirm my suspicions. That's when it took everything in me to not throw up the highball of amber liquid I'd just consumed. My heart, which I was so ready to lay at Fallon's feet, shriveled up and died in my chest. Then again, despite what my brain was telling it, it was still beating. The damn organ refused to accept what my eyes were seeing—the employment of one Ms. Fallon Brookes. Reading her file, I almost passed out, realizing this had been going on for almost the entire time we'd been dating.

All I can keep asking myself is, when did I let myself get soft? Should I have known better? Resisting the honeypots was part of my indoctrination when I trained for the Agency. Now, a girl barely out of the school room managed to slip past my defenses like I was groomed to be hers.

What if I'd really let her into my life? What other kind of traps could she have laid?

Scrubbing my fingers through my hair, I growl again, "I don't get it. Why would she be involved in something as heinous as this?"

Thorn reminds me, "You're making some pretty huge assumptions, Ethan. Have you questioned her? Asked why? There are always reasons."

"Don't give me this innocent until proven guilty crap, Thorn." That was my woman in there—the goddamn bitch. I want to wrap my fingers around her neck and squeeze until she gives me the answers I want.

"Which means your objectivity is shot," Thorn fires back. "You're basing your assumption Fallon is involved on the fact you have feelings for her. You have no evidence to prove it conclusively, do you?"

No, I have nothing to prove Fallon's one of the people after Leanne Miles, but there are far too many coincidences. My sister. Them meeting at a club in New York City. Fallon working at Devil's Lair. My voice is blistering when I fire back, "Fuck you, Thorn."

"Let my people work on a plan before you do something stupid." His voice is placating, which sparks my fury even further.

"I thought you weren't supposed to operate on US soil, which is how I keep getting dragged into your shit." I mimic his baritone and a famous Bruce Willis movie. "Come work for the Agency, you said. It will be fun, you said."

"Get your shit in check," Thorn orders me.

"You have a day. Then I'm going out there."

"That's a dumb fucking move."

"Why?"

"Because Sam and Qəza are putting the pieces of the puzzle together. Something doesn't add up."

I frown at Thorn's words. "You don't believe the evidence. It seems pretty clear cut to me."

"There's something off. Qaza's looking into Fallon Brookes specifically, Sam into Devil's Lair's employees."

"Whoop-dee-fucking-doo. Who the hell cares?"

His fist hits the desk. "I do! This isn't about you, Ethan. It's about so much more than just your broken heart—if that's even the case."

"You have doubts."

"I think there are explanations," he mediates.

"And I think there are absolutes."

"Which is part of why you left the Agency to begin with," he counters. "This whole business is a shade of gray."

I have to verbally restrain myself before I tell him where he can take his agency. But my hands fist on my desk and Thorn takes note of it. "You're hands off, Ethan."

"You're benching me?" The kick in the gut is just one more agony tonight. Though nothing as bad as when I figured out it was Fallon's hot as fuck voice trying to get me off—and succeeding—while I called into the Devil's Lair as my colleagues listened in.

"Just until I get more intel."

"Then why the fuck are you babysitting me? Call your other friends for intel and leave me to my fucking misery," I bellow.

He ignores me in typical Thorn fashion and instead pesters me about Fallon. "Why are you so convinced she's involved. Neither Qaza nor Sam can find any evidence that lights her up in their initial check."

"She's working there. That's enough." I rub my hand over the ache blooming in my heart.

Thorn hums contemplatively.

"What's that supposed to mean, Thorn?"

"What would your reaction be—right now—if I wanted to bring her in for questioning?"

Every drop of blood leaches from my face. I may be furious as hell at Fallon, but I don't want to see her go missing in an underground prison for the rest of her life. "No. Just...no."

"But you're so convinced of her guilt."

"Thorn!" I snap.

"She's yours, Ethan," he taunts in that fucking know-it-all way he has that's driven every agent who ever worked for him insane. "Just admit she got to you. It's happened before."

She got to me when she was eighteen years old. I refuse to admit the woman I knew as "Filia" got to me in any way. The bitter bite of betrayal surges through my veins.

Thorn makes a tsking noise. "I think you need to stop everything and think, but what do I know?" he asks then disconnects the call.

"Bastard." At that point, I'm not certain if I'm referring to Thorn or myself.

You. You're referring to yourself, asshole.

Shoving away from my desk, I whip out my cell phone and pull up my text string with Fallon, scrolling back a few days before I knew what I know now —that she's working for an organization that's in bed with criminals.

I knew she was far too young for me. Christ, she's my niece's best friend. She's a fleet of red flags I ignored because I wanted to be able to what? Stand on top of a foundation of lust to proclaim she was mine? Look where that got me. Every warning I gave myself about becoming involved with her pales to the fact there's a high probability she may be involved with illegal activities.

"I knew I should have resisted you," I say aloud as I read through the last few days of our texts. Based on the schedule at Devil's Lair I hacked, she's at work right now. I could log in and listen to her phone calls live, but I can't do it.

I just can't.

Especially after the last one where she cut out the heart of me. I recall each and every detail in full, unable to shove it out of my mind knowing it was *my* Fallon who so used it with a complete stranger.

A fantasy I came close to orgasming to because I knew it was her.

Only she didn't know it was me.

The disgust I feel right now is the only thing that pushes me through to complete this job so I can stop fighting the pain I know I'm setting myself up for. I also know I can't talk with her. I can't listen to her breathless sighs as she takes herself there. Instead, I set up a bot to text her around 2 AM when she's supposedly going to get off work at Galileo's to say, "Sleep well."

Because one of us needs to.

I'll be too busy trying to pull her proverbial fat out of the fryer so she can make more mistakes in her young life.

Just none that will include me after this.

CHAPTER FORTY-SIX

SEVEN VIRTUES, NORTH CAROLINA

Fallon

ETHAN:

Sleep well.

FALLON:

Are you still up?

SINCE I REPLIED BACK ALMOST IMMEDIATELY AFTER I RECEIVED Ethan's message, for a moment, I'm hopeful he'll respond. But as the minutes pass while I sit in my car outside Devil's Lair with no response, hope dies when there is not even an acknowledgment he's read my text. "What the hell has happened in the last few days?" Frustration eats at me to the point I type that into the text window and am about to hit Send, but decide I don't have the energy to hash it out with Ethan tonight.

Too many emotions are swirling toxically together in my heart and if I'm truthful, what I crave more than the potential healing that could be offered by a man I'm falling for is to forget my heart's agony. Even if oblivion can only last for a brief while.

As I sit in the lot at Devil's Lair, I know the sun's licking at my heels. By the time I make it to my door, I'll have just a few hours before I have to be back at the hospital with my mother if I want a chance to speak with her team of oncologists. With a heavy heart and a knot in my stomach that might rival the pain my mother complains about after her chemo, I toss my phone in the center console and put my car in gear to make my way from the warehouse at the fringes of Seven Virtues back to the center of the small town.

Exhausted as I am, it takes all my focus to drive the back roads. I have no desire to roll my car off the side of the Appalachian mountains. Nor do I feel like swerving into the side of them into a cliff face. Finally, I manage to navigate into the valley and breathe a sigh of relief when I pass by the perimeter of the university where I graduated from just a few short months ago. My lips curve when I recall the crazy joy I felt that night between finally completing my degree, the jaw dropping shock and awe my best friend once again caused in our small community, and most importantly, Ethan.

Ethan at my graduation.

Ethan at my side.

Ethan in my arms, my bed. Finally open to my heart.

Pulling into my reserved parking space behind Galileo's, I park the car, grab my cell and purse. Unlocking the security door, I climb the stairs and enter my apartment.

Thank the lord, the bar below has quieted down for the night. With the way I'm putting in twenty-hour days between my time at the hospital, the museum, and my repayment plan to Florence, everything is catching up to me.

Within seconds, I enter my bedroom and fall face first on my bed.

Fast asleep.

Four hours later, I'm showered, dressed and back at Seven Virtues Hospital with a smile on my face for my mother when I squeeze her delicate hand between mine. "You look better this morning."

My mother's face isn't quite so gray and flushed from the effects of yesterday's chemotherapy. "Truly a stunning compliment, Fal."

"I could have remarked on how sparkly your head looked beneath the lights."

My mother grins before casting lashless eyes upward. "It really is rude, isn't it? You would think they'd use a filter so my new cancer haircut wouldn't be so shocking."

We both laugh at her remark, continuing to cut up at everything from the color of the hospital walls to the way her gown pulls the color from her pallor to the too stringent nurses who won't let me sneak in a breakfast of biscuits and gravy and are not amused when I get busted using the whiteboard to draw a ticktacktoe game as we pass the time waiting on the oncology team. "You know, we use that area for serious information," I'm scolded.

My mother rolls her eyes before mouthing, "Top right," which is where she wants me to place her next X so she can block me from claiming the game. I glare at her over the head tyrant's shoulder before replying to the scowling face in front of me. "We haven't erased anything."

"See that you don't," is huffed out before the nurse scurries out of the room.

Mama and I laugh again and hope rises in my soul. *Maybe this time, it worked.* We continue our fierce battle of Xs and Os until the second her oncologist strides through the door after a sharp rap. Immediately, the tension in the room ratchets up, and our demeanor changes with the seriousness of his expression.

I know without him opening his mouth what he's about to say and I wish with all my heart I could share this burden with Ethan.

Hours later, I'm assisting the head of the holiday decoration team by accessing the records of all cataloged Biltmore Christmas museum artifacts. On a normal day, I'd be ecstatic knowing we're planning the formal dressing of the estate—giving a whole new meaning to the phrase "Christmas in July." But I'm severely subdued by the news I learned this morning.

I want to upend every single plant in the majestic Winter Garden and let them rot. I want to tear apart each and every one of the 24,000 books I know are housed inside George Vanderbilt's two-story library. I want to curl up on Edith Vanderbilt's French Renaissance settee and cry my heart out before smashing every window and reflective surface along the way out the door.

My mother isn't responding to the treatment. The treatment I fought for her to get.

Dry-eyed, I faced her oncologist to hear for myself the failure of modern medicine that was explained to us instead of bursting into hysterics. "So, you're saying the treatment—"

"Ms. Brookes, the treatment wasn't a guarantee. It was a hope. It had a small chance of working—something we conversed about when you came to my office to discuss it originally," Dr. Richard Smyth interjects.

Dick, is the first thought that comes to mind, as it was three months ago when he told me I had thirty days to get the money for my mother to even receive the medicine she's on since it wasn't covered under her insurance plan. I waved my hand back and forth. "Can you answer a simple question?"

"If it's possible." The doctor's eyes drift again to my legs, which are shown to their best advantage in my work uniform and heels. I hear Mama crying softly behind me, and between that and the lecherous look in front of me, I

want to hurl. Honestly, I don't give a flying fuck he's staring at my tits. If he wasn't, he'd have long left the room and fobbed me off on one of his minions. I'd never have learned the full details behind why this supposed new FDA miracle drug failed in my mother's case.

Clearing my throat so Dr. Smyth does his best to raise his eyes above my breasts. "You indicated my mother was an excellent candidate for the medication."

"Yes, but..."

"But what?" I asked.

"The cancer had already metastasized." A look of empathy crosses over his face when he addresses my mother. "I'm sorry, Helen. There must have been a lesion that didn't come up initially in your PET scan. You need to make plans—sooner rather than later."

My heart stops pumping fire and instead ices over in fear, afraid to ask what he means. Instead, I spin, wrapping my arms around my mother, rocking her back and forth as sobs wrack her body. I hiss at Dr. Smyth, "I-I thought you'd told me she had a chance."

Was it my own naivety that believed that she could be saved if I just sacrificed enough for her? After all, didn't I prove there wasn't anything I wouldn't do to save my mother's life? Judging by the doctor's face, my beliefs were a complete fallacy made up in my own mind.

He confirms my thinking. "Because of the lateness in her diagnosis, she's barely able to tolerate the therapy as it is."

My mother, showing she's the stronger of the two of us, asks, "How much longer do I have?"

He hesitates. "It's different for each patient. All I can say is time is of the essence."

While I absorb these awful truths, my mother clings to me. Unwilling to let her go, our heartbreak collides as our mingled tears drip down our faces.

Dr. Smyth's head twists and his jaw tics. "This is the part of my job I despise—when the science of medicine is supposed to work and it abysmally fails." With those words, he exits the room, leaving heartbreak and destruction in his wake.

"Fallon? Fallon, did you hear what I said?" Charlene waves a hand in front of my face.

I jerk out of my reverie. "I'm sorry. I zoned out for a moment. Let me see if I got everything. You would like to start with the tapestry room, then move to the Winter Garden to decorate?"

"Yes." She goes on to explain the general process of how we start decorating the enormous mansion beginning in mid-October for the festive holiday season, but I'm about as far from the holiday spirit as a person can be.

I'm feeling so alone. Surreptitiously, I glance down at my phone after giving it a nudge to wake it from sleep.

Nothing. Still nothing from Ethan.

Where is he?

What is going on?

CHAPTER FORTY-SEVEN

KENSINGTON, TEXAS

Ethan

Who knew my cell phone was haunted? #ghosted

—**@PRyanPOfficial**

#lesigh Here we go again.

—**@CuteandRich3**

IGNORE.

I press the button to decline Fallon's call again. My fingers resume dancing across the keyboard as I unearth more information about Devil's Lair. As I do, my fury swells with her even as disappointment mounts simultaneously. The only thing preventing my heart from being crushed beneath the weight of these opposing emotions is the job I was hired to do—the contract work for Thorn. Still, one question out of a million keeps pushing past the block I've thrown up.

"What the fuck would possess her to do this? She's never going to shed the humiliation that's going to be attached to her for the rest of her damn life when this comes out." The words are out of my mouth as I glare at my computer screen.

My phone rings again, and I growl savagely before I realize it's Thorn. I snarl, "What?"

"Qəza and Sam want to know your status."

"I'm almost all the way through analyzing the transcripts."

"And?" he demands.

I forgot what an insistent bastard he is. It's been less than three days since we last talked and he wants me to have analyzed close to three years worth of phone sex transcripts—which I first had to trigger to locate the crown prince's calls and then analyze with voice prints. "And I forgot what an impatient bastard you are."

"You used to be faster at this," he taunts before he proceeds to infuriate me. "Qəza is already done with her part."

"Well, isn't that nice when we're just running financials and coming up with profiles. Some of us are a bit hampered because you don't want footprints, so I'm downloading data to my system. Also, for what it's worth, I'd better not get the FBI knocking on my door as a result of transferring this data across state lines," I warn him.

I hear his fingers clicking furiously on his side. "Done. How much more time do you need?"

"Do you want me triggering any alarms in Devil's Lair's system that I'm there?" My voice is dripping with sarcasm.

"Testy much? Just call her and ask her why she's doing what she's doing. She'll ask how you know, you'll obfuscate. She'll be pissed. The end."

"How many times do I have to say this—I don't care!" My voice rises with each word until I'm shouting.

His chair creaks as he settles back. "I have a gut feeling it's not what you're thinking."

"Great. Your gut isn't going to clear Fallon until the data does. Until then, she's just as suspect as her boss, her trainer, and the other three operators."

He backs off. "How much more time do you need?"

I check my upper left monitor. "Another six hours."

"And to analyze the data?"

"A few more after that."

"Let me know what you find." He abruptly disconnects the call.

Ten hours later, I'm emotionally exhausted. I've analyzed the data and narrowed down the potential suspects to three. Data doesn't lie the way a woman's sweet lips can.

With that, I pick up my cell phone and text Fallon.

Ethan: I'll be there tomorrow.

Fallon: Thank god. I need you.

As I stare at the trail of data connecting the owner and Fallon's operator number to those being made against the crown prince's, I wonder if she'll be saying that after she sees me, and I tell her I never want to hear from her again.

CHAPTER FORTY-EIGHT

SEVEN VIRTUES, NORTH CAROLINA

Fallon

There is nothing better than a friend unless it's my best friend who showed up with La Maison du Chocolat.

—Moore You Want

IN THE FEW HOURS OF SLEEP I MANAGE THAT NIGHT, I HAVE A nightmare triggered by a conversation between me and my mother over wanting to tell Kensington about her diagnosis. Stretching for a few precious minutes in bed

I acknowledge her only ask of me is driving my soul into an early grave.

Throwing back the covers and shoving to my feet, I recall the vivid memories that raced through my eyes just before dawn.

There was a seemingly endless maze of corridors to navigate my way through the pristine corridors of Seven Virtues Hospital. I let out a rush of air when I burst into the late summer evening. Even though the touch of fall hasn't brushed the Asheville region yet, I still hug myself to ward off a chill.

Twisting, I shoot a fulminating glare at the building behind me—as if the inanimate object can absorb my fury from the past mingled with my present wrath. "God, I hate this place. All it does is try to suck the life out of those that I love."

A twisted image of my mother's face being drunk by a straw extended from darkened skies as her eyes fixated on mine was interrupted as a nameless face fights being wedged into the same glass container that resembled the collection of Galileo thermostats at the bar. Something is shouted at me I can't understand.

But even as it tried to take the life of my mother, warmth steals through me as Ethan's brawny arm slips around my waist. Waves of comfort crash over me, reminding me that despite the fact I can't share the details, I'm not alone. We gravitate together, he to offer comfort, the only thing my promise to the woman I love will permit him to in these desperate moments.

Contact, touch.

Love.

I didn't need words from him because I knew he was there for me at my best and worst, and this was certainly shaping up to be my worst. After all, what prepares you for the imminent crumbling of the strongest cornerstone of your world?

Grabbing his hand, I drag him away from the scene, racing around straws plunging down from the sky—each of them trying to jab us in the head— ready to drain one or both of us of our souls. Reaching my car, I urge him to get inside. I slide in effortlessly before I start the engine.

Only to find him not there.

Is it a sign I should betray my mother's wishes?

CHAPTER FORTY-NINE

Fallon

I refuse to be remembered in death as someone who didn't bring people joy. From now on, this is where you can come to for your music news.

—@PRyanPOfficial

Until you get dumped again.

—@CuteandRich3

"Mama, please," I beg.

For as frail as she is, the determination in her eyes doesn't waiver. "No. I don't want the Kensingtons to know."

Tears prick my eyes. "I swear to you, I won't ask them."

"I refuse..."

"I don't plan on asking Austyn for money. I...I just..."

"You just what, Fallon? You know that the first thing she's going to do is tell her mother."

"Not if I tell her not to!" I shout.

My mother goes on as if I haven't spoken. "Then the family will offer to do what they can to wipe away our burden. As if the money is what concerns me at this point."

Something in my face must alert my mother. Her expression turns caustic. "I told you already that if the hospital tries to hold you liable, the life insurance will cover it."

"I know."

"Then what is it?"

God, I can't believe I'm having to have this conversation with my mother. Surging to my feet, I storm over to the window and stare out at the campus of the Seven Virtues University from my mother's hospital room. Knowing I have precious few minutes before my mother's doctor comes in—Dr. Smyth being notorious for his punctuality—I note the clock on the tower is still three minutes slow. *God, how many days was I late to class because I relied upon the massive clock in the bell tower.* The whimsical thought comes and goes as I rub my forehead with my fingers while trying to break through the pride my mother wears like a superhero's cloak, even now.

As a single mother, she taught me to hold onto my pride at all costs. *"Fallon, the strongest commodity you'll ever have is your pride—the knowledge you accomplished your dreams without relying on another person."*

While I tucked her life lesson next to my heart, along with everything else she wanted me to learn, the agony of knowing I have little time left with her is making it hard for me to hold on to my sanity, much less my precious pride—both of which I'd easily give up to know my mother would live.

Still, I made her a promise—a promise she needs to release me from. Since she made it so I couldn't go to the Kensingtons for money and I instead took the job at Devil's Lair to offset her medical costs, I haven't shared anything about her medical condition. I'm alone as I absorb the insidious pain of my upcoming reality. Sure, a few colleagues at Devil's Lair are aware of it, but it's not the same as having Austyn to lean on as my world shatters.

As having Ethan know how much I need him more now than I ever needed him for any stupid hangover.

Ignoring the tiny spear of light that blooms inside me knowing he'll be here shortly after my shift ends at Devil's Lair, I return to sit next to my mother. Clasping her fragile hand between mine, I whisper, "Mama, Austyn loves you."

My mother shifts uncomfortably in her bed. "I know, darling."

"She'll be devastated if she doesn't get a chance to say goodbye." It's just that simple. For years when we lived in Kensington, if I wasn't at my home, I was at hers and vice versa. Austyn's mother became my second one, and my mother became hers. I lean forward and press my lips against our joined hands. "Would you deny her the chance to tell you she loves you?"

"Fallon...," she croaks.

"Wouldn't you be angry if the roles were reversed? Would you want me to be able to...to say...goodbye to...my other mother?"

My mother presses her lips together as tears run unchecked down her face. She pulls her hand free of mine. For a second I'm fearful she's going to deny my request until she uses her thumb to brush at my tears. "Just Austyn. Just her...for now."

I nod, grateful she bent enough to give me this. "And Mama Paige?"

Her fingers tangle in the ends of my hair. "Not till the end, Fal. Just...leave me some pride."

Resting my arms against the side of her bed, I meet her gaze just as three raps hit the door. "There's no place for pride when it comes to love."

As Dr. Smyth shoves open the door, I hear a faint, "I hope Ethan recognizes that before it's too late," which leaves my stomach nauseous before we get more bad news.

I have thirty minutes before my shift at Devil's Lair begins, and I can't put this call off any longer. Reaching for my cell, I note there have been no more texts from Ethan, which causes me a moment of concern, but knowing he's going to be in my arms later soothes the ache immediately. With a scoff, I reach for my phone and go to my contacts. As the call connects, I mutter, "I only have to suffer through a few hours of phone sex and breaking hearts until he gets here."

"I really hope you're not planning on going into great detail about how you and Uncle E sext each other," Austyn's infamous voice drawls. Before I can remark on that, she says a lot more seriously, "And after he finally managed to get his head out of his ass, I hope you don't plan on breaking his heart."

"I would never go into that kind of detail with you about the first and absolutely not to the second," I reassure her but even I can hear the quiver in my voice.

"What's wrong? Who do I need to maim?" Austyn demands.

At her immediate offer of harm for my pain, I burst into tears. Austyn says my name over and over, trying to calm me down. In the background, I hear her husband demanding to know what's wrong. "I don't know!" she shouts back.

After I finally manage to get myself under control, I sniffle before saying, "I'm okay." Her whoosh of relief comes too soon because that's when I drop the bomb, which causes her to start crying. "But Mama's not."

"Fallon? How bad is it?" she whimpers.

I'm certain my quivering breath can be heard over the phone line. "As bad as it gets."

Her shriek of "No!" has multiple people asking, "What's wrong?" on her side of the line.

I wish it was the same here. I wish I had Ethan to wrap his arms around me. But not now, I remind myself. Later.

Tonight.

Pulling myself together, I tell her everything that's been happening—from my mother's cancer to Florence and her offer of my second job. It's then I listen to my best friend's heart shatter right alongside mine. Once her tears have calmed, she asks me one thing, "What do you need?"

"For now, nothing."

"Fallon," a gentle reprimand.

"Austyn, right now, we don't need anything. I swear." *Because, like I told you, I agreed to sell my voice to make the medical payments,* I say silently. Then I catch her up on everything from the diagnosis to the treatment to the last two days and the bleakness that enveloped us both.

"I'm coming down," she declares resolutely.

"I figured you'd say something like that." For the first time in days, a hint of a smile curves my lips.

"You know anything I have, Mama has, whether its access to different doctors, money, just hugs, they're yours."

"I know." The tears I'm holding back cause my throat to tighten. "I'm not doing what I'm doing for the money, Austyn."

"Of course you're not," she tuts. "You're doing it to save the one person on earth you love more than anyone else."

Other than your uncle, I think, managing to keep those words unspoken. Instead, I remind her, "You know how to let yourself in when you get here."

"I do. Text me your schedule and I'll have drinks ready."

"That sounds heavenly right now."

We talk for a few more minutes before I realize I'm going to be late. With a sigh, I tell her I have to go. But before I hang up, I need for her to know something. "This isn't how I wanted to tell you."

"I'm just glad you convinced Mama Helen to tell me at all." That's my best friend, showing she knows me and my mother as well as she knows her own. That's how I knew she'd be fine about my extra job at doing what I have to at Devil's Lair. Hell, knowing Austyn the way I do, she'll likely write a song about it.

I just hope Ethan understands why I'm doing it—more importantly, why I had to keep it all a secret. Because as it is, I'll be risking the last few weeks of my mother's life just to tell him.

CHAPTER FIFTY

SEVEN VIRTUES, NORTH CAROLINA

Ethan

It's never too hot for hot chocolate, nor too cold for ice cream.

—Fab and Delish

THE FOG HAS ROLLED IN SINCE MY PLANE LANDED, SHROUDING THE mountainous region with a dangerous curtain to conceal important landmarks and signs.

Almost like the way Fallon did with me.

How could I have been so stupid to believe Fallon wouldn't fall to the sin of greed when she already fell to lust as if she'd been born nursing at its bosom? I slam my hand against the steering wheel, and the rental car I'm driving jerks in reaction, edging me closer to the dangerous cliff. "Whoa.

The idea is to get there and to let her know you know. Not to die in the process."

Dying can happen back home in Texas with a bottle of whiskey as I systematically erase every part of Fallon Brookes from my life.

I slow and take the turn down the road that leads me to the warehouse Sam traced the calls to while I was in the air. As my rented SUV rattles down the lane, individuals in full tactical gear approach in slow, practiced moves. Even as I coast to a stop, because despite the fact I'm armed and can handle myself, I curse Thorn as I call him on Speaker.

"What?" he snaps.

"Did someone forget to mention the tactical team guarding Devil's Lair?"

"There are guards?" His voice is shocked.

"Four surrounding me right now," I confirm.

"Fuck. Hold on."

My lips curve in amusement as my former boss puts me on hold. "Depending on who he's calling, I could be sold as a sex slave by the time he comes back."

"In your wildest dreams, Ethan. You took a wrong turn, you jackass."

"Not hard to do in this fog."

He snorts. "Well, it landed you on the backside of one of our training sites. Give them your phone so I can talk to the team leader."

Feeling like a complete rookie instead of someone who went through Thorn's special brand of torture, I roll down my window and hold out my cell. A gloved hand snatches my phone away and shortly thereafter a bark of laughter escapes the masked figure. Figuring Thorn's just given them the stand down procedure and then sold me out because of the damn fog, I know I'm about to take my rightful ribbing.

After my phone is handed back to me, the team lead solemnly repeats, "Sir, the director would like to know if you need backup on your assignment tonight since you're about a mile away from your turnoff."

I bare my teeth. "When you call Director Thornton back, you can tell him to suck my dick."

"No, thank you, sir. I'd really like to pass training." The agent-in-training's eyes gleam behind his mask. He points ahead and instructs me, "Go ahead about a quarter of a click. There will be a spot for you to turn around."

"Thank you."

Just as I'm about to roll up my window and get back on track, the future of the Agency calls out, "Don't drive off the mountain on your way out, sir. It's right in front of you when you hit the road."

God, is Thorn recruiting them as smartasses these days? My cheeks burn as I find the turnaround, turn the SUV around, and head back to the main road.

Once I get back onto the main road, a text from Thorn appears. I ask it to be read to me.

> THORN:
>
> Maybe this is a sign what you're about to do is a mistake. Give Sam and Qeza some more time to correlate your findings against their information. You may be wrong.

> ETHAN:
>
> Unlikely

> THORN:
>
> But possible.

I don't bother replying. It isn't his woman who is so clearly implicated. His wife builds secured facilities for a living. Sam goes home to a wife whose been lauded as a national hero. And Leanne has Castor and her husband—whom I've had the pleasure of getting to know pretty well over the years. He's as much of a straight shooter as I am.

And I'm supposed to bring Fallon into this mix? Finally, I harden my heart and tell Thorn exactly what I plan on doing.

> ETHAN:
>
> No, this ends tonight.

> THORN:
>
> Your call. I think it's the wrong one, but who am I to say. Oh, wait. I'm just the director of the...

I throw my phone on the seat, ignoring the remainder of Thorn's latest dig, and I find the correct turnoff. My eyes immediately land on Fallon's car in the parking lot of Devil's Lair. Parking next to her, I wait.

And wait.

According to her phone logs, I have a few hours until I need to surprise Fallon with my presence. As I wait, my thoughts turn inward as I try to figure out exactly how I will approach her. Unfortunately, I can't turn off my memory quite so easily from the last five years of wanting her. From falling in love with her.

I reach for my phone, pull up our text string, and scroll back as far as possible. I wince when I recall the way she reamed my ass out about Jess giving her a side hug at Austyn's birthday bash that I couldn't make because I was working on another job Thorn threw my way.

Fuck. As pissed as I am, the witch was right to call my ass out.

FALLON:

> Then you should have been here to put your own damn arm around me.

If I had been, would I be in the predicament I'm facing right now? I rub my hand over my heart as the pain radiates from the center of my chest. Fallon's been woven through the very fiber of my being since she was eighteen—how in the hell am I supposed to survive not having her in it? *Easy asshole. Think about the fact she's selling herself for money and assisting in blackmailing high profile clients*, my conscience prods me.

Up until a few days ago, I didn't know Fallon was working at Devil's Lair. I had no clue. It wasn't until I was on the phone and heard the way she described her new lingerie down to the last fucking detail—the same way she had done with me—that my antenna went on full alert.

Then I began to listen to the cadence in her voice.

I didn't want to do it, but I asked Sam to trace her cell, praying to God I was wrong, but when he confirmed it was smack dab in the middle of the Devil's Lair call center, I broke that night.

I honest to god broke.

The woman I've wanted with a fervor since she was barely legal was working as a phone sex operator. Selling her husky moans, the catch of her breath, the little gasp before she orgasmed.

Something I only just found out on the night she graduated from college.

"Fal, how could you do this to us, witch?" I ask aloud in the darkened vehicle. There's no answer, and I suspect when I ask her something similar when I see her, she's not going to be able to reply.

Still, I know this as well as I know my own name, ripping her out of my life is going to be like losing a limb.

CHAPTER FIFTY-ONE

SEVEN VIRTUES, NORTH CAROLINA

Fallon

When I started this blog during my uni years, I never could have predicted it would lead me to so much. Back then, I was set on a mild—oh, bugger it—a severe course of retribution.

I wanted to watch the world burn as I tossed the match on the petrol.

Now, I realize it was part of a grander plan to have my life intersect with the most important people in my life.

For that, I'd like to thank my family for always supporting me. My best mates, for never letting me give up, and you, my readers, for giving me a reason to go on every day.

Some days it took all of you for me to keep going.

—Moore You Want

"Fallon, can you come into my office for a moment?" Florence calls out.

Getting up from my chair, I head toward her office. She stands behind her desk and motions for me to close the door. "Sit down, Fallon."

I drop into the chair. "Is something wrong?"

"I spoke to my lawyers today."

My insides freeze. "About me?"

"Not about you specifically, about your situation. Have you and your mother spoken about family estate planning in light of everything that's going on?"

I snort. "What estate, Florence? Unless Mama won some secret lotto she never disclosed, there's just her bungalow, her car, and her life insurance policy."

"There's probably more."

"Now that you mention it, there might be some additional policies and crap from her employer, but I'm too exhausted to think of it all right now."

She comes around her desk and rests her hip against it. "Fallon, you should really speak with a probate lawyer to determine if you're going to have any responsibility to the hospital because I don't think you're going owe them a red cent despite the fact they're going to try to charge you for every sip of water your mother has taken out of one of their precious plastic cups."

I rear back. "Excuse me?"

She explains some high level information about probate law in North Carolina before lifting a hand to remind me, "But I'm not a lawyer, Fallon. Don't take my word as gospel."

I cross my arms over my chest, hugging myself, as it seems of late, I'm the only one who can give myself comfort. "Why are you telling me this?"

"Because you came in tonight with devastation written all over your face.

The last thing I want this place to be is a burden when there's no point in you working here."

"No point?"

"Fallon, the amount of money I've paid out is a pittance in comparison to the amount you negotiated. Am I wrong?"

My head drops and I'm unable to form words. Finally, I just give it a shake.

Her hand reaches over and squeezes my shoulder. "I was hoping that wasn't the case for your sake, but I suspected as much. How much time have they given her?"

"A month, max," I admit aloud.

"Fallon, I'm canceling your contract."

My head snaps up at her words. "But...I...you...my mama still needs to be in the hospital."

She leans forward until her face is all I see. "Listen to me, little girl. Consider my helping you is all those tips I should have given you on your shifts at Galileo's."

A watery laugh escapes. "Yeah. That might pay for one of her pills." As Florence indicated, hospital stays aren't cheap and as I learned, my mother doesn't have the greatest insurance even if she does have some.

"You don't need to be here trying to cater to someone's fantasy; you need to be clasping your reality as close as possible for as long as you can. If you're here when something happens, you'll look back later and regret not being with her. You're not going to be able to get this time back, despite how much you wish you could." Her eyes flash a desperate agony that sears through me. But just for a moment. After quirking me her patented lady of the boudoir smile, Florence tosses her blond hair back. "Besides, I need a tax break."

"You try to be such a hard ass."

"Ask anyone on that floor, honey. They'll tell you it's true," she drawls.

"No, it's not, Florence. You gave me hope. I hope sometime I can return the favor." I bite my lip to hold the tears away because I know if I start crying now, I won't stop. I have to get out of here. I stand up and reach in my pocket for my access card to Devil's Lair. "So, I guess this is it."

"What's the first thing you plan on doing when you get home since I'm throwing you out hours before you're supposed to be out of here?"

"Catch up on sleep," I immediately answer. But in my mind, the need to get a hold of Ethan is pulling at me hard. "I suppose I need to go get my things."

"Before you go." Florence reaches back and plucks up a piece of paper which she hands to me. "This is a list of the best probate lawyers in the area. Call any of them. Get your mama's affairs in order. They know to bill me."

I grind my teeth together as I fold the paper and slip it into my jeans pocket. "Thank you."

"You know, Fallon. You remind me of myself...before."

"Before what?"

"Just...before." That flash of agony flickers across her face before it's masked. "Now it's late and it's foggy. Get out of here and drive safe."

"Florence?"

"Yes?"

"Can I ask a personal question?"

"Do I have to answer?"

"When..." I start and stop because I can't quite get the words out. "When it's time, will you join us... after? You've become a friend, and I can't thank you enough for everything you've done." I can't say *after my mother dies.* The words aren't ready to pass my lips, just like I'm not ready to let my mother go from my heart.

Her blue eyes dampen and sadness overtakes her countenance. "Without question."

I open my mouth, but no more words of thanks can come out. At a time of desperation, this woman saved me from unknown despair and broken promises that would have irreparably damaged the last few months of my mother's life. Now, I'm about to walk out the doors of her lair unscathed.

Not able to save my mother, but able to make memories to hopefully heal my heart when I look back to our last days together.

Do I need more than that?

No, what I need are the people I love to know so I can finally break down and fall apart. *Sorry, Mama. It's time for me to lean on the people I love to get me through.* In this case, some promises are going to have to be broken.

CHAPTER FIFTY-TWO

Ethan

Conversation Starter: Is there anything you wouldn't do for love?

—Viego Martinez, Celebrity Blogger

THERE SHE IS. FUCK, SHE'S TWO HOURS EARLY.

I snatch up my phone and text Thorn.

ETHAN:
Things are about to go down.

THORN:
Don't. Do. It. Give us another hour.

ETHAN:
I need to tell her it's over in person.

THORN:

Let us confirm. That is an order.

I toss my phone back into the console. "Sorry, Thorn. There's letting you confirm Devil's Lair involvement and the fact my woman didn't come to me before pimping herself out for money."

That's the part I can't let go of. How am I supposed to move past it?

Rage, the likes I haven't experienced since I found out my baby sister was seventeen, pregnant, and left behind in our small town by her boyfriend boils the blood in my veins. I punch the steering wheel repeatedly as she picks her way through the well-lit parking lot. "How could you do this, witch? How could you hide something like this when this was supposed to be it—our end game after five long fucking years?"

I'm almost grateful when Fallon drops her keys and bends down to pick them up because it gives me a moment to get myself under control, to let the cool mask of indifference slip over me. Ultimately, the why doesn't matter. What matters is she did it to us. She torpedoed a hole in us before we ever began.

And I'm about to finish sinking our ship.

Reaching for the handle, I fling open the car door just as she approaches. It startles her into stumbling back, almost tripping over her sneaker-clad feet. I frown. She acts like a well-trained prostitute on the calls as Filia, yet she's wearing a Seven Virtues University sweatshirt and jeans with a worn pair of Converse? Thorn's words niggle at the back of my brain, but I shove them back. Instead, my voice is purely sardonic when I drawl, "Surprise."

I'm taken aback by her reaction, though. Instead of being embarrassed or shocked, her eyes flood with tears. Her lip trembles. Her purse falls to the ground seconds before her body hits mine with the force of a full broadside, slamming me back up against the door of my open vehicle. Fallon's voice warbles, "How did you know I needed you?" as her arms wrap around my waist.

Every protective instinct is telling me something happened inside Devil's Lair, that Fallon's in trouble. Begrudgingly, my arm pulls her closer, knowing that it is a final tribute to our long-lasting friendship more than the woman I believed I was in love with up until a few days ago. Fallon's fingernails score against my back as tears wet my shirt. Instinctively, my arms wrap around her tighter.

Still, I can't tell her everything's going to be all right. I won't offer her lies and platitudes.

Eventually, her weeping subsides and she pulls back enough to lift the hem of her shirt to dab at her eyes. Even having just cried a river of tears, her indigo blue eyes reflect the stars in the Appalachian Mountains. Her long blond hair is loose, flowing freely around her shoulders. I hate myself because a part of me wants nothing more than to sink my fingers into it as I lift her face up to mine to offer her solace.

But that's not why I'm here.

I slide my hands around my back and grip her hands before unlatching them from behind my back. I hold her hands tightly and stare down into her bleak face. "Why, Fallon?"

Her nose scrunches up, transforming pain into confusion. "Why what, E.?"

Her pretend ignorance triggers my fury just as my watch sends me a message from Thorn, "DON'T DO IT! STOP!" I grip her fingers and press her back away from me before coldness seeps into my voice. "Or maybe I should call you Filia?"

All the color drains from her face. "You know."

"You're damn right I know."

"I can explain." The words are spoken so hurriedly, her tongue trips over them.

"What were you thinking, Fallon?" My voice erupts in an explosion of fury in the quiet night. As soon as it does, the squawking of birds interrupts my next words as they smartly flee. They obviously sense a predator has trapped its prey and is about to move in for the kill. "Did you think I wouldn't find out you were working for those monsters?"

"Monsters?"

Her night-sky eyes widen before they liquify like the moon shining on water. "Please, let me tell you everything—"

I interrupt her hotly. "I don't want to hear your excuses, Fallon. You could have told me."

"I couldn't."

I sneer. "Why? It isn't part of their NDA."

"How do you even know what's part of their...never mind. There are other reasons." She steps forward, hand lifted as if she's going to touch me.

I take a giant step back, maintaining a distance between us. Her luscious lips part. Just as she's about to speak, I cut her off. "You've been lying to me."

"But, my mother—"

"I highly doubt something that serious is happening with Helen or I'd have heard about it. You must think I was born yesterday. Was it an excuse to buy new clothes? Handbags? Jealousy over your friend's newfound wealth finally get to you?" I don't know where these words are coming from, but the impact on Fallon is tremendous.

Her body lurches back with each statement until I'm afraid she's going to trip on a large stone. Fortunately, I'm saved from having to grab her when she shakes herself into awareness. Instead of answering my questions, she asks me one in return. "You're never wrong, are you, Ethan?"

Something curdles in my stomach, but I attribute it to cutting out the part of my heart that's rotting. "This is the kind of stupid choice a kid makes, Fallon. Not the type of sound decision reasoned out by the kind of woman I want to be with. It makes me wonder if what we had was just some down and dirty sex we needed to get out of our systems."

Fallon's expression shows me nothing. Instead, she stares at me, eyes tracing over every feature. Not saying a word. Uncomfortably, I finally hiss, "What are you doing?"

Her voice vibrates with something I can't quite name. There's a hush in the nature swirling around us, as if it's waiting for the crescendo of our implosion. When Fallon speaks, I'm certain people miles away can hear her despite the faintness of the words. "I hope you'll remember this moment as your before and after for the rest of your life. Of what you could have had with me and what you threw away by accusing me instead of asking me why I worked here in the first place. Because that never occurred to you, did it, Ethan?"

Without waiting for my answer, she races to the driver's side of her car, gets in, and engages the locks. Something like dread slithers through my gut when she turns over the engine and backs out of her spot—almost running over my foot in the process.

It could be seconds, minutes, fuck I might have been standing there for hours before I got into my own car. Reaching for my phone, I see there are ten missed messages from Thorn. All of them say the same thing.

THORN:

Whatever you do, DO NOT confront your girl.

My head slams back against the headrest. Too fucking late.

And after what I said just now, there's no way I can call her mine.

Not anymore.

CHAPTER FIFTY-THREE

Fallon

Heaven, hell. Some days they're mirrors of one another.

Especially if you live in Manhattan during rush hour.

—StellaNova

"My uncle did what?" Austyn's fury is palpable. Before I can answer, she pulls out her phone and sends a text.

"Who were you messaging?" I ask wearily. It's only been a few hours since Austyn let herself into my apartment

"My mother. I told her under no circumstances was she to share she's on her way here."

I glare at her. "Austyn—"

She shrugs unrepentantly at having shared the information with her mother. "Would you have kept it from Helen if it was my mother lying in that hospital bed?"

I can't lie. "No."

My best friend leans over and clasps my hand. "You've been there for me for the best and worst times of my life. Let me return the favor. Mama won't go see your mother until the end, but you'll have her nearby for support."

I stare at our entwined fingers, remembering when I met the girl who lived a few houses away in Kensington, Texas and knew she was going to be my best friend. At the time, Austyn was dressed in torn jeans, Converse Chucks, and a T-shirt that proclaimed she loved Brendan Blake. Her long hair was in a mass of braids which was pulled away from a face with fierce blue eyes. Her first words, after asking my name, were, *"What kind of music do you like?"*

I nodded down at her T-shirt and her smile burst across her face. "That's a good enough place to start."

"What about you?"

She cocked out a hip and grinned—something about her very attitude, those eyes, and her smile vaguely familiar but then I recall Mama pointing out Austyn's mama the other day. I brushed aside my musings as she said, "Want to come with me to a concert at the park? It's Founder's Day."

I stared at her blankly. "What's Founder's Day?"

She grabbed my hand. "It's only the most relaxed day around this prissy town. Say you'll come with me, Fallon."

I grinned at the exuberant pixie and dragged her behind me as I shouted, "Mama? I'm going to Founder's Day with a new friend."

My mother came to the door. "Oh, hello. I'm Fallon's mother."

Austyn held out her hand and introduced herself. "It's nice to meet you, Ms. Brookes. I'm Austyn Kensington."

I sputtered, "Kensington? Like where we're living?"

She shrugged. "It's no big deal."

If she didn't want to make hay over the fact this celebration was about her family, I wasn't about to. "Is that cool, Mama?"

"Sure, sweetheart. Just be home by supper."

Austyn waved to my mother before pointing to a field at the end of the street. "If we go through there, we can cut through my Gramps's yard. He won't mind and it won't take us long at all to get to the town center."

"Cool." Along the way, I found out Austyn's mother was at work and this was the first summer she wasn't "Tethered to one of her uncles' hips."

"What does your mama do?"

"Now? She's a doctor."

"She must be super smart."

"She's so much more than that." A shadow flits across Austyn's face before she stops walking and faces me, hands on her hips. "Listen, let me just get it out there. I'm bullied a lot."

Anger boiling beneath my skin sets my cheeks flaming. "Why?"

"Because the 'good' people of this town think it's an outrage that Dr. Paige Kensington had a baby when she was seventeen and wouldn't name the father." Austyn's body language dares me to say a word about her mother but something inside me relaxes.

I blurt out the first thing that comes to my mind upon hearing Austyn's tale of woe. "You don't have a dad too?"

"Seriously, Fallon, I...wait. Too? What happened to yours?"

"Car accident."

Austyn hooks her arm in mine and we resume walking. "How did you end up here?"

"Mama got a job in Austin...hey. Were you named after where you were born?"

She groans. "Can we save that story for another day?"

I grin. "Sure." I'm about to say more when we approach an enormous barn. Coming to the side, my voice whispers, "Whoa."

She winks, completely irreverent. "That's what we say to the horses."

"Austyn, do you have to check with someone before you're friends with me?"

Her dark brows wing upward. "Fallon, I love people for who they are, not what they have nor what they do."

Coming out of the memory, I find Austyn's concerned face with her now infamous rainbow hued hair flopping forward. "What were you thinking about?"

"The day we became friends. The things you said to me."

"Which part?"

"That you love people for who they are, not what they have nor what they do?"

Austyn swears ripely.

I'd let Austyn read the years' worth of texts between myself and Ethan before I told her what happened. It gave me time to go shower and wash the slimy feeling of being dirty off my skin. Pulling my knees to my chest, I lower my head and sob.

Austyn scoots closer and murmurs, "Men are assholes."

Sniffling, I manage, "Not all men. Just your uncle."

She amends her statement. "Uncle Ethan is an asshole."

"Promise me you won't tell him about why I did this." She hesitates. I turn ferocious eyes on her. "Promise me, Austyn."

"I promise...until after."

"Fair enough." Following a long silence, I whisper, "I gave up my pride in an attempt to save my mother's life and lost the man I love."

"Then I just have one thing to say to you."

"What's that?"

"It's the same thing you said a long time ago."

My head cocks to the side.

"Forgive me for paraphrasing, but the situation calls for it."

I wait while she clears her throat. "You'll be fine. You want to know how I know? Because no matter what, I'll be right by her side. Fallon doesn't need fame or fortune. She just needs love to heal. She's been my best friend since we were fifteen."

Tears fall down my face unheeded as I recall the words I said to Austyn's therapist when she was hospitalized after the car accident. I can't speak. "Let me not forget my favorite."

Swiping madly beneath my eyes, I push out, "What's that?"

"You fell in love with a douchebag. Someone you're better off not having in your life." Then her mask of evil fades, leaving her just as devastated by her uncle's actions as I am. "He's going to regret making you hurt, Fal."

If only I thought he would care. Instead, I lean forward, wrap my arms around my best friend, and rely on her to help replenish my strength since all of mine was depleted.

CHAPTER FIFTY-FOUR

KENSINGTON, TEXAS

Ethan

Saratoga Springs, N.Y. CEO Leanne Miles is pleased to announce a new internship program for Castor Industries. One internship per semester per location will be granted. Details regarding the application process must be *located* by applicants on the Castor website. The information is not under the standard 'Careers' link.

—Castor Newsroom

IT'S TWO DAYS LATER. I'VE STAYED DRUNK MOST OF THE TIME AND finally, after coming up for air, I reply to Thorn. What he tells me has me retching over the bowl. After rinsing my mouth out, I croak, "What?"

Thorn's voice is unmistakably cold when he replies, "I told you to wait for a reason."

"She wasn't there? Not for any of the calls?" My hand nudges my mouse to the side, waking my computer up. There she is, beautiful and smiling. Not blank and emotionless the way I left her two days ago in the parking lot of Devil's Lair.

"Not. A. Single. One. Qɘza triple checked her personal cell's movement. Although her extension was used, she, herself, was only at Devil's Lair for a few hours at night." A sneer enters his voice. "You know, long enough to field a few calls, including yours."

"Don't. It was part of a job."

"Did you tell her your role in it?"

My silence is the only answer that's needed. Thorn sneers, "Seems she wasn't the only one keeping secrets, was she, Ethan?"

"My secrets were classified!" I shout.

"There are ways you could have told her without blowing up national security if you'd come to me, but no. Not the great Ethan Kensington. Gee, doesn't this sound familiar. Isn't this why you quit the Agency in the first place? Found taking orders too restricting—that is the line of bullshit you threw at me, wasn't it?"

I wince, knowing every word he's hurling at me with perfect precision is the truth. There's no use in trying to argue because to try to use words against my former boss in this mood is fruitless. "She's in the clear?"

"She's so far clear, you have no idea." Thorn's anger is so hot I can feel it singe through the phone lines. Not since Qɘza went missing years ago have I heard him this livid. He takes several deep breaths before he regulates himself. "Consider yourself blessed if she ever speaks to you again."

Something sours in my stomach and tries to crawl its way up my throat. "Thorn..."

"Let alone forgive you."

"Tell me," I plead.

"You don't deserve to know. And don't try to get into her file. I've already had Qɘza flag anything to do with her or her family."

That makes me shoot straight up in my chair. He wouldn't do that without good reason. What is it that Thorn knows that I don't? He doesn't pause long enough for me to ask, instead demanding, "Did she share anything useful with you?"

Just her agony, her devastation. My voice is robotic when I give him a "No."

"Why not, Ethan?"

The memory of the way I tore into Fallon causes me to rub my hand against my chest in agony. For the past few days, I'd thought the organ that used to live there was gone. It turns out it was just in stasis while I mourned. *What must Fallon be feeling?*

"Why would Ms. Brookes be feeling anything other than an extreme desire to learn how you knew she was working there?" Thorn's low warning can be heard across the phone lines.

I swallow to shift the lump in my throat so I can respond. "She meant everything to me, Thorn." That's not quite right. Fallon is everything. I just forgot that for a moment in my very real fury over who she's been working for.

How she's been supporting herself.

Instead of giving her a chance to explain, I just went for the jugular. Knowing Fallon the way I do and her innate honesty, it wouldn't surprise me if her mother already knows about her daughter's association with Devil's Lair.

As honest as the day is long, Fallon wouldn't do something so farfetched as blackmail a Middle Eastern royal family member. Christ, I open the file and look at her access rights. She didn't have the ability to see who her clients were.

Then what drove me to attack her? The answer is as simple as my racing heart. I was jealous of her sharing even that little bit of herself with strangers—even with me.

I face-palm myself and want to see if it's a physical possibility to kick my own ass.

"I'm going to kick it for you," Thorn grunts, letting me know I've been speaking some of my thoughts aloud.

"I almost wish you would."

"You failed to do *what I ordered you to do* and wait for confirmation. Hence, you blew what could have been a necessary in."

I cringe before admitting, "You're right."

"And Ethan?"

"Yes?"

"Just for the record, had you waited until Qəza confirmed, you would have learned your Fallon was at her museum job for every single threat. We confirmed they were sent from inside the building when she wasn't within ten miles of the place. Maybe you wouldn't have blown up your personal relationship with the pretty little blond in the meanwhile." Thorn lodges the knife he's holding into my heart a little more before he disconnects the call.

I lean forward and brace my elbows against my knees knowing I didn't just cut my nose off to spite my face. I carved my heart out and ran over it back and forth with a tank. I can only imagine what Fallon must be feeling if I'm feeling this way.

Pulling up our text string, I send her one.

ETHAN:
I'm sorry, Fal. It was a huge shock.

ETHAN:
I found out about it because of something I'm working on that I'm not at liberty to discuss.

ETHAN:
I'd like to fly back out so we could talk about this in person.

ETHAN:
I truly want to make amends.

ETHAN:
Fal, baby. Please. Give me a chance to explain.

As quickly as I'm sending texts, I don't realize each and every message is coming back one at a time with an angry "Not Delivered" notification. My hands shake when I realize the implications immediately. "She blocked me."

Furious as Fallon was with me six months ago for not sharing with my family she and I had a friendship that existed outside the confines of our family parameters, she still never blocked me when she refused to talk to me for those two weeks. For her to have done so now tells me she doesn't want to listen to any apologies. She wants me out of her life.

Right now, I can't say I blame her.

"If I'd just let her speak, maybe this mess could have been avoided."

CHAPTER FIFTY-FIVE

SEVEN VIRTUES, NORTH CAROLINA

Fallon

Per the Mayo Clinic, broken heart syndrome is a heart condition often brought on by stressful situations and extreme emotions. It is usually temporary.

Usually.

—The Fireside Psychologist

I'M DESPERATELY TRYING TO KEEP MY MOTHER TETHERED TO THIS world. I'll do anything, say anything, to prolong a life that's being cut far too short, but there's one thing I know: the love flowing between us will last forever. I lay my head next to her hand and by a miracle, she manages to weakly thread her fingers through the crown of my hair. The memory of how she'd do something just like this when I was a little girl prompts me to ask a question I used to ask when I did anything to beat back the time to go to sleep.

Now, I'm trying to keep her talking as long as possible. "Mama, tell me again about Papa."

There's a weak cough. Out of the corner of my eye, I catch Paige reaching for the cup of water to offer Mama a sip. She rasps, "Thank you."

Paige murmurs a response and then slips back into the shadows. Mama continues to stroke my hair. "My Herb."

I pull up a mental image of my father. Tall, dark, with piercing blue eyes like mine, my memories of Herbert Brookes are little more than a man in pictures. But he was very real to my mother. "I'll never forget the first time I saw him."

"Which was when, Helen?" Paige asks.

I twist my head, uncaring if my hair becomes a nest of knots. I want to see my mother's smug little smile one last time when she admits, "When I"— her coughing interrupts her—"saw him at a bar. He was playing the guitar on stage. Snuck..." Another cough. "In to see him. Underage."

I can't prevent the giggle that escapes at the shock on Paige's face as her eyes bounce between the two of us—likely comparing our enjoyment of older men. "How much older was he?"

Then, because I can't help myself, I tease both Austyn's and my mother. "Mama doesn't enjoy her men to be as—seasoned—as I enjoy mine, Paige."

Mama's dull eyes brighten for a moment at me revealing my truth. Austyn cackles, but Paige doesn't get it, judging by the confusion written on her face. I ask my mama, "Did he fall for you right away?"

She wets her lips. "He...made fun...of me. Herb...hoped... I had more of a clue than my...twin."

Austyn gasps in outrage. "What twin?"

"Helen? You have a sister?" Paige is appalled as she glances around the room to not see another family member.

I grin. Since I know this story by heart, I help my mother tell it. "She doesn't. He was trying to flirt with her."

"What?" and "I don't understand" come out simultaneously.

"Yellow...suit," my mother manages before she nudges her oxygen cannula back down into place.

"Yellow plaid suit," I correct her. "With her blond hair and yellow plaid suit, my father was trying to compliment her by saying she looked like Alicia Silverstone."

At that point, both Paige and Austyn put it together and laugh. I stroke my hand up my mother's arm. "You gave him hell."

"Sure...did."

"He loved you for it," I remind her.

It takes her a few before she murmurs, "I was never sure why me."

"I know." I've said the same thing ever since she told me the story for the last twenty years. I know exactly why my father fell in love with my mother. He fell in love with the heart that was as bright as her trendy yellow plaid suit.

Her lips curve. "Half the girls in that bar were in love with him."

"He never saw anyone but you after he laid eyes on you the first time," I remind her, reaching back and capturing her hand with mine. I bring her hand to my cheek, nuzzling against it.

"He loved you, Fallon."

I swallow hard because the few pictures of my father and me showed he did indeed love me. He worshiped my mother and adored me. I searched for that expression in the eyes of every man I met and never came close to seeing it until Ethan. At least before. Now? Nothing will ever be the same.

Her hand falls away limply. My heart turns over in fear until I realize the *beep, beep* of her heart monitor is still going. A whoosh of air releases. "She fell asleep."

Austyn comes over to me and wraps her arms around me from behind. "You should try to get some too."

"I'll just doze."

"Fallon, you have to get some rest sometime," Paige admonishes me.

I shake my head vigorously. I know if I sleep, I'll end up back in the Devil's Lair parking lot, dying. And really, isn't it bad enough I'm going to have to bleed out a second time in such a short period of time? Do I really need to relive the death of my happily ever after while my once upon a time is taken from me?

CHAPTER FIFTY-SIX

KENSINGTON, TEXAS

Ethan

Brendan Blake pulled his niece through marriage, Grace Bianco, up on stage at Madison Square Garden tonight. Shocking the crowd, the two belted out a rendition of the Luke Bryan/Karen Fairchild duet, "Home Alone Tonight" that blew the roof off the place!

Who is Grace Bianco? Well, for one, she is a practicing anaplastologist. Also, the brilliant beauty is one of the Amaryllis heirs.

And she's not taken how?

—Sexy & Social, All the Scandal You Can Handle

TWO DAYS PASS, AND NOTHING ABOUT THEM IS GOOD DESPITE THE SUN streaming in my windows. In my mind, I'm haunted by Thorn's words.

What did I do?

Did I really act too hastily?

Was Fallon's worst crime working in a place where she sold her voice?

Then bitterness swamps through me again. I lift my leg and kick over a chair. "She knows our family. She should have come to me if she needed money."

But what if she couldn't? An insidious voice taunts me.

"That can't be right. There's nothing Fallon hasn't shared with me," I argue with myself. I just can't escape the memories of her trying to press in on me from all sides.

I snatch up my phone, desperate for contact. Any contact. Even if it's for her to tell me to get the hell out of her life.

I try texting her again to no avail.

"Where are you, witch? What are you doing?"

CHAPTER FIFTY-SEVEN

SEVEN VIRTUES, NORTH CAROLINA

Fallon

Every year, on the anniversary of my grandmother's passing, my grandfather and I drive to his cabin in Maine. We sit beneath the stars and look for the brightest one we've never seen with the naked eye.

We claim that is her reaching through to us from the celestial barrier that separates us from our loved ones after their passing. Grief and the bittersweet recriminations that are associated with it never truly disappear.

Much like new stars.

—StellaNova

Two Weeks Later

A WARM ARM WRAPS AROUND MY SHOULDER AS I STAND, LOOKING down at my mother's urn and the picture Austyn and Paige helped me pick to display next to it. It's from my Seven Virtues graduation and we're both beaming, laughing and sharing a secret in our eyes and with the quirk of our lips.

It was the way I grew up, always knowing she'd be there for me.

"How am I supposed to go on without her?" I ask Paige, knowing she's the one who came up to stand by my side.

"By embracing every moment, darling." Austyn's mother turns me to face her until she can cup my face. I want to flinch when Ethan's green eyes bore into mine but I control the impulse. "You heard her say that the other night."

I did. It was a few days before Mama succumbed to her cancer. Paige, Austyn, and I were camped out in Mama's hospice room like it was Austyn's and my freshman year at UT. Since we never knew when she'd be cognizant, we made certain one of us was always with her. Also, we transformed the room to resemble her living room as much as possible, bringing in Mama's favorite afghans, framed photographs, and munchies and drinks.

At one point, Mama—in one of her more lucid moments—asked Paige, "Will you look out for her?"

Paige leaned over and kissed my mother's cheek. "Helen, you don't even have to ask."

Mama's eyes welled up with tears. She shot a furtive glance at me before sharing, "She's in love..."

I jumped in at that point. "There's no need to go into that."

Mama frowned. "All I was going to ask is—should something come of it—if Paige would walk you down the aisle."

Christ, that moment. I ran a hand over my heart, trying to stop the bleeding that wouldn't stem. Austyn leaped up from her chair and guided me away from our mothers. My sobs couldn't be controlled.

In such a short period, I had everything, and it all blew away like dandelion seeds in the wind. Nothing more than wishes and dashed hope. A before and after.

That's all my life's come down to lately.

I push myself into Paige's arms. Even as the tears overwhelm me, I feel Austyn wrap her arms around my back in an effort to hold me together as we get through this short memorial before I figure out a way for my life to move on.

To embrace the after.

I'm uncertain how long we're standing there when there's a knock on the frame. "Ms. Brookes?"

I pull back and go to swipe beneath my eyes but Paige is at the ready with tissues. "Yes?"

"Guests are beginning to arrive."

I dab at my eyes as Austyn and Paige do the same. Uncaring if it might be selfish, I take one more moment, lean down, and press my lips against my mother's urn. If I close my eyes hard enough, maybe I can will myself back to before.

Later that evening, we're sitting at Mama's where we held the post service reception for her few coworkers and mine who came. Having long kicked off our shoes, I tuck my feet under my rear when Paige comes out of the kitchen with a bottle of wine and three wineglasses. After filling them, she passes one to Austyn and me, then lifts her glass and toasts, "To Helen. For never giving up."

I tap my glass against hers and Austyn's before I take a long pull of my drink.

It's then Paige asks me, "Are you ready to tell me why you didn't come to us the moment you knew she was ill?"

With a sigh, I relay my mother's wishes. Paige doesn't get irate. Instead, her lips quirk. "If I didn't have my husband or family, I'd likely feel the same. I'm not upset, Fallon. I just wanted to understand. Now, what about bills?"

Austyn slants me a furtive glance. I scoff and jerk my head in her direction but address Paige. "You mean the little prodigy didn't tell you?"

"She hinted at something unorthodox, but I'm not quite certain what that means."

Taking another drink, I tell Paige about Devil's Lair, how the proprietress was one of my former customers at the bar I used to work at. Her jaw drops. "You're kidding. They paid for your mother's medical treatment?"

"I never received a dime. In fact, they let me go from my contract early when...when..." I take another drink of wine.

"When they learned your mother wasn't going to make it?" Paige says as gently as possible.

Tears burn my eyes, but I manage to say, "Yes."

Paige takes a sip of her own drink. "Unorthodox, yes. But honest work, Fallon. You didn't commit any felonies. You had a job, and you worked hard in addition to maintaining your curator position and caring for an ailing mother. That just further demonstrates your incomparable strength as a woman."

Austyn's hand comes down flat against the wood coffee table before she hisses, "That's not what Uncle E. said."

"Austyn, don't," I plead.

"Ethan? What on earth does he have to..." Her eyes dart between her daughter and me. I can practically see the wheels turn in her mind, and when they stop on the correct combination, all the secrets are exposed like a slot machine spilling its coins. Her eyes widen in shock before she takes a longer drink of wine. "I see."

Resigned to explaining it to her, I shoot Austyn a filthy look. "We started out as friends."

"Most good relationships do," Paige remarks.

"What about the shitty ones?" Austyn mumbles, earning a stink eye from me.

Mentally giving her the finger, I explain to Paige the high and low points of my relationship with Ethan. "It changed for both of us after Austyn's accident. We were each other's rocks."

I take her through the different stages over the years—Ethan's jealousy, my own hurt he hadn't shared our friendship. "I told him he made me feel like his dirty little secret."

Austyn mutters something rude about her uncle beneath her breath. Her mother snaps, "Austyn!"

"We haven't got to the worst part yet, Mama," she warns her.

Paige guzzles some more wine and refills her glass, topping off both of ours. "Keep going."

I catch Paige up on how our relationship shifted—how we evolved. Despite her being okay with this, she still lifts her hands to her ears and chants, "La la la, I do not want to hear about my brother sexting."

"Deal with it, Mama. Once I figured it out, I had to," Austyn offers her no quarter.

"How long did you know, my darling daughter?"

Austyn chews on her lip before answering. "About her crush? Years. Fallon's always had a thing for older men."

I bob my head. "Truth."

Paige shoots a grin in my direction. "At least you have good taste."

The wine in my mouth turns bitter. "I *had* good taste, Paige."

"Fair enough. When did it become more between you two?"

"Truth?"

"Always."

"I think things changed the night of our graduation party." At their combined gasp, I hold up my hand. "Nothing happened. It was just Ethan who started looking at me differently."

Austyn pretends to hurl even as her mother tosses a pillow at her head. Austyn gasps. "Mama. For shame. You could have knocked over the wine."

Paige narrows her green eyes thoughtfully. "Now that you mention it, Fallon, I recall the shift. There was this look he'd get when your name was mentioned."

"Oh, wait. Let me demonstrate!" Austyn declares gleefully. She proceeds to imitate a basset hound. Just the sight of her yanking her chiseled cheeks down and her overly exaggerated pout causes me and Paige to snicker. Austyn winks at me before pointing out to her mother, "I wouldn't be laughing too hard there, Mama. You and Dad wore the same expression on your faces when you were falling for one another. Discreet you were not."

Rolling her eyes at her oldest child, Paige probes delicately, "So, there was an emotional...connection..."

"Intimacy," I supply helpfully, taking a sip of wine.

Paige scrunches her nose but soldiers on. "Yes, that. You two had that before there was...uh..." Her head tips back, and she asks my mother plaintively, "God, Helen. You didn't leave me *these* instructions. How did you handle this?"

"He wasn't her brother?" Austyn offers helpfully.

Paige glares at her oldest child. I roll my lips inward to gather my control before I relieve Paige of her discomfort. "If it helps, Mama was as shocked as you were at first."

Paige's hand rests on top of mine. "What did she say after that?"

"That Ethan is a fine example that God's a woman because looking at him could cause an orgasm." The words leap from my mouth without me censoring them.

Both Kensington women stare at me like I've lost my marbles before they flop back, screeching with laughter. Paige regains control first and blows a kiss skyward. "Bless you, Helen. Your answer was perfect."

"She trusted me to take care of myself and to protect my heart."

Austyn rests her hand against my leg. "And right now, you're wishing she hadn't?"

It all comes pouring out of me, all the pain and agony I've been subject to in addition to losing Mama. "Everything was perfect even after graduation. There I was, finally happy with Ethan. Then, I found out Mama was sick."

Paige puts the pieces together quickly. "And she refused to allow you to tell us."

"Yes."

"Charles Dickens said, 'There is something in sickness that breaks down the pride of manhood.'"

"Not in Mama."

"No. Yet, maybe your mother was trying to teach you a final life lesson amid her agony."

"What's that?"

Paige reaches over and clasps my hand. "It's one she and I discussed at length, one which Austyn knows as well."

I wait, knowing I'll finally get the answer I've been seeking after so long.

"Your mother wanted you to appreciate that you, Fallon Brookes, are a strong woman with or without a man in your life. You're determined to do what's right and damn the path you have to travel. You'll do anything for those you love. She didn't have time to teach you that herself, so she used the only thing left in this world to give you that lesson—as painful and cruel as it may have been at that moment."

"You really think so?" My voice is small when I question my mother's motives.

"Darling, if I didn't believe that, I wouldn't be sitting right here. Regardless, you have a tribe of people at your back. You don't have to fear what lies ahead of you. You're not alone."

Except I don't have Ethan. Not anymore.

A tear drops into my wineglass, causing a tiny ripple. Squeezing her fingers relentlessly, I tell her about how I cut off communication with Ethan. "I just couldn't handle more...words. Not when his actions showed me I meant so little to him."

"Understandable."

"Do you think I did the right thing?"

"I do. And Fallon?" Paige's expression is pure evil. "I hope every moment he's trying to reach you makes my brother suffer."

"All I did was block him. I know eventually I'll have to end things between us like a mature adult, but with facing losing Mama and then having him ambush me the last night I worked for Devil's Lair at the same time? All that time together, and he didn't trust me."

I swipe at my eyes before admitting, "I haven't told you both the things he said. Needless to say, he gutted me."

Paige looks at Austyn. "Are you speaking with your uncle?"

To my shock, Austyn shakes her head. "I refuse, Mama. With everything they went through before they were intimate, he didn't stop to think, 'This is my friend. Let me find out what's happened to drive her to do something like this?' They weren't some one-night stand at a club. He knew her."

"Yes, he did. And he should have known better."

"I'm sorry, Paige." I feel like I need to apologize for causing this strife in her family.

"Don't be. It's obvious to me Ethan just stopped emotionally maturing before he needed to." She lets out a heartfelt sigh of displeasure that causes Austyn to crack up. "On the other hand, it will make it completely understandable to people why he would be in love with someone at his same level of emotional maturity at such a young age."

Austyn somehow manages to hold her wine upright as she rolls back and forth on the floor, laughing. I'm not quite as amused as my soul feels like it has gaping wounds. I challenge Paige. "You're assuming I'm ever going to want him back."

"After I'm done kicking his ass, you might."

Dear lord, Ethan will have no idea what hit him.

Paige beams at me before holding out the wine. "More wine?"

I exchange my glass for the bottle. "Thank you."

I need to forget my heart's been shattered just for a night.

Tomorrow's soon enough to begin to locate the slivers of pieces.

CHAPTER FIFTY-EIGHT

KENSINGTON, TEXAS

Ethan

Saratoga Springs, N.Y. "They say 'Don't hate the player, hate the game.' Well, it was your choice to play against people better than you."

—Castor CEO Leanne Miles, when asked by a reporter about winning a new software bid.

IT'S BEEN A WEEK AND MY HATRED FOR THORN IS SPIRALING ALONG with my desperation to reach Fallon. He had Leanne pull some of her voodoo magic, so every time I try to search for Fallon, even on the open internet, the results are a bunch of Jimmy Fallon and the Roots classroom instrument videos.

No matter how many different ways I search for information to determine *why* Thorn is so protective and furious, Leanne finds a way to block me on every single one of my devices. The damn hoyden even managed to figure out my move to buy a new laptop and shut me down that way. She's gotten so nasty that she's leaving little notes in my dark web inbox to fully express her disdain.

To: "Whiskey"

From: "Qəza"

Subject: Filia

The first time I met her, I knew she was something special. No one goes for the guy who is a lovable geek but can't drive a Ferrari.

I like her. You're wrong. Therefore, you pay.

Leanne's creative side—a side she once shared with her deceased twin—must have been stirred up. Her next reminder of how I fucked up was in the simplest code ever designed—music lyrics.

To: "Whiskey"

From: "Qəza"

Subject: What you inspire others to create

You think you're a winner, but you're just a mess

Lost in the details, can't even guess

You're playing a game you just can't win

Messed with her heart, man, you're too dim, uh uh

Her third message was much more direct.

To: "Whiskey"

From: "Qəza"

Subject: Back OFF!

Stop trying to dig up information about her. You no longer have that right.

Do not make me come after you.

That one, I wrote back to.

To: "Qəza"

From: "Whiskey"

Subject: Re: Back OFF!

I fucked up. I need to make it right.

Her next email reply was a bunch of laughing emojis followed by:

To: "Whiskey"

From: "Qəza"

Subject: Back OFF!

Wear your body armor. You're going to need it.

Tossing back a slug of water, and not the whiskey I've been sating myself with so I can get some sleep night after night when memories of Fallon bombard me before I sleep, I pull up the text string between us that's gone on for five years. Since she blocked me, I've been re-reading a little at a time trying to figure out if she's given me any indication on how to get back in her good graces.

Last night I reread the section about how I should have been there myself if I was jealous of my older brother holding her so close at my niece's birthday party in New York. "You were right, witch." *Right about so many things, but I never told you that, did I?*

Berating myself, I scan my apartment above my shop, trying to think if there's anything I can bring to convince her of what she means to me. Something that will show her how much I'm sorry? Or will words be enough? I'm still wondering if there's even a possibility of her forgiving me for the shit I spewed?

Then there's the clawing fear she blanks out on me in the same manner she did that night and turns and leaves.

Cursing the fact the earliest flight I can get to Asheville is tomorrow morning, I'm doing everything I can to be prepared to head out the second the family dinner Paige organized at my father's house is over and done. I plan on staying at the airport tonight, placing myself one step closer to her. I don't care if I don't sleep. All that matters is being on Fallon's doorstep the minute she opens her eyes.

Until then, I'm rereading our conversations since her graduation at Seven Virtues, in between the times I'd fly out to see her. Each and every one made me recognize how carelessly I destroyed her trust and, more importantly, her love.

FALLON:

What do you want to do to me?

ETHAN:

I want to bind your hands above your head. I want your eyes covered with the softest silk.

FALLON:

So you want me helpless?

ETHAN:

No. I want you to feel me in ways you've never imagined.

FALLON:

You're making me ache, E

ETHAN:

Join the club, Fal. My dick's so swollen behind my jeans.

FALLON:

Take it out for me...

FALLON:

I want to taste you.

ETHAN:

I think that can be arranged, witch.

FALLON:

Every inch of you from the top of your head, behind your neck, down your back. I want to burn you in my memory.

ETHAN:

What we're doing, it's wrong.

FALLON:

Who is it hurting, Ethan?

ETHAN:

You? I don't want to lead you on, Fal.

FALLON:

Give me some credit, E.

ETHAN:

Fallon...

FALLON:

I can hear that scolding tone, E. Are you thinking about spanking me?

ETHAN:

Damn you, yes. I want to light up that sweet little ass of yours.

FALLON:

I'm leaning over and lifting up the back of my skirt...

Five years. It's been five excruciating years since the vivacious blonde who could charm a rattlesnake off a rock it was sunning on captivated me as if I were her next prey. Yet, she had no idea of the hold she had on me until I pointed that out to her. "Fallon, I swear to you, I'll fix us."

It's a promise, a vow.

One I don't intend on breaking.

After I realized random fucking wasn't going to take away the ache for the one woman I wanted, I gave up having sex since well before that night I blew up at her for taking that friendly photo with my brother. Instead, I realized no other woman would do.

Hurling my phone away from me so it lands on the couch, I lift the water and down another guzzle . *How the hell was I supposed to know what was really going on? That's easy, you fucktard. You knew her. She's not the type to expose herself like she does with you to anyone else.*

Now my subconscious decides to make an appearance. I fall to my knees in agony because I do know her. I know her drive, her determination, her absolute ethical morality.

You blew it to hell instead of asking her why she was working there. I finally admit the truth to myself because I am terrified of being hurt again.

Thus I come to the crux of my problem—being hurt by women. Being devastated in the wake of their leaving me. More recently, the aftereffects of being lied to amid terrible circumstances I can't control. And finding out what truly happened to my sister and her husband, even taking the steps to fall for Fallon scared the piss out of me. Then to realize she, too, was lying to me was enough for me to abandon the relationship—and her. Only to find out I was the douchebag because I didn't give her all of me.

Including my trust. That's not Fallon's fault. It's because that was taken from me long before I became involved with her. Still, she's paying the price for it.

I cross the room and pick up a framed photograph of my brother and me with our arms wrapped around a beautiful woman, equally enthralled with her as she was with us. We had no way of knowing that just days later, she'd be taken from us.

Our mother, Melissa.

For years, our father told us she'd died as the result of a cut she didn't treat properly from a fence. It caused an infection they couldn't administer the proper antibiotics to because she was pregnant with our baby sister, Paige. Apparently, after Paige was safely delivered, they tried to do their best to rescue our mother and failed.

It was a lie.

She was in a brutal car wreck caused by a drunk driver the day before Paige was born. But the lies and betrayals told for close to forty years after almost broke our family apart. I learned from him the truth is as plain as the nose on your face. That most people don't have honor or integrity, and won't keep their word.

Those are the life lessons I learned at Tyson Kensington's knee.

Staring down at the picture of my mother, Jesse, and me, I wonder aloud, "What would you have taught us, Mama? How would you have taught us all to believe in doing the right thing, no matter the cost. To be honorable. To seek out the truth regardless of how hard it cost me personally?" Then I blurt out, "What would you have thought about me and Fallon?"

A wave of shame washes over me when I realize I've held this photo a hundred times since Fallon and I became an us, yet I've never asked my mother that question. She once accused me of being ashamed of her, but she had it wrong. I'm the one she should be ashamed of, with a father who would have sooner let his family fall apart than admit to his own culpability.

Fallon's everything with her unending capability to bring out the best in everyone around her—including me. From the moment I met her indigo blue eyes in my rearview mirror, she's been the one person I haven't wanted to disappoint, also making her the one person I can't quite quit. She's the antidote to superficial relationships and meaningless conversations.

She's the one person I need in my life.

And I threw her away because of what?

Forcing myself to relive the last few weeks, I go over every piece of evidence. I come to the same conclusion *Qəza* did—I didn't piece together the facts. Most importantly, I didn't factor in the woman I've known for the last five years.

I grab my phone, knowing exactly when we had this conversation.

ETHAN:

So, are you living it up with every Phi Beta Douchebag there is?

FALLON:

<yawn> They're more like Pansy Boring Doormats.

ETHAN:

Cold, witch.

FALLON:

Truth, E.

ETHAN:

What do you want out of a man then?

FALLON:

You said it.

ETHAN:

Want?

FALLON:

A man. I want someone who I can rely upon to build a family with. I want the kind of love that scores my soul.

ETHAN:

When you find it tell me.

FALLON:

You think you haven't seen it? What about your sister?

ETHAN:

Fair.

FALLON:

There might be another…

ETHAN:

Who?

FALLON:

Lips are sealed.

ETHAN:

Keeping secrets, witch? I'll get it out of you, eventually.

FALLON:

Maybe you will, maybe you won't.

FALLON:

It boils down to this, E.

FALLON:

I what my mother had. It may not have lasted forever, but what she felt for my father was worth every emotion she buried with him.

> **FALLON:**
> What? Nothing to say?

> **ETHAN:**
> I'm trying to rationalize if that kind of love exists.

> **FALLON:**
> That's your problem.

> **ETHAN:**
> Problem?

> **FALLON:**
> Love isn't rational. Neither is what you'll do to keep it.

"Christ, I had the answer the whole fucking time." My phone drops out of my hands and clatters to the floor, unharmed. I let out a scream of primal rage, my fury at myself so encompassing I can't believe I didn't put the pieces together.

Something's happened and Fallon's trying to protect someone she loves. That's why she took the job at Devil's Lair. Swooping down, I frantically text Thorn only to receive a bunch of applause emojis in response.

> **THORN:**
> Now, if only you'd thought like this before you made an unmitigated ass of yourself.

> **ETHAN:**
> Fuck you, Thorn. Tell me what happened.

Fallon wants exactly one thing and it has nothing to do with the gross accusations I flung at her in the parking lot of Devil's Lair. She wants love. Because of my knee-jerk reaction, I've sentenced myself to hell—a life without Fallon in it in any capacity.

Knowing my demands are likely to go unanswered, I try to call my niece. Then, on a Hail Mary attempt, I call my sister. Both of them ignore me— par for the course the last few days. I'm about to call Paige's husband when I realize the whole family will be here in a matter of hours to celebrate my father's birthday.

That will be soon enough.

I hope.

CHAPTER FIFTY-NINE

Ethan

Conversation starter: Does some food taste better the next day?

—Fab and Delish

THE MOMENT I ENTER THE ROOM, THE FEMALE CONTINGENCY OF MY family—my sister and niece—proceed to sharpen their emotional claws against my heart by talking nonstop about their time this past week with Fallon in Seven Virtues.

"What the hell do you mean, you've been in Seven Virtues?"

Austyn, never one to watch her smart mouth, snarks, "Have you ever heard of the feature called 'Find My'? We do share a family plan. If you were so determined to locate where I was, you could have found me at any time."

Fuck, if she doesn't have me by the short hairs. While I'm stewing in my own incompetence, Austyn has the audacity to show photos to everyone, but she snagged her phone back before it reached me.

Sending me a vicious smile, something I'd have attributed to her father, except her mother's wearing one just like it, Austyn drawls, "You don't want to see photos of Mama and me hanging around with a stupid kid who makes stupid choices. Wouldn't want to waste your time, Uncle E."

As much as part of me wants to strangle her, the other part of me can't help the surge of gratefulness she flew to see Fallon. Still, if Austyn's trying to wound me, she can't. She has no idea of the level of pain I'm in.

That's when a concerned Jesse asks Austyn, "How's Fallon holding up since her mama's memorial?"

My head snaps in his direction as my jaw drops. Did he say what I think he just said?

No. My mind rejects Jesse's words as truth. That is, until Austyn's head bows, the light of battle dissipating from her bright blue eyes. "About as well as can be expected. It's only been a few weeks." When she finishes speaking, her head falls to her husband's shoulder, seeking support from a loved one—knowing Mitch will be there. The way I wasn't there for Fallon.

Oh god. Helen's gone.

The cogs of my brain stutter to life again and as they're ca-chunking they're also making my stomach churn.

What have I done?

Jesse mutters, "If I'd have known, I'd have been there."

Paige leans over and grips his hand. "It's all good, Jess. Helen was specific about who she wanted there. She didn't want to add any *further* burden to Fallon." Nodding at her own husband before aiming a tender look at her daughter. "Just imagine if Beckett showed up?"

As I'm trying to process the words, my fork, having just stabbed a bite of food, clatters to the plate, forgotten. "She lost her mother? How? Was it sudden?"

Austyn and Paige ignore me. My only ally in the room is apparently my father, who is wearing an expression that is just as bewildered as my own. Mitch answers us both, but only after he sees Tyson's confusion. "Cancer.

Despite every hump Fallon busted to afford the cost of treatment not covered by her mother's insurance, she was too far gone by the time it was found. Her body couldn't handle it."

My hand is already itching to reach into my pocket for my cell to demand Leanne or Sam find a way to lift this ridiculous block Fallon dropped between us so I can offer her my condolences when my niece's hostile voice freezes my movements. "I'm just so grateful she was able to spend those last few weeks with Helen without any interruptions. She left her second job—you know, the one where she worked at Devil's Lair?"

Just hearing the name of that organization has me erupting. "You knew?"

Austyn eyes skew me like icicles. "Of course I did. In fact, she never actually received a paycheck from them. They paid for all her mother's medical expenses in lieu of her taking money while she was alive. The owner urged her out when it became apparent Helen was going downhill."

In my head, over and over, I see Thorn's desperate text right before the one I found of Fallon's.

> THORN:
>
> Let us confirm. That is an order.
>
> FALLON:
>
> Love isn't rational. Neither is what you'll do to keep it.

She wasn't working there because of the childish reasons I accused her of, she was trying to save her mother's life. I don't realize I've spoken aloud until Paige's soft "Yes" slams into me with the power of a death strike. I shove back from the table, even the few inches separating me from the wood's edge too close for me to be comfortable to breathe.

This is what Thorn was keeping from me. I've never wanted to murder someone so badly in my life as I did my former boss, but despite him holding back the information, I know where the real blame squarely sits.

On me.

"God. Oh god," I rasp. My body shakes under the urge to strike something, the need to, what? Cry? Yeah, that's a distinct possibility. I threw away something good and precious.

"Ethan, son? Are you all right?"

I may never be all right again. Still, I need to know what my family does. My eyes skewer my niece in pieces. "You knew what she was doing?"

Silence descends around the table. I'm certain Mitch is debating how to beat me senseless when Austyn hisses, "Why don't you share with us what *you* think she was doing, Uncle Ethan?"

I shove my chair back so hard it falls behind me. "The worst, okay? I damn well assumed the worst."

Malevolence gleams in her eyes as she drawls, "I already know that. Want to know how? I *asked.*"

Running my hands through my hair, I begin to pace. "Austyn, she works—worked—for a phone sex hotline."

"So what?"

In deference to the assignment, I limit my words. "This particular one is...questionable."

"Questionable, how?"

"I can't share."

She flicks her middle finger at me, dismissing me.

"The fact she was a phone sex operator didn't have you worried?" I shout, needing to redirect some of my righteous pain before I collapse from beneath the weight of it. Surely someone can see where that might have derailed me.

Austyn stares at me, slack jawed. I'm certain I got my point across when she bursts into gales of laughter. "Oh, that's rich. Truly."

"What's so damn funny?"

"Fallon's done nothing more than what I do."

"I think it's a bit *more* than that," I emphasize.

"All she had to do is sell her voice, Uncle Ethan. What's the big fucking difference?"

"You don't have men jacking off to yours," I shout.

"Like hell I don't," my niece purrs.

Her husband growls. "Thanks for that mental image, baby."

"You're a musician!" I bellow.

"So? I still do it for money."

"So did she," I grit out.

"Her reasons behind it are a lot more noble than mine and completely cancel out any potential morally gray ick factors, in my opinion."

I'm about to point them out when Jesse, the fucker, raises his hand. I bite out, "What?"

"I just want to know how you were even aware of it."

"Stay out of this, Jess," I warn him.

Instead of helping, their lack of anger over the revelation about what could have been my and Fallon's coming out only fuels my own. "You don't know everything you think you do about Fallon, Austyn."

Austyn rolls her eyes at me. "Come on, Uncle E. There isn't a thing about Fal I don't know."

"How about the fact I've been talking to her constantly since you two graduated high school?"

My niece snorts in derision. "Like I didn't figure that out? Please. She'd get this stupid ass smile on her face when you'd text her."

My hands slap down on the table before I thunder, "And you were okay with it?"

"As long as you cared about her, then why wouldn't I be?" Austyn confounds me by asking in return.

Even as my sister nods emphatically along with my niece's words, I feel the blood drain from my face. My brother-in-law, Beckett, just shakes his head before offering up his own words of experience. "Ethan? I rarely offer advice as I'm not the best role model—"

"What do you have to say about this?" I snarl.

"If you don't want to wonder what every day of your life could have been like with her, I'd be doing everything possible to fix your mistake. Otherwise, you'll find yourself twenty years later waking up at night grateful you were gifted a second chance."

Without a word, I shove back from the table. Just as I make it to the door, one voice stops me. "Ethan."

God, my father. He hasn't butted in until now other than to ask about Fallon's mother.

I turn my head to meet his. My voice is noticeably cooler when I ask, "Yes?"

"If I had another hour with your mother, I'd give up everything to take it." His eyes harden. "If you're given one, don't be a fool and waste it."

Wincing at the memory of our confrontation in the parking lot of Devil's Lair, I cringe. She's been steeping in pain, agony, and bitterness for the last two weeks. I wonder if there's a chance in hell of getting Fallon to talk to me before she slams the door in my face.

The answer is simple. I didn't trust my heart.

Now, I have to try to get Fallon to listen to me. It's hers to do with what she will.

It always will be hers.

No one else's.

CHAPTER SIXTY

Ethan

DJ Kensington, her husband, and her parents were spotted in their hometown having a beer at a local dive named Rodeo Ralphs. Locally famous for their ghost pepper wings, the three native Texans dove in while being monitored by Kensington's husband.

—Viego Martinez, Celebrity Blogger

FOR YEARS, EVEN AS I FOUGHT AGAINST THE ELECTRICITY THAT simmered between me and Fallon, I never expected to find the depth of the woman beneath the self-deprecating sense of humor, the mocking insinuations, and brilliant mind. All too soon, she disappeared.

Out of my sphere.

She should have been out of my mind, but that wasn't how it worked.

Instead, I found myself consumed with where she was and what she was doing. I had an overwhelming need to stake a claim on her and, in fighting it, lost my damn mind. I wasted years keeping us trapped in between two electronic boxes because I was too stupid to realize the people who loved us, truly loved us, wouldn't give a damn about anything except our happiness. I forced us into assigned roles I'd designated for us out of what? Fear? Fear of what? Falling in love? I did that anyway and look where it got me.

By forcing us to remain captive, I never gave us a chance to become who we were supposed to be. I stole from us our chance at true happiness.

Then, because of my fears, at the first sign of my world crashing down, when I believed she did something that didn't jive with the woman I'd built up on the screen of my phone, I didn't just knock her off the pedestal I'd made out of computer towers and anchored with wires. I took a sledgehammer to the whole monument I'd built her up on. "Overreacted isn't a strong enough word for what you did," I berate myself.

Since I walked out of the family dinner a few nights ago, I've researched the fuck about phone sex operators. Christ, most of them are so clinical about it. It's like they've mentally disconnected themselves from their clients. Is that what Fallon was like with her callers? Thinking of it like that makes what we did together on those calls easier to swallow.

That she picked green because it was easy to remember.

That she chose lace because she happened to be wearing it.

That she used that memory because we'd just talked about it. Even then, she didn't taint it, I realize. She changed it.

Fuck, if what I'm reading is right, she was likely on a treadmill to get the breathless pants out at just the right moment. I'm so disgusted with myself that I want to get on a plane as fast as possible to apologize. If everything I've found is true, what's the worst she did? Talk dirty to some mega-wealthy people to fulfill their fantasies to save her mother's life?

Caused me to get aroused because I *knew* it was her?

My inner voice admonishes me sharply, *Isn't the greater sin yours because you knowingly betrayed her?*

I shove the thought to the back of my mind. First things first, I corral myself. Fallon. She's all that matters and she's in pain. Take care of your woman.

As for what I hurled at her, who the fuck am I to judge if she wanted more money even if it wasn't for the most noble of reasons? After Thorn confirmed Fallon was in no way behind the attempted extortion, I should have had a discussion with her instead of acting like a spoiled man-child.

Again, I hate admitting that motherfucker was right.

Relegated again to donkey work of searching the dark web for more information about the trafficking ring and Devil's Lair, I can't ask for updates the way I demanded them before.

I royally fucked myself with my woman and my employer because of what?

I mumble, "Jealousy. Sheer unadulterated jealousy."

Jesse's voice intrudes my thoughts. "Well, it's about time you admitted to it, brother."

My head swivels in his direction and I gape at him.

"You're a fucking fool, Ethan. For whatever you did to have Paige and Austyn so incensed, to have Fallon so unwilling to return to Kensington to heal—"

His words stop my forward momentum. I croak out, "She won't come back?"

He shakes his head. "I asked Paige if getting away from Seven Virtues would be better for her for a little while. Apparently, she and Austyn thought the same thing. Fallon turned them down flat. So congratulations, brother. Whatever you did to her crushed her at the absolute worst moment in time."

"I know." My voice sounds shredded to my own ears.

In facing the facts, I admit the truth. I was a stupid moron, fucking jealous, and hurt for no reason. I haven't shared my source of additional income with Fallon, so why should she? We weren't there yet. Even still, Fallon had reasons—reasons I never took the time to find out about. If she didn't come to me, there must have been a reason.

Considering the moment I made her mine, to me everything I have— especially my heart—became hers. She and I obviously need to talk about more than just my apology for my asinine behavior.

The need to get to Fallon as fast as possible is pressing at me. Hard.

To beg, to apologize. To give her a safe place to grieve.

And when the time is right, to ask for another chance.

CHAPTER SIXTY-ONE

SEVEN VIRTUES, NORTH CAROLINA

Fallon

There is no wrong way to grieve, just as there is no wrong way to live. So long as you honor the person in a way that's healthy.

—Beautiful Today

I'M FACETIMING AUSTYN WHILE CLEANING OUT MY MOTHER'S kitchen. "So, he knows."

"He knows and from all accounts, he's flying to you as fast as a commercial airline will get him there."

The surge of bitterness and resentment that rises through me almost overcomes the sadness that's become my constant shadow. "Why bother?"

"I think you should hear it from him."

"You're assuming I don't take Mama's cast iron skillet and brain him with it." I heft up the item in question and swing it like a tennis racket with a two-handed forehand to show Austyn.

"Now, why would you contaminate something that means so much to you?"

"I'm questioning whether a lot of things mean anything to me right now." I lift the phone to show her the stacks upon stacks of Tupperware that are still in their original boxes. "I'm beginning to think my mother's kitchen cabinets are like Mooney's magical trunk in Harry Potter."

Austyn's eyes bulge. "One...two...six? Six boxes? Are you certain she wasn't selling it?"

I let my legs give out and sit down on the kitchen tile to rest my back against the dishwasher. "No. Not entirely. I haven't hit the office yet. When I do, I'll let you know for certain."

"Find anything interesting?" Austyn asks.

I stretch my arms high above my head and bend forward until my forehead touches the floor. "Yep."

"Like what?"

"Her black box."

"Her what?"

I lift myself up and prop up on my elbows. "Remember when you and I were in college and we swore to each other that if the other one died, no one was allowed into our dorm room until..."

Austyn's face is appropriately horrified. "No!"

"Oh yes. Want to know what was in it?"

"No. Yes! No. What am I saying? Of course I want to."

"Exactly what you'd expect," I drawl. "In no way was I shocked by the lube or the vibrators. I mean, my mother had me at twenty-five. Come on. You should expect to find your own parents..."

"La la la, I can't hear you. The world does *not* need to know if Beckett Miller and Paige Kensington ever had a toy box."

"And there was something else." Just thinking about it causes my lips to curve and my heart to clench simultaneously—a sensation I'm getting used to with every minute that extends between my mother's passing.

"What's that?"

"A letter addressed to me."

Austyn's choking for air. "Your mother left you letters in her toy box?"

Oh, the look on her face is going to be priceless. "Actually, *your* mother left me a letter from *my* mother in her toy box."

Austyn's face turns as purple as her braids. "Shut. The. Front. Door."

"I can't lie."

"Have you read it?"

"Not yet, but it's your mothers handwriting on the envelop."

"Do you want to read it now?" That's my best friend—my ride or die. I know for a fact she's on her way to jump on a plane to head back to New York, but if I need her, she'll stop right where she is—literally—to listen to me read my mother's words aloud.

I'm about to take her up on the offer when the doorbell rings. "If there's a god, she's at the door with my pizza."

"Let me let you go. We're about to board. I'll call you from the plane."

I begin weaving through rooms. "Thank your mama for me."

"Only if I can do it in front of my dad. He'll get a kick out of where she hid the letter and I'll get a kick knowing they're going to have to hide their box better." She murmurs to her husband who barks out a laugh.

"I love you, Austyn. Thank you for being here when I needed you."

"If there's one thing you don't need to thank me for, it's that." The second Austyn disconnects, I pocket my phone and fling open the door.

I wish I'd looked out the side pane to see who was on the other side because standing in front of me is a destroyed Ethan.

I go with my first instinct and immediately tighten the muscles in my arm so I can slam the door in his face.

CHAPTER SIXTY-TWO

Ethan

Who's hungry?

—@PRyanPOfficial

That's your inspired post today?

—Viego Martinez, Celebrity Blogger

Crap. I meant to send that as a text.

—@PRyanPOfficial

There are days, buddy. I just can't with you.

—Viego Martinez, Celebrity Blogger

My hand shoots out to stop the forward momentum of the

door Fallon's determined to use to take off part of my facial features. I immediately begin begging, "Please, witch. Let me offer my condolences."

Her eyes glance off mine before her voice, likely colder than the recesses of space, "Accepted, Mr. Kensington. Thank you for stopping by. Now, please, if you'd be so kind as to remove yourself from this property."

I step closer to her, more drawn to her now than I was the first moment I felt the arc of attraction over five years ago. "Fallon, I'd like to speak with you."

Just then, I'd like to think divine intervention granted me a reprieve or perhaps her mother intervened. A local delivery kid came up, struggling with ten boxes of pizza. "Delivery for 10 Mountain View Circle Terrace."

Fallon opened the door wider, eyes bulging. "I ordered pizza, yes. But I ordered a single pie, not enough to feed the Seven Virtues University basketball team!"

"Lady, once the orders are in my car, they've been validated. It says to deliver ten extra cheese pizzas with pepperoni to this address."

Fallon pulls up her app and shoves her phone in his face. "One! I ordered one pizza. What the hell am I supposed to do with the other nine?"

The kid, obviously immune to irate customers, drones in a bored voice, "You can keep the order or reject it. Those are your options."

"You mean to tell me I can't take one and send the rest back?" She's outraged.

"No."

"Listen, are you keeping the pizzas?"

"Well, I suppose if I want to eat—" she begins only to be cut off.

"Have a nice day." The kid jogs back to his car.

"I'll be calling your manager," she shouts after him, making me want to grin because if it wasn't for all of her years in the retail industry, she likely would have taken this kid's head off.

He should feel grateful. Lord knows, I do because now I can offer, "Do you want help carrying those inside?"

"Where am I supposed to put ten pizzas?" Her voice sounds so bewildered and lost that my heart aches.

"I don't know. Eat them?"

She shoots me a filthy glare that has so much more behind it than nine extra pizzas. I want to recoil from the pain and anger in it, but I persevere when she snaps, "Be grateful you have some use right now, Mr. Kensington, or I wouldn't be letting you past the front door."

"I'll take whatever opportunity is presented to me just to talk with you for five minutes."

"Fine. Get these pizzas into my mama's..." Her head dips to the side and her jaw locks.

I want to sweep her into my arms to offer her a place to release her pain about Helen's death, but I strongly suspect it wouldn't be welcome. Not right now, at least.

"Just get them and follow me," she concludes.

I lift the boxes easily after swinging my laptop bag over my shoulder. "Lead the way, witch."

Abruptly, Fallon comes to a stop somewhere between her mother's formal living and dining rooms. "Let's be clear, *Mister* Kensington. I'm not your witch, your sweetheart, your babe, nothing. I am absolutely nothing to you except some stupid kid you had sex with. Are we clear?"

My heart cracks open with regret. I'm still holding the stupid pizzas when I ask her, "Will you let me apologize?"

"For what?"

"For the things—"

She cuts me off. "We did? For great sex? There's no need." We walk into the kitchen and she lifts half the boxes and places them on the table. Removing the remaining stack from my arms, she places them beside the others before flipping the lid on the top box and taking a piece out.

My stomach growls in protest at the smell of the cheese and spice combination that fills the air. I haven't had more than mini-pretzels and a few Cokes since I boarded the flight in Austin this morning. I'm starving, and the woman I'm in love with is surrounded by dinner for forty yet wouldn't be inclined to offer me a bite of food if giving it to me meant saving me from certain death.

Of that I'm sure.

Lowering the tip of the pizza into her mouth, Fallon reaches for her phone. She fiddles with it for a minute before dropping it on top of the box. After she chews, she glances at it pointedly before she presses it. "You have five minutes, Mr. Kensington. Then I want you to get the hell out of my life and stay out."

I scramble to find words that will convince her to let me stay longer than her five-minute timer. "You could have come to me, Fallon."

She immediately shakes her head. "No, I couldn't."

My brows snap together. "Why the hell not?"

"That's between me and my mother." When she doesn't offer any further reason, I just gape at her. She snaps her fingers beneath my nose to get my attention. "Tick tock. Your time is running out."

"I can't apologize enough, Fallon. You were trying to tell me that night the money you were making at Devil's Lair was for your mother and..."

Bitter laughter escapes her sweet lips. "And what? Nothing's changed."

I emphasize, "Everything's changed."

"Really? Tell me why?"

"Fallon, you were telling the truth."

"I tried to tell you the truth the night you showed up, but you wouldn't let me get a word in edgewise. What does it matter?"

I'm flummoxed. She drops her half-eaten piece of pizza in the box and lashes out at me. "What did you think, Ethan? I'd be so devastated over my mother's death I'd open my arms and accept you back into my life with your worthless excuses and half-assed trust??"

"The only thing I thought about was apologizing to you."

She slams her hand down on the phone to stop the timer. "Then fucking apologize."

"I'm *sorry*, Fallon."

"For what?"

"For thinking you were one of them?"

"One of who?" she snarls.

"One of the people we've been investigating inside Devil's Lair!" I thunder.

It's so quiet in her mother's kitchen I think I hear the grease popping on the still scorching pizzas. I go to clarify my remarks, but Fallon holds up her hand to stop my words. "Let me get this straight."

I nod, a tiny knot of terror forming in the pit of my stomach.

"You were investigating Devil's Lair?" Before I can say a word, she demands, "Yes or no answers, please."

Oh, shit. "Yes."

"And you knew I worked there?"

"Not at..."

"Yes or no," she snaps.

"Yes."

"Instead of asking me about it, you tried to make me bleed by eviscerating me." Before I can provide affirmation, she sneers. "Sorry if the fact I'm still standing offends you."

"Fal..."

She makes a slicing motion in the air. "I'm asking the questions."

I snap my mouth shut and wait. I pray she doesn't go down the path I think she's headed because if she does, it's nowhere good.

Her chest heaving, Fallon stares me dead in the eye. "After knowing me for over five years, after talking to me almost every single day—either via text or phone—you still thought I could be that person? That I was jealous of my best friend in the entire world? The person who was *here* when my mother died. The person whose life-threatening injuries brought us closer. Somewhere in your twisted mind, you gave credence to the shit you accused me of that night?"

My "Yes" is riddled with shame because I did and I can't deny it.

Her head ducks to the side, and she hits the timer to start it again. It starts counting back from thirty-two.

"I suspect in your thorough research you called in to Devil's Lair, didn't you?"

No, no, no. Not this. Anything but this. "Fallon..." I plead.

"Answer the fucking question, Ethan!" she screams.

"Yes."

"Did you like the way I talked to you?" Her voice turns into "Filia's"—a seductive purr.

I can't lie. If I do, she'll never believe me again. "At first, No. Once I realized it was you? Yes."

"You fucking hypocrite."

"What? How can you say that?"

"These people who work there aren't there to get their rocks off. They're there out of need. Do you think they like doing that kind of work? That they want their children to grow up to do that?"

His lips tighten at the corners. "I'll concede some of them are like that."

"Yet you have the goddamn nerve to stand here and convince me they did something wrong? The people who stood by me? That I was wrong because I dared to use my voice to *try to save my mother*. Yet, it's perfectly fine for the high and mighty Ethan Kensington to get hard because he was looking out for the greater good? Fuck you, Ethan. Fuck you and fuck whomever you were working for."

Fallon storms out of the kitchen. I've no choice but to follow her. Still, I can't help but bellow her name to try to stop her.

She whirls on me like I'm fresh chum in shark-infested waters. "Get out of my mother's house."

I lift my hand to touch her cheek, but she slaps my hand away so hard I feel the sting radiate up my arm. Tears fall down her cheeks as she reaches for the handle of the front door. She flings the door open and stands next to it. She points at her mother's porch, a silent demand for me to leave.

Not wanting to push her further, I cross over the threshold. Fallon's tears are still falling fast and furious and I want nothing more than to hold her, to make things right. But I savaged that.

Me.

Not anyone else, not her mother's death.

She reminds me of just that. "A few weeks ago, I'd have given anything to have you here."

"I'm here now, Fallon."

"Funny, now it means absolute crap."

Her gorgeous indigo eyes hold mine as she slams the door in my face.

CHAPTER SIXTY-THREE

Fallon

> **The mementos you collect over time tell a story not about your taste but about your history. Don't try to manipulate them to match your space, but allow your space to organically grow from them.**
>
> **—Beautiful Today**

BACK AT MY APARTMENT, I DROP ANOTHER BOX OF PIZZA AS WELL AS the box of things I needed from my mother's on the counter with a thud. The overwhelming feeling I endured as I sorted through my mother's possessions sent me rushing to the bathroom to puke up my breakfast more than once.

Then I found the letter in her toy box, which struck me as exactly what my mother would ask Paige to do to alleviate my tension at such a horrible time. For a moment, it made me recall what it was like when I confessed to her that I had feelings beyond friendship for Ethan.

"Mama, I don't know what to do." I buried my face in my upturned knees. *"We just started out as friendly acquaintances."*

"When did it become more—for you, that is."

"When Austyn was hurt. We leaned on each other and I got to see this side of him I didn't know was there." Relaxing back, I explain. *"Ethan's always so self-contained. He'd do anything for anyone, but rarely does he let his walls down."*

"And he did with you? It made you feel needed, wanted?"

I nod. *"It showed me the kind of man I want."*

"Is it the kind of man you want or is he the man you want?"

"I've thought of that. I haven't met anyone else who comes close to making me feel the same way."

She draws back a little before smirking at me. *"Not even the art TA?"*

I groan, recalling the fact I told her about the scorching sex I had after I modeled nude. *"There are times I regret oversharing with you."*

She pulled me tight against her side. *"I don't. I cherish every single gray hair you've given me."*

I burst into laughter before squeezing her so hard she protests. *"Me too, Mama."*

Her hand tangles in my ponytail. *"Does Ethan know how you feel?"*

"Not that I'm aware of." Wryly, I add, *"I'm certain he'd go running for the hills if he did."*

She hummed. Silence descended between us and Mama rocked me back and forth. Something poked at my skin. I grumbled, *"Ow! What's that?"*

Mama blushed. *"Nothing you need to worry about, young lady."*

I groan. *"Mama, I just confessed to having some pretty significant feelings for a man twenty years my senior. Is there a taboo topic between us?"*

"Well, sweetheart, let's just say that's the box you want to immediately dispose of in the event of..."

"Stop."

"But, Fallon, I thought there was no such thing as a taboo topic?" Mama intones innocently. Too innocently.

I glare into eyes that are the exact shade of my own. "I really don't want to know about your preferred toys."

She tugs me closer. "A later conversation perhaps when you're not in the middle of an existential crisis?"

Now, I'm holding a letter that came from that very box because Paige reminded me I needed to open it and properly dispose of the contents before the estate people went through every nook and cranny to price my mother's life. "That's not something you want them finding, sweetheart."

It wasn't. And yet, due to her and my mother's shenanigans, my mother's words may be what gets me through tonight after my confrontation with Ethan. Leaving all the rest of the combined frames and documents I need to sort through on the counter before I meet with the probate attorneys tomorrow, I snatch it up and head into the living room to read it.

A few seconds later, my legs are tucked beneath me and my finger has slit the envelope open. I'm taken aback when I lift the multiple pages out, knowing my mother wasn't strong enough at the end. "When did she write this?" I ask the empty room.

I soon find out she had an accomplice.

My darling, Fallon,

Forgive my ramblings.

You're only a few miles down the road at work as I ask Paige to pen this for me. As your mother, I couldn't be more proud of you and all you've accomplished. I need you to know that, to believe it. Wherever you are in your life when you're reading this, please understand you are a gift and from the moment you were born, I have loved you from the very core of my heart.

No matter where I am, or what you are doing, I am so proud of the woman you are, Fallon. I truly am.

As I'm speaking, I can see the vast mountains from my hospice bed. They're waiting for me—a reminder they took your father from us far too many years ago. Yet, they're also telling me a story of endurance—that you'll survive after I'm long gone. Staring at the mountains offers a sense of people I know I'm never going to experience again except in the precious few moments when you're telling me you love me.

It's nowhere near as much as I love you.

My heart is in tatters that I made you suffer this alone now that Paige and Austyn are here. How could I do this to you, Fallon? Because my pride was in shreds? What malarkey. Yet, you shouldered this burden alone. From what Paige says, not even Ethan knows.

If you haven't told him, you should.

There's no place for pride in love, my Fallon. It's one of the many reasons I'm grateful you never took after either your father or me in that regard. Oh, I've encouraged you to be a strong, hard-headed, determined woman who has no qualms about going after what she wants, but to be too stubborn to ask for help? Your father would have been much like me, refusing to ask for help. Still, I hope he forgives me when I see him again for adding to your burden. He will be furious with me for not allowing you to share your pain. He would never have stood for such foolishness. He may have been a prideful man, but he was a good one.

Much like your Ethan is.

Despite you thinking you can keep a secret, I know how you accrued the money to supplement my treatment, Fallon. As I dictate this letter to Paige, tears fall down my face. I'm humbled my grown daughter would go to such lengths to save my life. You could be jeopardizing your future, but that doesn't matter to you.

I do, I matter because you love me.

I know you're likely wondering how I found out. It's not that hard, sweetheart. Your boss—Florence?—came by to see me after you went to get food the other day. She wanted to reassure me any debt would be canceled out after...well, after.

I must confess, darling, I'm concerned about your working conditions—and judging by Paige's face, so is she. But, going on my gut instinct, I trust this Florence to hold her promise to me and you.

After she left, Paige started talking about your strength and heart. We both agree, you have a soul that deserves to fly, to soar. She reassured me she'd help you however you may need it.

If nothing else, she relieved my mind, as she knew it would.

There are other letters you'll receive when the time is right, but for now, I want to talk to you about what happens after.

Loving after death.

It's both horribly simplistic and beautifully difficult—I need you to keep holding on to life. Long before I got ill, I made up a list of things I wanted to see in my life. I almost got through them.

Watch Fallon ride a bike.

Watch her go to her prom.

See her graduate high school.

Be at her college graduation.

Meet the man she's in love with.

The only ones I won't be able to check off are walking

you down the aisle and meeting any future grandchildren, should that be your path in life.

Don't hide yourself away, my Fallon. Don't. Make up your own list of all the things you want from your life. Then live after me. Live for me. Live the way I lived for your father even when there were days I wasn't sure if I'd be able to lift my head off the pillow until you stood at my side and asked me if I was hungry. Live to find love. Live for love. Live because you love.

Above all, Fal? Live for you. Fall in love with yourself. Having loved you almost a quarter of a century, I know you're worth the greatest love there is.

Eternal.

I have to end this now, darling. I'm tired. Sometimes, the exhaustion is unbearable. Still, if there was one person I'd continue to fight for, it would be you.

Know I'll be waiting to give you a hug in the after. So will your father.

All my love. Always.

Mama.

By the time I'm done, tears are dripping down my face. I lay my mother's precious words to the side and do what I've wanted to do since I woke up this morning.

I let loose all the emotion bottled up inside me. It's too much for me to handle on my own. I cry because I lost my mother. I cry because I lost Ethan.

And I cry because I'm certain about what to do next. I unblock Ethan. Despite everything, he is Austyn's uncle and there will be times he may need to get a hold of me. Even if we imploded, we'll always have a connection through her.

But that's it.

It's time to find out who Fallon Brookes is without Ethan Kensington in her life.

CHAPTER SIXTY-FOUR

Fallon

"Curses on the Mend" is one of the few songs I can say that brings me to my knees every time I hear it. It rates right up there with "Little Sister" by #brendanblake

I'm so ecstatic about the new collaboration, ladies!

#djkensington   #amandareidel   #wildcardmusic #fiercewomen

—Moore You Want

THE NEXT TWO WEEKS DRAG BY AS I TRY TO READJUST TO MY LIFE, WHICH was so busy being so empty. I no longer have anywhere to rush to, no conflicts with schedules to balance against visits to hospitals. I'm not trying to text the man I love with enough frequency to give him what's left of the heart that's dying with every breath my mother took. All is calm and none of my life is bright.

I want to disappear, but I can't. After reading my mother's letter, I made myself a vow. I'd live for her—for us, I amend. I stand in front of the mirror, adjusting my white blouse beneath my navy suit jacket before telling my image, "I promise, Mama. I will fall in love with myself even if no one else thinks I'm worth it."

Turning away from my image, I flick off the lights and head out of my apartment with a travel mug so I can make it to the curator's office on the Biltmore Estate before the tourist traffic clogs the roads.

Just as I lock my door, my sanitation team finishes with my can. I give them a quick wave and pull the can up next to my door. Even that simple move reminds me of Ethan. I haven't heard from him other than two bouquets of flowers with a card that had a benign "Thinking about you, —E" written on them. It's like he's trying to assuage his guilt with the most expensive flower arrangements he can order.

Flowers remind me far too much of the funeral I just hosted for my mother. And it's not like the words he wrote meant enough for me to not chuck them along with the vases.

I hope the sanitation team appreciates the less than pungent fumes from my bin as they drive up and down the streets of Seven Virtues doing a job few appreciate. As for me, I feel nothing for Ethan's lame ass attempt to reach out except an expanding void where my senses used to live.

Or maybe that's where my emotions once did. It's hard to tell the difference.

Sliding into my car, I get behind the wheel and mentally steel myself to return to work. Pulling out onto the quiet street, I don't know if this is a good idea or not. I just know I can't spend another day crying—especially when what I'm crying over is no longer clear. Is my grief solely about my mother, or is the loss of Ethan just as prominent?

I shove that thought aside as I pass the boulder that indicates my turnoff approaching. Slowing down, I take one of the unmarked roads to employee parking. Just as I park the car, I receive a text.

Ethan: Witch, please. Let's meet for coffee.

Powering down my phone, I don't bother responding, the same way I haven't responded to his other attempts to engage me in between his flower deliveries. Leaving it in my car, since I know no one who doesn't have my work extension will bother to try to reach me while I'm at work, I slide out of the car and lock it before starting the lengthy walk on the trail from the employee lot to the main estate. It's as if our entire relationship didn't implode outside of Devil's Lair and then disintegrate on the porch of my mother's home.

Recalling Austyn's last call to check on me, I remember we broached the very topic of Ethan pushing too hard. She probed delicately. "Have you heard from Uncle E?"

"He's tried." I gave her a low down of his "attempts."

She snorted. "What a lame jackass. I would have thought he had more game than that."

I told her bluntly, "I don't have the emotional wherewithal to deal with the way he hurt me right now, Austyn."

Her voice softened noticeably, "No. Of course not."

"But you think I should talk with him? More than I already have?"

"I think there's a reason for him doing the things he did," was her response.

Considering she suffered the worst kind of suffering due to male protectiveness, I begrudgingly agreed but cautioned, "On my terms. I'm not ready."

She immediately agreed. "Absolutely. How are you supposed to heal if he doesn't give you space?"

At least I know Austyn isn't colluding with her uncle, I think grimly as I climb the last few steps and enter the estate garden. A feeling of peace settles over me as the monstrous home Cornelius Vanderbilt built in the late 1800s appears. Quickening my pace now that I'm on even ground, I flash my badge once I reach the estate.

Once inside, I promptly push thoughts of Ethan Kensington aside because I have a job to do.

CHAPTER SIXTY-FIVE

Ethan

Some days, I imagine happiness within larger families can best be portrayed by an episode of Game of Thrones.

—Viego Martinez, Celebrity Blogger

"I don't know what to do!" I shout at my niece.

"What do you mean you don't know what to do?" Why is it that I've never realized her voice can be exceptionally grating when my niece, who has perfect pitch, shrieks? "It's been a week, Uncle E. What *have* you done?"

I rattle off the list. "I've sent her flowers. I've sent her meals. I tried to email her..."

Austyn has the audacity to laugh at me. "Yeah. She's no longer checking that email address."

"Well, how the fuck was I supposed to know that?" I growl.

That's when Austyn loses her absolute shit. "Because you're supposed to know *her*, Ethan. What do you think matters to Fallon right now? What is making her heart tick, even just a little?"

And just like that, I know what I need to do to show her she's on my mind.

"Mr. Kensington," Dr. Clarabel Lam shakes her head remorsefully. "You know I can't discuss a former patient with you unless permitted to by the next of kin."

"I knew Helen Brookes, and I'm in love with her daughter. I would just like information on where I, and potentially my family, can best do good in her memory."

"Oh. I see. Would you give me a moment?"

"Of course." I stand uncomfortably in one of the family rooms in Seven Virtues Hospital, remembering the last time I was here. When Fallon had wrapped her arms around me. Comforting me.

Offering me peace and shelter against my fears.

"Who did that for you, witch?" I murmur.

Just as the question comes out, the door opens and Dr. Lam reenters with a man dressed in a suit clutching a tablet. "Mr. Kensington, this is Horace Edith. He is in charge of philanthropy and planned giving at Seven Virtues. He can answer any questions you may have in honoring the late Mrs. Brookes."

I tip my head in thanks before holding out my hand to the man. I shake his hand and find it to be soft in mine. His voice is just as diminutive. "How much were you thinking to donate, Mr. Kensington?"

I jerk my head to the side. "How much does it take to get one of those hunks of stone?"

His eyes light with greedy excitement. "About ten million dollars."

Mine bug out. While I would love to give that kind of donation to honor Helen, I might have to kidnap my brother-in-law and his buddy Brendan Blake to sing a tribute concert for the sole purpose to do so. "What will fifty K get me?" I don't mind cashing out one of my CDs to do this. I want to make certain that Fallon knows there is nothing I won't do to make up for the harm I've done to her at such a precarious time.

"Why don't I show you?" He flips open his tablet and shows me the honor wall of clouds that decorate the waiting area. "Each one is personally engraved with whatever the family wishes."

I nod. "Yeah, this works."

"Excellent." He types away for a few minutes, asking me pertinent billing questions. When it comes time for the engraving, he prompts me by saying, "Many of our generous donors use scripture verses..."

"No. It needs to be more meaningful than that." I shift my weight before I give him the details.

"Excellent. And this donation is anonymous, you said? We're just to notify Ms. Brookes when it's mounted?"

"That's correct."

CHAPTER SIXTY-SIX

Fallon

We're coming up on the season where every charity miraculously finds money to send you a fifty-two-page, glossy catalog explaining why you should donate money to them instead of buying your family gifts.

Listen, if you need that last minute tax donation, Send Me An Angel can always use funding. I can vouch for the board, personally. And they won't send you a catalog to recycle.

—StellaNova

I ROLL MY EYES WHEN I RECEIVE ANOTHER CALL FROM SEVEN VIRTUES Hospital as I'm boxing up my mother's belongings I want to keep. The Angel House charity is coming tomorrow for her estate sale and they told me I need to remove anything I don't want to be sold.

I had to call Austyn earlier because I wanted to ask how one should go about disposing of sex toys. She screeched, "How in the hell should I know?"

"Well, ask your mother! She's a doctor and would know if I need a biohazard bag or some crap!"

Fortunately Paige came on the line and reassured both of us that a regular trash bag was acceptable. She also let me know additional letters from my mother are in her possession, which is an enormous relief. "I honestly was worried about that. That I would somehow miss where they were hidden."

"Well, don't be, sweetheart. I have the rest of them in safekeeping."

Still, the voicemail from the hospital is worrisome. I'm tempted to ignore it, but it's not from the regular scheduling number. I press the play button and hear, "Ms. Brookes, this is Horace Edith from philanthropy and planned giving at Seven Virtues Hospital. We wanted to again offer our condolences on your loss..."

I roll my eyes and I wait for him to request a donation. My thumb hovers over the button to delete the message.

"...the plaque to honor your mother is ready. We'd like to unveil it to you before anyone else. If you could call me back, we'll arrange a time." He rattles off a phone number.

The second he does, I hit pause on the message and dial his number, my fingers shaking. *What plaque?* Is this something Seven Virtues does for every lost patient?

"It can't be. The walls, the ceilings, hell, the floor, would be lined in metal." I finish reasoning that out just as he picks up.

"Horace Edith."

"Mr. Edith, this is Fallon Brookes."

"Ms. Brookes. Again, please accept our condolences on your loss."

"Thank you." I want to scream from the deepest part of my soul whenever someone says that, because it doesn't quite feel real. Taking a deep breath, I ask, "Can you tell me how my mother came to receive a plaque?"

"There was an anonymous donation. And the sentiment is simply exquisite."

Suspecting this is something Austyn or her parents likely did, I resign myself to accepting it gracefully. "You've seen it?"

"It's been mounted. We would like for you to come see it before we reveal it to anyone else."

Taking a deep breath that this is another trauma I'll endure alone, I make plans to be at the hospital bright and early the next morning.

The first person I see when I get off the elevator is Clarabel. I swoop in and give her a swift hug before she can escape. "I never had the chance to thank you for everything you did."

She hooks her arm through mine. "I wish there was more I could say and do, Fallon."

"Isn't your time here almost up?" I remind her that her program was only for one year.

"Just about."

"Where are you going after this?"

Just as she's about to answer, a man scurries forward. "Ms. Brookes?"

I catch Clarabel rolling her eyes next to me and that makes me the tiniest more relaxed. I hold out my hand. "Yes. I'm Fallon Brookes."

"Horace Edith. Please, join me." He pulls me forward to the wall of clouds that catches the stream of sun every day illuminating the patient waiting room. There's a rolling safety ladder in place with cones all around it. Patients and caregivers alike are eyeing me speculatively as I approach the base of the steps. Horace points to the one cloud exposed. "Once you read the cloud, we'll free the others again."

Clarabel gives my arm a quick squeeze. Releasing her, I climb the six steps and stand on the platform. That's when I see my mother's name and her birth and death dates. Followed by a quote from Mitch Albom's *The Five People You Meet in Heaven*. Tears pool in my eyes and blurs the script.

Life has to end. Love doesn't.

A sob rips from me as if a part of me is intended to float to the clouds with the agony of seeing that plaque. I turn to sit down on the top of the platform before navigating the stairs and I catch sight of him lingering in the far end of the hall.

I don't have to guess who did this.

Ethan did.

His chin lifts before he rolls his body off the door jamb and he disappears.

I want to clamber down the steps and ask how he can shout such vitriol and still care for my heart. I want to know how he can honor my mother and me yet demean the manner in which I tried to save her. I want to give him hell for what he said and smother him with love for this precious gift. A gift that no matter what, reminds me I'll never be alone because I'll always have love.

But he just left me to think.

CHAPTER SIXTY-SEVEN

Ethan

I don't understand winter in the South.

—@PRyanPOfficial

That's because it doesn't exist. Shoot.

—@CuteandRich3

What?

—@PRyanPOfficial

I just got sand stuck to my skin.

—@CuteandRich3

Let me know where you are and I'll brush it off.

—@PRyanPOfficial

Aww, Ryan. Are you finally asking me out?

—@CuteandRich3

Would you say yes?

—@PRyanPOfficial

IT DOESN'T TAKE MUCH TO PICK THE LOCK TO GET INTO THE SHED ON Helen's property. I just hope she has the tools I need so I don't waste time renting them. Fortunately, everything is there from a relatively new lawn mower to hedge trimmers to gardening gloves. Dragging everything I need out, I shut the door,

As I stand in the quiet solitude of her mother's backyard, memories flood my mind like a relentless tide, pulling me back to a time long ago, when life was simpler, and forgiveness came easier.

Maybe it's the solitude or the scent of freshly cut grass and the gentle rustle of leaves whispering in the breeze that transport me to memories of doing chores over the weekend on our family farm in Kensington. I can almost feel the warmth of the ceaseless sun on my skin as I remember countless hours spent tending the animals and the dreams that never quite came to fruition after my mother died.

Mowing Helen's lawn is therapeutic, allowing me the mental space to sort out what happened—why I blew up at Fallon and what triggered it. I know I need to talk with someone about it, but the Agency has rules in place for these types of conversations. I need a way to atone for my mistakes and reclaim the relationship I lost.

But can it be that simple?

Each blade of grass I trim, each weed I pull, is a silent prayer for Fallon to open her heart enough to listen, a prayer that she gives me a chance to mend the divide between us. I don't want to be, but in my head are the lessons my father taught me and the values instilled in me through hard work and determination. But most of all, I'm reminded of the power of love and the lengths we'll go to in order to protect the ones we hold dear.

"Ethan, one day, son, you're going to fall in love."

"I hope so, Dad."

His hand comes down on my shoulder. "Son, when you're wrong—and you will be—don't be too prideful to admit it."

I slash out at the tears leaking down my cheeks as I collect the grass clippings. That's when I hear her gasp.

"What are you doing here?"

As I sit beside her, I realize this moment is about rebuilding trust, about healing wounds that run deeper than I ever imagined. As I look into wary eyes, I know that no matter what the future holds, I'll carry the lessons of the way I hurt this part of my heart with me.

Forever.

For in this quiet corner of the world, surrounded by the echoes of the promises we'd started to build, I've found Fallon's happiness means more to me than my own. When I touch her face, she stiffens—a clear indicator my touch isn't welcome. I offer her a sad smile before withdrawing my hand. The weight of my remorse and regret weigh heavily on my chest but it's nothing in comparison to the devastation pulsating at me from her indigo blue eyes.

Eyes, I'm certain, I'll dream of for the rest of my life. "I can't begin to express how sorry I am, for everything."

"Ethan." Her voice is low and riddled with warning.

"I should have come to you instead of not trusting who I know you are. I didn't trust my instincts, didn't trust us. I invaded your privacy, hurt you when you were already in agony, and maligned your character. For what? To find out you were set up? Something that would have taken me hours to confirm if I'd known by asking?" I scuff my boot in the gravel leading up to the porch steps.

When she looks over at me, her gaze softens slightly. In her eyes, I see a glimmer of forgiveness peeking out, buried beneath the pain. I fumble on. "I know I can never fully make it right, but I need to try. I want to show you that I'm committed to making amends. It was recently pointed out to me that I've given you a lot of words over the years but nothing to back them up."

Reaching out tentatively, I touch her hand, relieved when she doesn't pull away. Her touch is like a lifeline, grounding me in this moment of vulnerability. "I've been doing a lot of thinking."

Her smart mouth quickly sasses, "Did it hurt?"

That moment of her natural brazenness flaring causes my grin to flash briefly. I realize it's the first smile I've had since we imploded. No, since I blew us up. Then just as quickly as it appears, it's gone—just like she is. I should have done a better job of cherishing them both while I had them. I know the ache of that is going to live inside of me for the rest of my life, however we end up. Still playing with her fingers, I admit, "I realized I had no right to judge you, regardless of your reasons. I *knew* you and I should have known better."

Her lips tremble slightly, and I feel my heart clench with the weight of what she says. "That's just it. I did think you knew me."

I bow my head in shame, unable to hold her gaze.

"I had promised Mama. Ethan, you were my rock—even if you didn't know it. Every day, I'd wake up fearing today would be the day I'm going to get the call she's gone. I lived my life in fear. Afraid of Mama dying. Afraid of losing you, of being alone. And yes, I was afraid of losing the job at Devil's Lair."

"I know it's no excuse, but...I couldn't bear the thought of you sharing that part of...us...with strangers."

She reaches for my hands. "Would it help you to know what it was like working there?"

I glance out over the perfectly manicured lawn and nod. "Maybe knowing is better than not. Because my imagination is killing me."

Fallon walks me through a typical shift and I find myself laughing at all my misconceptions being thrown out the window. In fact, when she mentions utilizing a fly swatter against the desk to mimic spanking, I can't help but double over laughing. "Creative little bunch, aren't you?"

She shrugged. "It was a job."

Clasping her chin so she can't look away, I give her back the strength I callously ripped away with petulant words. "I see that now." Taking a deep breath, I steel myself for her response, knowing that my fate hangs in the balance after I lay my heart on the line. "Fallon, I have a lot to make up for.

But if you think there's a time in the future when you could possibly forgive me..."

"Ethan, I..."

I lay my finger across her lips. "Witch, that's why I'm here. To earn my forgiveness. To show you that I'm not just the man who made a mistake, but the man who will not only say anything to earn your forgiveness but who will earn it."

Silence stretches between us, broken only by the soft sounds of nature. Her eyes shimmer with unshed tears as she looks at me, really looks at me, for the first time since that awful night. Then her arms wrap around my sweaty body. Scooting closer, she lays her head directly against my chest.

"You bought her a cloud."

Immediately, I deflect the conversation away from what I did, "An anonymous donor did."

"Uh-huh." She skewers me with a side eye I try not to react to. Then she rests against me. "You mowed my mother's lawn..."

"I know it's not enough, but... it's a start. I want to help you and support you in any way I can. I want to be there for you, if you'll let me." I hold my breath, waiting for her response, my heart thundering in my chest. When she finally twists her head to meet my eyes, what I see there is like a lifeline, pulling me back from the brink of despair.

"Maybe...maybe we can try to be friends again. Take it slow, see where it leads."

Hope surges within me, but I know there's still a long road ahead. Nodding, I meet her gaze with determination shining in my eyes.

"I'll take whatever chance you're willing to give me. I promise I won't let you down again."

As we sit there, surrounded by the echoes of the past and the promise of the future, I know that forgiveness won't come easy—but for the first time in a long time, I'm willing to fight for it. That's when she lets out a heartfelt sigh. "I'm afraid."

"To trust me?"

She nods. "Right now, everything you do causes my heart to brace. I have to guard myself against our past and live in my present. I'm constantly on guard."

I rub my chest where my heart lives, certain a kick from one of the horses on my family's farm would have hurt less. "Christ." Until that moment, I was not certain I understood the battle I was facing.

Still, because she's Fallon, she rescues me. "But maybe, for the first time since this happened, I don't fear the future."

CHAPTER SIXTY-EIGHT

Fallon

Conversation Starter: Are you afraid of trying or giving up?

—Viego Martinez, Celebrity Blogger

I'M CURLED UP ON THE COUCH WITH AUSTYN ON FACETIME AS SHE implores me to consider what she's saying. "I don't know, Austyn. Right now, the idea of New York City just seems overwhelming." Particularly since I want to hide in the dark, away from everything and everyone.

Austyn's voice is filled with excitement and determination. "Come on, Fal. It will be good for you. You'll have plenty of people here and won't be so alone."

I think about the people I have left in Seven Virtues—Ruby, Layla, Caroline, Levi, and people tied to Devil's Lair or to the hospital. I let out an involuntary shudder. Austyn, catching it, lifts her hands. "I get it, I do. But think about it—new opportunities, new experiences. But it's a chance to start fresh. You can't tell me that doesn't sound appealing."

I sigh, torn between the familiarity of Seven Virtues and the allure of being lost amid millions of people. "What about my job?" Despite being Mom's sole benefactor, I want to save that money for the special events.

Buying my first home.

Getting married.

Having a baby.

Then I cringe. Right. Like those things are going to happen now that the picture isn't fully developed on who will be in my life. With things so up in the air between Ethan and I, and being unable to imagine anyone else fulfilling those roles, I've lost more than just him. I've lost the vision I had of my future. But working at Biltmore is my final dream I haven't let go of yet. Through all this, I've managed to hold on to a piece of myself.

Austyn saves me from my depression. "Your job isn't everything, and you know it. Maybe it's time for a change. You've been through so much, Fal. Moving to New York could be just what you need to heal." Then she suggests slyly, "And who says it has to be the city."

"What do you mean?"

She gives me an idea I never thought of, causing my jaw to drop. "Why didn't I think of that?"

Her face morphs into one of tenderness. "Fal, you've been taking hit after hit. Why would that even be on your radar?"

The mention of my recent losses sends shooting pangs of grief through my heart. I struggle to hold back tears. "I just... I don't know if I can do it. I need to think."

"I understand, I do. But I also know you, Fallon. Remember what I said. You're stronger than you think. And besides, you won't be alone. You'll have all of us nearby."

What's left unsaid is, *just not Ethan.* The absence of those words makes my chest hurt. I rub my thighs with my sweaty palms even as my mind spins with possibilities and doubts. "I'm not saying yes or no. I'll consider it, okay? I promise."

"That's all I ask. Just promise me you'll at least think about it."

After we disconnect the call, I feel relief from the pressure, but there's something there that's been missing since the night Ethan ripped out my heart.

Hope.

Excitement.

Maybe Austyn's right. Maybe starting over in New York could be exactly what I need.

Curious, I log into my employee portal at work and search "Transfers." I'm surprised when I find pages of information to read. My heart thuds in my chest as I realize that maybe a few people who love me are orchestrating my healing from somewhere I can't get to.

At least not yet.

If you're listening, thank you, Mama and Dad. For everything. Especially for loving me.

With that, I can't help but feel that glimmer of hope burst into something brighter.

CHAPTER SIXTY-NINE

Ethan

According to Forbes, a collapse in home sales spurred by rising interest rates will continue into next year. On the bright side, a lesser demand for existing homes will allow those of you with a handy nature to personalize your dream home.

—Beautiful Today

The "For Sale" sign goes up in the front yard of Fallon's mother's house five days later. For the last three, there's been an estate sale. I've been on the phone with Austyn continuously while Fallon took off for parts unknown. She assured me, "Fallon went through everything at her mother's house, Uncle E. Truly, if she wanted it, she's boxed it up."

"But what about the house itself?"

My niece sputters. "Are you offering to buy her mother's home for her?"

"If she wants to hold onto the memories, yes." I'm standing outside the three-bedroom, two-bath with the detached garage.

"Oh, Ethan." I hear my sister's voice through the line.

I grunt. "A little heads up I'm on speaker next time, kid?"

Austyn makes a non-committal sound. "Ungrateful brat."

"Love you too, Uncle E."

Paige jumps in. "Ethan, while I think your gesture certainly shows you're thinking about Fallon—"

"Way more than before you completely screwed things up!" Austyn shouts.

"Yes, well. Austyn's right. You still need to explain why things happened."

I sit down on the front stoop of her mother's home and warn, "The first person who will hear the full explanation will be Fallon."

"I think that's fair. Would you like to speak with a professional?"

"No, Paige. It was work."

"Work?" Paige parrots.

"Work. And no, I can't, nor will I, get into more than that unless I'm speaking directly with the woman I love."

"Then what's the house about, Ethan?" she queries.

I answer unhesitatingly. "She's just lost so much recently. Too much. I...I didn't want her to lose this too. If it was important to her."

There's a distinct sniffle in the background. Paige clears her throat. "Well, I think your motives are genuine. Don't give up, Ethan."

"I won't. You're certain about the house?"

Both Paige and Austyn come back with, "Very!"

"Fine."

"But, Uncle E.?"

"Yeah, kid?"

"It's nice to see you're using your heart to think."

Sighing, I tell her, "Maybe I should have used my head instead of my heart."

"What makes you say that?" she asks curiously.

"If I'd done what I was told—waited instead of reacting out of misplaced pride, I wouldn't be in this mess. I'd still be with Fallon. Sure, I'd have been furious—initially—at the idea of her withholding this from me, but I'd like to think I would have discussed it with her instead of going off half-cocked." A pregnant pause at the other end of the line tells me what my sister and niece think. I clear my throat. "Anyway. I have to go."

After leaving Fallon's mother's house, I drive around until I reach the cemetery. This isn't my first visit to speak with Helen, and I'm fairly certain it won't be my last.

I pull up next to the barrel of flower holders and the worn table with a hole to collect flower clippings and a spigot attached to grey water. After getting the flowers arranged, I make my way over to her newly placed tombstone.

Helen Vale Brookes
Beloved Wife, Mother, Friend

I set the spiked vase into the ground before greeting her as if she were resting against the stone instead of lying beneath it. "Hey, Helen. I don't know what to say."

How about telling me how you didn't keep your promise?

"I completely fucked up," I admit aloud. A gust of wind bends the deciduous trees, the residual wind whipping my hair around my head. Crouching down, a hand on the top of the stone, I tell her everything—not leaving a detail out.

Not even when the wind turns into rain.

Or the rain turns into sheets of water.

I remain crouched down and confess how I pursued justice instead of love—and not even a justice I personally sought. Finally I conclude my torrent of words by standing, my fingers slipping away. "You can't be more disappointed in me than I am with myself, Helen. Fallon's been a part of my heart for years. And in a matter of minutes, I threw us away—who we were, who we were meant to be." Swallowing hard, I accept the truth. "I just want her to be happy again. If that means letting her go, so be it."

Leaning down, I press a kiss to the top of the wet stone. "My biggest regret is I wasn't there for her when she needed me the most—when she lost you."

Having said what I need to, I return to my full height and leave Helen to either dispense more of her wrath or to leave me alone. Maybe it's not Helen who's listening, but I manage to make it back to my rental unscathed. Driving through Seven Virtues, I get a feel for Fallon's life here these past few years. I admire the beauty of the town, the spectacular views, the slice of heaven nestled into the Appalachian mountainside.

I wonder if where she plans on going next—if I could be happy there. Really it doesn't matter. Because there's no way I'll be happy without my heart and I'm never leaving my heart behind while there's still breath in my body.

Not ever again.

CHAPTER SEVENTY

NEW YORK CITY, NEW YORK

Fallon

DJ Kensington and her best friend, Fallon Brookes—who made national headlines when the two broke the internet at a small bar in Seven Virtues, North Carolina—were spotted strolling arm-in-arm down the streets of Manhattan today with a platoon of bodyguards.

For those thinking there might be a Manhattan repeat, we're sorry to burst your bubble. Brookes is only in town for a quick visit.

—StellaNova

"IF YOU'D HAVE ASKED ME TEN YEARS AGO, NEVER IN MY WILDEST fantasies could I ever have imagined I'd be in superstar Beckett Miller's living room drinking wine," I drawl. I also never imagined the particular cluster of women surrounding me dissecting the pros and cons of my relocating to New York as part of Austyn's plan to revive me due to the aftereffects of my affair with Ethan.

Austyn rolls her eyes. "And you definitely crushed on my father."

Recalling a time when I distracted her with a new magazine cover our senior year, I smirk. "Oh yeah."

Paige just laughs at us before turning to the tiny dynamo at her side.

Taking a sip from my glass, I admire the strong women grouped in clusters around the large space. Excluding the fact it's Beckett's place, there's serious power and wealth in this room. The kind you see on TMZ, ET, and StellaNova.

Speaking of StellaNova, I drawl to Ursula "Sula" Moore, wife of StellaNova's owner. "Do we need to sign NDAs when we're in your presence or something?"

This sets the remaining women in the room laughing. Sula, who hasn't lost her faint British accent despite years of globetrotting as one of the world's most renowned project managers for varying Fortune 500 companies, including the one her father used to operate, snickers. "No, Fallon. What happens during Girl's Night Out..."

"Stays away from our husbands," the rest of the women chant before breaking into laughter.

Sula winks at me from across the room before reaching for a platter of chocolate brownies I heard were supplied by Amaryllis Bakery and helping herself to two.

Carys Burke-Lennon, Beckett Miller's attorney and one of Paige's best friends, eyes her narrowly. "Why are you not drinking?"

"I am," she protests. With immaculate precision, she chops her brownie into perfect chunks before dropping the pieces into her wineglass. Lifting the goblet to her lips, she takes a "drink" before chewing with precision. "See?"

Carys leaps to her feet and points accusingly at Angela Burke—her sister-in-law—who is trying to restrain her smile behind a glass of full-bodied merlot. "She's pregnant again and you didn't say a word?"

Angie lifts her hands in self-defense. "To be fair, I knew before her husband."

The "How?" and "What?" come from every direction. Angie flashes the flushed Sula a wink. "I got a 9-1-1 call from Sula when Ward, the kids, and I were driving up to the beach house in Rhode Island. Sula accidentally left her early pregnancy test on the guest bathroom counter. She wanted me to overnight it to her."

I raise my hand. Carys calls on me. "I love she raises her hand. Yes, Fallon."

Addressing my question to Sula, I wonder, "Why would you not just pee on another stick?"

Angie toasts me. "Which is exactly what I told her since I didn't think FedEx would be too thrilled to have something with urine overnighted in the mail."

By this point, we're all doubled over laughing. That's when the elevator dings and Paige remarks, "Oh, good. Lee made it."

I scrunch my brow. "Lee?"

Austyn reaches for my hand and squeezes it hard. "Leanne Miles—owner of Castor, a government contractor who specializes in software development. Uncle Ethan's done work with her in the past." At my obvious tension, she reminds me, "You've met her before."

"I have?"

The woman in question stops in front of me and Austyn. I blink rapidly because she's memorable. After Austyn springs up to hug her, I get to my feet slowly and continue to study her carefully. Like Sarah McLachlan's "Building a Mystery" the energy from this woman calls to me—dangerous and tempting. Much the same way Ethan's has just with a uniquely feminine twist.

Even as she rubs her hand on her extended baby bump, pieces of a puzzle are snapping into place. I don't question the conclusions I'm drawing in my head because somehow I know they're right. Ethan. Work. Leanne. They're all tied together. Somehow, this vivacious woman is responsible for part of my pain. I can feel it.

I know it.

Taking a step back from her offered hand, I place my glass on the end table and confront her. "You were one of the people involved with what Ethan was doing, and you have the gall to show up here?"

There are gasps of shock around the room at my blatant confrontation.

Leanne's face morphs from cautious pleasure into deep regret. "No, Fallon. Harming you was never intentional."

"You can go to hell." I turn to head to the guest wing, where I'm temporarily staying.

Leanne grabs my wrist to stop my progress. "It wasn't you he was investigating, Fallon. It was Devil's Lair."

"Why?" I shout. "Can someone answer that?"

Pain swirls in her eyes. "Soon. Just please hold on to your faith in us a little longer."

"Lady, the only thing I know about you is you have good taste in movies, and you're in cahoots with my ex-lover. Give me one reason I shouldn't spit on you right now for assisting Ethan in kicking me when I was at my absolute lowest?"

"These women." She looks around the room, eyes lingering on Paige and Austyn. "They know me, Fallon. They know who I am, what I used to do, what I do now."

I tap my foot. "Which is?"

A gusty sigh escapes. "When I was younger, I was a special operative."

I blink. "Excuse me? Like spy shit?"

She cautiously releases my wrist. "Not in the traditional sense. I could—can —hack into anything. Let's just say I was at a crossroads in my life when Uncle Sam made me an offer I couldn't dare refuse."

"And this involves me, how?"

"Because I never intended to cause you harm."

I feel hands gently rest on my shoulders before a familiar scent wraps around me. Paige. I lean back against her as she whispers in my ear, "I trust her, Fal. I truly do. You're safe here. Nothing you say will be repeated. Leanne is our Secret Keeper."

A bitter laugh escapes. Leanne flinches at the sound. Moving around the room, she sits next to Carys before explaining, "I tried to get him to talk to you that night."

I can't restrain the bitter laugh that escapes. "Oh, he talked all right. Did he ever tell you what he said?"

Hesitantly, Leanne shakes her head.

His accusation is burned in my brain. I quote Ethan's words for the group, giving them the snide twist he did. *"I highly doubt something that serious is happening with Helen or I'd have heard about it. You must think I was born yesterday. Was it an excuse to buy new clothes? Handbags? Jealousy over your friend's newfound wealth finally get to you?"*

Austyn snarls. Paige drops her head in her hands. Carys offers, "We can sue him for slander," which earns her a cool glance from Paige but gives me something to think about. Angie and Sula's faces mirror what I'm feeling but it's Leanne who ends up cradling me when I give myself the grace to let the first sob release. It's Leanne who knows what I went through because in some odd way, she was a part of it—not that I understand the details.

Then she murmurs something that makes me pause. "Ethan may be one of the most brilliant men I've ever met, but he's acting just like my husband Kane when he sat outside of my apartment for months moping when I ran away after a death threat he refused to listen to."

I offer a faint, "Excuse me?"

Leanne flips her hand back and forth. "At least by then, I had Kane trained enough to have learned from his mistakes and finally got off his ass to do something productive. What's Ethan been doing—other than exhibiting he's been blessed with more of a 'Y' chromosome than most thus, logically, screwing up his life even further by just existing?"

Her direct observation breaks the complicated tension that has permeated the room since she walked in. Even before she shares, "I wrote him a song about you."

"You did what? Why?"

Austyn claps her hands together. "What artist did you use for inspiration?"

Leanne's lips curve into a cat-like smile. "The baby and I were getting jiggy with it when I was sending your uncle hate email about not waiting for information about Fallon."

I arch my brow. "Oh?" I mean, what could she have composed to have this room full of women cackling like evil witches on Halloween. But I still don't give in.

With that, Leanne belts out her opinion of Ethan's boneheadedness making it damn hard to maintain my earlier feelings.

I meet her eyes before I burst into laughter.

Much later that evening, just before she heads down the elevator, Leanne pulls me aside. "I shouldn't be telling you this."

I can't help the sweet bitterness that enters my voice when I reply, "No one tells me much of anything."

Her hand squeezes mine. "I know. Truthfully, we can't. Not yet. But, I'd like to give you two things to think about."

"What?"

"First, Ethan was called in to work on this assignment by a mutual friend because—again—my life may be threatened. Well, my life and my little one's." She smooths her hand over her baby bump.

My eyes widen. "And Devil's Lair's involvement?"

She shakes her head. "I can't speak of it. I have a...colleague. A protege of sorts who will be going to Seven Virtues to beef up their security."

"That's kind of you." I take a deep breath to tamp down my resentment before doing what's right for the people I grew to care about. "Leanne, there are some good people who work there."

"Then you won't mind passing their names on to me? Once I've vetted them, it would be good to work with them."

My head ducks. She steps closer. "Fallon, I know trust is the most precious commodity there is and once it's broken, it's never the same."

"That's the truth."

"What you will find, what I found, is that it can be better than it was before. Men are dumb and we should throw things at them—true. But when they learn lessons as hard as these, they rarely make the same one twice."

My eyes snap in her direction. Her smile is sincere. "Remember, I do know this from experience."

"Thank you."

"The second thing I wanted to share is don't let what happened tarnish your ability to believe in people—particularly Ethan."

I step back and glare. "That's not really your decision to make."

"No, but there are few men in this world with the level of integrity he holds."

I scoff at that.

"Fallon, he was livid and a complete asshole—no question. But did he ever mention bringing in the police? The FBI? Any type of authorities?"

I hesitate and wrack my memory. "Well...no."

"That's because you were his primary focus, not me. Not this baby. You. Despite his grossly misplaced fury, his focus was always about you from the moment he knew you were involved in this mess. Romantic? Trusting? Hardly. Real? Eye-opening? Absolutely."

I don't even know I'm crying until Leanne dabs at the tears on my cheeks. "Think about what you would have done—what you really would have done in a similar situation. If you'd caught him—say in a chat flirting with a woman—with no obvious explanation." With that, she steps into the elevator.

I open and close my mouth, uncertain about how to respond when the doors begin to close on her. She waits until they're almost shut before shouting out, "Riley rules!"

With that proclamation, I find myself laughing at the end of an emotional evening.

And wind up awake the whole night thinking.

CHAPTER SEVENTY-ONE

Ethan

Whiskey vs. whisky. There is a difference. To summarize, whiskey refers to grain spirits distilled in Ireland and the United States. Whisky refers to Scottish, Canadian, or Japanese grain spirits.

—Fab and Delish

SITTING IN MY HOTEL ROOM, I DIAL A NUMBER I RARELY USE. Normally, the bastard is the one calling me. Before I can be blasted for using it, I go on the attack, "You couldn't bend your precious rules, you bastard? You couldn't tell me the truth before my life turned to complete shit?"

Thorn releases a sigh before excusing himself to whomever the fuck he's with. "Let me get somewhere I can talk."

"Fine." My voice is flat, devoid of emotion.

When Thorn comes back on a few minutes later, he informs me, "I went to the secure space. You're good to talk freely, Ethan."

"I have nothing to say to you that I haven't said already."

"Then why the fuck did you call me?" He's bewildered as if I'm as single-minded as him when it comes to completing a mission.

"Why didn't you tell me about Fallon's mother?"

"Why did it matter? You—" he starts.

"Because she matters to *me*!" I roar.

There's absolute silence on the other end of the line before Thorn comes off his high horse to add one and one together to get two and not complete some complex theoretical thought process questioning whether one exists. I know this because it's half a second before he spits, "Fuck!"

A painful burn starts at the top of my eyelids. I swallow the watermelon size lump around my throat before I say, "I...I should have told you Fallon's the type of woman who would do anything for someone she loves."

"Ethan." This time Thorn's voice is as raw as mine is.

"She...Helen, not Fallon. She was the most non-judgmental person I'd ever met."

Something tickles my cheek. I swipe it away impatiently. "Apparently, all the money she was supposed to earn from Devil's Lair went to paying her mother's medical bills."

His voice is gruff when he gently confirms, "That's what Qaza found after she did a deeper dive on your woman."

My woman. Christ, Leanne realized what Fallon was doing so easily when I couldn't align the pieces due to the jumbled emotions screwing my head up. All I knew was there were pieces of my woman being given away and it rocked my world. My eyes are leaking a steady stream of salty liquid down my face. "I'm not certain you can call her that any longer."

"Because you're a dick?"

"Not to mention the fact she said I'm a fucking hypocrite. She's right. Who the hell am I to accuse her of heinous activity when mine was worse?" The laugh I let escape holds no humor.

"You did what you did because you were hired to. It was classified. Isn't that what you said?" I hear Thorn's chair creak as he settles in for a longer conversation.

"It started that way." I stand and pace. "God, I can't take this. I feel completely out of control."

There's a tension filled silence before Thorn asks a question that's been on his mind for years. "What changed you, Ethan? What pushed you from being one of the best agents I had into a renegade I couldn't control?"

Suddenly, I can't keep the words to myself any longer. "The lies! Christ, it was the damn lies. It was like a whole house fell down on me again, only this time it landed on my fucking chest."

Silence stretches between us until Thorn probes, "Because of Fallon?"

"No. Long before I fell for her." Realizing I was finally going to have to admit to the whole truth, I give my former director the truth he's been after, "About five years ago, something was revealed in my family."

Thorn is the head of the Agency for a reason. "Something that was detrimental to you being an agent?"

"Something that made me unable to trust my judgment."

"What was it?"

I brief him on the events about my mother's death. Thorn's a prick but not a complete bastard. "Christ, Ethan. What a clusterfuck. You had no idea of your father's lies?"

"No, but apparently your buddies at Hudson Investigations found enough evidence for my father to admit the truth to my sister. It's what caused his heart attack—why I departed from the Agency." I can't keep the bitterness out of my voice.

"Why you never asked to come back."

"How could I? The man who raised me to be an honorable man who believed in my intuition about people deliberately destroyed my sister's life. How was I to trust my instincts as an agent after that?"

"Truth?"

"Please."

"You made the right decision. If I can't trust you one hundred percent, if you can't trust yourself, you're useless to me as an agent." I'm stunned when Thorn surprisingly agrees with my decision after all this time. His next words don't surprise me at all. "But you were never happy in the field. You're too much like Qəza—you do your best hunting behind a keyboard."

"Is this where I say thank you?"

"Fuck you. Your problem with Fallon is a dumpster fire only you can put out."

Just hearing her name sends pain radiating through my system. It's like someone has my nuts hooked up to a battery and turned on the juice just to see my body sizzle in agony. I must have made some agonized moan because Thorn says, "Unlike your decision to walk away from the Agency, I think you'd be a stupid jackass to let something like this come between you and your woman."

"I accused her of being jealous of the money her best friend's now earning and then admitted I got off on it when it was me on the other end of the phone. I swear if we weren't standing in her recently deceased mother's home, she'd have done more than throw me out."

He makes a *pfft* sound as if what I've done isn't quite so bad.

"Is this experience talking?" I dare to ask.

"Let's just say I'm eternally grateful for the life I have and the fact my wife is upstairs," he admits.

The words are a painful punch to my already bruised heart. "I don't know what to say to get her back."

"Sometimes, life is a game we like to call Show and Tell. From what I understand from my sources—"

"Qəza."

He neither acknowledges or denies my claim because it could just have easily been Sam who shot him the intel about my years of talking with Fallon. "You've spent half a decade talking. Why don't you try showing the woman you're in love with how you feel about her?"

"How do I tell her some of it without telling her the whole?" I groan.

"Leave that up to me." Without waiting for my response, Thorn disconnects the call.

Leaving me wondering what the hell he's planning.

I fall asleep in the hotel room chair, waking with a horrible pain radiating from my neck and down my arm. But the one good thing is it gives me an idea of where to start. The only question I have is whether Jesse can handle my father on his own because I'm sure as fuck not leaving Fallon now that I'm here.

Maybe forever is enough time for her to eventually feel the waves of love instead of the pain I doled her way.

CHAPTER SEVENTY-TWO

Fallon

Wondering if it's time for a new job? Well, we can't answer that for you. All we can offer are some thoughts for you to consider:

You feel dread going to work;

You feel constant stress and fatigue;

Your work culture is permeating other areas of your life—aka, toxicity;

Your values no longer align.

—The Fireside Psychologist

After a week in New York, I've returned to work to finish out my time before my transfer. I'm reminded of the loss of my mother constantly because of well-meaning "I'm so sorry for your loss" comments. It's not that people are trying to be hurtful, it's just that each one feels like a tiny stab in my heart, given so frequently, there's no time for any scabbing in between.

I'm more than ready to head home to continue packing by the time my day's over. My boss did little more than mutter a "Run away," before I stood from my chair, grabbed my bag, and sprinted for the exit.

As the sun shines down over the impressive formal gardens, the tightness in my chest begins to ease as I slow my pace. Unlike this morning, I take time to admire the perennials as well as the hydrangeas, now in full bloom. Paired with the vitex and the weeping sourwoods, I stop dead in my tracks. I never thought I'd relate to flowers after my mother's funeral but these? There's a note of awe in my tone when I voice, "It's like the garden's feeling my pain."

A voice interrupts my introspection. "It's not just the flowers that are doing that, witch."

I still. Ethan's voice, infiltrating another of my safe spaces, sends spiraling emotions cascading through me particularly since due to Leanne's words, he's been on my mind constantly since I returned from New York.

I whirl around to face him head on and brace myself to be confronted again, only to have my bitterness temporarily washed away by the abject sorrow on his face. Or the pride in his voice when he nods at me before saying, "Being a curator looks good on you."

Still unwilling to let him completely off the hook, I question, "Did someone send you here to investigate *this* job choice, Ethan?"

He has the good grace to wince. "No. I just wanted to see you."

I wait for him to say more, but instead, he makes his way toward me at a slow and steady pace. I edge myself backward until he leaps forward and snatches me around the waist. Breathless, I slam my hands up between us. Before I can even formulate the words to yell at him, he steps back. His voice is on the precipice of lifelessness when he informs me, "You need to be more careful, Fallon. You were about to fall."

Twisting my head, I see where I was about to back down a set of eight marble stairs. No, it might not have been a fatal fall, but it still would have been painful. "Thank you."

"There's no need to thank me. I just…"

"Just what?"

"I just didn't want to see you hurt."

"You're the one who hurt me!" I shout.

If the cure for agony is pain, then I'm seeing every ounce of agony Ethan is suffering by the expression on his face. He pleads, "Fallon, I know I'm likely the last person you want to spend time with but can we go somewhere and talk."

A colleague on the restoration team calls out, "Night, Fallon!"

"Night. See you tomorrow," I call back before returning my attention to Ethan—an Ethan whose jaw is clenched so tightly, the bones might snap. Coolly, I prompt, "You were saying?"

"I want to apologize."

"You already have." I use my most bored voice, one I save for pesky insects who annoy me. "What else do you have to say?"

I swear, if Ethan doesn't need dental work when this is over, it won't be because of my lack of trying. His teeth visibly click together. Still, when his jaw unlocks, his words almost cause me to fall again. "I have the authority to tell you anything you want to know."

Like a veil of fog being lifted from the estate in the early morning, some of Ethan's words at my mother's come back to me. He was investigating Devil's Lair. He infiltrated an organization that, regardless of whether they end up being sinners or saints, gave my mother a chance to live. In the process, it crushed my heart. But I have to push back from him because the stupid organ doesn't fully get it since it's rapidly beating. Irritated with myself, my voice is a growl when I inform him, "My place. One hour. Don't be late."

I note his body posture slumps just before I walk away. My heart wails even as my head tries to make sense of what happened. *Oh, Ethan, why couldn't you just talk to me before?*

But finally I'll have the explanations I need to move on.

Before I continue packing.

CHAPTER SEVENTY-THREE

Ethan

SHE SAID YES!

—@**PRyanPOfficial**

Of course, you had to tell the whole world? Now, where are you taking me?

—@**CuteandRich3**

I PULL IN NEXT TO FALLON'S CAR BEHIND GALILEO'S. SHUTTING OFF my vehicle, I suck in a deep breath as I stare up at her window. The curtains flutter, telling me she's aware I arrived. Minutes later, she comes downstairs and her security door opens. It's another reminder of her lack of trust, knowing she doesn't even trust me with her door code. Before everything, she'd have texted me the code and met me at the top of the stairs like she did the night of her graduation.

Knowing I'm unworthy of even a six-digit number is just another bruise on my heart, but I know I deserve every single one of the kicks I'm enduring. Still, I alight from the car and make my way to her. Staring down into her eyes, my voice drops of its own accord. "I appreciate you making the time to speak with me."

She turns without a word and climbs the stairs up to her apartment. I follow behind her, entranced by the natural sway of her hips as she jogs ahead of me. Once we cross the threshold of her apartment, I come to a dead stop.

All around are packing boxes of varying shapes and sizes. My throat swells up and threatens to cut off my oxygen supply to my brain. "You...you're moving?"

She rolls her eyes as she squeezes between smaller book boxes as if to say, *Way to notice, Captain Obvious.* Making her way to her couch, she perches on the edge of the arm. "You said you had the authority to tell me everything? I'd like to know why you were spying on my life."

"It didn't start like that." Slowly, meticulously, I explain to her what I really do. The threats against another former agent. How we stumbled upon cracking into Devil's Lair. And how someone was using "Filia's" access code.

When I get to that part, Fallon noticeably pales. Her whole demeanor changes and she slides off the arm of the sofa when I share how I accessed the files that linked her to being "Filia." Her hands visibly shake, but still she skewers me with her eyes. "Why couldn't you explain it to me just like this before?"

I crouch down in front of her and lay my hands over hers. "It's national security, Fal."

"Explain *that* to me because the closest thing I understand about national security is secret tunnels used in *National Treasure* to see the back of the Declaration of Independence."

I have to bite back a smile because I recall how Leanne said they bonded over that very thing. I squeeze her fingers. "It means there's certain information I—we, that is, people who have access to the data—can't share with the public. I was waiting to get the authorization to be able to share this with you."

She's thoughtful for a moment. "And this agency you work for..."

I'm quick to correct her. "Used to work for. I only do odd jobs for them now and then."

"How long did you work for them?"

I give her a brief rundown of how I got started in the navy, put in fifteen years, and then, "When I got out, that's when the Agency recruited me but I didn't last there long."

"Why's that?" Her head cocks to the side.

I open my mouth, but I can't force the words out.

Her brows draw together. "Ethan?"

Nervously, I try to pass it off. "It's not a big deal."

"Ethan," she pushes, albeit gently.

I push to my feet and shove my fingers through my hair. Finally I summon up my courage to admit, "The lies. I couldn't live with constant lies. Not on top of what was happening at home after my father betrayed us all. Christ, Fal, he was the man I looked to as a damn hero my whole life and then—"

"A lifetime of his lies were exposed." Looking over my shoulder, I find she's lifted both of her hands to her lips and tears are welling in her eyes. Instead of pity, there's regret and something I hope I'm not misinterpreting.

It looks an awful lot like understanding.

Feeling like a weight has lifted off my chest, I lean against a stack of boxes and sigh, "Yes."

Fallon nods. She gets to her feet and reaches into her pocket. Her head ducks as her fingers fly. She must have received a text while we were talking. I briefly wonder if it's her movers when I feel a vibration against my chest.

Next to my heart.

Cautiously, I reach for my phone and slip it out of my pocket.

It's her.

My eyes flash toward hers and she glances down at my phone when all I see is a street name. Seconds later, I receive another bit of information.

FALLON:

Centerport, NY

FALLON:

My address when I move.

FALLON:

I'm transferring to Vanderbilt Eagle's Nest.

FALLON:

Fresh start. Closer to what's left of my family.

Once the dots stop moving, I lift my head and find her eyes on me. I hold hers for what seems like an eternity before I type back.

ETHAN:

I'd like to help you move in.

FALLON:

I wouldn't turn it down; that's for certain.

ETHAN:

That's good to know.

ETHAN:

Gives us a chance to really spend some time together.

ETHAN:

Talking.

FALLON:

I'd like that.

ETHAN:

But I have to make a quick trip first.

FALLON:

Where are you going?

ETHAN:

Life's too short not to get answers.

ETHAN:

I think it's time I get them from my father.

Fallon's head snaps in my direction the second she reads my last text. Her cheeks are flushed, making me wonder if this is what her face has looked like every time we've had a text exchange over the last five years. *Christ, I'm such a fucking moron.*

"You're not going to hear me argue with that," she tells me, letting me know I spoke my thoughts aloud.

I take a step in her direction and she doesn't retreat. Another one, and still another until I'm directly in front of her. "I know I have to continue to earn back your trust, witch."

She nods, but the corner of her lip quirks. "How do you plan on doing that?"

I tuck a piece of loose hair behind her ear. "Your mama tried to make me promise not to hurt you."

She snorts. "That went over real well." Then she stills as my words penetrate. Her next words are whispered. "When did she say that to you?"

"The night you graduated."

Her lashes lower and a lone tear drips down her cheek. I sweep it away with my thumb, knowing Helen's loss will live with Fallon for a long time. Tipping her chin up, I ask, "Want to know what I said back to her?"

"Yes."

"I can only promise to try, Fallon."

Her breath shudders out. "I learned that the hard way, E."

"I'd like to amend what I said to her."

"You can't promise to not hurt me."

"I wasn't going to." Her head snaps up and for a moment, her eyes flash. *There she is.* There's my witch, the woman who captivated me with a single look through my rearview mirror. "What I'd like to amend is that I can't promise not to hurt you, but I can promise I'm never going to stop loving you."

Her head falls forward until her forehead rests on my heart for a moment before she tips her head back again. After a while of her studying my face, her lips finally curve. "Then I guess I'll see you at some point in New York?"

I press my lips to her forehead, giving myself a moment to gather strength for what I know is to come. Then I make a promise I know I can keep. "As soon as possible."

CHAPTER SEVENTY-FOUR

KENSINGTON, TEXAS

Ethan

For me, letting go of my anger was a great deal easier than letting go of his perceived ambivalence.

—Ursula "Sula" Moore, in an interview about her late father, software giant West Moore

---

BEFORE I GO TO SEE MY FATHER, I TAKE CARE OF WRAPPING UP MY life in town. I contact a former navy buddy who recently moved to town to see if he wants to buy my building. When he asks why, I explain, "I'm moving to New York."

"Doesn't seem like your cup of tea, Kensington."

"There's a woman," I begin.

Before I can continue to tell him about Fallon, his silver eyes flash with humor. "Of course there is. Is her pussy good enough to go chasing after..."

I had him up in a chokehold against a wall within seconds. With my hand pressed against his jaw, I murmur directly into his ear. "Don't speak about my future wife that way."

He gurgles for a few moments as I continue to cut off air to his windpipe. Finally, he manages to get out, "I'm." Gasp. "Sorry."

I let him drop before I do something that will keep me from Fallon any longer than necessary. Or that will require Thorn's intervention. God only knows I don't want to be indebted to his ass any more than I am. As it is, I'm getting daily pings from him asking how Fallon is, if I've told her everything. And if she's forgiven me.

Since I can't give him an affirmative on all three of them, I continue to ignore him.

As I drive out to the home I grew up in, I think back to my earliest childhood memories on Kensington Farm. How my mama used to love flowers. How she'd hold my hand as we walked amid the sunflowers that grew behind the barns.

Mama. Until Paige came home a few years ago to confront my father, I'd forgotten about those memories. I'd shut her out. I'd let my father's lies replace the warmth that Melissa Kensington had bestowed upon us.

What would our lives have been like if she'd lived? I ask myself, not for the first time since we found out the truth.

After Paige had the strength and purpose to confront our father about the truth surrounding our mother's death, it caused thirty years of lies to unfurl. It also caused thirty years of love to come into question. What Tyson Kensington did shook the foundation of our lives, making Paige believe she killed our mother. Lying to her when she fell pregnant as a teen when she tried to search for the baby's father. Denying her the chance to have a family with her now husband.

Lies.

For what?

I turn down the driveway that leads to the big house. Parking my car in the semi-circle, I sit for a few minutes with the car running before turning off the ignition and sliding out. I stare at the home I lived in for the first eighteen years of my life and the only word that floats through my head is the one that escapes my lips is, "Lies."

That's when I hear Jesse's voice, "It wasn't all lies, brother. There were just too many told to us."

Turning, I see him standing a few feet away. We've always been close but there's some things we've never discussed over beers at Rodeo Ralphs. I jerk my chin up. "Have you forgiven the old man?"

"Forgiven? Yes." I open my mouth to speak when Jess lifts his palm and I see the diamond brightness in his eyes. "Forgotten? I can't say I'll ever forget the night I drove up and Paige was right there railing at him for ruining her life. He was so adamant he was right."

"That's what I can't reconcile." My tone is hushed as we stand shoulder to shoulder, looking up at the deck.

"What?"

A rush of air leaves my lungs. "He lied, and he lied, and he lied."

Jesse faces me. "Yes. He did."

My hands fist at my sides.

"Ethan, what's the problem?"

"Where is the old man?"

"These days? He's probably on the back porch...hey! Where are you going?" Jesse shouts as I bound up the stairs.

I don't answer him as I walk around the wrap-around porch until I spy my father sitting in a rocker. His head turns in my direction slowly as I make my approach. It strikes me suddenly how much his heart condition has affected him. Once upon a time, Tyson would have had his pistol cocked and aimed at any potential intruder. I'd have felt proud of my father for standing his ground, for protecting his honor.

Lies.

I'm so much like him it scares the fuck out of me.

I don't want to end up like him—brittle and damaged. Willing to hurt the precious parts my heart out of a misguided sense of righteousness.

It stops. Right now.

My steps slow as I approach. I move in front of him until I'm the only thing he sees. His face lifts and something stops me from just saying what I came to say and leaving. I did that once to Fallon with disastrous results.

I need to talk to him, to find out why.

Instead, I drop into the rocker across from his and set it in motion, not saying a word. Waiting for him to speak first.

It doesn't take long. "You and your mother used to sit right there."

"I have a faint memory of her reading me books. Maybe some of that occurred right here. Then again, maybe you're just lying to me about her."

He flinches. "Have a lot to say sorry for."

"You lied, Dad." I stop the motion of my chair. "Why?"

His face takes on a thoughtful cast. "Pain. Pride. Take your pick."

Despite my feelings for what my father did to our family, my empathy for the body my father's trapped in makes me ask, "Let me try to translate? You felt like less of a man because she got into that wreck? Because you couldn't bring her back and Paige was born?"

He stares deep into my eyes before giving me a slow nod. "Over the years, I began to resent..."

Because I know him well, it's easy for me to complete his sentence. "Paige. Because she looked like Mama?"

Nod.

"Acted like her?"

Nod.

I swallow and ask the toughest, "Fell in love?"

His eyes close. For a long moment, I think he's drifted asleep until I track a lone tear down his cheek. "Why should the son of the bast..."

"Bastards?"

Nod.

"Why should the son of the bastards who took Mama fall in love with the girl who looked just like her? Is that what you were trying to say?"

Nod. Another tear falls. "Wrong. Loves Paige. Austyn. Me too. Wrong."

"Yeah, Dad. You were wrong."

Shame wars with love when he admits, "Lied. But miss your mama. Still. "

"Dad, yes, you lied. But your lies?" I shake my head. "They didn't just touch Paige, Austyn, and Beckett. Those lies touched Jesse. Me. Those lies were far-reaching."

His tears are falling ceaselessly now. He reaches for a tissue, but his hand is trembling. I lean over and hand it to him, appreciating what Jesse said now differently. Sitting back in my chair, I study the man whose behavior I let cloud a large part of my adult life. "I'm not certain I'll ever forget what you did in the name of love."

He accepts my words with a slight inclination of his head. But who am I, another liar, to sit in judgment? My father told lies and broke apart multiple relationships because of love? I did it because of my job, uncaring of the fact that I broke the heart of the woman I love in the process. "The problem is, you raised a son who lied for a living, so I know how much lying hurts. It gets so you don't know what you said to who. It makes it so you don't know who you are. You say the wrong thing at the wrong time and then live in a world of regret eating away at your soul."

His eyes bulge out and his lips part. "So, it's not up to me to forgive or forget what you did, Dad. The only person who can do that is waiting for you on the other side. And trust me, if she's anything like Paige, Austyn, and Fallon, Mama's gonna be pissed. I hope you have your apology A-game ready. You're going to need it."

He swallows repeatedly before he rasps, "Love you, son. All of you. Still sorry."

I lean forward and lean my forehead against his. "I know."

I know he is because I am.

I just have a longer chance to make it up to the woman I love. I hope.

CHAPTER SEVENTY-FIVE

SUFFOLK COUNTY, NEW YORK

Ethan

Improved open and honest communication is one of the key elements to rebuilding trust after it has been broken.

—**The Fireside Psychologist**

HAVING A BROTHER-IN-LAW WITH A PRIVATE JET MAKES FLYING around the country very convenient, I muse as I step off his plane at Long Island MacArthur Airport where there's a private car waiting to take me the twenty miles to where Fallon's new home is. While I'm kicked back in the car, I send text.

ETHAN:

What are your plans today, witch?

FALLON:

I've decided if I unpack another box, I'm going to lose my mind.

Concerned she may not be home when I arrive, I probe for some additional information.

ETHAN:

Are you heading to the beach?

FALLON:

Right now, I have no intention of leaving my bed.

FALLON:

Not until I decide I want food.

FALLON:

Then I'll DoorDash something.

FALLON:

What about you?

FALLON:

How have things been in Texas?

God, even after everything, she still gives enough of a damn to worry about the demons I confronted. It just causes me to realize I'll never fully shed the guilt for the pain I put her through. And that's okay. After all, the sting, the ache of knowing what I've still yet to earn back gives me the motivation to cherish it. Because I know if Fallon gives me a second chance, I won't let anything come between us—not a job, not our families. Nothing. Replying back to her, I give her the truth, I just don't tell her where I am.

Closer than she may be ready for.

ETHAN:

Driving at the moment.

ETHAN:

Why don't you let me order you something.

ETHAN:

You know—a welcome to the house lunch.

FALLON:

Not turning down free food, E.

ETHAN:

Even from me?

FALLON:

Ethan...

ETHAN:

Fal?

FALLON:

We really need to talk.

ETHAN:

Later?

FALLON:

Feed me first. You know what I like.

What I hope you like better than the food is the fact I'm delivering it to you personally. Instead of letting my pounding heart overwhelm me, I find the Mill Pond restaurant and place an order for pick up that will last us for several meals. I might be too optimistic, but even if she throws me out of her life, I'll know I had the chance to take care of her one last time.

Leaning back against the seat after I advise the driver we'll need to make a quick stop, I reminisce over our relationship. Like our love, there have been mistakes on both sides—admittedly, a hell of a lot more on mine. My mouth quirks up on the side.

After my discussion with my father, I spoke with Jesse and told him about my plans. To say he wasn't shocked is an understatement. His smirk was all-knowing even before he pulled me close and gave me a huge hug as I made my way through the house searching for what was presently residing in the breast of my jacket pocket. "Paige and Austyn have been blowing up my phone," he admitted.

I rolled my eyes. "Is nothing sacred in this family?"

Cheerfully, he admitted, "Not really." That's when he found what I was looking for in point two seconds before handing it to me. "Is that all you want?"

I looked down at what was in the palm of my hand. "It's the only thing I'll need."

Hopefully.

The driver slows down as we approach the restaurant before dashing out to pick up the order. He makes his way back to the car at a much slower pace, stowing the bags along with my suitcase in the trunk. Everything else I own is in a storage unit in Kensington, just waiting for me to give Jesse the high sign on where to ship it.

I pray it's to this seaside piece of heaven. But first, I have to tell Fallon the truth about me.

Just a few minutes later, we pull up to a beautifully appointed Cape-style house I know from our texts Fallon's renting while she decides if she wants to make New York her permanent home. When we spoke on the phone, I couldn't help but tease her that she sounded like her Realtor as she enthused about how it was "located in the largest privately owned beach on the North Shore of Long Island. I have access to a community dock, boat ramp, and, Ethan, you won't believe this!"

Dutifully, I asked, "What's that, witch?"

"It's walkable to local shops."

"There goes your paycheck," I deadpanned.

"Hush. Not to mention bars and restaurants."

"What about the house, Fal?"

"It has four bedrooms and an office, three bathrooms, an enormous kitchen with a separate dining and living room area, a walk-out basement, and a flat backyard perfect for the whole family to gather. Hold on." She then texted me the listing and I had to admit it was close to perfect. I like the idea of renting to determine if this is really the place we're meant to be. Ultimately, it's Fallon's choice and all I want for the rest of my life is to ensure my Fallon has everything she desires because, after everything, she deserves her slice of perfection.

Lord knows if she accepts me back into her heart, the man she loves won't be.

Somewhat impatiently, I wait for the driver to bring my bag and the food to Fallon's front door. After handing him a hefty tip, I whip out my phone.

ETHAN:

Food should be arriving.

ETHAN:

ETA 2 min.

FALLON:

Thanks for the heads up and for lunch! 😊

I groan in anticipation as I count down sixty seconds before ringing the bell. Through the wooden door, her voice shouts, "Be right there."

My stomach cramps as I wait for her.

The door flies open and she's within reach. Her eyes flare as she takes me in. Her lips part as she visually inspects me from head to toe.

Then, in typical Fallon fashion, she drawls, "Well, if I'd known you were coming, let alone dressing as a throwback to my graduation night, I might have unpacked my formal dresses."

I clear my throat and ask tentatively, "Good surprise?"

I'm almost knocked back a step when she throws open her arms for me to step into. Wasting no time, I wrap her up tight and bury my nose in her neck. Holding on for dear life, I just breathe in her scent.

That's when she starts wiggling around. "Witch? What is it?"

"I hate to say this..."

I loosen my arms. "What?"

"Is there something in your pocket jabbing me or are you really that happy to see me?"

I want to howl with laughter, but she and I need to talk. "Why don't you invite me in and let's talk?"

CHAPTER SEVENTY-SIX

Fallon

I left the question open because the response was so overwhelming. There isn't much most of you wouldn't do for love.

Your lucky families.

—Viego Martinez, Celebrity Blogger

My home looks like the game Tetris landed in random locations. Not to mention, when the pieces touched down, they exploded. After Ethan's text, the only thing I wanted to do was curl up in bed and flush out all of the conflicting emotions once and for all but now I need to throw on clothes so I can meet the delivery driver.

Grumbling, I shove myself out of bed and tug on a pair of shorts and a top before glaring at the half-opened box still on the chair. My eyes circle around the almost pristine sanctuary I've created in muted grays, crisp white, with a dash of orange—courtesy of Austyn and Paige dragging me to HomeGoods last weekend. Even as I make my way over to the box, I can't restrain the snicker as I recall Beckett Miller up on a ladder, hanging my curtain rod along with Austyn's husband. "There are just some things you're not meant to forget," I say aloud as I unpack the box I carefully put together from my mother's.

Lifting her jewelry box, I notice a white edge sticking out the side. Frowning, I set it on the bed before lifting the lid.

My heart catches when I see my name in her bold writing.

Hand shaking, I touch the envelope as if it's going to disappear, a figment of an overactive imagination. But the texture of the paper sends chills up my spine. Lifting it carefully, I sink to the floor with my back to the upholstered footboard of my bed. Using a nail to slit the back of the seal, I read:

Dearest Fallon,

I don't know where I'll be when you read this. Likely, I'll be somewhere beyond your physical reach. I'm not writing this because I'm giving up hope, darling, but because I'm realistic.

As each day passes, I'm coming to terms with my prognosis. I've asked the medical staff to keep certain information from you because some lies are kinder than the truth. Often a non-answer is kinder than the answer itself. Either way, it's going to hurt like hell to leave you, but the knowledge you don't have to suffer inside my head every single minute makes it easier to bear. Trust me, there's an enormous difference between acknowledging what you know to be true, accepting it, and the way a person reacts to it. As humans, facing pain, lies are something we're not equipped for. Few have the strength to move past the betrayal and look at the reason why.

I hope I've raised you to do that or by now to trust I knew what I was doing so I'm not tainting your memories of how much I love you. Even from where I am, watching over you with your father finally back at my side.

If I'm not already gone, sweetheart, I'm dying. That's the long and short of it. I knew it from the moment they diagnosed me, but I was selfish enough to hold on to every scrap of hope you ensured was presented to me because I wanted nothing more than to see the shine of love flicker in your eyes for one more minute, hour.

A single day.

You're the reason I kept perpetuating the lie of strength when I was ready to let go of this body so many months ago. Your love was better than any medicine. Your fearlessness.

I'm so proud of the woman you've become, Fallon. Don't be afraid to go after what you want in your future. Just be certain you're making that decision because you chose it to make you happy, to fulfill some deep-seated dream you haven't had the chance to share, or because you love.

Especially because of love.

Oh, baby girl, I wish I had more time. Just trust your instincts and know I'm always with you where you need me most.

Your heart.

Love,

Mama

"How did you know I'd need you, Mama?" My hands crinkle the edges of the letter as I draw my knees to my chest. What do I want? I know I need to listen to Ethan and give him a chance to fully explain his actions. I can't move in any direction until I do.

When I receive his incoming text, a large part of me aches. The part of me that's tired of superficial conversations. The part of me that misses us—even the Ethan and Fallon from years ago. The honesty, the trust, even the pain. At least those emotions I knew were real.

ETHAN:

Food should be arriving soon.

ETHAN:

ETA 2 min.

FALLON:

Thanks for the heads up and for lunch! :)

I reach the door just in time for the bell to ring. I don't even realize I'm still clutching my mother's letter until I go for the knob. I fold it carefully and tuck it in the pocket of my shorts. I fling the door open, ready to find a DoorDash driver holding out a plastic bag.

What I find instead causes air to back up into my lungs.

God, the man can fill out a suit like no other and this one? It's burned into my brain. The navy blue clings as lovingly to his legs and molds his shoulders as it did at my high school graduation, my college one. It especially looked lovely tossed so cavalierly on the floor of my apartment the first night we made love.

It was the suit he wore the weekend he came to talk to me about my mother's death.

It's riddled with memories, good and bad—just like our relationship.

I can't stop my heart from pounding as I give him a full once-over since his hands are loaded with takeout bags. When I finally find my voice, I drawl, "Well, if I'd known you were coming, let alone dressing as a throwback to my graduation night, I might have unpacked my formal dresses."

He clears his voice before tentatively asking, "Good surprise?"

I think about my mother's letter, the one burning a hole in my pocket. A letter where she admits to lying to me out of love. It makes what happened between me and Ethan not so black and white—not so over. Instead of answering his question, I open my arms for him to step into or not.

His choice. His move.

He drops the food and scoops me up. Burying his nose in my neck, we stand on my front stoop for a long time holding onto the past? The present? Hoping for a future? I need to know.

That's when I'm jabbed in the rib by a sharp edge. The first time it happens, I ignore it. But the second, I start to wiggle out of Ethan's embrace. Concerned, he rears his head back. "Witch? What is it?"

"I hate to say this..."

"What?"

"Is there something in your pocket jabbing me or are you really that happy to see me?"

"Why don't you invite me in and let's talk?"

I step back and invite him in.

CHAPTER SEVENTY-SEVEN

Fallon

HOT! From Wildcard Entertainment's Kristoffer Wild, Wildcard Media Representative, Paula Stone, and DJ Kensington's legal representative, Carys Burke-Lennan.

Stone, "We're excited to announce DJ Kensington has released the name of her first single from her new album, 'Winding Path,' which will release before her collaboration with Amanda Reidel."

Lennan, "'Love's Pursuit' will drop on your favorite streaming platform one week from today."

Wilde, "Plans have been made for a worldwide stadium

tour. Once the single drops, both Wildcard and Kensington's websites will list the locations."

The world can't wait to hear your magical vocals.

#djkensington #wildcard #lovespursuit

—StellaNova

ETHAN ASKS ME IF I WANT TO EAT BEFORE OR AFTER WE TALK. I decline food but ask if he's thirsty. "I wouldn't mind something to drink."

Walking into the kitchen, I pull out a pitcher of sweet tea and a couple of glasses before carrying both into my somewhat inhabitable living room. Pouring a glass for each of us, I gesture for him to sit, but he declines. "I've been cooped up between the flight and to get to you."

Sipping on my drink, I quirk a brow at the underlying desperation in his tone. "What for?"

At my question, his face blanks. "What do you mean, 'What for?'"

"What do you want the outcome of this conversation to be, Ethan?"

Never in a million years did I expect what happens next. Ethan drops to his knees before shuffling over to me. Uncrossing my legs, he spreads them apart and maneuvers himself in between them. "You back in my life, however I can get it."

"I already am," I counter because, after our discussion at my apartment in Seven Virtues and my subsequent chat with Leanne, I don't hold the same kind of resentment I did. I can logically see where the evidence wasn't good.

What hurt was he didn't trust in me—in us—enough to confront me with it.

His fingers graze the side of my temple. "Maybe in here, you have. But here"—his fingers trail down to the curvature of my breast where my heart's thumping wildly—"I owe your heart an explanation. That's why I had to get one of my own."

Confused, my brows draw together. "What do you mean?"

Instead of answering me, Ethan reaches into his pocket. For one horrifying moment, I think he's going to pull out a ring box. While a few months ago, nothing would have made me happier, now I'm terrified I'm going to have to say no.

Instead, he pulls out a small silver picture frame and hands it to me without saying a word.

I study it and frown. "Why did you bring me a picture of your sister and..."

"Not Paige, Fal. Look again."

My throat closes up when I piece together the age of the photo and the fact that the little boy whose hand the woman's holding isn't one of the dark-haired, blue-eyed children Paige has had.

It's the man on his knees in front of me. Absentmindedly, I cup his cheek while I study how carefree he looks holding his mother's hand as they tromp through a field of sunflowers together. "You look so happy."

"Next to the time I'm with you, I think that's the last time I was." He studies the photo intently. "Do you know that's also the last time I was certain my life wasn't based on a lie?"

"What?" While I'm still struggling to understand, Ethan takes the photo and places it on the nearest table. That's when he explains the details of his job in the navy—including how he met Sam Aiken and Parker Thornton. I recognize their names from when he explained the situation involved in his hunting down the individuals at Devil's Lair that might be behind Leanne's death threats.

He explains the years of field operative work he did for the Agency, using Kensington as his home base, until the world crashed down when all of Tyson's lies were exposed. How his father admitted to years of lies, of punishing Paige for being the spitting image of her deceased mother, how Tyson went off the rails when Paige became pregnant by Beckett—when he too was a symbol of the people who took his wife from him.

"How did you leave things with him?" I ask, concerned not only for Ethan but also for the whole family.

Ethan, who has long since dropped his head into my lap, shudders. "I said, 'The problem is, you raised a son who lied for a living, so I know how much lying hurts. It gets so you don't know what you said to who. It makes it so you don't know who you are. You say the wrong thing at the wrong time and then live in a world of regret eating away at your soul.'"

I lift my hand to my mouth, fisting it against my lips in an attempt to stifle the sob that wants to escape.

"I walked away from the Agency because I was tired of lying. After I was pulled back in because I owe—owed," he corrects himself, "Thorn so much, I became that man again."

"And that was?"

"A liar." He lifts his head and I'm shocked to find tears falling down his face. "Witch, the only way I deserve to apologize to you is on my knees."

"Ethan," I protest.

But his fingers stop absolution from being granted too early. After I hear them, I'm glad they do. "From the first night, we've never lied to each other. Even when it might have been easier. Even when it might have hurt less."

I hesitantly agree, thinking of the women he's dated, the men I've been with. The friendship we maintained that bloomed into something more before it imploded.

He glances over at the picture of himself with his mother. "I want to be the man worthy of holding that woman's hand and yours. The only way to do that is to stop lying and to promise you the truth."

"What does that mean?"

His eyes lock onto mine. "It means I no longer call Kensington home. It means I accepted a job working for Sam at Hudson Investigation. I can live in Alaska, North Carolina, the city...or right here in Centerport." He holds his breath.

Waiting.

I think about the letter from my mother I haven't had a chance to show him. The opportunity for us to be a regular couple. This is a chance for us to start over.

I don't realize I've shared these things aloud until he lifts himself up until we're face-to-face, lip-to-lip. "All of that, witch, and more. All that matters to me is that you know I fully intend to pursue you and make you fall in love with me again."

I shake my head.

His face falls. He swallows hard before he manages, "You just want to be friends?"

This time, it's me who scoots closer. I thread my fingers in the hair that's slightly lighter near his temples. Pulling him closer, I brush my lips lightly against his before admitting, "I never fell out of love with you, Ethan. That's why it hurt so damn much when—"

He doesn't give me a chance to finish my sentence. He's pulled me off the sofa and onto his lap. His lips, at first powerfully devouring, finally begin dropping light kisses around my face as he murmurs, "I love you," over and over. As if he says it enough it will penetrate.

I don't plan on stopping him any time soon. Still, I'm not ready for the breakneck free-for-all we lived through before. Pushing my hand against his chest, I ask, "So, what's your plan?"

At that, he stands before placing me on my feet. "Just you wait and see."

I study his face solemnly for a long moment, reconciling the man I fell in love with at eighteen, the man who became my friend, my lover, and then a complete stranger. Still, deep down, maybe I always knew there was a piece of him with me. Tentatively, I broach a subject I hope it's not too soon to mention. "I have two questions."

"What are they?"

I chew on my lip before working up the nerve to ask, "What's going to happen to Devil's Lair? You made it sound like they were into something awful. Then Leanne implied..."

He lays his finger across my lips. "That's still an ongoing investigation, witch. I can't share much but what I can is an agent Sam and Leanne trust with their lives is going to help them out."

"Florence? Becca?" I think of all the others who might be caught in the crossfire and left destitute.

He scrubs his cheek against mine before murmuring against my ear. "Sam's daughter will be by their side. Rachel is the best at what she does. She won't let them get hurt"

The pressure inside my chest releases. I can feel his smile against my cheek before he asks, "What's number two?"

"Whiskey." Quickly, I share, "Maybe it was your voice. Maybe...I don't know."

He jerks his face back, brows lower into a *V*. Ethan's voice is serious when he asks, "What about whiskey, Fallon?"

My head ducks to the side before I admit shyly, "In my head, whenever you'd call Devil's Lair, I'd started calling you Whiskey. Me, all the operators, we all had nicknames for our callers. That's what I used to call you."

To my astonishment, Ethan tosses his head back and roars with laughter. I slap my hand against his chest. "It's not that funny."

"Actually," he starts. Then he leans down and whispers in my ear. By the time he's done, my body's molded against his, and my mind is whirling at how I unknowingly gave him a nickname that was the drink he used to consume on every call *and* was his Agency code name. "No way. You're kidding, right?"

He pulls back and flashes a smile at me I've dreamed about for five long years. "There's no way I'd kid about something like that. When you meet him, ask Thorn to confirm it."

When I meet him. His words imply I will be a part of his world for a long time to come.

When we first met, I never meant to pursue Ethan Kensington. I'm just grateful, in the end, we each followed our own path and still managed to be right here.

With each other.

EPILOGUE
SUFFOLK COUNTY, NEW YORK

Fallon

One Year Later

I STARE DOWN AT THE LINES ON THE TEST BEFORE ASKING THE HOUSE, "Any words of wisdom?"

Kids are the one topic Ethan and I haven't touched on in the year since we've reconciled. Like he promised, he and I started from scratch. Openly dating, we ate at some of Centerport's finest restaurants, danced at their festivals, and strolled hand in hand along the beach.

And because I never wanted to fall into the trap we ended up in, Ethan agreed to counseling. When I broached the subject with him, he was reluctant at first. That is until I played my ace card and said, "The woman holding your hand in this picture would never have allowed you to get to a place where you felt like you were nothing but a liar. The woman who wants to hold your hand for the rest of your life wants to make sure you've made peace with it."

He called the counselor the next day, not me.

I didn't just participate in our joint sessions. In my own individual sessions, I learned how to handle the loss of my mother in a healthy way and identified when it's okay for me to break a promise so I don't end up devastated or being the person to bring about destruction. I also now acknowledge what triggers will set me off about what Ethan did to destroy us the first time around, despite my forgiveness having been granted due to the work we put into our joint sessions.

Ethan attacked his therapy much like he did a black hat. In learning he could only control his actions, he needed the tools to control his reactions when they were outside his control. He also accepted he needs to be more forthcoming—particularly with me. Most importantly he accepted it's okay to be emotional—particularly over loss. Not only was he grieving the loss of his mother, he grieved the loss of the man he knew his father to be. One night, while we were lying in bed, his eyes were welled with tears as he wept over the senseless loss of his childhood.

I explained, "You didn't lose the memories, E. You just lost how you perceived them."

He pulled me tightly against him, holding me in place for a long period of time. "So, it wasn't all a lie."

I shook my head. "I think for that, you'd have to talk with Paige and Jesse to get their perspective."

So he did. Due to those talks, he, his brother, and his sister are closer than ever. As for me and Austyn, dynamite may have to blast the two of us apart, even if she does needle me about becoming her "Aunt Fallon."

One of these days. Not today. I glance down at the test results. "And depending on how Ethan reacts, who knows if that will ever happen."

Instead of flipping out, I use the tools from therapy to consider how I'm going to tell him. "Ethan, there's something we need to talk about..."

Nah, it sounds too cold. Too clinical. Then I snap my fingers. "Maybe I'll take him down to the beach!"

It's on those walks that we get into some heavy discussions. Maybe that's why the first time we slept together months after we reconciled, we forgot the condom. That or the fact that I had just baked a cake and placed it proudly in the center of the dining room table.

I swear I did it subconsciously because Ethan and I were coming back for dessert at my house, but we never left to have dinner. Instead, he rucked up the back of my dress, grabbed hold of my panties with his teeth, and dragged them down my legs.

I didn't worry about it too much. After all, Ethan pulled out before coming all over the cheeks of my ass.

But the little lines on my test tell me I should have been a bit more concerned. "What the hell am I going to tell him?"

Then, as if I conjured him, he is leaning against the open door jamb. "Tell who, what, witch?"

I don't even hesitate. Lies are an absolute non-starter between us. Instead of trying to find the right words, I just hand him the test and remain sitting on the toilet with my pants kicked into the corner as I wait for his reaction.

It doesn't take long.

He flings the test over his head into the hall and reaches for me. Hauling me up, he plops me down into the center of our vanity. His hands clasp either side of my face before he plunders my mouth with his tongue. He murmurs, "Undo my pants, baby."

Suddenly, needing my man's cock inside me sounds like the perfect way to celebrate our impending parenthood. Breathlessly as I work at the tab and button, I remind him why he's dressed in a suit, "You have that meeting in the city."

He groans before reaching into his suit pocket. Pressing a button, he tucks the phone against his chin. He doesn't waste a second before he rips open my shirt and quickly unhooks the front closure to my bra. I let out a moan when his hands wander to my sensitive breasts. "Yeah, Sam. You're on your own. Why? Fal just found out she's pregnant."

He grins down at me lecherously before he rubs the head of his cock through the juices of my soaked pussy, knowing he's on the phone and I'm spread before him like a damn sexual buffet. I hear Sam's voice through the phone before Ethan says, "Damn right, I'm not going anywhere," and then ends the call.

Much like my pregnancy test, his phone lands somewhere in the hall. Then Ethan thrusts inside me in one slow, smooth glide. My arms and legs wrap around him. Breathlessly, I manage to ask before I'm incapable of thinking, "I take it you're happy?"

He cants his hips forward and I feel his cock grow inside of me. "Happy? Witch, I'm not certain I'll ever be this overjoyed again."

A little over six months later, Ethan realized he was wrong. That was when our identical twin daughters—Helen and Melissa—were placed into his arms for the first time. Tears of joy flowed freely down his cheeks then and again later that same day when they were placed in their only grandparent's arms—Tyson's.

As we've learned through the pursuit of our lives together, not every moment is filled with happiness. Sometimes we stumble, but always, we're stumbling while holding onto each other.

And that's what's perfect.

WANT MORE?
BONUS SCENE

FALLON AND AUSTYN COME FULL CIRCLE IN THE FEW MOMENTS before Fallon's wedding to Ethan. This takes place six months after the epilogue concludes.

Read about Fallon thoughts as she makes her way down the aisle to become Fallon Kensington.

Click here to have the bonus scene sent to your device. Additional information may be required to gain access to the file.

PERFECT ASSUMPTION

For the last ten years, Angela Fahey has struggled with fears and the kind vulnerability necessary to fall in love. She's held strong to the conviction love was meant for someone else until one day something slipped.

Ward Burke, a handsome lawyer who doesn't need to work if the scandal sheets declaring him a billionaire are anything to go by, has never noticed her before now. Or so she thinks.

Who knew dropping a cup of coffee all over her grumpy boss may have been the best thing to happen to both of them?

Purchase your copy on Amazon.com or traceyjerald.com!

ACKNOWLEDGMENTS

Nathan, I love you. Every day, that feeling grows even more.

To my son, you've gone through so much this year. Pursue your happiness and never let it go.

Mom, Thank you for always encouraging me trying even the smallest pursuit growing up. I love you.

Jen, all our car rides and duets with the Indigo Girls led to the scene with Fallon and Austyn. Power of Two, forever. I love you.

To all Meows, now, forever, always. I love each and every one of you.

Amy, Kristin, and Dawn, thank you for always sharing your strength, your wisdom, and your love. Thank you for always being there.

To Missy Borucki, thank you for understanding the crazy phone call from London! You rock. XOXO.

To Holly Malgieri, to my twin. For making everything shine, just the way you do.

To photographer Wander Aguiar, Andrey Bahia, Jenny Flores, and Donna Lathan, always my heartfelt thanks!

To my cover designer, Deborah Bradseth, you did it again! XOXO

To Gel, at Tempting Illustrations, MUAH. Thank you!

To the team at Foreword PR, thank you for helping keep me juggling everything, every day.

Linda Russell, thank you for never letting me down. You know how much I love you.

Finally, to you, my readers, I am overwhelmed by your support. Always. You have my eternal gratitude for your emails, comments, and reviews. I love hearing from every one of you. Thank you for choosing to read my words.

ABOUT THE AUTHOR

It began when Tracey stayed out for hours making up stories in her head as she biked around her neighborhood in Connecticut. Writing, always a passion, started interfering with her life when she started rewriting ends of books instead of finishing papers during college. After all, what was more important, a happily ever after or Greek mythology?

Eventually, she combined both when she wrote the Amaryllis Series.

With over 125,000 copies of her work worldwide, Tracey's collection of contemporary romance and women's fiction is available on Amazon.com and free on kindleunlimited. This includes her best-selling Amaryllis Series, Midas Series and Glacier Adventure Series. She has over twenty-five books in print and has participated in several anthologies for reader pleasure as well as charity.

Tracey is dedicated to her own happily ever after, having been married since 2007. She and her husband have one son who is as addicted to his Fortnite as his mother is to Starbucks.

When she's not busy with her family or writing, Tracey can be found in her home in north Florida drinking coffee, reading, training for a runDisney event, and feeding her addiction to HGTV.

If you want to interact with Tracey daily, join her Facebook Reader Group as well!